The Bloody English Women of the Maison Puce

Also by Jill Laurimore

Dinosaur Days

The Bloody English Women of the Maison Puce

Jill Laurimore

MICHAEL JOSEPH
LONDON

MICHAEL JOSEPH

Published by the Penguin Group
Penguin Books Ltd, 27 Wrights Lane, London W8 5TZ, England
Penguin Putnam Inc., 375 Hudson Street, New York, New York 10014, USA
Penguin Books Australia Ltd, Ringwood, Victoria, Australia
Penguin Books Canada Ltd, 10 Alcorn Avenue, Toronto, Ontario, Canada M4V 3B2
Penguin Books India (P) Ltd, 11 Community Centre,
Panchsheel Park, New Delhi – 110 017, India
Penguin Books (NZ) Ltd, Cnr Rosedale and Airborne Roads,
Albany, Auckland, New Zealand
Penguin Books (South Africa) (Pty) Ltd, 5 Watkins Street,
Denver Ext 4, Johannesburg 2094, South Africa

Penguin Books Ltd, Registered Offices: Harmondsworth, Middlesex, England

First published 2001
1

This is a work of fiction, and none of the
characters are based on or portray any
real people, alive or dead.

Set in Monotype Fournier 12.5/14.75pt
Typeset by Intype London Ltd
Printed in Great Britain by Clays Ltd, St Ives plc

A CIP catalogue record for this book is available from the British Library

ISBN 0–718–14471–6

For my mother Louise with love

Acknowledgements

For their mixture of wisdom, patience, flair and good humour, I send a raft of gratitude to the following – my editors Louise Moore and Harriet Evans, and the rest of the terrific team at Michael Joseph and Penguin: my agent Annabel Hardman at PFD; Jon, Sophie and Dido Laurimore; William Hamlyn and Huw Llewellyn for their quick thinking; the late Victoria Davidson – in happy memory of a dear, wise friend; and my mother Louise, to whom this book is dedicated.

1

May Day

'Alice! *Aleese!*'

Round the corner comes Josette Lamartine, shouting as she trips lightly over the cobbles (as in the Light Fantastic – an air she's cultivated carefully: such a youthful spring in the step, never mind she won't see sixty again). Stops – looks up . . . tapping the foot – gold-sandalled, red-shiny lacquered toes – what an instep – what an ankle – could credit a girl of seventeen – impatient now – glaring up at the shutters – *knows* she's there.

'ALEESE!' And once more in a despairing bellow, 'Aleese BARNES! Come! We will go to Juan-les-Pins – take taxi – we will go to Boom-Boom – we will 'ave COCKTAIL!'

Not a sound from above. The shutters remain fixed, but the rim of light is tell-tale – gives the game away. Josette steps back, craning her neck to try and improve the angle of vision, peers up to the first floor to see if she can catch the faintest movement behind the peeling grey louvres. Nothing, though: just that rim of light – and silence, a gap of quiet within the background hum of traffic and the plash of the sea against the rocks below the promenade.

She has one last go. 'Aleese! We will 'ave cocktail

–'*ARVEY WALLBANGER*! We will 'ave *FUN*!'

A dog barks, a klaxon sounds down in the square, but the shutters remain closed. Josette shrugs. These women – these *Eeenglish* women – so mystifying. You think you've made a *rendezvous* – a pleasant little arrangement, nothing difficult. But no, they don't seem to understand – there's no dealing with them. And they could have shared the cost of the taxi. For a moment she thinks she'll have to take the bus after all. She looks regretfully at the golden leather pencil straps encircling her feet, the high thin heels, and sighs, oh la-la – too fine, too insubstantial for the bus. She'll have to afford it somehow, and she trips down the slope to ambush a cab.

*

So what's happening here? Step back and take a look at this tall and ancient house squeezed into a narrow alley. Scan across its vine-curtained frontage and then back up to the window at which Josette was glaring. Where the heck, then, is this Alice Barnes?

Perhaps she's out: left the light on to deter possible burglars – a rational explanation, for the Côte d'Azur is known to be a hive of larceny. Or perhaps as a welcome glow to greet her lonely return to the flat late at night, that would do too. But no: Josette knows she's there, and Josette's instincts are spot on – for if you can be said to loiter with intent in your own bathroom that's what Alice is doing right now, glued (only metaphorically, she hopes) to the closed lid of the lavatory with her crotch smothered in Immac, her legs splayed out as far as the narrowness of the space will allow, for fear of doing terminal damage to her labia.

Feeling pathetic, of course. What a tit. She must have misunderstood. Once again in a mixed Franglais conversation she must have missed a vital word – or in this case mentally added, '*peut-être*' to a proposed outing to the hot spots of Juan-les-Pins. For, seriously, she'd only thought it was an idea, not a concrete plan, or of course she'd have made more of an effort, not marooned herself in this depilatory no-man's-land, scarcely able to move, let alone get as far as the window and offer up some sort of explanation. And what sort of explanation *could* one offer with Immac beginning to froth and bubble dangerously round the nether regions? Do Not Rub In, warn the instructions on the packet (as if one would). Do Not Guess The Time Allowed. Use a Watch. Ahhh, well, there they've got her. She has a watch, of course, but she's left it on the other side of the room – not the shower room, that's only three feet across, but the *only* other room, the rest of the flat, the tiny studio she now calls home. She's gone and left her watch over there, *past the window*, below which Josette Lamartine is bellowing. So she can't go and get it, even if she could walk, and she has a horrible feeling that the cream has been on for long enough – even for the woman with pubic hair like Brillo pads. Something of an exaggeration, but come to think of it, considering all she's been through one way and another, should she, on top of everything else, *really* have to suffer pubes practically down to her knees in the smooth gleaming New Millennium world of the Bikini Line – justice or what?

And now the telephone rings. Wouldn't you know it? Rings and rings and rings, insistent as toothache. She thinks of leaving it – for the moment. But this moment's going on for far too long. Whoever it is won't give up. Another six rings and by now she's thinking of the children – images of accidents, death and destruction flashing by. *Where were you? We rang and rang*. Family guilt will always get her in the end – she *can't* just ignore the call, so in one mighty heave she throws herself off the lavatory, cracking both knees against the enclosing tiles, and then, with legs held as wide apart as possible, shimmies crab-like across to the telephone, ducking as low as she can in the circumstances, past the shutters in case Josette is still down there ready to pick her out. She grabs at the receiver just as she realizes that, of course, it's probably Josette on the line, calling from the box on the rue d'Alphonse Daudet trying to catch her out.

So it's a relief when she hears only dialling tone – whoever it was has given up. She wonders if France Telecom has a last-number recall service like 1471 at home (and thus catches herself out, for *here* is supposed to be 'home' now, isn't it?), something else she'll have to find out about – yet another tentative enquiry to be made in her creaking French (*excusez-moi*, *Monsieur*, *mais pourriez-vous m'indiquer . . .*? and how many times has she done *that* these last months, her dictionary clutched grimly in hand?).

She's just starting the shimmy back to the bathroom when it starts again. Reluctantly she picks up the receiver.

'*Allô*?' (One must at least attempt a touch of Frenchness at this stage and a BBC English 'Helleou?' never sounds quite up to snuff.)

'Mum?' It's a puzzled-sounding Gavin. 'Is that you?'

'Yes – hello, darling.'

'Oh, you *are* there – I'd given up. Just thought I'd have another go in case I'd dialled the wrong number first time around.'

'I'm here – sorry – couldn't get to the phone – tied up.'

And he sniggers. The cheek of it. 'Busy,' she adds, firmly.

'Sounds as if it's going all right, then.' He giggles again.

'Yes.' But there's a lot of defensiveness in that 'yes' – even she can hear it.

'You're all right, then, are you?' he insists – and seems to mean it.

'Well, yes . . . fine. Has its ups and downs, of course,' she says, surprisingly touched to be asked.

'Sorry I wasn't around when you were back in London. Work's a bit of a bummer just now – can't seem to grab myself a moment.'

'I'm sure.'

'Getting settled?'

'Sort of – it takes time . . .' And *how* – what an understatement. And where to begin if he really wants to know?

'Good. That's terrific.' But now she rather wishes he *would* ask – just a little bit anyway, so that she can launch into the constant, on-going struggle of it all: the admin and bureaucracy, the queuing up at the *mairie*, the *taxe foncière* versus the *taxe d'habitation*, the intricacies of all this foreignness which so far she's managed alone.

'Got yourself kitted out and all that?'

'Do you mean furniture?'

'And all that stuff.'

'More or less – quite cosy, really . . .' But somewhere down below – her below – a voice is calling. A burning sort of voice – the Immac voice warning her, On No Account Leave Longer Than 10 Minutes and she's left it . . . how long? How long since she was lurking on the lavatory with Josette Lamartine baying for her blood? 'Actually, darling, I'll have to call you back – something's come up,' but in reality something's coming down, descending her thighs in a slithery slide.

'But I'm just off out – got a meeting. I only wanted to be sure you were settling in all right – '

Again how touching, she thinks.

' – because,' he goes on, 'I was wondering if you could put me up – not for definite – only I may have to get down for Cannes probably in the first week.'

'I'm sorry?'

'Cannes – for the Film Festival – with this new project.'

'Which project?'

'Only it might be *really* helpful – you could, couldn't you?'

'Well – of course you're very welcome darling, but . . .' ('but' because he isn't, not at all – that's just what a mother *has* to say) ' . . . but I don't think you've any idea how small it is here.'

'Yeah, you've said.'

'But I don't think you've quite grasped – '

'It's just a bed for the night – maybe a couple or three.'

'I know, darling but that's it – there isn't one, that's what I mean, only mine.'

'The *floor*'s what I mean – with a mattress'll suit me fine.'

'But there isn't one.'

'Mum, stop being so literally minded, will you? You've got a floor, right?'

'Yes. Oh, yes. I've got a floor.'

'Well, there you are, then. I'll stump up for the Li-lo – if I need to – may never happen.'

'But I'm not all that near, you know. Cannes must be at least forty minutes away – worse if the traffic's bad.'

'Well, that's a lot closer than London and it could be *really* helpful if the shit hits the fan.'

What? Alice doesn't like the sound of this at all. (What shit? Whose?)

'Right,' is what she says out loud, then lamely, 'But wouldn't a hotel actually *in* Cannes be a better proposition?'

'Yes, Mum, I dare say – but I ain't got the readies – right – yup?'

Which leaves her silent, wondering yet again why they'd spent such a lot on his education.

'So it's OK, then? Thanks, Mum – you're a doll.'

*

A doll with a red, raw crotch.

Once she's stood in the shower and washed off the cream, she pats the skin delicately, anxiously dabbing at it with a towel, then stands looking at the result. There is only one way to do this, for the long glass is screwed to the inside of the bathroom door, which has to open outwards, or it would smash against the washbasin. And for the same reason, she can't stand and examine herself from the private safety of the bathroom with the door closed, for there is barely enough space for her not particularly buxom buttocks to interpose themselves between the said mirrored door and the edge of said washbasin. Anyone of size eighteen or over would have to concede defeat and either see to their ablutions at an angle of forty-five degrees by the loo or go for semi-publicity by leaving the door ajar. To get a full-blown view therefore, Alice has to swing the door wide open and stand in the middle of the floor with her back against the sofabed (the *only* bed, Gavin).

A forlorn sight. A saggy, baggy creature with those beginnings of humanoid zebra-stripes where she's caught the early season sun whilst still mostly fully clothed. How do so many of the French manage, then – that permanent all-over soft taupe shade which reaches right round the tender underneaths of arms and in between the toes? Even now, when the season is at its earliest, there they are, arriving down on the beach, the sea still cold to them (but, then, they've never tried swimming at Aldeburgh in July), slipping out of their dresses to reveal skin of even fawn tones, with none of these pinkish trout-on-the-turn shades which stare back at Alice now – not to mention this new V-shaped area, which glows painfully a vivid shade of smoked salmon on white bread. Irony piled on irony, for the sole purpose of this bodily pruning was to make herself *more* respectable for the beach – not to display such a humiliating mark of Cain.

This wasn't the picture she'd had of herself last August when, still reeling and bruised from the arrival of the decree nisi, she'd discovered Vieilleville for the first time – and fell for her Dream of Glory.

2

Alice Alone

So what's brought Alice here to her tiny studio flat in Vieilleville, contemplating the wreck of her body?

Scroll back to last August, and here she is again, sitting at the kitchen table of her sort-of friend Deirdre in Bristol, weeping all over the decree nisi, which has just arrived in the morning mail.

'What you need is a holiday,' says Deirdre, smugly safe in her coupledom of twenty-five years. But then, had Alice not been equally smug, sitting on her own marital nest-egg of twenty-*nine*-years-together – solid, immovable as a giant boulder? How could anything, bar death, break them now? Anything bar death and Hillary Aldyce it turned out.

Hillary Aldyce – never known as 'Hill' or 'Hillie', Hill-ar-y – Philip's practice nurse, not a patient, of course, or that could have spelt possible strikings off the Medical Register, but bad enough for all that. Philip the Immaculate, Philip, the self-proclaimed premium gynaecologist and obstetrician south west of the M4 corridor, had, so it turned out, been eyeing up Ms Aldyce all this time, across the prone bodies of numerous respectable West Country ladies, who wouldn't have noticed anything, of course – not with their eyes averted against the embarrassing indignities of stirrups and speculums.

And he's been doing so well, since he set up in private practice. All those NHS years they'd lived through together, those worthy, honest, shattering years – junior doctor, houseman and registrar – were becoming a distant memory. The *soi-disant* Premium Gynaecologist of the West could now practise in relatively civilized hours and in extremely civilized surroundings, his consulting rooms smothered in pale grey Wilton, and even his babies mostly organized to arrive via inducement and Caesareans during a standard working day. And word spread like that proverbial old wildfire. Nothing like a friendly, sympathetic, but also gravely *distinguished* gynaecologist, for bolstering the nervous dispositions of women who wanted little more than to get the hell out of his office as healthily as possible, *decorum intacta*.

His relatively recent rise and rise was why, of course, she was lying on her back on top of eighteen feet of scaffolding when he dropped his little bombshell.

It was his idea to leave their old house in Hotwells, the small Georgian terrace she'd loved and nurtured since they'd first moved there in 1972 when she was expecting the twins. It was their first non-rented property and technically *theirs* – though the mortgage had seemed so eye-wateringly vast, their monthly repayments so frightening, that she'd felt it was the Abbey National's for years, until inflation drained the figures of their intimidating power.

Then, for a while, with the mortgage paid off, it was

truly theirs, breeding a quiet sense of solid security in Alice's soul. Until suddenly it seemed it would no longer *do* – not for His Royal Gynaeship it wouldn't. HRG had his eye on one of those Italianate nineteenth-century villas at the top of Clifton where the Downs begin – a detached one too, the Villa Guardi, its name immovably carved into one of the Bath stone pillars by the pavement, almost unheard-of for its rarity and expense. But now the profligacy could all be justified on the grounds of intelligent need, for the house could evidently serve double duty for the practice, the fanciful cloister on the south elevation being a perfect annexe for new consulting rooms, terribly convenient, and saving *thousands* in rent.

She'd tried to get excited about the project, although ponderous stone mid-Victoriana had never sent her spirits soaring. In the old house in Hotwells, the narrow, dark hall had its original panelling, which she'd lovingly painted in shades of washed-out blues, long before the rag-rolled mania of the eighties held sway. The long thin garden, its head in the shade, was a mysterious jungle she'd ingeniously created with pots and creepers. It was all to her scale – and so, she'd always thought, to his too – its five emaciated storeys hopelessly impractical for the bringing up of children and yet triumphantly succeeding in just that very task, both of them up and grown, thoroughly fledged, gone away with complex lives of their own.

This new house had a wide, fat, bald expanse of lawn, edged in laurels and crowned in the middle by a vast, unforgiving monkey-puzzle tree. She'd wondered if they could fell it, only to discover dismayingly that it was *listed*

– guarded in perpetuity by the Council's edict. So there it stood, its bracts bristling like razor blades against the morning sky.

The house might have been a sensible necessity in the eyes of HRG, but the new mortgage payments were so gargantuan as to set off palpitations if you hadn't got your wits about you, and once it had become an inescapable *fait accompli*, the financial pincers set in. It seemed there was money available for the new consulting rooms, because that was all tax-deductible. But the depressing sixties kitchen, its chipped shiny cupboards picked out in scarlet Formica, was going to have to stay (and why not, from Philip's point of view – *he* never went into it), certainly for the present and possibly for the duration. Ditto the acid-yellow bathrooms with greying grout. It therefore went without saying (was, in fact, tacitly demanded) that her usual labours with paintbrush and wallpaper paste were expected – and pronto. There was an unexpressed gloss that went roughly along the lines of 'Well, what on earth *else* does she have to do, for God's sake?' it always being clearly understood that the Finest Gynae in the West could *not* be expected to wield the Polyfilla knife when his hands must be saved for the delicacy of a scalpel.

And fondly she'd loved him for it all, in an almost cosy, mothering way (what a mistake), indulging him in his vision of himself, and forcing her mind towards feelings of gratitude for his brilliance, management and drive – like an idiot, ignoring the pomposity and hubris. So thoroughly grateful was she that she found herself eighteen feet up the scaffolding in the huge entrance hall picking out the egg and dart mouldings in gold leaf. This was not *her* idea or taste. She'd have preferred doing the whole lot in Farrow and Ball's matt 'Hound Lemon'. But this was to be a shared hall, half of it leading to the consulting rooms, and the needs of private-practice fee-payers leaned towards glister, it seemed – glister, yet more pale grey Wilton and current issues of *Country Life* and *Vogue*.

So there she was, lying up on the scaffolding boards, suspended over the ornate engobe-tiled floor, trying not to cough or even breathe too heavily because gold leaf is such a tricky substance – one sneeze and you can send a pricy sheet uselessly off into the ether – when he'd said, 'I'm leaving you,' just like that, with no fancy additions, no attempt at a preamble. And she hadn't thought she'd heard him – and shouted now, whilst still keeping her head and arm very still, shouted, but for the same reason trying to keep her breath off the leaf, 'You're early – do you want some tea?' because she herself was gasping for a cup but hoped that for once he'd take the hint and go and switch the kettle on himself. And he'd shouted back, much louder this time, 'I'm leaving you for Hillary Aldyce' – and she'd thought it was a joke, and let out a kind of snorting laugh, which did indeed send a whole sheet of gold floating off, down and across, where it collapsed and stuck to one of the prongs of the grandiose iron chandelier they'd recently installed.

No joke this, though. If only. And he wasn't even being technically truthful when he so baldly spilt the beans, for what he really meant was that *she* was going to be cornered into leaving him, for *he* had no intention of moving out of the echoing spaces of the Villa Guardi – not with the ink barely dry on the contract, not when he was only now reaching the apogee, the magnum opus of his life. Not on your nelly.

No. *She* was the one who was going to have to do the leaving, because she didn't have any baggage or ties – not now the children were grown-up. Ten years ago it would have been different. Then she'd have been allowed – even expected – to maintain the existing family home as a secure base for them, if not for herself. But suddenly at the age of fifty-one, and rapidly embroiled in the process of an uncontested 'quickie' divorce, she found herself, in the eyes of the law, a non-person – not even a practising mother: a soon-to-be-ex wife with no visible function.

In the divorce petition, her request for financial support came under the quaint-sounding name of 'A Prayer for Ancillary Relief'. In response, Philip's sole concession to her financial contribution to the marriage was: 'She answered the telephone – sometimes.' This after half a lifetime of shared enthusiasm and endeavour, baby-induced sleepless nights (their own and his patients'), meals without number, washing, decorating, and doing most of his appointments, typing and accounts (not to mention presents and birthday cards for his mother, friends – and even Hillary Bloody Aldyce). In between she'd tried to squeeze her charity work – what Philip always termed her 'Mrs Bountifuls' – rattling collecting tins and organizing sales of work and raffles for the hospice and the homeless, trying to do what she could to pay back a little of the largesse she had been granted herself.

As a life, hers didn't seem to have amounted to much, particularly in relation to Philip's. His career suddenly assumed a magnificent stature all of its own, for there's something about surgeons, something so impossibly mysterious and arcane about what they do, which is so utterly *not* what the rest of us can do, that they are rendered God-like even to (perhaps *especially* to) ageing judges with furry arteries.

Even her own lawyer, who'd seemed moderately supportive to begin with, started to tell Alice that she must be sensible, for it was clearly absurd to expect a renowned medic to give up his home and place of work, when he was *so* busy and under *such* pressure – possibly even at this very minute saving the life or sanity of some hapless female.

There was also the uncomfortable detail that the modest total joint ownership of the tall, thin house in Hotwells had been transposed into the gigantic new debt for the Villa Guardi – so suddenly there wasn't really anything very substantial *to* split. Sometimes in the miserable middles of the night when she lay awake turning and re-turning the whole sad saga in her mind, she wondered if he hadn't in fact arranged it all, carefully disentangling her from the solid, saleable and splittable reality of the old house, and sending her into the quicksand mortgaged world of the new. But then she'd banish such thinking. He couldn't have been that calculating surely – she couldn't think such base thoughts of the man who was, after all, the father of her children, could she? Well, actually sometimes she could.

The Court – as in Divorce Court – were really quite impressed with Philip's solution, for he agreed to add to his existing financial burdens by taking out a second mortgage to provide Alice with a lump sum – modest, perhaps, if expected to provide both a home and some sort of income, but generous in the circumstances. True, the arrangement specifically excluded her from access to his pension for her old age, but that was just the way of it. And she could get a little job – she's not that old – get herself trained for something. There were surely little jobs around . . . in a shop or something? He can't be expected to keep her going as some sort of permanent backpack when he's got all the weight of his new family to worry about. For that's the other detail that didn't quite come out that first day of his confession; Hillary Aldyce was pregnant, and it seemed it was the knowledge of this pregnancy which prompted that confession, for no child of *his* was going to be born a bastard if he could help it – not likely. Hence all the rush. Otherwise he'd probably have waited a bit – well, at *least* until the gilding of the hall ceiling was finished . . . heaven alone knew who he'd get to do it now.

It was a lot to take in. A seething mass of pride had to be swallowed just to get through each day. If Alice's nature had been more public – if she could more openly, as it were, have washed her dirty linen – she could have made things very nasty indeed for HRG. Quite apart from the instinctive ickiness of gynaecologists regarding *any* woman's body with a less than thoroughly detached eye (and hand), there was the little embarrassment of the pregnancy, which was *unplanned*. Not the best advertisement for the man whose IUDs are rumoured to fit like a glove. Ohhh, no. But then Philip knew Alice very well – almost better than he knew himself – and he was so right, for the worm didn't turn. The worm was too embarrassed and self-blaming to have the energy to turn, and instead felt more and more worm-like, burrowing back down the hill to Hotwells, to stay with Deirdre and her husband as a paying guest.

*

There's nothing comfortable or familiar about Hotwells now, though.

Alice, who has until quite recently been mistress and organizer of her own space and establishment, feels displaced and awkward, like one of those unwanted old maids of nineteenth-century literature – Cousin Bette or a middle-aged Jane Eyre before Mr Rochester. Deirdre is welcoming enough in theory – but there is definitely a touch of exultation, of the old *Schadenfreude*, going on, despite the often repeated cries that Philip's behaviour is outrageous. Alice senses an egging-on of her private misery, a constant tweaking and tempting out of her tale of woe on a grinding, daily basis, for the more precarious her own world, the more sane and settled seems Deirdre's.

She starts in a desultory kind of way to flat-hunt, and is depressed anew by the available spaces in her price range, so dank and cheerless in comparison to her previous life – a life that sings out, a dismal chorus, from every familiar paving-stone and pillar-box, regurgitating her sense of loss and failure. So it's then, with the decree nisi lying open on the kitchen table oozing defeat all over Alice's ego that Deirdre counsels a holiday – and Alice, to her own surprise, agrees.

Toss a coin. Where would you go (within the confines of a pretty limited budget) that promises in your wildest fantasies, laughter, light and, yes, why not admit it?, *glamour* – about time – some glamour in your life? Not Greece – the language too tricky, the Shirley Valentine jokes too near the bone. Not Spain or Majorca – too unfairly tinged with package deals and lager louts. Not France, which until now in Alice's life has always meant the Dordogne, crammed with memories of all those get-to-me-by-family-Volvo summers. But then there's another France, almost divorced from the rest and never yet visited by Alice, truly alien territory, the Côte d'Azur. That world with its own mythology: Somerset Maugham and David Niven; Grace Kelly and Cary Grant; Scott and Zelda – palm trees . . . casinos . . . wine and song. So she books straight away – irrationally light-headed in a sudden burst of freedom – Heathrow to Nice. No careful preamble or customary boning-up from guidebooks, all spur of the moment, the hotel plucked almost at random – likes its name – the Auberge de la Rose, facing the Baie des Anges. Sounds promising, though. Sounds bliss.

3

At the *Auberge*

But it isn't. *Quelle erreur.*

A frazzled, disorientating bus ride in the broiling August heat takes her too few stops along the *autoroute* from the airport, and deposits her at a large pinkish bungalow with a neon rosebud on its façade. Around it in a regimented fan stand ranks of mobile homes tricked out with thatched roofs, each standing on its own raw plot of hard-baked sandy soil. These were described as separate cottages in the travel agent's blurb, had sounded charming – '*chaumières individuelles*' – surrounding a swimming-pool. The pool had been the only illustration, and jolly nice it looked too – dazzling turquoise water, surrounded by happy people sipping icy-looking drinks beneath thatched parasols. Well, the thatch was accurate – the Auberge de la Rose is pretty big on thatch.

On that first afternoon, and refusing to let the dank flannel of disappointment invade her psyche, Alice dumps her case in her allotted caravan, and decides to head straight out to the beach – get a look at the Mediterranean, that's what she needs. Dip her toe in its warm balm, catch the magic, soothe her soul.

She goes out of the gates and looks towards the sea.

'Within a stone's throw' was the description in the brochure – Well, she thinks, just about if you have the throwing arm of Goliath. It stretches thinly blue in a horizontal line across her vision, and is held at bay by intervening bands of dual carriageway, B roads, railway track and pebbly foreshore. The traffic swishes by relentlessly, never slowing. There is no pavement, only a broken line of crumbled kerbstone, dusty rubble, snaking cables and placards indicating roadworks. There is no sign of a crossing. The Auberge de la Rose seems trapped, marooned amid a cat's cradle of other people's transportation, all rushing past and away as fast as possible, and who can blame them?

Eventually, having trudged past garages and giant furniture shops like aircraft hangars, she finds an underpass, which leads in convoluted, lengthy fashion to the water. She is baking and dusty by the time she reaches the wide expanse of stony beach, kicks off her sandals and wades into the shallows of the Baie des Anges.

It's a name that holds a special resonance somewhere in the back of her mind. Years ago she'd seen that film with Jeanne Moreau – an art-house sort of flick. Philip had taken her to one of those cinemas they called flea-pits. In those ancient pre-video days, you went to Odeons and ABCs for proper mainstream films from the Technicolor Woods (Holly and Pine). But if you wanted a flavour of the *nouvelle vague* or the *dolce vita* – if you wanted Godard, Truffaut or Fellini outside London – you had to go to the nearest local flea-pit, the Cameo, Rialto or Roxy.

Baie des Anges – hadn't seen it in years. Not sure she can even remember the plot all that well, but nevertheless it's left its mark. Jeanne Moreau, with lustrous, smudgy, kohl-rimmed eyes and that extraordinary soft cushion of a mouth, spinning roulette wheels, swelling music to underscore the mood of doomed passion, and all against the backdrop of the huge sweep of the bay, and the architectural complexity of Nice itself. Although the film's plot may have faded, the mood of watching it has not. Sitting on the back row, almost lying, really, with legs stretched out, the heavy uncut moquette of the seat scratching her bare mini-skirted legs (don't think about the fleas, though – mere thought being quite enough to bring out psychosomatic bumps) and Philip, with his hand on the back of her neck, lightly stroking, tangling his fingers in her hair. Most underrated of erogenous zones, the neck. So that's the bell of recollection – watching Jeanne Moreau – absorbed in her dilemma – soaking up the glamour of her pain, while in Alice's own solid world, love and life were just hanging there, ripe for the taking. But the dream was never meant to look like this. Moreau could never have celebrated lovers' doom in such a setting. The real Nice seems to be way over there, swimming disconcertingly in heat haze above the sea. In the middle distance, planes loom up every few minutes out of the waves like mirages, heading away from, or into, the promontory of the airport. And here where she stands is just a long, sloping, raw and empty bank of hot, sharp pebbles. A lone fisherman is setting up his rod – echoes of the banks of the Avon. He's even got one of those little green canvas stools – and can that be, surely not, a *Thermos*? Two dogs are scavenging at the water's edge – at least, with their rangy, dingo-like bodies they don't look particularly

Anglo-Saxon but they don't look exactly French either. They are playing with something – tossing it into waves, then retrieving. Alice moves nearer to see what it is. A Coca-Cola tin. It couldn't even be Orangina.

That night she gets her first look at the other guests, and wishes she hadn't. High August, high season – and families running riot. The *auberge*, it turns out, is just two steps up from camping and one along from a motel. It caters to coach parties and has a large car park at the back of the *chaumières individuelles*, past the thin screen of umbrella pines. Just before sundown, the families pour in, mountainous piles of tanned flesh, in bouncy groups: Germans, Italians, Swedes, but mostly Brits – masses of them.

And what an unattractive species we seem to be *en masse*, we Brits, she finds herself reluctantly thinking later, once they've been herded into dinner in the cavernous hall labelled 'La Brasserie'. Everyone seems to order steaks from the large plastic-laminated menus – steaks and *frites*, more *frites* than seem possible for the good of the planet. The children, still mostly bathing-suited and in jelly-sandals, shriek and giggle, stick their forks into steak *haché* with its accompanying tomato sauce, falling off their chairs in hysterics. Alice sits alone in a corner, tackling her *moules marinières* (surprisingly good, despite the jolly-camper atmosphere), and recognizes with a new sense of humiliation that she's never felt so old and out of it until this moment.

'Kevin, come 'ere,' yells a young woman to her small son. She has a huge Pre-Raphaelite mop of peroxided hair, which she keeps flicking off her shoulders. 'Come 'ere and

I'll smack yer,' she adds. Kevin, all of eight, with *frites* jammed in his mouth on either side, pretending to be a vampire, looks pretty resistant to this invitation, as his mother waves her steak knife vaguely in his direction. He dives off across the restaurant under the paper tablecloths. His mother smiles at his departing steely little body and catches Alice's eye. 'They get so excited. I blame the telly – or maybe it's the beef. I don't give it him at home, what with mad cows.' She shrugs, then adds fondly, ''E's a little bugger, though, in'e?' And she laughs.

That night, Alice sits outside her *chaumière*'s door at the plastic table provided, gently pickling her senses on the bottle of rosé *vin de table* she's bought at the *auberge*'s own little mini-mart. Just occasionally the burble of conversation and bursts of giggles die down for long enough to hear the background song of the cicadas and the insistent croaking of what must be frogs. But only occasionally. In between come snatches of English pop songs she doesn't really recognize. A raucous chorus echoes repeatedly – something about feeling 'horny' or maybe it's 'honey'? She'd lost any pretence at interest in pop once the children left home – but could that be Oasis . . . maybe Blur? Then shrieks of cackling laughter again – and electronic beeps, some computer game, dragged all the way down from Basildon or Basingstoke or wherever, and peppering the hot Riviera air with its demanding cyber song.

At last she is pickled enough to allow the disappointment in. What a letdown. The Côte d'Azur? What price Willy Maugham and the Villa Mauresque then? What price Grace and Rainier, Sacha and Bardot? Can this be all there is –

all that's left for us ordinary mortals after the gods of commerce have had their fill?

*

That night she sleeps, though – heavily, almost comatose, as if physically struck by a rock, rather than the subtler weapons of the mind, and wakes up oddly alert, and game for adventure. But there's been no corresponding miracle at the Auberge de la Rose – it hasn't transmuted into St Tropez. The shrieking laughter and loud tabloid Brit jokes are just as intrusive.

Logic, of course, tells her she should leave as soon as possible, but then logic wouldn't have to pay for the suggestion. The whole ten days at the *auberge* are already ticking away as a substantial debt on her credit card, squeezed out of a tight budget, so however disappointing, it will just have to do. And then, thinking she is heading back down to the sea, she discovers the railway station.

Through the underpass, turn right, climb the slope and there it is: small, pink and planted with tubs of oleander and palms, a station in Toytown, utterly divorced from Railtrack and Temple Meads. The timetable is practical enough, though, and beautifully clear and simple. Small local trains evidently wind their way along the coast with admirable regularity and economy of fare, between St-Raphaël and Ventimiglia, just over the Italian border, stopping at all the little towns, as well as Nice, Cannes, Antibes and Monaco – even the names are mouth-watering.

And that's how the exploration begins. Every morning she scoots out of the *auberge*'s grim compound without even stopping for coffee, jumps on a train, and lands herself at a new destination. Because much of the railway line was laid long before the many-layered criss-crossings of the roads, it cuts through much of the ugly ribbon-development sprawl and lands her right in the heart of each community. And once away from the traffic, the apartment blocks and the shopping malls, it seems that the spirit of Scott and Zelda is here after all.

By now armed with a copy of the *Guide Michelin*, she explores narrow, heat-drenched streets for a few hours, sliding into the cool shadows of churches and cathedrals for respite, whilst all the time planning for the delight of lunch. Lone dinners at the *auberge* are a miserable disaster, but these lunches more than make up for them – these lunches are a miracle. The whole region seems dedicated to the gods of scoff – more so than anywhere in her previous French experience. The streets are dotted with *pâtisseries*, their windows laid out in ranks of drool-inducing lusciousness, arranged as abstract art. Crystallized fruits have whole sugar palaces devoted to their display – like precious jewels. *Charcuteries*, with their ranks of prepared dishes, make a mockery of bothering to cook at home. And then there are the crowning glories – the markets.

Each town seems to have a market so heavily blessed it might be a paradigm for the Garden of Eden. Small local farmers and gardeners join the professional traders and pile up their largesse. Everything is so fresh out of the ground you can still see the dew. Bunches of basil scent the air so headily it feels like a drug. Twenty varieties of salad leaf each proclaim their name and provenance. Dozens of cheeses vie with rings and garlands of *saucisson*; tubs of olives, larded with garlic and chillies and herbs, line up next to barrels of pickles and platters of spice. Nectarines, peaches and melons and strawberries, mulberries even, are heaped up in a state of heavy ripeness never seen at home. The aromas of food scent every corner – and the pursuit of food seems the determined goal of every passer-by.

Each town is also crammed with delectable-looking restaurants, under awnings, settled into corners of beautiful squares, on the pavements of bustling streets or quaysides, displaying their all-inclusive menus – very reasonable – on stands aimed at catching your attention. So many restaurants. So much food. How to choose? Shall it be the 85-franc basic or should she push the boat out for the 145-franc bonanza featuring stuffed oysters and confit of duck? Which should have the bounty of her custom? She becomes rapidly expert at picking, balancing menu against location and coming up with winners every time.

There is no shame in lunching alone, it seems. Even French women lunch alone, unselfconsciously tucking into three courses and whole bottles of decent wine without demur. Of course, during the day, the eating alone gives out a different set of signals. Behind the scenes, a 'monsieur' might be (indeed, probably was) indicated – a husband, possibly even a lover, but he was *busy* – well, naturally – busy earning the loot to pay for this little luxury of a lunch. But Alice, having also happily waded through yet another menu, feels herself released from the nightly humiliation of eating alone in La Brasserie. By the time she gets back to the *auberge* she is thankfully too tired and too well fed to need anything but sleep.

So that's how she finds Vieilleville – alighting at the rather unpromising station of its younger sister Bonneville-sur-Mer with its ranks of pink and amber concrete apartment blocks, but trusting in the *Michelin*'s advice. As suggested, she heads down the slope towards the high stone walls by the sea. Through the huge gate, up the steps to the battlements, and she's instantly immersed in another world, an ancient town impossibly perched over the sea, just as promised.

A complex tapestry of sun and shade – greys, amethyst and topaz-coloured stones. A maze of undulating streets and alleys, tightly packed with tall old buildings; rusty red clay roofs; flowers seeming to pour from every window – magenta, carmine and indigo; cascading curtains of bougainvillaea, jasmine and plumbago – and all backed by the brilliance of the sky and sea. Different blues – turquoise balanced against cobalt, navy, cerulean – each of such clarity that they quite literally steal away her breath for a moment as she rounds a corner and catches the vision anew. Aaaah, she goes – so briefly, just to herself, a little gasp – but this is surely so beautiful and could never be taken for granted.

She explores a little further. There are a couple of elegant squares dotted with tall palm trees, benches and places to play *boules*. There's an elegant promenade, with civic plantings of orange strelizias and red canna lilies and below that a sandy beach. Beyond the breakwater is the remains of an old fishing port, now mostly transposed into a yacht marina. Tongues of concrete reach out into the harbour to provide safe mooring for dozens of boats, glittering in the midday sun. A few fishermen are left though, just below the town walls, fiddling around on the quay with nets and floats as if to lend authenticity and justify the staggering display of marine life she's seen slithering around under the market's awnings just up the street.

And thus the thought begins – so quickly, a fantasy at first, an idle game as she comes to the end of another scrumptious outdoor lunch, sipping a *digestif* to go with the *express*, smiling and nodding at Madame across the way, who's brought her little dog as company, and watched him being fed a dish of penne pasta in tomato sauce, served actually *on* the table in a stainless-steel bowl – imagine *that* in a Clifton teashop. This is a place on a human scale, Alice thinks, and if only I lived here – if only I could be part of this – I'd be different – rescued – redeemed, involved, complete.

And then – well, there it is, right in the middle of the estate agent's window, the Agence Gerontin, written up on a card '*Studio – Bon État – Tout Rénové – Cuisine Équipée*', with a photograph of the building, and a price roughly half that of the miserable basement she'd inspected in Bristol only last week.

She only goes in on a whim, boosted by the whole *pichet* of house red and that slug of *eau de vie* she'd somehow managed to consume over lunch. Slips through the door, points to the card in the window, asks for details in her halting French, nothing more than that. Expects a sheet of paper with a photograph at the top, something she can moon over once she gets home – only moon, that's all she's really thinking of.

But Monsieur Gerontin doesn't seem to realize she's just acting out a day-dream, takes her quite seriously – and doesn't provide printed details. Instead, before she's quite cottoned on, he is preparing to take her round to see the flat straight away – no nonsense with appointments – is ushering her out, locking up behind him, a one-man band rattling with keys.

It isn't far, and just as well, for her French isn't up to much in the way of small-talk. She has a go with the weather, but more or less grinds to a halt after '*Il fait très chaud.*' She doesn't take in much of the exterior of the building, apart from its curtain of smothering vines, and just dives into the cool of a dark hallway with gratitude. It is almost circular, with steep stairs spiralling up. Narrow slits of windows like arrow-holes cast the only light and a rope hangs from a central vertical wooden beam, to act as a banister.

'Mast,' says Monsieur Gerontin, patting the beam approvingly.

'Mast?' says Alice.

'Mast. Of *sheep.*'

'Sheep?'

'*Bateau.*'

'Oh. Ship's mast?' says Alice.

'Sheep's mast. *Verrry* old.' And very romantic. She likes the sound of that.

She follows him up and round. At the first landing he stops, unlocks a door and pushes her in. He himself stays outside, and a long time later she wonders if he hadn't done that on purpose, to make the space seem slightly less minuscule. It is unfurnished, a bare, white-painted narrow room with a disproportionately high ceiling, which makes it feel as if it is carved out of something originally bigger. The walls are rough-cast, the floor newly tiled in a fired-earthish way, and in the bottom left corner is a modern galley kitchen, fitted into an alcove – really just a glorified sink unit inset with fridge and hob. Next to it is the only internal door, which opens to the sliver of a shower room, taking up no greater depth than the kitchen. One small space has been effectively sliced to form the whole. It smells strongly of damp plaster and fresh paint – the builders can surely only just have left.

Alice opens the sole window and flings back the shutters. The view is disappointing – just a wall on the other side of the alley. But it's rather a nice wall, smothered with vine leaves and supporting an old iron street lamp; a lizard is splayed out on its top. She hangs out over the sill, looking down into the street, sniffing the air. The sun slants sideways between the rooftops, just catching the occasional window-box stuffed with pelargoniums. If this were mine, I'd have my own window-boxes – my own pelargoniums.

Out on the landing Monsieur clears his throat and looks at his watch. She is expected to say something.

'It's rather small,' is what she comes up with.

'*Small*,' says Monsieur Gerontin, with a cartoonesque Gallic shrug.

'*Petit*,' says Alice, to her subsequent shame.

'Madame, I know ze meaning of "small". But for this part of Vieilleville at this price is – *comment veut dire*? –

énorme, and a bargain – *à saisir. Neverrrr* again at thees price and *tout rénové* – all new, you will 'ave nothing to do. Is not easy to find in Vieilleville – in Bonneville, yes, you can get new apartment wiz use of tennis and *piscine*, of course, but 'ere is *verrry* special. You 'ave all ze ambience – all ze culture – and ze price eez good . . . and wiz ze *sous la table* even better.'

'The what?'

'*Comment veut dire*?' Monsieur Gerontin ruffles his brow and searches around the room for inspiration. 'Ze "under ze table".'

'Under the *table*?' asks Alice, nonplussed.

'Is usual 'ere in France – everybody does it.'

'Does what?'

'You make a price for ze *notaire* in public – little price – zen you make another price in cash – bigger price. Zen you –'ow you say? "Split ze difference" yes? It 'elps ze seller wiz 'is taxes – tax is *verrry* difficult, no?'

'Is it legal?'

'*Pardon*?' Monsieur Gerontin is already heading out to the landing again.

'I don't know if I could do anything like that . . .'

'Madame – wizout "*sous la table*" will be *verrry* difficult. *Impossible*.'

Longing to escape his sceptical stare, she makes her excuses to get away and goes down to the beach. It's a horseshoe of sand, currently crammed with a hot, cheerful riot of high-season sunbathers and swimmers, and backed by rocks which lead in turn up to the promenade on the old town walls. She perches herself on one of these rocks, in the shaded lee of the wall, and scrabbles at her calculator, working and reworking the exchange rate – and yes, it seems to be true: however often she redoes the arithmetic, it looks as if it really would be possible. She could buy the studio in *bon état*, and surely be left with quite a bit more of a lump sum than she'd thus far been planning. She'd have to sort something out, of course – a building society, an ISA, an annuity, one of those things anyway . . . details she can think about later. But it would be possible. It could be done.

The next morning she returns to Vieilleville to take another look, feeling much more sober and practical, but the crazy magic of the idea re-intoxicates. She goes first to the rue d'Espoir to examine the building more carefully. It really is pretty – like something out of a fairy story, half castle, half house. There are staircase towers at either side, each with its own front door. The one at this end leads to what she's already beginning to feel is *her* landing, and then on to the floor immediately above. She'd asked Monsieur Gerontin where the other one led – 'To ze *appartement de grand standing*,' he said, making it sound way, way above her, and not just because of its physical location. Its door has just a single bell-push next to the answerphone grill, but the one down here has three, two of which are labelled. 'Prosper' (as in Prosper Mérimée – *Carmen* had been one of her O level set texts) and 'Grange' as in 'Madame Legrange' in *Allons-y*, the book they'd used at her prep school all those years ago (*Voici Madame Legrange. Madame Legrange ouvre la porte . . .*'). A house full of locals, a life of Gallic charm.

Her sense of practicality doesn't entirely desert her – not yet. She does *mention* the word 'surveyor' when she goes back to see Monsieur Gerontin ('*visite d'expert*', it said in the dictionary, which hadn't sounded specific enough to her ears – what *sort* of expert? the possibility of choice is a bit unnerving), but his look of exasperated amazement is enough to make her instantly bury the thought. After all, she reasons, the flat itself is clearly newly done up with bathroom and kitchen fittings appetizingly unused – the shower tray still bears its sticky labels, for goodness' sake. True, as far as she could tell in the dim light, the hallway is surprisingly shabby. All the doors are painted the same sad gun-metal grey splotched with dollops of other colours, as if someone has gone around deliberately flicking emulsion for the hell of it, and the walls are pitted and bruised. Monsieur Gerontin sees her examining them and waves his arm expansively to cover the whole area – '*Tout rénové* – six months at ze most. You can see the plans in my *bureau* – *six*.' and he holds up the correct number of digits to prove it.

And then things move pretty swiftly. She sits in Monsieur Gerontin's office, at his desk, under his beady gaze, using his telephone to get through to both her bank and the building society. She will be signing what is evidently called a *compromis de vente* in the next couple of days, before she returns to England, and that signing, plus an accompanying deposit of 10 per cent, will set the whole process, more or less irrevocably, on its way. From then on, if she tries to back out of the deal she'll lose the deposit, but conversely, should the vendor want to wriggle out of it, he'll have to pay her double. It's a bit hairy, but at the same time rather satisfying. Little room for gazumping and the solid quality of the deal appeals to her sense of a new self – the newly *released* Alice Barnes, who doesn't prevaricate, who doesn't *ask*, not in the sense of asking permission anyway, who doesn't need to bother with that old stuff any more.

She would quite like the children's blessing, though – or that of any child she could reach. But she knows that Gavin is away somewhere on location in his capacity as second assistant director (or maybe it was third?), so it will be all down to trying to reach Lally for a cheering blast of approval. She doesn't want to borrow Monsieur Gerontin's office telephone again – too public. But there are no private phones in the *chaumières* at the Auberge de la Rose, and struggling to use alien call-boxes, with the wrong change, trying to reverse charges, makes it all seem terribly difficult. Then when at last she does reach Lally's number by dubiously swiping her credit card in a state-of-the-art call-box in the place de la République, she only gets the answering-machine. Blast.

'Hello, darling,' self-consciously – she hates these machines, 'it's Mummy' (God, that sounds wet – perhaps she should have said 'your mother' or 'Alice'?) loathes the feeling that her bumbling hesitations are caught in time by the tape at the other end, 'calling from France. I'm having a lovely time – um – well, I'll have to – um – actually I've got a happening – but – well, I'll have to talk to you once I'm back,' all this said rather reproachfully – she's aware of her tone – as if Lally is squatting there, refusing to pick up the receiver.

4

On Approval

'Well, good for you,' says Deirdre, but her tone is watery. 'Gosh. Well, there's a turn-up.' And she whistles. She doesn't usually whistle.

Alice is back in Hotwells under her guise as unwilling paying guest, leaning excitedly across Deirdre's kitchen table – the very same table that was the tragic repository for the decree nisi those few weeks ago.

'You think I've been rash,' says Alice, who also feels she's been a little on the impulsive side, and is looking for confirmation and back-up here, not deflation of her personal balloon.

'Well . . . it is a little *sudden* – and is it exactly *you*?'

'What do you mean "*you*"?' says Alice.

'I mean *you*, that's what I mean, *you* living on the Riviera.'

She's jealous, Alice realizes, with a tiny stab of satisfaction. She's *green*.

'It's not as if you've ever lived abroad before – not like Bill and me with Kuwait.'

Deirdre and Bill had lived in Kuwait for ten whole months in the early seventies, tax-free, courtesy of one of the big oil companies, and Deirdre has never got over the glory of it all – the marble bathrooms and chauffeur-driven cars, the cocktail parties at the Embassy. Deirdre thus *knows* about life. 'I mean you've always been *here*,' she now adds, by way of good measure.

'Not always.'

'Devon doesn't count as *abroad*, Alice. Devon's only down the road.'

Well, she has a point there. Still, it's not as if growing up in Exeter has been the sum total of Alice's five decades on the planet – not quite. There was the stint in London at St Hilda's Secretarial in Belsize Park, not to mention the job at St Jude's Hospital in Student Admissions, working as PA to the Dean of Studies, which was how Philip Barnes came breezing into her life in the first place. And after that, an awful lot of trailing around, at first as willing and eager girlfriend, and gradually melting into long-term willing helpmate, plus useful additional breadwinner in those leanest years.

They'd lived all over the country for short stints, according to which bit of Philip's career next needed refuelling. She'd become a very dab hand at packing tea-chests, then unpacking them again in double-quick time, adding her own original touches to turn the latest grotty rented flat into yet another haven. Still, Deirdre's right, she's never really pushed out the boundaries of her life's experience – she's never had cause or inclination. Surely all the more reason to start pushing now.

'Well, I've been and gone and done it,' she says. 'There's no going back.'

'What do you mean?'

'I've got the whole process started, and it's different in

France – none of this shilly-shallying around. Once you've signed the agreement, that's it – you're committed.'

And she is too. The speed of her decision is still intoxicating – so liberating after all the years of tagging behind Philip's mind-set like an obedient spaniel. But she's certainly gone and burnt her boats now – or at least 10 per cent of them – and if she thinks about it too precisely, a pit of apprehension threatens to open up. So, with Deirdre sounding less than enthusiastic, the gathering of family approval for her decision is beginning to feel essential.

She decides to explain face to face: even when you are in the same country telephones are so difficult – you get no sense of body language. Gavin is still away on location, but as it's really more Lally's support she's seeking, she goes up to London anyway to meet during her lunch-hour from work. Lally is in recruitment in the City – seems to be doing quite well. Shares a rented house in Clapham with a bunch of other girls. Has a boyfriend called Hamish in PR whom Alice has yet to meet. Since the disruption of the divorce there's been far too little opportunity for family get-togethers – and nowhere to hold them either.

Over Prêt à Manger sandwiches, she tells her tale.

'God – Mummy. Wow!' says Lally, and she starts to choke on her hummus and red-pepper wrap. 'I mean that's amazing. God. What does Daddy think?'

'I don't *know*,' says Alice, instantly irritated. 'I haven't asked *him*. Why on earth would I?'

'Sorry,' says Lally, 'I should've thought – it's just so automatic. I suppose I'm still not used to it – not yet,' and her eyes fill with tears. Recently Alice has been so taken up with the misery and disruption of her own life that she's tended to forget that the children might be feeling a little battered too. They seem so grown-up and centred on their newly developing worlds of work and relationships, that she's assumed the state of war between their parents was just something peripheral and out of focus.

'Anyway,' says Lally, 'tell me all about it – I want to hear every detail,' and then she looks at her watch. The brevity of her lunch-hour, really more of a lunch-forty-minutes, is the reason they're perching on Prêt's chrome stools rather than relaxing somewhere over a plate of pasta. This gesture, though, however fleeting, has the effect of putting Alice off her stride. She's thought about the whole adventure so much, but now she's got to gabble it out in a few minutes, baldly stating facts, when the whole thing is really made up of feelings and visions – almost nameless, formless hopes. So it comes out rather drily: Vieilleville, how different it was from the horrors of the holiday auberge, Monsieur Gerontin, the building, the flat . . .

'But how can you afford it, Mummy? I thought the French Riviera was all pure millionaires' stuff.'

'If you have a villa, of course, or a large apartment, yes, of course it's expensive, terribly – well, no more than London I suppose – but this isn't anything like that. This is in a very old building right in the middle of the town and it's tiny . . . Sort of – well, sort of a bedsit, really.'

'A bedsit?' says Lally, really quite carefully, as if the words might shatter.

'A studio, that's what they call them – better than a bedsit, really. It's got its own bathroom and everything . . .'

'Yes, Mummy, I know what a studio is,' Lally is sounding impatient now, 'but honestly – I mean surely, for you at your sort of age and stage – '

'What?' says Alice, really quite sharply.

'Well, what I *mean* is – what about home?'

'In what sense?'

'*Home*. For us. I mean for you too. All of us . . .'

'Well, Vieilleville will be my home . . .'

'But what about Bristol . . . and us? What about our *stuff*?'

'It's still all packed up in the Villa Guardi.'

'I know that. I just thought somehow that once you'd got yourself settled somewhere – well, you know – that it could be *home* again, I suppose . . . You will have somewhere that can count as home here too – in England – won't you?'

'I won't be able to afford anything else. I think the Villa Guardi will have to do for that – for you, I mean . . .' Alice lets her voice trail away. 'Have you been down there yet to see them – Daddy and . . . you know . . . Hillary Aldyce?'

'No, I *haven't*,' Lally snaps.

'I'm sorry – I didn't mean to pry' (only she did – of course she did), 'only I just wondered – while I was away or something – you'd have been perfectly justified. He is still your father.'

'I do know that – I'm perfectly aware – I just haven't felt – I mean, I tried phoning – apart from anything else I needed my old black taffeta puffball for an eighties party so I thought maybe Hillary might be able to find it and bung it in the post . . . but you know . . . Oh . . . oh, *God*,' and a huge tear overspills Lally's eye and rolls slowly down her cheek. 'Bugger. I'll bugger up my makeup and I've got an interview at two. Blast.' She looks at her watch again. 'I'm sorry, darling, I'll have to go – I would have met you after work only I've got to meet clients. I'm sorry.' She jumps down from the stool and gives a huge sniff, thus pulling herself fiercely together. 'It sounds terrific, honestly it does, marvellous – I'm sorry,' and she gives Alice a big hug and charges out into Bishopsgate.

She thinks I'm losing my marbles, thinks Alice, and goes to get another cappuccino and a square of pecan pie. Maybe she's just being greedy, but doubts are already beginning to stir, and she doesn't want to brave the reality of the route back to Paddington – not yet.

*

She's losing her marbles, thinks Lally, scudding along Cheapside to her office, hoping she'll have time to mend her face and hot-tong her hair before her 2 p.m. with the personnel people from Deutsche Inc. 'I'll have to try and get hold of Gav – talk some sense . . .'

*

'Cool,' says Gavin later that night. At last he's switched his mobile on and she's been able to reach him somewhere in the Yorkshire Dales.

'How can you say that? It's crazy – she's just sort of doing it on the rebound – she doesn't know anyone there or anything.'

'Cool. No, really. Fan-dabby-doosey – '

'Oh, do speak English, Gav. This is our *mother* we're talking about.'

'I *know* – and like I said, it's *cool*. We should be grateful.'

'Why?'

'That she wants to start a new life and all that. What Dad's doing is a real cold baked potato, right?, a slap in the face with a wet haddock, yeah? This'll be like, you know –'

'What?'

'Get her off our hands.'

'*What*?'

'Off the hook, right? That's what I mean – get her started, something new. She's not that old – who knows what could happen?'

'That's what I mean – that's what worries me – and she'll have nowhere here, no bolthole.'

'She'll have us, yeah?' says Gavin. 'Why don't you stop moping and think of all those free holidays?'

*

Back in Bristol, waiting for the *notaire* in France to do his legal stuff, Alice has several weeks for her own doubts to fester. Despite the supposed efficiency of French property conveyancing, it looks as if the deal is dragging on just the way it does in England. She feels more and more like a sad old gooseberry hanging around Deirdre's house, waiting for vital letters that don't arrive. Mostly she is longing to get on with it all, but at the same time horrible doubts will keep creeping in and making her feel sick and empty. But then, as the autumnal leaves fall, and the gales begin their annual offensive, a snapshot of Vieilleville tends to click into her mind, and she can see again the colours of the place, sniff the aromas and feel the warmth on her skin. Surely it's going to be all right.

Of course there is also a lot to find out, and after the initial rashness of her decision, she decides she'd better sober up and absorb some relevant information. Research in the local library produces a book called *French Dressing – A Survivor's Guide* – not as totally reassuring as she'd hoped. Until now she'd thought that with the new great freedoms of the EU, with their common borders, laws and regulations, they were all supposed to be one great big happy family. Surely, as a British citizen, she could effect such a move without the need for any formalities or regulation. After all, one scarcely seems to need passports any more – at least, no one seems to check them all that carefully.

Now, however, she feels a bit sick to discover that she'll require several official sanctions, the most pressing of which, a residents' permit called a *carte de séjour*, is an absolute legal necessity and must be applied for within three months of arrival. The book is quite hot on the topic, and not very reassuring about the potential for getting embroiled with French officialdom, describing it as full of 'jobsworths'. Evidently nearly a quarter of all French people work for the government, but only have 10 per cent of the total workload, leading to all sorts of bureaucratic meddling. Alice rereads that statistic several times, and hopes it's an exaggeration for dramatic effect – it's quite a jokey sort of book. On the opposite page it lists all sorts of documents and certificates she's going to need, everything from birth to divorce with all the other bits in between, each to be translated by someone on the French Embassy's 'approved list', and then each translation in turn to be certified as accurate by the Embassy itself. It's all going to cost a bomb and take an age. As a first step, she goes out and orders herself a copy of *French Dressing* – she can see it's going to become her Bible.

It's a lonely time. She can't really share any of these doubts with anyone. Deirdre and Bill are already far too full of I-told-you-sos to be any sort of help, and most of her other friends seem to have melted away since the divorce – or, rather, they all seem to have turned out to be Philip's friends after all. A bit hard, considering he never lifted a finger to entertain anyone, and something she can't quite understand. Of course they'd always socialized as a couple, but even so, she'd have thought that people like the Morleys and the Johnsons were really more her friends than his. And yet Jessie Morley was really strange when she saw her in Whiteladies Road the other day. Alice crossed over to say hello – dodging all the traffic, wanted to know how the boys were getting on at uni – and Jessie was really distant and peculiar, made Alice feel paranoiac about halitosis or something. But then, of course, Freddie Morley is a work colleague of Philip's – as are most of their friends when you get right down to it, which means that they nearly all already know Hillary Aldyce in her professional capacity. And, now Alice comes to think of it, apart from having got rid of her, nothing has really changed for him, has it? He's still lording it up at the Villa Guardi, while she's down here with Deirdre living out of suitcases. So, yes, it's a lonely time all right.

She knows she really ought to tell her father, not that she has any hope he'll be clear-headed enough to have anything very helpful to offer but she feels she ought to let him know what she's up to and maybe even get his blessing. But she's kept putting it off. Since he remarried six years ago, Brenda-the-New-Wife has kept all comers firmly at bay. Poor Brenda, she can't have got quite what she bargained for when she married the retired, widowed solicitor from Exeter with his golf-club membership and penchant for all-in luxury holidays on Tenerife. A brainstem stroke, rapidly followed by some form of dementia – though nobody actually mentioned Alzheimer's – meant she'd turned into a nursemaid rather than the Queen of Rotary. It must have been very disappointing, though in public at least she seemed to thrive on her status and kept her charge hedged around with anxious care.

It is Brenda who answers the phone.

'Dad's not too clever today,' she says, 'but I'll tell him you called.'

'Couldn't I have a quick word with him?' asks Alice.

'No, dearie, I wouldn't – he's really not too clever. Heart's a bit dicky now.'

'Should I come down?'

'No, dearie, he couldn't take the strain.'

'I wouldn't bother him – just to say hello. Maybe I could take you both out for lunch – give you a bit of a break?'

'No, dearie. As I said, he's not too clever. Another time maybe.'

'Only I've got some news – I'm moving to France.'

'That's nice, dearie.'

'I'm sure he'd want to know.'

'Well, as I say . . .'

When Alice hangs up, she wonders if she shouldn't have fought harder against this prohibition and gone to see him anyway. But, then, supposing she did and he had a coronary? It's not as if he seemed to have had the slightest interest in her even when Mother was still alive. She can't ever recall exchanging any confidences with him. All the confiding was done with Mother and was lost the day she died bizarrely of measles at the ripe old age of forty-nine. At least, it had seemed ripe then, to an eighteen-year-old Alice, enjoying the time of her life in Swinging London. How odd and sad to think that she is now already older than Mother had been at the time of her abrupt demise.

That night, over supper, Bill asks her what she thinks she'll be *doing* in France. The trouble is, she doesn't really have much of a concrete answer – so far it's all been a matter of instinct. So she says, with what she hopes sounds like confident scorn, 'Live of course!' and he says, 'It's all very well in theory but have you thought it *through*?' and then leaves this horrible don't-say-I-didn't-warn-you kind of pause just hanging around over Deirdre's sticky toffee pudding. And, of course, the trouble is that she hasn't – in fact, she hasn't any idea of what 'through' might equal in this instance.

*

She is just at the stage of having serious doubts, questioning what the hell she's letting herself in for, when something decisive happens.

She's walking up one of those steep hills towards Clifton, on an errand for Deirdre, a visit to the organic greengrocer – anything to feel useful in this odd homeless, aimless lacuna in her life. It's pouring with rain – more than mere pouring, in fact, much more like those artificial sheets of the stuff you see in films, when you can almost hear the director's shout of 'Cue rain – action!' so she has her head down and is looking at the individual paving stones and the streams running down her trenchcoat, when a car screeches up just behind her so that she feels she has to look – then wishes she hadn't. It is Philip's Jaguar, and Philip within, immaculate in grey worsted – the rain might as well be a mirage for all it touches him – and now the electric window is sliding down.

'Hello, *love*!' he calls, quite cavalierly gay (in the old sense of the word, of course). 'Aren't you going to congratulate me? I'm a daddy again! Twins. Boys.'

And she literally doesn't know what to say. 'Well, bugger me,' is the only thing readily on her tongue. The tactless cheek of the man instantly drains her brain of any suitably cutting response. His face is pink with delight. He seems genuinely certain that she will share in his triumph too and she's darned if she'll let her sense of outrage into the open for air. She has more dignity than *that*. Well, actually she doesn't – that's the problem: she doesn't think she has a shred of dignity left anywhere to clothe her poor old naked ego, but he needn't know that, need he? Still, the word 'congratulations' would choke her so she opts for health instead – always a reliable get-out, and quite adult in the circumstances. 'How is Hillary?' is what she says, for after all one was properly brought up, wasn't one? and her dear, dead mother would surely have been proud.

'Oh, fine, fine,' says Philip. 'A little sore, of course – Caesarean. One of them was breech.'

I'll bet she is, thinks Alice, I'll *bet* she's sore, with instant recollection of their own twins' births, twenty-five years ago, one of them a breech, and no Caesarean for her, only forceps – insides never been *quite* up to scratch ever since. How typically inconsiderate of Philip to have the twin chromosome so firmly available, and to implant it in other people's wombs with such tiresome regularity.

'Can I give you a lift?' he then asks, but doesn't sound awfully keen. Alice looks at the pristine fawn leather seats of the car that only quite recently she'd thought of as almost *hers*, and then down at her soaking trenchcoat with its rivulets of water still streaming, and declines.

'No, thanks, I'm enjoying the walk,' she says airily, and tosses a dismissive wave. Being Philip, he does not of course press the point, and with her departing shouted 'Give my best to Hillary' (now that was civilized, wasn't it?), she watches the Jaguar purr on up the hill.

So then she *knows* she has to go – and knows that she's been right. She has to do something drastic, something to catapult her up, out and away – comfortable half-measures won't do.

5

Sous La Table

Vieilleville in December doesn't seem quite the same.

Alice arrives on the eighteenth, initially relieved to be escaping the tyranny of Yule. As always and for ever, the whole of Britain is already drowning in the hysteria of its annual festive rite. Every newspaper and magazine is weighted with a 'Countdown to Christmas' supplement, thus inducing quiet panic within the souls of women the length of the land. Possible Purgatory awaits all those who fail the test or buck the preordained timetable. If your monster chestnut-stuffed bird misses the 7 a.m. oven deadline, you get the whole shebang out of synch. How then can you start lunch at one thirty in time for the Queen's Speech at three, followed by the inexorable run-up to tea with *The Wizard of Oz* on BBC2, accompanied by individual holly-leaf-decorated mincemeat puff-pastry bites? How? *How*? Oh, the *groan* of it.

So the prospect of Vieilleville is enticing. It's a well-known fact that the French have lots of festivals and thus don't need to hurl their all into this one major orgy of gastric familial celebration. But the reality is . . . well, a little odd. It's true that compared to the multi-coloured light-infested shriek of home this town looks restrained, just the occasional elegant window display, and here and there a nativity scene – otherwise on the whole, a distinct sense of life as normal. But that life doesn't seem to be quite the warm, transparent vision of her recent summer memory. From flowery, parasolled bower, it has metamorphosed into chilly, blustery citadel with rain sweeping off the hills, driving the populace indoors. Even the café pavement tables are stashed in wet plastic heaps.

Somewhere in the back of Alice's mind has always lurked the notion of eternal Riviera warmth. Wasn't it a fact that our Victorian ancestors considered the 'season' on the Côte d'Azur to be a winter one, a blessed relief from foggy bronchial Britannia – but then, of course, they wore such a lot of clothes, didn't they? Either that or the climate must have changed, for this isn't a place designed for the cold. There is too much stone around – and too few radiators. The stone, which seemed so perfect for absorption of August heat, is now slippery, impervious and deadeningly chilled.

Alice puts up at the only hotel in the old town, picturesquely planted on the edge of the main square and devoid of central heating. In her room there is an elderly fan heater mounted on the wall. It wheezes through the night, leaching out a tepid warmth and a strong aroma of singeing dust. She rues the lack of sweaters in her luggage, and clutches her thin raincoat tightly round her chest on her way to the *notaire*'s office for the big signing.

In any case she is feeling a bit queasy. Inside the clutched mac is a briefcase rammed against her breastbone. It holds her large Larousse dictionary in case she has any last-minute vocab emergencies when faced with the legal documents, and a brown padded envelope stuffed with used banknotes. She feels ludicrously obvious – as if she has a Belisha beacon labelled 'Guilty' strapped to her head. She also feels vulnerable – a sitting duck ripe for mugging at every turn in the road.

Initially she'd completely ignored Monsieur Gerontin's mention of the 'under the table' payment, on the basis that it sounded far-fetched and if she looked vague and clueless enough he'd eventually give up and let it drop. However, on this particular subject, his use of English suddenly became far more fluent – he'd even phoned her a couple of times in Bristol and managed to get past Deirdre, who spoke no French at all, in order to re-clarify the situation. Madame Barnes *did* understand, did she not, that the price agreed on paper did *not* include the additional sum they had discussed – she did – she *did*? Well, all right, so she did – but she very much rather wished she didn't. *French Dressing – A Survivor's Guide* didn't mention this situation in the main text, but described it briefly in a footnote attached to the section labelled 'Matters of Tax'. The content of this note seemed intended as a firm warning, but the tone was one of helpless shoulder-shrugging. In the face of Monsieur Gerontin's steady determination, she decides in the end to try to adopt the same tone herself, which is why she's carrying a Jiffybag of French francs through the streets of Vieilleville at 10 a.m. on a wet Tuesday.

*

In the *notaire*'s office, Alice and Monsieur Gerontin are seated at either end of a large desk. The *notaire* is a kindly old gent with a smattering of English, and between the three of them and the Larousse, they creak their way through the various documents. Alice had thought she'd be meeting the vendor at last, but it turns out that Monsieur Gerontin *himself* is the vendor – something which she'd somehow missed in all their communications thus far. She also finds out that the building has a name, Maison Puce, as well as a street number. *Puce*, she remembers, is 'flea' – it's always cropping up in the context of flea-markets – *marché aux puces*. A couple of times she's seen a gathering of bric-à-brac stalls down in the place d'Espoir, so perhaps that's the connection. Now doesn't seem to be the time or place to ask – there's too much serious business going on. Still, she likes the idea of living in a named house – it makes it seem extra special – and she signs the papers with additional gusto.

Towards the end of the proceedings, the *notaire* excuses himself and disappears into what seems to be his own personal *cabinet de toilette* – an elderly chap, suspect bladder?

As soon as he's gone, Monsieur Gerontin whips down to her end of the desk.

'You 'ave it? Ze *sous-la-table*?'

'Now?' asks Alice. 'Won't Monsieur be coming back?' There's a background chorus of flushing.

'He will stay long enough,' says Monsieur Gerontin enigmatically. He takes the Jiffybag and retreats back down to his end of the desk where he starts counting, whipping expertly through the notes like a bank-teller. Obviously par for his particular course.

'I can assure you it's all there,' says Alice, feeling like a pompously upright citizen in the face of this open deception.

Monsieur finishes and stuffs the entire bag inside his jacket, where it gives him a lop-sided one-bosomed look. Surely the *notaire* will notice? And where *is* the *notaire*? The flushing stopped some time ago.

'You 'ave a bargain,' says Monsieur Gerontin, smiling and leaning back, so that the bulge on his chest sticks out more than ever. 'Is *verrry* good price.' He clears his throat noisily.

'I hope so,' says Alice. 'It needs to be. I hope you realize I'm doing this on an absolute shoe-string?'

Maybe the throat-clearing is a signal, for the *notaire* returns abruptly, looking sprightly, not like a man who's been taken embarrassingly short. Alice feels the presence of the money bulge on Monsieur Gerontin's chest, almost as if it has developed an infrared beam and is sending its light straight into the *notaire*'s eyes. She can feel herself starting to blush. 'I was telling Monsieur Gerontin,' she continues, by way of distraction, 'that I'm doing this on a shoe-string' (part of which is in that Jiffybag right now – what *have* I done? is what she was thinking).

The *notaire* and Monsieur regard each other – at a loss. They know what 'shoe' is, they understand the meaning of 'string', but the significance of both together?

'*Fil de soulier – peut-être*?' suggests Alice, but, catching their look of puzzled pain, lets it drop.

*

So that was it. All it took. Alice Barnes is now a property owner in France. Madame Barnes of Maison Puce, numero

8, rue d'Espoir, Vieilleville. She moves in the following day – if it can be called 'moving in', for all she has by way of possessions so far are her suitcase, a duvet, a nicked hotel toothmug and a bottle of warm supermarket champagne. Her personal bits and pieces can't be delivered from England until well into January because of the Christmas strangulation back home, but she feels she can't get out of the hotel fast enough – partly to economize and partly to have a taste of being in her very own space again, a luxury she hasn't experienced since she moved out of the Villa Guardi and down the hill to Deirdre's.

She can't exactly pretend it's all that much fun, though. That night she sleeps rolled up in the duvet on the freezing tiled floor, and wakes up stiff and sore, realizing that her first priority is to get a heater and a sofabed. She'd already decided to buy most of her furniture down here. The nicest bits of hers were anyway left at the Villa Guardi as part of the divorce settlement, and it would be expensive and awkward to transport the rest of it from Bristol. Better to have a completely new start.

Vieilleville itself doesn't really go in for much in the way of practical shopping, something she hadn't really noticed until now when she tries to buy basics like a bucket and mop. So she has to trail up to Bonneville-sur-Mer's slightly bigger stores. There's a place there like Woolworth's for day-to-day necessities, and also one or two *bricolages* for hardware, but nothing like heaters or furniture anywhere. Vieilleville itself specializes, of course, in food, and apart from that has quantities of pharmacies and beauty parlours – the maintenance of the body's exterior presumably being paramount, once it has been so well fed and watered. It also has antiques shops, a few galleries, a bookshop or two, and lots of small boutiques specializing in lingerie and/or particularly esoteric linen – for bed and table. Alice can thus buy innumerable embroidered breakfast sets or plunge bras with matching thongs, if she wanted them, but not a single dustpan or broom.

She takes the bus towards Nice in search of the big furniture shops she remembers from last summer. The *autoroute* goes past the Auberge de la Rose. It is shut up now for the winter, its neon rosebud extinguished. As the bus swooshes past through the rain, she can't help thinking a little bitterly that its owners, fattened on all those summer receipts, are probably holed up somewhere sensible – like the Caribbean.

But some way beyond the *auberge* she finds what she's after, those giant furniture warehouses draped with banners screaming their wares. Meubles Galore boasts right across its front that it gives 'Le Big Discount'. What price Franglais, then? And what hope for all the Anglophones trying hard to avoid it? Inside it also offers something called 'Home Service', which turns out to mean delivery. She picks out a pretty yellow sofabed, on the astonishing basis that they are prepared to deliver it the very next day, even so close to Christmas, then prays, as her credit card is swiped, that it can be squeezed round the spiral stairs of the Maison Puce. The next warehouse along, TéléElectro, produces a convector heater, which she takes with her, wrapped up in a double thickness of plastic bag against the wet. She heaves it all the way back to Vieilleville, via two changes of bus with a forty-five-minute wait in the pouring rain stranded on some traffic island in the middle of nowhere. No – so far, you certainly couldn't call this fun.

The next day is 23 December. Back at home mock-snowy peaks of royal icing would be setting hard on a million Christmas cakes, toy departments would be depleted of all available stocks of the latest hideous toy craze, and here in Vieilleville, the van from Meubles Galore arrives to deliver Alice's sofabed. The men park across the bottom of the rue d'Espoir, thus successfully blocking two lines of traffic. Within moments great streams of furious little Fiats and Renaults are buzzing like angry wasps and honking their horns, but the men take no notice at all. Alice wrings her hands, as outside the racket grows, and inside the men curse, heave and squeeze – until at last the sofabed is pushed round the last curve of the stair and emerges with a little pop. Once installed it offers a single glowing pool of comfort in what is otherwise still a rather bleak habitat.

Alice would love to crack open a bottle with the men, wants to thank them and would also relish a little human contact. But they have to hurry on, more deliveries, and down in the street the backed-up traffic is threatening to blow – so instead she sends them on their way with what she hopes is a decent tip and shouts of '*Joyeux Noël*' (the right thing to say? or possibly a *faux pas* – but then, come to think of it, does even *faux pas* have the same shade of meaning here? Heavens, but there's going to be a lot to find out).

December 24 – Christmas Eve. This time last year she was up to her armpits in chestnut stuffing and brandy butter, wrapping last-minute presents, and today she is sitting cross-legged on the lone luxury of the sofa taking stock. She has a rotisseried chicken from the man down by the market and some of his own crisps, huge and salty, *fait à la maison*, another bottle of that supermarket champagne, a bucket, a saucepan, a fish-slice, a mop and, most essential of all, the electric convector heater going at full blast right now.

Not bad, really. She turns her Walkman to 'speakerphone' and switches it on. BBC World Service: 'Once in Royal David's City' pipes out, the boy soprano's famous solo, the unmistakable sound of King's College Choir and the Festival of Nine Lessons and Carols. She catches herself just in time – stops the beginnings of regret from taking hold, smothers the impulse to weep. Wouldn't do at all. Things are fine. Things are *dandy*.

'Happy Christmas, Mum.'

'Happy Christmas, darling.'

'You're all right?'

'Fine, darling. Yes. Fine. Thanks for accepting the charges.' Alice is in the call-box on the quay, for despite her urgings of FranceTelecom, the phone has not been connected at the flat. The glass of the box is steaming up and outside the rain still pours and the sea is being whipped into frothy waves.

'Could hardly refuse, could I, Mum?' Gav laughs heartily down the line.

In the background she can hear sounds of a crowd, music, not King's College this time, more like – could it possibly be? – 'Santa Claus Is Coming To Town'? *Gav*? 'It sounds as if you're having fun – what's the music?'

'Oh, nothing, Mum. Retro-chic kitsch stuff. Sandy's brought a CD round – the Ronettes, I think. Thought we'd try to get in the spirit of the thing.'

'Yes. Terrific.'

'Cos it's a bit strange, really, don't you think?'

'In what way?'

'Well, you know, you're there. And like we're here, yup? And Dad's got this whole new life we're not even part of and, well – like only last year we were all together, Lally and me back down to Bristol, claimed back our own bedrooms, dug out our old *Star Wars* posters – you know what I mean? Doesn't seem real, does it?'

'No. I don't suppose it does.'

'What'll you be doing? Lunch with the locals?'

'Something like that.'

'Get you. I can see it all – I've got this picture – sitting in the sun with a glass of kir.'

'Umm.'

'Do they eat the same sort of stuff at Christmas?'

'I'm not sure – yet. Not judging from the shops – they seem to be full of *foie gras*, and *bûches de Noël* in the *pâtisseries*. Christmas Eve is the big night for them of course – le Réveillon. They have this thing called the *Treize Desserts* – the Thirteen Puddings.'

'That sounds good.'

'Yes, it's very traditional, I believe – lots of different nuts and dried fruits and a special sort of bread.'

'Oh . . . bread. Bet they don't eat cold-turkey-jelly-roast-potato sandwiches.'

'Bet they don't.' A waft of nostalgia hits her. Cold-turkey-jelly-roast-potato had always been Gavin's favourite post-Christmas treat. He'd been known to binge.

'So you'd better get off, then,' he says now, 'to whatever you're doing?'

'Yes.' He wants to get rid of me, she thinks. But she doesn't want to let go. 'Who's cooking your Christmas dinner, then?'

'*I* am.'

'Gavin, I am impressed. I thought you'd have some hapless girl in tow at the very least.'

'Get real, Mum – that attitude went out with Fanny Cradock.'

'Turkey's been in the oven for ages, then? Up to the mark with your countdown?'

'What?'

'To Christmas? Surely you've been subjected – even the *Grauniad* must do one?'

'Actually we're having goose.'

'Oh. Goose.' (Without *her*?)

'Thought it would make a change.'

'Yes. No turkey-jelly sandwiches for you, then, this year.'

'No. Goose jelly, maybe – maybe not, though. But there you go.'

'Is Lally there?'

'She's gone up to Norfolk to stay with Hamish's family.'

'Right. Have you heard anything from the Villa Guardi?'

'No.'

'Not even a card?'

'No.'

'Me neither . . . Well, you're right. It is a bit odd. We're all split up.'

'Yup.'

'Refreshing, really.'

'Yup. I'm sorry, Mum, there's the doorbell. I'll have to go.'

'Sure. Happy Christmas, darling.'

'Happy Christmas, Mum.'

*

Walking back through the streets of Vieilleville, away from the seafront as quickly as possible to avoid the wind, slinking through the alleys, sneaking looks through ground-floor windows, families at table – even in a land which does most of its celebrating on Christmas Eve there's no escape. Throughout Christendom kith and kin are gathered today – families are what it's all supposed to be about. And where is hers?

What is Philip doing now, at home in the lofty drawing room of the Villa Guardi with Hillary Aldyce, the new Mrs Barnes, and the twin Barnes boys? What has he called them – she's never asked? Are they opening presents around a tall tree, stylishly hung with real cranberries, ribbons and baubles in shades of cream? Is the room even decorated yet? When she'd been heaved out, down the hill to Deirdre's, it was still painted poisonous infirmary green. Had Philip hired builders to complete her task? Surely Hillary Aldyce hadn't been sent up the step-ladder at nine months gone, paint roller in hand? Well, actually, knowing Philip, quite possibly she had. And cheerfulness suddenly breaks in. Bugger the being alone. Who gives a damn? Bugger the groaning tables of fare. And Up with Freedom.

Walking back down the rue d'Espoir, she gets a good look at the house. The façade is now laid bare, the leafless stems of the vines making a bizarre network which reveals the pockmarked weather-beaten condition of the plaster beneath. This is a state of affairs which was totally hidden in August by the thick curtain of green. Also hidden then was the sprinkling of bas-reliefs – stucco garlands that wind from window to window and round the twin towers at either end, echoing the real vines. Now the relief designs show up clearly. Over each window and door is a worn carved stone frame. There are two designs – one of a twisted serpent, and the other of some sort of insect. She'd thought perhaps these were bees, but perhaps after all they might be fleas. That would make the whole notion of a link with the flea-market very ancient, wouldn't it? Had they been going that long? She'll make some enquiries – perhaps one of the other residents will know.

So far the rest of the building has seemed empty – a bit spooky, this. She'd assumed it would be full of all her new neighbours, but in these few days, she's seen neither lights nor people, heard nothing. Hers are the only windows not permanently shuttered. Immediately below her flat, on the ground floor, the closed shutters look particularly weather-beaten, whilst on the second floor they look quite smart, with various hanging baskets on hooks around the sill. Above that it's quite hard to get much of a sense of what happens because the narrowness of the street prevents her from getting far enough back to have a good look. She inspects the bell-pushes again. The one at the other end still hasn't been labelled – but then neither has hers at Flat 2; she hasn't got round to it yet. Everyone must be away for the festivities. But she can be patient now – time will tell.

6

Territorial Rights

Someone has moved in at last – downstairs. The previous night, Alice heard scraping noises, and when she crept down to take a peek, saw a light under the door of Flat 1. Presumably this is 'Prosper' (as in Mérimée?). Then, in the morning, she finds both a motor scooter and a large gingery dog parked out in the communal hallway. Neither of these is a visual improvement. They take up all the available space and have to be negotiated with care. Alice assumes – no, Alice *hopes* – that they are both temporary arrivals?

One day on, and Alice still hasn't met her new neighbour, though the dog and scooter are turning into permanent features. The dog is a bit sinister for she has to squeeze past him to get out and he usually growls. When she tries smiling and murmuring, '*Bon chien*,' he lifts his lips to reveal a fine set of yellow fangs, which she can all too clearly envisage embedded in her calf. When he isn't growling, he sits outside Flat 1's door, looking beseechingly up at its impenetrability, and whimpers.

In the afternoon she hears the front door bang and rushes over to her window, just in time to see a young woman turning the corner into the square. She's a small, dark, skinny person, spindly legs sticking out of clumpy black lace-ups, with a straggly mat of hair – not exactly '*bon chic bon genre*' as touted in the pages of 'Madame Figaro' and worn by most of the young girls round here. Alice hadn't known the French went in for grunge.

The mixture of dog and bike in the hall makes it look tattier than ever and a pair of puddles is developing – one of saliva, the other of oil. Alice knows she ought to say something, but it's difficult. The last thing she wants is to start off a new neighbourly relationship with a complaint – awful to get off on the wrong foot like that. Also, she's acutely aware that her French isn't up to an argument. She's working on it, of course – every day. From schoolgirl memory and various modern textbooks, she's trying to recall all those lost conjugations and which verbs take *être*, not to mention the blasted subjunctive, but it's still disappointingly halting and stiff. What she needs is *practice* – fluency will only come if she really immerses herself in local life. The trouble is, it's all a bit chicken-and-eggish. She can't enter local life without good French and she can't get more fluent without the local life. All the more reason for *not* antagonizing this new neighbour. She decides to try listening out more carefully for the various comings and goings to see if she can just bump into her in the hall as if by accident . . . try and keep the whole thing light and informal.

Two days later and she's still failed to meet Mademoiselle Prosper in the house. She does spot her outside, though – on the scooter, pop-popping slowly along the quay with the dog loping behind. She seems to know lots of people, keeps stopping to chat – plenty of vigorous French arm-waving.

Alice follows her right down to the end where some of the bigger yachts are moored. For a moment she wonders if she should introduce herself, but feels funny about it. As she hasn't yet met Mademoiselle Prosper 'properly', she realizes that the very act of recognition will expose her as the snooper she's become.

So instead she stands watching the girl park both dog and scooter by a gangplank and go aboard a big yacht with crescent moon flag and Arabic name. Alice has had plenty of time in her lonely wanderings to explore the quays and marvel at these floating palaces. It's become something of a private game for her, particularly at dusk, when the interiors start to be lit up and she can see through into shining wood-panelled cabins. They seem utterly mysterious and unattainable to her, part of another untouchable, parallel universe. So it's intriguing that this young woman, her immediate neighbour, seems part of that world. Tantalizing – a potential entrée for Alice, a source of hope?

The next morning, however, Alice comes down to find the dog slumped right across the stairs, blocking her exit. Every time she tries to slip past, he raises his lip and growls. Her patience snaps and she's hit by a full blast of righteous British indignation. If you *must* keep a dog in such an unsuitable place (and there are no parks to speak of in Vieilleville – no wonder avoiding dog *merde* is something of a town sport) – anyway, if you *must* be so self-indulgent, the least you can do is look after the poor creature properly. Leaving him outside your own space to rot up other people's simply isn't on. Simply isn't.

She gathers up her nerve and a residue of French vocab,

steps over the growling animal, and knocks on the door. It's opened only a crack, and an angry, sleepy-looking eye is inserted. The voice says, '*Oui?*' very coldly. Alice sticks a smile on her face and tries to exude warm and friendly body language to show she's basically a good egg. Then she does her best to explain the dog problem and the general gumming-up of the hallway.

The girl lets her finish, then launches into a French cascade, of which Alice only catches every tenth word or so. Ten per cent is quite enough, however, to get the general gist. Mademoiselle is *outraged* that Alice should be insulting Frédéric – a real coochy-coo of a pooch is jolly old 'Frédéric' – and he *can't* be shut up in her studio all day as he suffers from *la claustrophobie* (even Alice can translate that one) and that basically she can lump it (something along the lines of '*Il faut bien que vous acceptiez sans rien dire*' etc.). As the dog has moved away by now from the bottom step and is trying to infiltrate the flat, Alice takes the opportunity to back up the stairs, keeping the smile firmly mortared to her face, and offering a self-deprecating wave as she disappears round the bend.

She goes into her own flat and is just about to close the door when the dog gives an extra loud whine – really a howl – and the door below opens again. A female voice says, 'Oh, belt up, Fred – and fuck off while you're about it.' The accent is pure London Estuary Twang. Alice shoots downstairs again. The hall is empty except for the dog, now backed up against the scooter, growling anew. Alice says, 'Belt up, Fred,' and is gratified that he flops down immediately, looking depressed. She raps on the door.

'*Oui*?' The door is opened wider this time, and a sink piled high with dirty pots is revealed, as well as a furious Mademoiselle P. '*Oui*?' she rasps.

'You're English,' says Alice.

'So what?' says the girl.

'You might have told me,' says Alice.

'Why?' says the girl.

'I thought you were French,' says Alice.

'That was bloody obvious,' says the girl, and laughs.

'But you let me say all that stuff – bang on and on in French, when you *knew* – '

'It was bloody funny – you should have heard yourself.'

'I did.'

'I don't know how I kept a straight face.'

'At least I try,' says Alice. 'The French like one to try.'

'I think they expect a better grasp than yours, don't you?'

Alice's sense of embarrassment evaporates in a blast of rage. 'Now, just you listen – it's not on, I mean it, braving a snarling Alsatian every time you want to pop out. It's not on at all. Kindly keep him under control.' Oh dear – so much for the blast of rage. Even to herself she only sounds like Disgusted of Tonbridge Wells.

'He *is* under control. And he's not an Alsatian, he's a mongrel. And he's not mine. I just got dumped. He came off one of the boats – from Senegal or somewhere. He was a gun-runner's mutt, weren't you, Fred?' and she lets out a torrent of French in his direction. The dog is so delighted to be noticed that he starts squirming towards them on his belly, his tail sweeping the floor. 'The trouble is he's fallen for me. I've tried leaving him down on the beach but he always comes back and howls on the doorstep. And he can't stay in the flat all day – he eats the furniture and makes the place stink and, anyway, some of my pupils are allergic – '

'*Pupils?*' asks Alice – useless to muzzle her sense of surprise.

'English as a foreign language. And I do a bit of French too – for ex-pats with no grasp, like you. You could do with my services – I might do you a special, reduced rate for quantity and being on the premises. I'm Imogen by the way – Imogen Prosper.' This is said as in 'save and prosper' and not as in 'Prosper Mérimée' after all. What a let-down.

*

After a horrible night's night tossing and turning, Alice decides she'd better go down and make her peace with the girl. She feels more foolish than angry. By mistaking the girl's nationality she's been wrong-footed as well as disappointed. And how ironic to be thrown together with someone like this – English yet not the sort of person she'd ever know at home, reminds her of those gum-chewing types who hang round Broadmead shopping centre on Saturday afternoons, shouting after the boys and dropping litter. Still, having at least a shared language with full access to its nuances, is empowering, and she feels on much more solid ground than yesterday as she raps on the door.

Imogen Prosper doesn't look at all welcoming, but Alice continues regardless.

'I think we'd better talk – may I come in?'

She's curious, of course, to see inside the flat and compare it with her own. This space is equally small, and it hasn't been modernized. The walls are the colour of old nicotine, the big old china sink is as piled high as yesterday, and a plastic concertina door half hanging off its runners, leads to what she assumes is the bathroom. The room is chaotically untidy – books, newspapers, scattered clothes and full ashtrays cover every surface. A Formica table is sway-backed under the weight, and in the opposite corner is a small stack of metal chairs. There's nowhere else to sit except on the bed, and Alice lowers herself gingerly on to the edge of it, while Imogen squats on the floor and lights a Gitanes. The dog has used the diversion of Alice to slip in and is already prostrating himself, wiggling on his belly towards Imogen's lap.

Alice uses him to break the ice. 'He obviously adores you.'

'Yeah.' She's not making this easy.

'I felt I should come and introduce myself properly. We got off on the wrong tack yesterday.'

'Did we?' Imogen blows out a puff of smoke, and sticks out her lower jaw. No she's certainly not making it easy.

'I'd like to start again. If you don't mind.'

The girl says nothing, almost adolescent in her sulkiness.

Alice remembers that she herself is supposed to be a mature woman, so opts for carrying on regardless. 'Right. Well, my name is Alice Barnes. I'm from Bristol, recently divorced, just bought the flat upstairs.'

'For holidays?'

'What?'

'You *have* only bought it for holidays?'

'Oh, no. Not at all. I've bought it to live. Here.'

'Permanently?'

'Well, yes.'

'Oh, God. Not another one.'

'What do you mean?'

'Another bloody English woman. We're all English – me, Verona Grange on the second floor and now you. Didn't Gerontin tell you?'

'No, he didn't say anything. I thought I was going to be living with French people.'

'I *was* living with French people – or as good as. I've been here nearly six years. It used to be lovely – all shabby and genuine.'

'Full of French, you mean?'

'Algerian mostly – a few *pieds noirs* up the street, otherwise Arabs. Lovely. Everybody kept themselves to themselves. Mostly tenants – rents were cheap. There was a nice old boy up in your flat until the winter before last, working on a building site over at Sophia Antipolis – used to get jobs all over the shop – but he slipped a disc, had to go back to Oran, and that's the way it is now. As soon as Gerontin gets one of them empty, he tarts them up and there you go – another bloody English woman. He says he's always broke, but he can't be. It's all money with him – and he runs our *syndic*. Never does any repairs.'

'You're making it sound as if he's got some sort of conspiracy going . . .'

'Well, he has – he must have.'

'But I don't understand – do you mean aimed specifically at the British?'

'Yeah, the tourist market.'

'But he couldn't have targeted *me* – I only found the card in his window by accident and French locals could just as easily have got there before me. It was only the luck of the draw.'

Imogen laughs. 'No French "local", as you put it, would ever be interested in this place – not smart people, anyway, and at Gerontin's prices they'd have to be a *bit* on the smart side.'

'But I'd understood that it was rather reasonable,' says Alice faintly. 'A bit of a bargain.'

'They wouldn't be seen dead in the Maison Puce – it doesn't have the right cachet for the French.'

'Because of the flea-market? I thought that rather added to its charm.'

'What do you mean?'

'"*Puce*"?'

'It's nothing to do with the market, it's a sort of mixed-up play on words – *pou* meaning "louse" and *pus* meaning "pus", and sort of connotations of *putain* as well. It was the old whorehouse – shows what they felt about the poor cows who had to do the whoring, doesn't it? Glows with respect.'

'Really?' Alice's mouth is drying up. 'So this place was a sort of brothel?'

'Not "sort of", it was – right up to the First World War as far as I know.'

Alice tries to search around for something positive to say. On her old Bristol medical-dinner-party circuit the correct response would have been 'How *fascinating*,' and she hears herself say it now, before she can stop it popping out.

'Eeoh, yess,' says Imogen, in unpleasant imitation. 'It is – simply *fascinating*. Actually, why would it be so *fascinating*? I think it's sad. You've only got to think of the women – shut up in these little rooms, servicing their clients. It's like a little ghetto, marked out with the sculptures on the walls – you've noticed them?'

'You mean the plasterwork outside – the reliefs?'

'Yeah. Pubic lice and corkscrew willies – nice, isn't it? *Fascinating*.'

Alice has slumped slightly against the bed-head.

'Don't go getting comfortable,' says Imogen sharply. 'I've got a class in ten minutes. And I'm not a mixer, you know. In case you thought I was. You might as well get that straight. Don't go thinking I'm a mixer.'

'Of course not,' says Alice, rousing herself. 'Neither am I.'

*

After she's got rid of Alice Barnes, Imogen pushes back the table and lifts three of the metal chairs from the small stack in the corner, bangs them down in a row across the floor. It's such a tight squeeze that they only just fit in between the edge of the bed and the wall.

She's still seething – at the Barnes woman, at her own situation, at herself for letting the likes of the Barnes woman get to her. But, God, she's feeling trapped – so trapped, worse than ever. All the sense of freedom she used to have here is being destroyed. Another of these women, dried up, strung out – and *posh*. On top of everything else why do they have to be so sodding *posh*?

It's beginning to feel like there's nowhere left for her to go. As ever, she'd loathed her Christmas break back in that hideous pink house in Purley, stuck with her mum, wading through the beige shag pile, forced to wear party hats and pull crackers with smelly old Uncle Perce. The only thing that kept her sane was the thought of getting back here as soon as she could hack it – 'hacking it', in this case, meaning that she had to hang around looking willing until she could wangle the next maintenance cheque from her mother. Didn't make the Christmas crap any more bearable, though – made it worse if anything, trapped by her own poverty into family obligation. Seems to be her status quo, though – can't seem to shift it any old how. Not as if her teaching does much more than keep her in fags and pay her mobile bills.

For a moment she thinks she ought to do the washing-up – get it out of the way, so's it won't distract. Then she thinks, What the hell – and turns the chairs round the other way to face the door. She's got two deckhands off the *Lady Karla* today – Abdul and Khalim – and the Chinese cook from Malacca. They ought to tackle tenses, that's what she's promised them – I am pissed off, I will be pissed off, I shall have been pissed off . . . well and truly.

7
Sunflowers

The famed Riviera winter warmth and light haven't yet materialized. Most days have been grey and dank, though occasionally the clouds have cracked open to reveal an azure ceiling, which teases and hints at happier possibilities. The Vieillois hate it too – and turn out to be just as weather-conscious as the Brits – are appalled, complain, and ask what the world is coming to, as they stand in line under sodden awnings in the market, their mouths turned down at the corners like figures in a cartoon.

Only the local ladies-who-lunch don't seem to mind, for now's their chance to bring out their fur coats. After years of living with British anti-fur-trade propaganda, these are a scandalous vision to Alice. It's so weird to see cohorts of fitch and fox and mink on parade. Presumably owing to their expense when brand new, they're mostly cut, oblivious to current fashions, as chunky trapezoids with matching fur pom-pom drawstrings bouncing at the neck, giving the normally elegant women an unfortunate squat appearance, like hairy brown Munchkins. Alice is caught out. She'd been so certain of warmth down here that she hasn't even brought a heavy cloth coat from home, and is loath to shell out for a chicly expensive French one now, at a time when she's having to spend so much on getting her flat right. In the streets, she shivers in her mac and hurries to get her errands over as quickly as possible. For the moment, at least, the town has lost any attraction as a place for lingering exploration.

She settles to work on her flat. Her few tea-chests of basic possessions have arrived expensively via a carrier from Bristol. At last she can begin to think of having her own books and photographs around her, though as there are no built-in cupboards she has to start by returning to the aircraft hangar shops to buy herself some flat-pack wardrobes and shelves for storage. Once she's managed to get these upright and more or less functional, via instructions in an infuriating mixture of French and Taiwanese, the little room takes on a disturbingly utilitarian look, with about as much character as a student hostel. It's dark too. The view of the vine-covered wall across the alley, which had looked so fresh and green in the heat of last August, is bald of leaves, grey and ugly, absorbing any available light rather than projecting it back. It's a job to think how to handle this cold, narrow, unprepossessing space.

Down in the flea-market is a stall specializing in what seem to be local fabrics, bolts of Provençal cotton – buttercup, scarlet, emerald, ultramarine – all printed with miniature paisley sprigs. It's on one of these damp and lonely mornings that she discovers the sunflowers: one roll of cloth printed all over with life-sized blooms in photographic detail. She buys enough to make full-length curtains, a big throw, cushion covers, the lot, and lacking a sewing-machine, finds a woman in the rue d'Alphonse

Daudet, who advertises on a postcard in the launderette, to make them up for her. While she waits the two weeks for them to be ready, she starts painting the cupboards, coating the basic white melamine of the flat-packs to give it a distressed background, then adding individual sunflowers in acrylics to all the doors.

*

She finds herself yearning for good old BBC Radio 4 to while away the hours of manual labour. It's only now that it's far away and unobtainable that she realizes what a comfort it's always been. For years the background hum of the *Today* programme, *Woman's Hour*, *Afternoon Theatre*, *The News Quiz*, *I'm Sorry I Haven't a Clue* and *A Good Read* have punctuated her domestic life. Now she thinks about it, she's pretty sure she'd been listening to *P. M.* on the day she was up the scaffolding when Philip came home and dumped her.

She's more or less sussed out how to get hold of the BBC World Service on short-wave, but she's finding it hard to get a good signal and, in any case, it's definitely not the same. It carries with it a sense of decorum and dignity, as if on its very best behaviour for the benefit of all those foreign listeners – wholly at odds with the familiar daily outpouring of Radio 4. Although welcome, it's much more like an Edwardian aunt in her public Sunday best. She's thought about getting a television, but there doesn't seem to be any access to an aerial in the building, and the programmes she's spied on sets in various bars and cafés have yet to whet her appetite for TF1 or Canal+ – she feels she can do without episodes of *Perry Mason* or *Dynasty* dubbed into French.

Then one day, fiddling around with the radio dial, and knowing that, however good for her, an afternoon of France Inter is not going to hit the spot, she discovers Riviera Radio, a service for Anglophone expats, broadcast from Monaco. It's a mixture of pop music and local news, information and commercials – a sort of souped-up Radio Luxembourg of childhood memory, and she becomes rapidly, infuriatingly, addicted. Shouldn't she be listening to French and not yet another rendition of 'Easy Lover' or 'Yellow Submarine'? But as it also broadcasts regular news reports from the World Service, she can kid herself that she's keeping up with essential current affairs.

What really fascinates her, though, are the hints and perceptions of other expat lives. She'd had no idea there was such a community down here, living all over the place – along the coast and well into the back country and mountains. Americans, Australians, New Zealanders, English-speaking Scandinavians, as well as Brits, take part in the phone-ins, calling from all over the area and revealing little vignettes of a transient life. People try to flog their cars, barbecues, furniture, cats and computers before leaving for the next place, chatting over the airways, giving a picture of lives that seem totally unattached to the native French milieu.

The commercials exhort her to visit English bookshops, American steak-houses, install complex security systems, entrust her fortune to specialist investment banks (only those with at least a spare million French francs need apply . . .). Then, on the hour, the World Service news broadcasts are a bizarre mixture of sweeping, apocalyptic international events – terrorist attacks, bombings, earthquakes, wars, refugees, misery – interspersed with reports of more particular news from home – clashes in the House of Commons on welfare reform or town planning. Neither the sweep of global horror nor the parochial nit-picking of British life seem now to have any relevance to her. Locked away, alone in her little space, concentrating on her own narrow span of survival, she feels utterly divorced, not just from Philip but from all the rest of humanity too.

By the end of January, she's virtually finished. The sad grey world outside has been temporarily driven away by the riot of yellow and green within. She'd got carried away, really – started to let the sunflowers spill over, off the cupboard doors and on to the walls. She's even painted a few on the ceiling. In a typically recherché Vieilleville boutique she's found some artificial silk ones on wire stems and uses them for tie-backs and jokey finials for her curtain rail. She feels flushed with achievement – but only for a day. As soon as she's had a chance to clean out the paint from under her fingernails, she's hit by a waft of panic. Now what? What's to do? What's her life? *Where*'s her life? The lives revealed on Riviera Radio have no connection for her, but neither do the lives of her French neighbours. For years she's read in travelogues and cookery books of the warm, welcoming inclusiveness of French domestic life. Every documentary you saw seemed to end with a scene around a large table, the sharing of a feast, the clinking of glasses. But any idea of her involvement and absorption into this locale seems as unlikely and foolish as a fairy-tale. It's a life still on hold, with no shape. She's just getting by.

*

In order to ease the atmosphere a bit with Imogen Prosper, she offers to walk the dog, who still spends much of the day whimpering in the hall. Imogen scarcely cracks a smile, certainly doesn't warm to the suggestion (the cow), but says she'll hang his lead on the scooter so that Alice can take him straight out without coming knocking on her door, bothering her – particularly important if she's teaching (the *cow*). At least, now that Fred sees her as a sort of token aunt, he's stopped growling. Instead when she walks past she has to ward off his boisterous leaps of hopeful excitement. Alice heaves – Imo seethes – January scratches to its close.

Then at last comes a really lustrous day. The cloud rolls back to the horizon, the light is clear right to the snow-tipped Alps, and the sky settles around them all in a great turquoise mantle, as if it had never gone away. Everyone is instantly cheered – the pavement cafés up and running, a general mood of renewal. Alice takes Fred for a walk and lands up at La Barque on the quay for coffee.

'Excuse me – is free?' The woman asks in English, but is clearly French. Slender, tall, enviably lightly tanned, with ash-blonde hair expertly styled into a helmet quiff, a thin cream wool coat, wrists weighted with jangling gold, she's the very antithesis of the little Munchkin women. She lowers herself gracefully into the other chair at the table, and lets out a sigh of ease. 'Oh, so good to relax – we deserve *thees*, no?' She turns to face Alice, and regards her through dark tortoiseshell sunspecs, with big gold medallions on either wing. It's a wonderful accent – straight out of *Inspector Clouseau*. 'After all zat *wezzzzer* we deserve a leetle break – was 'orrible. I thought eeet would *nevverr* end . . . but, of course, for you *Eenglish* is just like home, no?'

'How did you know I was English?'

'I *always* know. I can tell. By ze shoes.'

Alice looks down at her feet. She is wearing a pair of quite smart Russell and Bromley's – not perhaps in their first flush of youth but surely not reeking Perfidious Albion either.

'But zen I *know* ze Eeenglish,' the woman continues, 'from ze bottom of my 'eart – I *adore* ze Eeenglish.'

Well, this is a bit cheering. Blow me, thinks Alice, an anglophile emerging from the woodwork. Knock me down with the *plume de ma tante*. 'You know England well, then?' she asks, almost having to force her lips into action. Casual conversations have been so very rare recently that her facial muscles seem to have lost the knack.

'*Nevverrr* – I 'ave never been there. I make ze plans sometimes – I make a leetle *rendezvous* to meet wiz my friends, but some'ow, it *neverrr* 'appens.'

'Well, I must congratulate you on your use of the language in that case. I can't tell you the times I've been in France over the years and I still can't make small-talk.'

The woman looks puzzled at last. '*Small*-talk?'

'Just chatting like this – *bavarder*? Would that be the word?'

'It will do – you see I can understand you perfectly. You are perhaps not as bad as you sink . . . *Small*-talk – we 'ave ze same – *petite conversation*. Always I like to learn a *leetle* more – we can 'elp each ozzer, yes?'

'Sounds a good idea,' says Alice, cheered. Contact starts here and now, she thinks – at last a connection is made. 'Do you live here?' she asks – hoping, yes, please do actually live here.

'Sometimes. I go all over ze place. I am *flibbertigibbet* – that's a good word, no? I learn it from my lover –'e was an Eeenglish man. I *love* Eeenglish man – most of all I love zem. You, of course, live in ze Maison Puce.' This is said so suddenly, so matter-of-factly, that it brings Alice down with a bump. She hasn't felt noticed or remarked these last weeks. On the contrary she's felt ignored and invisible, so how and why does this woman know?

'Why do you say that? Why "of course"?'

'Everybody know zat – ze Maison Puce is full of *Eeenglish* women – and I have seen you wiz ze dog.'

'Do you know Mademoiselle Prosper?' Alice asks, having to curb the reflex which still makes her want to fit the name with 'Mérimée'.

'Imogen – ha,' the woman honks. 'You don' want to 'ave anysing to do wiz zat one – she is a *nasty* piece of work. She 'as no money – she is, you know, not *clean*.' The woman makes it sound as if this is cleanliness in a biblical sense. She raises her eyebrows up over the sunspecs and tuts loudly.

Alice immediately feels a paradoxical sense of alliance with Imogen – national pride rearing up. After all, she may be a cow, and her housekeeping standards may leave something to be desired, but that's not exactly on a par with *vice* – which is what the woman seems to be indicating. So much for loving ze Eeenglish.

'You are from Londres?'

'No, Bristol. In the south-west.'

'*Bristol* . . .' The woman absorbs this for a moment, then adds, 'Bristol is very nice, I think?'

'Very – it's close to Bath. Have you heard of Bath?'

The woman beams. '*Bath* – now Bath I know is *verry* nice. Your Bristol is close by?'

'Very.'

'Is good. Is *verrry* good. I will call on you,' says the woman. 'We will make arrangements – we will 'ave *dinnerrr*, you will meet my friends. You play bridge, of course?'

'No – oh, no, I don't play bridge.'

'You are doctor's widow, yes?'

This is getting sinister. How noticed has she, in fact, been?

'Divorcée,' Alice says firmly.

'But married to a doctor?' the woman insists.

'Yes – a gynaecologist.'

'And you *don't* play bridge? Are you sure?' The woman looks truly aghast.

'Quite sure,' says Alice, even more firmly.

'But you do play backgammon?' the woman adds reassuringly.

'No. No backgammon either.'

'Well . . .' The woman sighs, and Alice gets the full drift of her disappointment. 'It cannot be 'elped. Maybe we will teach you,' she looks hard at Alice, who as it happens, loathes all games and doesn't care if it shows, 'but zen again, maybe not.' She gets up. 'I am Josette Lamartine – *enchantée*.' She holds out her hand. 'I will be in communication wiz you,' and she trips off along the quay just as the waiter arrives to take her order.

Alice watches the elegant form disappearing into the maze of masts and hulls along the marina, and hopes she hasn't blown it. Perhaps she shouldn't have been so honest about her lack of interest in games. If all the woman needs is a bridge partner, then any hope of a connection is already going up in smoke.

Josette is disappointed – there's no doubt about it. It's been the same with so many of these English women. They're a bit of a puzzle, but with each new arrival, she lives in hope and has another go. Surely *one* of these days will arrive in Vieilleville the sort of civilized, *bien élevées* women she remembers from her teenage sorties to the British embassies out East. Hong Kong, New Delhi – those were the days. The men so elegant in their white dress uniforms, you could swoon, a life of ordered splendour, sophisticated. The very idea of *those* women not playing bridge was laughable. For *those* women, the ones who had taught her all those years ago, such a confession of ignorance would have been unthinkable. What *was* life for them without bridge? And the men had played it too – her adored Billy Prescott-Smythe had had a nice little earner going with it, swept the board, kept his women enthralled and his club bar bill at bay. Billy-Boy – her adored Billy-Boy – *mon Dieu*, what a man, the model of handsome military perfection. Tragic, of course, that he'd been so under his mother's thumb.

What she'd said to Alice about her adoration of the English is true, though the women who come down here alone to Vieilleville are a bit of a puzzle. Of course, she doesn't often meet those with husbands, for they don't tend to live in the centre of town. If they have husbands in tow, they have cars and busy structures to their lives – usually buying villas or large apartments up in the hills. But who with any sense of style or the rightness of things would pick the Maison Puce as their Eden? You'd have to be a little touched, wouldn't you? The size of those studios is laughable, the drains always suspect. So they've got that Verona woman, so big and lumpy she has to dress in a tent, and that awful little gamine Imogen, so cocky with her fluent French in that terrible Marseilles accent – and now this Alice Barnes . . . all these incomers, and not a single invitation to stay in England from *any* of them. You'd think *one* of them would have a beautiful country house – the sort of place you see in the films, Agatha Christie, that sort of thing. The type of place Billy-Boy used to describe when they were dreaming about their future together – croquet on the lawn, a silver kettle, a cake-stand and a butler. Perhaps with Alice it will be different – though it's not a very promising start.

8

Verona

'Alice Barnes? Verona Grange from upstairs – Flat three? What a delight – may I come in?'

It's a moon face, large and flat with tiny features quite sparsely dotted about in approximately the right places, but leaving a lot of rosy flesh in between. Beneath it is a large body – not fat precisely, simply big, tall and giving a hint of solid bone beneath its covering of practical cloth. A full corduroy skirt, a navy Guernsey, a striped pie-crust collar poking up around the neck.

'Isn't this *super*? I couldn't *believe* it when Imogen told me – another one to join the club. It's too delightful – at this rate we'll have to draw up rules and appoint a committee! Oh, I say you're beginning to settle in – well done. Quite a business, isn't it? What pretty sunflowers. My goodness, yes. Mind you, if you'd waited I could probably have got you a discount. For soft furnishings *I* always go to Chez Dorinda in Cannes. She's English too, actually, married to a Frenchman – she's a simply super girl – one of the children born deaf so it's been terribly hard on her – business isn't always quite what it should be so one tries to support when one can, and her stock's really quite up to the mark and she usually gives me a very good deal. But no – I mean yes – any advice you need do just ask – only too glad to help. It's always a bit of a trial, I think – especially with the cultural differences – even with the best will in the world. Of course, it was different for me because to an extent I had a head start as we'd always had the villa – well, really it was more of a *bastide*, if you know what I mean, not in the least grand, up in the hills, water from a well, that sort of thing. We shared with the Pilkingtons and the Hemery-Blythes – always ructions – but at least it gave me a *taste* – and once you've had the taste it's really quite hard to have to do without. And after I was left alone – Edmund died two years ago – two years next Thursday actually – terribly sudden, just about to take early retirement, had a heart attack in bed. Woke up and there he was – stone-cold. As you can imagine a shock to the system – never quite the same. As I was saying, after I was left alone it was really quite hard to think of doing without – but of course I could hardly *begin* to think of keeping on my share of the *bastide* – far too expensive on a widow's pension – it's scandalous, really, what they expect by way of a drop in standards – and why shouldn't a widow want to keep things on as they were, if you think about it? Only logical. Anyway, that's how I came to be here. So now I'm back I was planning a little *peek-neek* and wondered if you'd care to join me? I'll ask Imogen too but don't bank on it – she's such a funny little thing. Shall we say one o'clock? I'll knock on your door – no, don't bring anything at all, I've got the lot – bit of a treat. I'll see you later. This *is* nice, isn't it?'

*

'This *is* nice, isn't it?' says Verona.

The picnic turns out to be a parody of summers at Weston-super-Mare for they are sitting on the beach below the rocks on a tartan travelling rug, eating pork pie and Hula-hoops. Pudding is laid out in front of them already – a Mr Kipling bakewell tart still in its box.

'I always like to do this the first day I'm back – I call it "Goodies from Home" day,' says Verona. 'After that I tend to go all native and it's *salades niçoises* all the way – though I *do* think there are things one secretly craves down here, don't you? Despite all the wonderful variety, there's a moment when *olives cassées au fenouil* simply can't take the place of a Hayward's pickled onion, don't you think? Particularly if one's feeling low or got a cold or something. I always bring heaps of Marmite and Heinz tinned macaroni in case of flu – they've got their uses in certain circumstances. Of course, one can get some of these things down here too now, what with there being so many of us scattered about. There's a place in Antibes which does the full range – baked beans and salad cream, the lot.

'So you haven't got your *carte de séjour* sorted? Oh, well, not to worry – I don't suppose it matters. No, I never bother because I'm never down here long enough in one go – they give you three months' grace and I can only ever stay for about a month at a time because of the Old Folk back in Hove. Still going strong – Mummy'll be eighty-nine in August and Daddy's just had his ninety-second – wonderful, really, though of course it's a bit of a tie. Not so bad when Edmund was still alive – he was harder-hearted than I am, I'm afraid, but then of course they weren't *his* parents.

He was orphaned during the war – doodle-bug almost at the end, too frightful, really, though he always said it saved him such a lot of hassle once he'd got the full benefit of mine. Are yours still alive – father's remarried? Well, that's fortunate if she's hale and hearty – shoulders the burden – unless you had any expectations in the monetary sense? Whereas I really am tied – have to go back and check up on mine. They're in sheltered accommodation – *almost* like home, but they always complain . . . Have a Jaffa Cake, why don't you?'

Alice wonders if Verona Grange has an 'off' switch. The babble of conversation is even smothering the rhythm of the sea. Already Alice seems to know most of Verona's life story – the unexpected widowing, the previous life at Haywards Heath, getting Edmund off on the seven-fifteen into Victoria daily so's he could get to Price Waterhouse, or was it Touche?, one of those accountancy firms anyway. Her son Theo, something big in the City, lives in Pont Street, her aged parents and her flat in Hove, 'near the sea – very pleasant, really, though a flat isn't what one's used to.'

Alice looks out at this sea – today particularly sparkling, the waves a deep indigo, fringed in froth, white boats scudding across the horizon. 'It's so beautiful,' she says, by now desperate to get off the subject of Hove and/or Mr Heinz's 57 Varieties.

'Of course,' says Verona. 'It's what one came here for.'

'I didn't,' says Alice. 'I came here to get a life – just like that phrase everybody uses now. "Get a life," they say, don't they? – with such scorn. It's always people who have a life already who use it.'

'Who *think* they have a life, you mean,' says Verona. 'But it isn't like that. Life doesn't just stand around waiting – it moves on. *I* had a life in Haywards Heath – with a man, not worrying about the Old Folk. I had a life but it moved on.'

*

The next morning Alice decides to go to Antibes. She's heard there's an English-language bookshop there – might be useful to track it down – and perhaps it's time she gave herself a cultural treat: the Picasso Museum sounds promising.

'Good morning, thought I heard you stirring.' Verona comes hurrying round the bend of the stairs just as Alice is shutting her door. She's swinging a shopping basket. 'Shall we venture forth?'

'Actually I'm off out – to Antibes. There's a bookshop there.'

'Of *course* – Heidi's – been going there for years. What a good idea – I could do with some birthday cards, always forget to bring them down. Hang on while I get my hat, will you, and if I were you I should bring a headscarf. I poked my head out just now and the wind's got a real touch of the mistral about it – won't be a sec.'

Her sense of delight is transparent. Before Alice can muster a single solid excuse (other than the truth, of course, which is that she'd much rather go alone), Verona has whisked up the stairs again. She's back in a trice, still carrying her basket, a woolly hat pulled well down over her ears, an umbrella clamped under her arm. 'This *is* fun, isn't it?'

Half an hour later, and they are both on the train. Alice stares determinedly through the window, trying to absorb the atmosphere, but it's almost impossible. The French conversations of her fellow travellers, which she'd hoped to earwig, are drowned out. Verona has hit on a hobby-horse subject and spends the entire journey comparing Vieilleville's market prices with Tesco's and Waitrose – cheerfully boring for Britain, though the rest of the carriage seems riveted to every word.

Once they arrive, Alice wants to walk straight down to the town, get some decent time in the Picasso Museum before it closes for lunch. Verona, however, has other ideas. 'I have something to show you,' she says, almost in a whisper. 'A shrine.'

They land up, not as Alice is expecting at some ancient stone chapel but standing outside a large 1960s block of flats, its balconies decked with flapping scarlet awnings.

'Graham's House,' says Verona, still in a whisper, and nudges Alice with her elbow. 'Can't you feel it?'

'Feel what?'

'*Him*. Graham Green – he lived here for years, you know.'

'Oh – yes, I had heard. This is the building? It's not . . .'

'What?'

'I don't know. Not what I would have expected. It seems a bit dull and anonymous, somehow, for a famous writer.'

'That was the point, I think – for him. I like to come

past when I'm here – it's a sort of talisman. I find his work terribly erotic, don't you?'

'Well . . . perhaps I don't know it that well. I think I've only read *Brighton Rock* and *Our Man in Havana* – a long time ago.'

'But you couldn't forget – of course you couldn't. It's very *taut*, don't you think?'

'Well . . . yes . . . I suppose so . . .' says Alice, a bit taken aback at all this sudden intensity from a woman whose subject matter forty minutes ago had been a detailed run-down on own-brand mustards.

By the time they get down to the old town, it's gone half past eleven.

'Better leave the museum for this afternoon,' says Verona. 'Trust me – you'll need the time. Come and have a coffee at Café Felix.'

They are served outside. It's perhaps still a bit wintry for this – the wind is getting up, sending splashes from the nearby fountain in their direction – but Verona insists.

'This was Graham's favourite place, you know,' she whispers loudly. 'He came here almost every day for lunch – in full *public* view. That was his usual table – over there. Don't you think that's amazing?'

'Well, yes, I suppose so,' says Alice, who doesn't really think it's all *that* amazing. Presumably the man had to eat somewhere.

'I always come here every time I come to Antibes – pay my respects. I feel I get a sense of his spirit, somehow, that he's really here again.'

'Did you know him, then?'

'Well, no – not exactly. Though I always *felt* I did. I *saw* him here several times, tried to introduce myself once, but it must have been a bad moment – in the middle of his lunch, you know – though I would have loved to tell him what he meant to me . . . and how I really *understood* . . .'

'Understood what?'

'The eroticism beneath the skin.'

'Oh – right.' Alice, feeling embarrassed, lets it drop and starts looking around, watching the traffic as it snakes past the café tables.

'How are *you* coping, Alice – without your husband?'

'What?' Verona's face has gone very mournful. 'Well . . . I mean obviously it's not been easy,' says Alice, 'it's taking some getting used to – but I'm surprising myself in some ways. I think perhaps I'm more practical than I thought I was.'

'I don't mean in that sense, dear.'

'No?'

'I mean,' Verona leans forward, hissing loudly, 'in the bedroom department.'

'Oh – *that*.' Alice doesn't know quite where to put herself. She hardly knows the woman, and in any case, sitting here in all her woolly-pully lumpiness, she's such an unlikely sexual confidante. 'Well, to be perfectly honest,' she says, 'I haven't had a lot of time to think about what you call the "bedroom department" – I've just had too many practical things to sort out.'

'Really?' says Verona. '*Really?* Oh, I miss it. I miss it dreadfully.'

'Well, I suppose it's different for you – I mean, you were

still together when your husband died, weren't you? You weren't rejected like me . . .' Alice is embarrassed to see moisture beginning to well in Verona's sad eyes, and continues more briskly, 'I mean it's no great tragedy, but I think I'm still sort of *reeling* – and I suppose I'm very angry. I mean, Philip's not dead. He's still here – and he doesn't want me. And it's made such a rubbishy nonsense of all those years together, all that life we shared and struggled through – *together* – it's all just chucked out of the window. It's such a waste. And for what? Just sex? Is sex with Hillary Aldyce so very much more amazing than sex with me? I mean, I thought ours was all right – no, that's not fair, it was better than that, I thought it was *good*. Of course maybe it became a bit predictable, but after thirty years it's rather hard to ring the changes, don't you think? I could hardly have started swinging from the light fittings or something, could I? I'd have felt such a fool.'

'Oh, that's totally the wrong attitude,' says Verona. 'You have to seize all those inhibitions and stuff them in life's laundry basket – on with the scarlet suspenders, that's what I always did.'

'*Did* you, Verona? Did you really?'

'Oh, yes. Absolutely. Well, at least until he died – well, actually even after if it comes to that. Monsieur!' Verona wants to pay the bill.

'What do mean "after"?'

'Well, when I woke up and found Edmund gone – '

'Gone?'

'Dead – but that's just what it's like. It was just as if the light had gone out. So it was the middle of the night and I knew there was nothing to do – I mean no resuscitation or anything, as I said he'd *gone* – so do you know what I did?'

'Called an ambulance?'

'I got up and put on my red suspenders and lay back down with him and cuddled him all the rest of the night – tried to keep him warm – and do you know, for a while it was just as if he was still there and would roll over any moment and want to make love to me. And then in the morning of course I had to call the GP and hand him over to the undertakers – so he wasn't mine any longer. So you see I'm missing it dreadfully. It's part of the reason I wanted to keep a place on down here – well, that and to have somewhere for my son Theo, because you see it *used* to be full of the best sort of men – one's own kind . . . but they seem to be very thin on the ground these days. When we had the *bastide* I always used to hope we'd just bump into Dirk Bogarde at drinks parties or whatever – but there you are, everyone worthwhile seems either dead or fled. In some ways it's a bit of a disappointment.'

As it turns out, the Picasso Museum is closed on Tuesdays – so that's a disappointment too. Though as Verona carries away quantities of Heidi's birthday cards plus two pots of Branston from the English supermarket she, at least, seems to have found some compensations.

*

Pretty well as soon as Verona arrived back here from England, Imo sensed that the game was up *vis-à-vis* the parking of Fred and her scooter. Not that she doesn't resent it – the sodding interference. Why make such a fuss about the look of the place? It's not exactly the Ritz as it is and she can't see that her scooter makes sod-all difference. Probably improves it if anything – scooter's quite smart, as it happens, bought dirt cheap but nearly new off that Croatian boy who was having to make a run for it. Nifty shade of lilac – brightens the place up a bit, if you'd only look at it logically. And also, *logically*, it's her hallway too – the others seem to forget that and they could park *their* scooters if they wanted – if they had them – not her fault they don't. But if they did she wouldn't go interfering – she'd be cool.

With Alice she's been prepared to put up a stony front – but with Verona it's not so easy. Not that Verona's not a wimp and wouldn't say boo to a goose but, for all that, she is the mother of Theo, so it's best not to get her back up – well, no more than absolutely necessary to maintain sanity. Because Theo's a bit of all right. Well, really, Theo's a bit *better* than all right, as it happens. I mean OK – so he's ludicrously la-di-da and takes a bit of adapting to, and his *body* may leave a lot to be desired – talk about love handles (all those swanky City lunches, though looking at his mother it's probably in the genes) – but, and this is the point, though he might be a bit excessive in the kilogram department, he's also excessively generous – when the mood takes him. And he's *rolling* in it – which makes him very *much* a bit of all right. The usual sort of men she knows, the deck-hands and stewards from the yachts, barely run to a couple of Guinnesses at the Irish bar by way of a treat. But with Theo around, dinners at the Negresco in Nice and nights in Monte Carlo are an almost daily offering. And then, fortunately, he has a healthy sexual appetite – and despite Verona's proud, sticky cooings about her adored boy, there are *some* needs which not even a loving mother can satisfy. So there's nothing for it but to stay cool when Verona comes a-knocking.

'Imo – Imo dear, word to the wise?'

'Yes?'

'It's just I thought we'd got this all sorted out last November – before I went back to Hove? The business of the scooter?'

'What? – Oh, *that* – yeah, I'd forgotten,' says Imo airily, just as if she hadn't been giving the subject a good and thorough going-over.

'We *had* decided if you remember, dear, that you were going to keep it down in your *cave*, and given that you're the only one of us with the luxury of a cellar, it's only *fair*.'

'Yeah, but it's a bloody nuisance having to push it up and down the ramp, and it's hard work too – you should try it.'

'Well, yes, dear, I can see it's not the most convenient arrangement for you – but then having it stuck out here isn't at all convenient either, not for us. I'm sure Alice thinks so too – and it's not as if you didn't agree. I really thought it was all settled – and now on top of the scooter we've got this business of the dog. Hardly hygienic.'

'Hardly the fucking plague either,' is what Imo wants to say, but doesn't. Calmer counsels prevail. 'But it's the allergies, you see,' she says, trying to look soulful, 'for my pupils. It's the hair, not that he sheds a lot, it's the microscopic filaments – red eyes, streaming noses – and I've got to earn my living.' (Unlike *some* of us, she might have added, but doesn't – keep it calm, keep it cool.)

And it works. Appeals to Verona's sense of fair play and trying to see the other side.

'Well, I suppose we could come to some sort of accommodation about the dog – perhaps he could stay out here on your teaching days? That would give you a reasonable sort of gap – let the allergens settle down or whatever they do – but the rest of the time it's only right he should live in his own home. *Yours* – right? Either that or you'll have to get rid of him – and the scooter will really have to go back down in your cellar.'

'All right.'

'I *mean* it, Imo.'

'All right. I said all right.'

'Yes. Right . . . well.' Verona's a bit uneasy at this rapid caving-in. 'It's only fair – you do see?'

Christ, yes. How many more times? 'Yes, Verona, I'll put it down in the *cave*.'

Verona seems to accept this at last. 'Thank you, dear,' and she turns to go.

'How's Theo by the way?' asks Imo, trying to make this sound like the wisp of an afterthought.

'Fine,' says Verona, whipping round quite sharply. 'He's fine – terribly busy, of course, flying all over the world these days.'

'So he won't have time to get down?'

'Of course he'll make time – he knows what it means to me to see him down here, enjoying himself. Brings back all those happy childhood memories.'

'Oh, yeah,' says Imo, as she starts to close her door, 'right – yeah – of course.' But surely on her face is the hint of a smile.

*

What's she got to smile about? thinks Verona, as she climbs back up the stairs. It's unsettling. That encounter should have registered as a victory – the dog and scooter problem put in its place. Instead of which Verona's feeling uncomfortable, as if she's had one put over – wrongfooted, again.

Sometimes she wonders if getting this place in Vieilleville hasn't been a bit of a mistake. It was all so much easier up at the *bastide* – those days were such fun, what with having to fight for space with the Pilkingtons and the Hemery-Blythes, always loads of people around, and then if it was the school hols, the children too. Theo used to love the *bastide* when he was a boy – had a bit of a thing for Henrietta Hemery-Blythe too, pity that never came to anything. If they'd only married, Verona could have maintained her connection with the place. Probably be a few grandchildren around by now too. But it wasn't to be – James Hemery-Blythe got really quite unpleasant when Edmund had his little fall from grace, always made sure they were never down at the same time after that. And then Henrietta went and married that chap in the Guards. And of course it was really very naughty of Edmund to land them in the soup like that – so unfair for Theo to be caught in the fall-out. He's found it hard to forgive. And then Edmund going and dying on them, with nothing really sorted out – hard to keep a scandal like that under wraps.

Vieilleville had seemed a good idea back then – a compromise solution – something of the old life to hang on to. But Theo doesn't seem to like it all that much, does he? Hardly ever comes down – and even when he does, it seems to be only when she has to be back in Hove seeing to the Old Folk. And she'd bought the platform bed specifically so that he could *share* the flat with her. Perhaps he's got too grand now really – prefers hotels. Sad, though, it's not the same. And if there's one thing she likes, it's a good old chin-wag.

It's been hard to make friends. Imo's so abrasive you never know quite what to expect, and she doesn't really know any of the locals. Well, apart from Josette Lamartine and her cronies – but Verona sometimes gets the feeling that they're sort of laughing at her. So hard to tell when they start rattling away in French – but it always makes her feel a bit uneasy. She is *capable* of being hurt, though you'd never think so with the way people insult her sometimes. Edmund always had a bit of a biting tongue – hypercritical – but she'd never let him know she minded, just let it wash over her. 'She Never Took Offence' could be engraved on her headstone, really.

But maybe things are looking up. This Alice Barnes now – a pleasant, quiet sort of woman. A real friend in the offing. Could make all the difference to life down here – and obviously lonely. She'll need leading by the hand. Nothing nicer.

9

Points of Contact

Alice has Verona overload. After two weeks it's turning into a full-scale nightmare. The trouble is she's always there – or, rather, always *here*, right here at the door, bringing with her a great effusive ballooning of goodwill, impossible to burst. Alice is pretty sure she listens out for her comings and goings – just as Alice herself had done when she was trying to meet Imogen Prosper 'as if by accident'. Only Verona doesn't really bother to make anything look like an accident: she just arrives, and immediately wants to join in. Alice can't even seem to put the rubbish out on her own any more. If Verona spots her, she comes bounding out to 'keep her company' down as far as the municipal wheelie-bin in the place d'Espoir. It's desperate.

When Alice does occasionally manage to get out on her own, Verona seems to pop up like a jack-in-the-box all over the place – 'Oh, *there* you are,' she calls, across the street, as if she's been deliberately hunting her. No amount of tactful wiggling seems to work – she just can't be shaken off. Last week she wrecked a trip to Menton, yesterday she caught Alice on her way back from the market and suggested another little *peek-neek*. When Alice declined, claiming a headache, Verona was back at her door within three minutes brandishing a choice of aspirin, ibuprofen or paracetamol and then stood there until Alice swallowed some of the blasted things, even though, of course, her head was in perfectly good nick – it was just the first pretext that came to mind.

Alice is starting to feel persecuted – she finds herself lying awake at night, trying to invent a series of excuses, so as to have them all ready to trip off her tongue whenever needed. But it's not that easy. She has none of the usual reasons – pressure of work or other social engagements. Verona knows perfectly well she has neither. Too late now to invent some imaginary activity which might appear to take up her time. And how else to put her off? Be honest? 'I *vant* to be alone' – but that's the trouble: Alice doesn't necessarily *vant* to be alone, she just doesn't *vant* to be with Verona. She's feeling drained by the non-stop chat – and also, if she dares admit it, she feels tainted by Verona's awful dowdy middle-aged murkiness. Until now, Alice has been trying quite hard with her appearance – quite specifically as a reaction to Philip having dumped her for Hillary Aldyce. But tramping round the streets with Verona seems to drag her over some invisible line and makes her think of tight perms and Crimplene – talk about downhill all the way.

Tonight, however, Alice is in for a change – at last. Josette Lamartine bumped into her this afternoon on one of her rare Verona-free outings and asked her to meet a friend for dinner at the Taverne Vieilloise. This friend of hers, Augustine (or was it Albertine – something like that?), '*lurve* ze Eeenglish too – you will adore her, and she will adore you too.'

Alice feels like a dog let off the lead – she's about to run barking wild.

*

She dresses up as near to the nines as possible in her good black trouser-suit from Dingle's, barely lets her latch click as she closes the door, so as not to alert Verona, then slips downstairs in her bare feet feeling like a naughty schoolgirl. The effect is ruined by Fred, who's stuck out in the hall again and greets her with a howl of delight. She runs to the front door, sticks on her shoes and makes a dash for it, deliberately turning left, the long way round up the rue d'Espoir and keeping in the shadows to avoid Verona's scrutiny from her upstairs window. This is getting ridiculous.

*

Augustine turns out to be a Josette clone – very elegant, and the absolute opposite end of the style spectrum from Verona's homespun beige. There's the usual solid, tinted hair, the quilted Chanel bag on its jangling chains (counterfeit? though it looks real enough) and, as ever, lots and lots of gold. Josette warned this afternoon, when she was issuing her invitation, that the woman had had a 'sad, sad life –'orrible 'usband – a pig – not *sympathique* –'e force 'er to do many, many things, 'orrible,' which really had Alice guessing. But now she meets her face to face, she looks normal enough – not at all *damaged*. A very jolly sort, really.

They speak mostly English, though Alice is dying to

have a go with her French. The trouble is, the moment she tries she gets bogged down with tenses and great gaps in her vocabulary. It's pretty embarrassing and brings the whole conversation down to a crawl. The women seem very understanding and say they'd actually prefer to practise their English – so that seems to be that. Every ten minutes or so, they look at each other and launch into a torrent of very fast French, which leaves Alice struggling and feeling a bit foolish. Then they turn back to her and start off again in English.

Unfortunately, while Alice is dying to talk about the real nitty-gritty of their lives in Vieilleville – the really practical stuff like plumbers and bureaucracy and anything they might know about the Maison Puce – they just want to talk about Princess Stephanie and no-trump strategies. Alice doesn't have much to contribute to either, whatever the language.

Then something odd happens. They'd asked for the bill and Augustine (or was it Adrienne?) suddenly jumps up and says she has an urgent appointment. Then Josette seems to melt away. At first Alice thinks she's gone off to the loo, which is down in the basement, but she's away for ages. By this time the waiter has been hanging around looking hopeful, so Alice decides she may as well take the initiative for once and signs on her credit card. The bill is particularly expensive by Vieilleville standards as Josette and Augustine were scornful of the all-in menus, which they deemed *touristique*, and they'd had the *à la carte* instead. Josette eventually returns – had not been to the loo at all, it seems, looks rather scandalized that Alice could have thought her guilty of such an appalling lapse in manners. No – she'd met some friends downstairs and just had to catch up. Alice explains what she's done with the bill, expecting Josette to divvy up her portion (and Augustine's too for that matter) but Josette just says, ''Ow *lovely* – zat was very sweet of you, my *leetle* Aleese,' and she kisses her on both cheeks, jumps up, and leaves. Alice is left alone, gasping – and nearly six hundred and forty francs the poorer.

Alice looks out for Josette all the next day, but can't spot her anywhere. She still doesn't know where she lives, and she doesn't have her phone number, though of course she's asked. Maybe Josette didn't hear the question, for she just looked straight through her, and after Alice had asked a couple of times, it began to seem rude to persist.

So far, Josette has just seemed to appear like magic – a sort of genie from the lamp – but she must live around here somewhere. She's always on foot, and always so beautifully dressed with never a hair out of place, so her home must be quite near. Alice did try asking again last night, but she's starting to notice that the French don't seem all that keen on revealing anything like direct information. If she asks questions straight out – for example, about this business of the *carte de séjour* – people look uncomfortable and there's often an embarrassed little silence, as if she's crossed some forbidden barrier of acceptable behaviour. She'd tried this topic last night – during pudding – but noticed that both Josette and Augustine hurriedly turned their attention to their spoons, clearing their throats, as if she'd farted or something.

If she'd managed to find Josette she was going to ask her

to contribute towards last night, but as the day passes, she begins to think better of the idea – it's all too embarrassing. Put it down to experience and be a little more guarded next time. There is also the problem of Verona who, despite Alice's efforts at secrecy last night, seems to know she's been out and arrives at her door first thing, wanting to hear every detail with particular emphasis on the menu – 'Oh, you *didn't* choose the lavender *crème brûlée*? Oh, my dear, you should have had the *nougat glace* – theirs is the best. If I'd known where you were going I could have warned you – what a *pity*.' If she finds out that Alice got landed with the whole bill, she'll probably march her back to the Taverne Vieilloise like some avenging nanny and demand her money back. Definitely best to keep mum.

*

'Imo?'

'Yes, Alice?'

'Could you spare me a minute?'

'No.'

'Only I was just wondering . . .'

'Yes?'

'Well, it's Verona – I wonder if you have the same problem . . .'

'What?'

'Well, she's just – well, she's a bit much sometimes . . .'

'Sometimes?'

'And I wondered how you cope.'

'Easy. I tell her to fuck off.'

'I meant *apart* from telling her that.'

'Oh. Well, apart from that – no, I don't know.'

*

At least Verona may be a helpful point of contact to decipher this odd epistle from Monsieur Gerontin. It arrived this morning and, try as she might, Alice still can't wangle any sense out of it.

The daily arrival of the post has its own eccentricities. There is no letterbox in the main front door, as one might expect. Instead, each flat has its own small metal box attached to the crumbling hall wall inside. The postman has a key and lets himself in. In fact, he has a huge bunch of keys – one for every house in this part of the town – and he keeps it dangling from his belt buckle, letting himself in as need be. It's totally baffling. Why? Why have to endure this extraordinary rigmarole of fishing out correct key for appropriate lock, when the mere installation of slits in all the doors would relieve him of the trouble? Alice has wondered, even asked Josette, but the only response was that blank one, indicating that it's somehow *Alice* who's got it all wrong. Another mystery for her to accept without demur. Once again put it down to *Frenchness* – that'll do.

This morning's post has produced, as well as the letter from Monsieur Gerontin, a clump of envelopes with disturbing logos – Visa, Mastercard and her bank statement. Sod's law to have them all arrive at once. Not that she *ought* to feel disturbed. Not at all – for God's sake, woman, grow up. It's only money. And it's not as if she couldn't justify her expenditure recently. It's all been necessary – everyone knows that setting up a new home is expensive – it's not as if she's been *profligate* . . . has she? Nevertheless, she leaves the envelopes unopened and pokes them under a stack of magazines – what the eye does not see et cetera . . .

The epistle from the Agence Gerontin is a completely indecipherable graph. It seems to be hand-drawn in ink – or perhaps it's Roneoed (but does anyone have such a thing as a Roneo any more with the universal advent of the PC?). But this graph isn't even typed. This graph is so far removed from the world of the inkjet printer that it has something of the substance of an antique – a curiosity. There's a list of names running down the left-hand side, none of which is legible. Then across the top some percentage symbols and a word at the end that has subsided into a black smudge. The accompanying note in French is, however, typewritten – unfortunately. For she can clearly read that Monsieur Gerontin presents his '*compliments les plus distingués*' and looks forward to receiving her cheque for the enclosed amount at her earliest convenience. Ugh.

Alice climbs the stairs to Verona's landing – funny, after days of trying to hide, to be actively seeking her out. Verona lets her in with the usual beam of transparent delight. She's wearing a vast orange muu-muu, and a towelling turban.

'Friday night's Amami night – only this time it's Wednesday morning. Come in, dear, just giving myself a going-over.'

Alice hands over Monsieur Gerontin's graph and Verona holds it at arm's length, trying to get some focus. 'Oh, it's just the usual – the annual list of charges for the co-proprietorship – it always comes about this time of year.'

'But what does it mean?'

'It's just the *syndic* – every *copropriété* has one and in our case it's Monsieur Gerontin. He collects the money for insurance, water, the communal electricity for out in the hall, that sort of thing.'

'I realize that – but what are the actual figures?'

'Well . . .' Verona holds the paper even further out, then brings it up close to her nose, squinting. 'It's no good. I'll have to find my specs.' She disappears into her bathroom and comes back with the specs lopsidedly poked into the folds of the turban. She has another look – holds it in, holds it out. 'Oh dear – yes – it does seem even worse than usual. We'll have to ask him.'

'But have you any idea of what it usually is? The amounts, I mean.'

'Well, it varies – it's done on a percentage basis. Imo's is the smallest square metrage, then I suppose you'd be next. Then, of course, mine is slightly larger.'

'Is it?'

Alice has never really taken in much about Verona's flat. It's so stuffed with possessions that it feels, if possible, even smaller than her own. Half the space is taken up by a wooden platform with a ladder at the far end. A sofabed in maroon Dralon nestles underneath, and is framed on either side by matching curtains hung from the platform, and ruched up with lots of gold bobble fringe. With a full complement of matching, fringed lampshades, the whole effect is basically Home Counties *circa* 1962 with, lurking beneath, a good dollop of tart's boudoir. All a bit unlikely – but perhaps fitting in view of the origins of the Maison Puce.

The platform, which is covered by a double mattress, is

supposed to be Verona's spare bed in case of visitors. But it's hard to see quite where she could tuck them, for the whole area is piled with cardboard boxes, stuffed plastic carrier-bags and piles of newspapers – 'The dear old *Tory-graph*' bought at vast expense (and one day late, having been airlifted in from the UK) from the *tabac* on the quay, and thus far too precious to chuck out until thoroughly read and digested.

'I tell you what,' says Verona, 'I'll get out last year's and see if we can make some sense of that.'

She climbs the ladder while Alice subsides on to the sofa below. There's a circular table at this end, covered with flounced cloth down to the floor and displaying ranks of framed photographs. A younger, thinner but no less rosy Verona appears in lots of these, often with a boy in various stages of development from chubby toddler to commanding youth. In a couple, a thin, grey man with beaky features appears holding the boy – the late great Edmund, perhaps?

From above, enormous rustlings are going on, mixed with huffs and little gasps of breath and muttering.

'Now, let me see – I'm *sure* it was here – oh – now – no – golly, what a muddle – ah, yes, – no – oh, I could have sworn – *ahhh* . . .' Recognizing the call of victory, Alice gets up and watches as Verona backs down the ladder carrying a Marks & Spencer carrier-bag. 'Here we are – last year's. I knew I had them to hand.' She settles on the sofa and rifles through the contents of the bag, producing numerous documents, examining them for a moment, then rejecting them in favour of the next. 'Right – yes. Here it is – oh . . .' She sounds disappointed, hands the paper over to Alice.

'But it's just as illegible as this year's.'

'Yes . . . it does seem to be.'

'Can you remember what you usually pay?'

'Well, I'm not sure that I can. I normally send all this sort of stuff to my accountant in Hove and he deals with it. It's not a lot, I don't think . . .'

'What about these names down the side?'

'That's all of *us*, dear.'

'Is it?' Alice has another go – and, yes, perhaps embedded in those squiggles is the germ of her own surname. 'What's this column at the end – the one with the big smudge?'

Verona compares the paper with last year's. 'Oh, that's just "*Travaux*" – the work to be done on the building.'

'What work?'

'All the renovations, dear – the stairs and the walls, that sort of thing.'

'The things Monsieur Gerontin has plans for? The ones he showed me in his office?'

'That would be them.'

'But what are all these figures? There's the number seventy thousand in my column – that's over seven thousand pounds.'

Verona has another squint. 'Perhaps it's in euros,' she says helpfully.

'That would be even more. What's it for? I'd understood that all the renovations are already in hand, paid for.'

'Not necessarily.'

'What?'

'But don't worry, dear, this crops up every year. They'll never be done – nothing's ever organized. I've been here two years and I can't even get the doorphone mended.'

Not in the least comforted by this additional piece of news, Alice goes back to examining the graph. 'What's this blank space here?'

'Oh, well, that would be the big apartment on the top floor – it's a duplex, you know, they've been doing it up for ages, all sorts of building noise and mess all through last summer. Nobody's bought it yet – I don't think.'

'Well, who owns it now?'

'What?'

'Somebody must own it. Why isn't their name listed? Who's been having all the building work done?'

'Oh, I don't know – Monsieur Gerontin's in charge, I think.'

'Do you think he owns it?'

'It's possible.'

'Only he owned mine.'

'Yes, I think he might have owned mine too – but it was all a bit of a muddle. To tell you the truth it never made complete sense – but then Theo came along to the *notaire* with me so I knew there wasn't anything to worry about.'

'Did you have to do "under the table"?'

'Shhh, dear, some things are just not spoken.'

*

Back in her own flat, Alice tries to forget the disturbing muddle of Monsieur Gerontin's graph, and makes herself a pot of coffee. Every time she walks past the pile of magazines, she can feel the reproach of the unopened envelopes as a sinking little thump in the pit of her stomach. This is loony. She is being *loony*. It's not even as if she's been on the razzle. She lifts the corner of the pile and pulls out the first envelope. Her bank statement. She slips her finger under the edge of the flap and opens it, then flips back the pages briskly. Oh, God. She *can't* have spent that much – it must be a mistake. Bloody computers.

She sits down now and makes herself go through it more carefully, the whole horrible list, and realizes it's all too miserably accurate. And these aren't even the expenses of setting up the flat – most of those bills will be listed in the credit-card statements she hasn't even opened yet. No: this horror is just the result of using her debit card, swiping it with abandon and not keeping a proper track. Most of the debits listed were to do with ordinary daily Vieilleville life, a conglomeration of innocuous little amounts. Lots of restaurants and cafés, of course, which at the time had seemed so very reasonable in comparison with prices back home. And then all those innocent little local shopping trips and the general travelling around. It's all added up to a huge unwieldy sum. The ghastly reality is that her income doesn't begin to cover it all. She's going to have to draw on some of her capital – and even she knows that's the start of the slippery slope to ruin.

10

Bearding the Lion

The weeks are slipping by. It's already March, and on top of her financial quakes, Alice is sinkingly aware that her application deadline for a *carte de séjour* is approaching fast. She keeps putting it off, half hoping it will melt away. When it doesn't, she inwardly excuses her procrastination – surely it would be wise to get some more direct and solid information from people who've actually been through the process, rather than relying solely on the guidance of *French Dressing – A Survivor's Guide*? But so far she's had no luck in finding such an informant. For once Verona is silent. Having never considered herself a resident, she has no advice on the subject – not even an opinion. Almost as if to emphasize this point, she's now gone back to England for ten days – something to organize for her Old Folk.

Occasionally Alice runs into fellow Brits quite casually in the town, but once she brings the conversation round to officialdom, they seem to freeze. She never hears anything about it on Riviera Radio, though she does wonder if perhaps she could advertise for advice on one of their phone-ins. But the general paranoia is catching, makes her increasingly wary, and it would be pretty embarrassing to stick her head over the parapet like that. There must be a more private way.

One day she has the brainwave of trying to find Verona's soft-furnishings friend in Cannes – the woman with the French husband and deaf child. Ironic that just when she's needed Verona is no longer on hand to give advice. Nevertheless Alice tracks down the shop – Chez Dorinda in the old Le Suquet part of the town. She has to buy several metres of Provençal cotton she doesn't need, in order to get talking, and the result isn't all that helpful. Dorinda has taken French nationality and consequently doesn't need a *carte de séjour*. She's effusive about the quality of French health care, but otherwise has strong views on dealing with officials – says it can be a nightmare. They have an all-encompassing name, *fonctionnaires*, which covers more or less anybody Brits would think of as government employees. They have an extraordinary amount of individual power, are not all that well paid but, as a hefty compensation, are virtually dismissal-proof. Land yourself with a tricky one, Dorinda indicates, and you may as well land yourself in Hell. Her parting shot, as Alice leaves with her unwanted packet of cloth, is 'Good luck – you'll need it,' which doesn't necessarily help.

*

Back at the Maison Puce, Alice goes in search of additional lore. Surely Imo must be in the same boat, living here full time, working and so on?

'Could you spare me a moment, Imo?'

'No.'

'Only I just wondered . . .'

'What?'

'Well, if you had any advice about the people at the *mairie*?'

'What about them?'

'I've got to apply for my *carte de séjour* any day now and I wondered if you could give me any pointers – just run through the process with me?'

'Why?'

'Well, just in case there's anything I need to know.'

'No – why do you want a *carte de séjour*?'

'Well, it's not a case of *wanting* one, is it? I mean I have to – it's illegal not to have one, isn't it, quite a serious offence?'

'Who's going to know?'

'I couldn't live like that, not knowing I was *supposed* to have one. I think you're meant to carry them with you all the time, aren't you, produce them on demand?'

'Nobody's going to ask you.'

'I'd be on tenterhooks constantly – and then if I needed anything official at all it would be hopeless. What about medical help?'

'Go private.'

'I couldn't begin to afford that.'

'Well, then, use your E111 form – the hospital will accept that. Don't *be* a resident – go home every so often, like Verona, see your dentist or your hairdresser or whatever people like you do, catch up with all your little kiddie-winkies.'

'But *this* is my home, Imo.'

'Yeah – right – but like not *really*.'

'Yes – *really*. I haven't got anywhere else to go.'

'Oh.'

'So if you could give me any tips – I mean, what was it like for you?'

'Look, I've already told you – I haven't got time for this, I'm up to my eyes, okay? Why don't you just leave well alone?'

*

Imo closes her door very crisply in Alice's face – but considering the turmoil she's causing, Alice should consider herself lucky not to have it slammed.

Imo's in a muck sweat. *Fuck*. That bloody woman – asking questions, nosing around. Why's she want to be a crummy *resident*? It's pathetic – the stupid woman can't even speak the bloody language. And what does she mean, this is her home? Don't make me laugh. Of course she's got somewhere else. They've *all* got somewhere else. People like Alice don't know what it's like to live on the edge. And isn't it typical of her sort? Got to be so fucking *correct*. Can't leave things alone – just get by. Don't they ever understand that's what most of us do, *just get by*? It's all totally out of order. Well out. Stirring up the pot – a pot that doesn't need stirring, thank you very much. And it's not nice to think of the eyes of the *mairie* officials turning their focus on the residents of the Maison Puce. Not nice at all.

Maybe she shouldn't have been so rude, though, because

now she thinks of it she's going to have to speak to Alice, make sure she only gives the address as 8 rue d'Espoir – maybe not as noticeable as 'Maison Puce'?

*

In her mind, Alice labels it D-Day. Having read and re-read the account in *French Dressing – A Survivor's Guide*, she sets off for the Bonneville-sur-Mer town hall, a.k.a. the *mairie*, with the following documents:

birth certificate
marriage certificate
decree absolute
passport, plus six copies of the personal information pages
four passport-sized photos (particularly weird – they make her look like a gangster's moll with catarrh)
building society passbook
bank letter (attesting to her solvency – ha, ha, ha)
air-ticket to prove date of entry
telephone and electricity bills to prove residence
– everything translated where necessary, certified, stamped and in triplicate

She arrives at about 9.30 a.m. The *carte de séjour* section is in a separate compound, round the back, and is already packed and heaving, mostly with foreign language students newly arrived for the spring/summer terms. She queues for thirty minutes, before cottoning on that there's a sort of raffle-ticket system – rather like supermarket deli counters at home. It turns out that today's quota of tickets has already been given out – at 8 a.m. – so it's no go.

She tries to find an official, but they're all on the other side of a high chain-link fence. It's a bit like a zoo, but with a real sense of confusion as to which side is observing the other more closely. Then a nice girl from New Zealand, who already has a ticket, suggests Alice should try and get here by 7 a.m. tomorrow, also that she should bring a book – *War and Peace* is her suggestion, which Alice takes as an example of healthy antipodean wit.

The next morning she arrives at 7 a.m. armed to the teeth, as yesterday, with all documents, only to find that today the tickets are not to be handed out until 8.30 a.m. precisely. In the meantime they are all supposed to form an orderly queue. Alice has a sense that perhaps, after all, *War and Peace* won't be long enough: maybe she's going to need the whole of Proust. At 8.25 a.m. a small man sidles up to the other side of the fence and stands waiting. There's a tangible increase in tension as the whole queue prepares to pounce. At 8.30 a.m. by the clanging of the *mairie* clock, he announces that today's tickets are only for students starting their courses next week. There's an instant sprint for the fence from the most unlikely mature-looking individuals, whose student days must surely have ended round about 1971 – and Alice is lost in the throng.

On day three, Alice again arrives at 7 a.m, this time dressed as a student lookalike and prepared to lie through her teeth, sell her soul, *anything*, just so long as she can get herself face to face with a *bona-fide fonctionnaire*. She needn't have bothered, for when the official arrives for the 8.30 a.m. handout, he announces that only non-students will be seen today.

Alice leaps forward, pulling off the baseball cap she was using for disguise, and at last a ticket is poked at her through the fence. It's not quite the open sesame she'd envisaged, but does let her into the inner sanctum, where she queues again. At 11.45 a.m. she's at last called forward.

The dreaded *fonctionnaire* is in reality a dishy, charming young man, who goes through her documents with care, then carries them away and returns, telling her to come back after lunch as they're just closing. The nice New Zealander had warned her never to let her documents out of her sight, but no other solution seems available. If she claims her papers back, she'll have to start the whole process over again from scratch . . .

In the afternoon, she returns to queue again, this time without needing a ticket, and is called up to see another man – small and irritable, perhaps with a touch of *mal au foie* left over from lunch, because he keeps rubbing his tum and mopping his sweaty brow. He examines the forms Alice had so carefully filled out this morning, carries them away, then returns. There is a problem. Madame Barnes has not provided the names/dates of birth/places of birth of all four of her grandparents – would she kindly write them down now? Horror. Alice hasn't the faintest idea of any of the relevant dates and she's not even certain of her maternal grandmother's maiden name – one of the Macs, she's sure of that, but Macintosh or Mactavish? Could it possibly matter? Monsieur looks deeply suspicious – then asks her if she's ever been in prison. When she says, 'No,' he looks even more deeply suspicious and tells her to prove it. How? Monsieur shrugs and the interview is over.

Wrung out with rage and frustration, Alice totters back down to Vieilleville, clutching her great file of documents, and spots Josette outside the Café Papillon.

*

Josette is very curious about these English women as a species – why such an incessant thirst for information?

Alice has already quizzed her several times about this *carte de séjour* business – as if she'd know such a thing, and if she did, as if she'd talk about it. Doesn't Alice realize that there are certain things you keep to yourself or which maybe you share only with your family or closest friends – and by closest, read decades, *years* of intimacy with people you've known since childhood if possible, not someone with whom you've just shared the occasional dinner?

But then today she's been at it again – comes barging into a very enjoyable (and private) *tête-à-tête* Josette is having with Augustine and Marie-Albertine at the Café Papillon, and starts ranting on about her grandparents! The very idea – the naïveté of it – the rudeness, laughing at the French system, cursing it too. Josette feels really quite embarrassed for her friends – as if *any* self-respecting French woman wouldn't know this most basic detail of her lineage. Alice laughs and says an Exeter solicitor's daughter doesn't have a sense of lineage (so maybe she's not so *bien élevée* after all – explains a lot – what a disappointment, and Josette's been nursing high hopes of this one). And to cap it all she doesn't even offer them a drink – just has her own *citron pressé*, pays for it and slinks away. *Mon Dieu!*

*

Alice feels banjaxed by this grandparents business. When she poured it all out to Josette and her friends this afternoon, they didn't seem to understand at all. She'd thought they might sympathize, agree with her it was a bit of a sick joke, but they'd simply seemed scandalized at her ignorance. When she said that her life hadn't given her any profound sense of ancestry, Augustine (or maybe it was the other one) said it was nothing to do with grandeur of lineage – in fact, quite the contrary since the Revolution – simply a pride in family connection. A French peasant farmer or a road-sweeper was as likely to know his own forebears as a duke or marquis. No such sense for Alice, though, when she tries to telephone her father. Once again she gets Brenda-the-New-Wife.

'Sorry, dearie, Dad's not too clever.'

'Again?'

'More or less daily.'

'Only I've got this problem . . .' Alice tries to explain the grandparent dilemma. Presumably there are certificates around somewhere, marriage lines and so on, her mother's birth certificate, something that might give a clue?

But Brenda-the-New-Wife is cagey. Says she'd had a really good clear-out when they'd moved to Cedar Retirement Village, as although it's 'very pleasant', there isn't room to swing a cat.

'But surely important documents would have been saved?'

'Depends on your definition.'

'Well, birth certificates – they'd be really important, wouldn't they?'

'Not really, dear, not if you're dead.'

So it's all a bit bleak. Sitting here on her sunflower yellow sofa, gazing at her sunflower walls, *sans carte*, *sans* money – beginning to feel like *sans* everything. It looks as if she'd better go home and sort a few things out.

11

Abroad Thoughts from Home

Alice buys a one-way plane ticket back to London, special offer with easyJet. Having no idea how long she'll need to stay, a return would be an extravagance.

With a sense of fleeing the coop, she sits in the departure lounge of Nice airport examining her fellow passengers. The French are so clearly marked out with their relentless elegance and chic, a cliché borne out by fact. Good-quality leather accessories might almost be their tribal identity – not a tatty plastic carrier between them. Alice feels she's been making a real effort in this direction herself – well, at least until the arrival of the horror bank statement reined in her spending. Despite her money worries, she is conscious of wanting to prove to those she's left back home in England that a little of this lustre has begun to rub off on her. But already she can tell that, in the eyes of these *bona-fide* French, she doesn't begin to pass the test. À la Josette, they can suss out us lowlier mortals 'by ze shoes' or their equivalent. It's a most specific skill, which doesn't seem to cross cultural barriers.

The waiting Brits are also pretty clearly marked out – though to a man (and woman) they've obviously been affected by this place. The Côte d'Azur has worked its usual sorcery. It just *does* something to people, however brief their stay. Despite everything that could drive you mad here – the whole gamut, from crime to the scream and shriek of the building sites and raw concrete – all just melts away under the spread of its intensely sensual magic. So that, expecting any moment to be called for boarding, even the slumped, unattractive middle-aged couple across the carpeted way is temporarily changed. Holding hands, the woman is absent-mindedly stroking his bare hairy knee (ghastly shorts, of course – what price chic?), her own large belly scarcely contained by her belt. Would she be doing this in public in Woking or the Wirral? Of course not. The Côte has worked its wonders – and just for a moment they're Abelard and Heloïse, not Darby and Joan.

So despite the churning worry of what she has done, hasn't done, but most certainly *should* have done, Alice experiences again a glimpse of that original magic she'd sensed last summer and feels a loss of light and lightness as they take off, circle over the blur of the sea and head north.

As ever when Alice is airborne, her mind turns to imminent death. She's always thought you'd have to be totally thick, however experienced a traveller, *not* to contemplate your own demise when flying, even if only briefly, even if only at take-off and landing. Now they are flying over mountains – the Massif Central perhaps? – and she looks down into great ridges of rock and ice. In comparison, their plane seems as tiny and inconsequential as a mosquito, just waiting for fate to take a swat. And yet here they all are, a hundred or so of them, brimful of hopes, fears, expectations and each the total sum of their own personal histories.

A realization creeps over her. This is the first time she has flown, and known for certain that if she died, right this very moment, it wouldn't matter. Until now, she's always felt her death would be a disaster for the family – but not any more. Suddenly *she* doesn't matter any more – except to herself. Her death wouldn't make the slightest difference to any of them. For better or worse, they're all set now and could carry on regardless. This should be depressing, shouldn't it?, but in reality she feels an overwhelming sense of relief – a real relinquishing of a long-held burden. Whatever pigs' dinner she may be making of her life now, it is at least *her* pigs' dinner and nobody else's.

Arriving at Luton airport on a sodden, gun-metal March afternoon, queuing for the bus to the station – it should all be vile. Then suddenly a great whiff of daffodils and wet grass defeats the stink of diesel fuel. Spring: gently unfurling English spring with none of Vieilleville's abrupt puff of brilliant emerald green. Nostalgia, of course. Home?

*

Initially Alice goes to stay at Gavin's shared, rented house in Fulham. She's never been there before, but it's always sounded quite smart – certainly a modish area now. Gav is away on location again, somewhere up Ben Nevis this time, shooting the stunt climbing for *Days of Death*, but he'd been relaxed and generous about her 'using his pad'. 'No probs, Mum. My room's empty – get there after seven and someone should be in. I'll leave a set of keys.'

She has two hours to hang around Fulham Road hampered by her trolley case and trying not to spend too much money. Not easy – there's a limit to how long you can linger over a single cappuccino, and the luggage is a real giveaway when she tries to infiltrate a trendy gallery. When at last she gets to the house, she finds Gavin's sharers – four enormous young men who all seemed to be called 'Rob' (you didn't get 'Bob' any more she'd noticed) all slumped in front of a vast television with quadrophonic sound watching football.

The Rob who's let her in immediately collapses back with the others on to the sofa, mesmerized by the screen and drinking beer from the bottle. It's so long since Alice has seen British television that she might have relished joining them, but she can't pretend she's been yearning for *Big Match Live*, and although they look comfortable enough ignoring her, she feels awkward and decides on an early night.

Gav's room is a *little* disappointing. The scattered unwashed underwear is disheartening, as is the overall funny smell hanging about. At first she doesn't recognize it . . . then suddenly it's quite familiar, tugging at strings of her memory. Oh, yes, *pot* – pot smoke infiltrating the atmosphere. Gav's lank curtains are almost thickened by the smell. She tries not to mind that he's made so little effort on her behalf, then feels a stab of irritation – if the boot was on the other foot . . .

She searches out the kitchen for a much-needed cup of tea and immediately wishes she hadn't. The blue lino crackles with spilt sugar, turned in places to adhesive syrup;

the fridge door is glutinous with grease – and this is the place that produced Gav's Christmas goose?

But it's the bathroom that finally defeats her. She tries hard to ignore the squelchy, speckled carpet underfoot and the pools of sodden grey flannels weeping round the edge of the washbasin, but the alien pubic hairs scattered across the bath break the camel's back, and after an itch-filled sleepless night, she rings Lally in the morning and asks to stay.

Lally's house is fully occupied, which is why Alice didn't come here in the first place. It's definitely a question of sleeping on the futon in the sitting room and trying to make herself scarce. Lally is absolutely welcoming and absolutely stretched. There's some vast drama at work – two major brokerage firms are merging and the City is already metaphorically awash with the blood of sacked ex-whiz kids terrified of their colossal mortgage commitments and screaming down their mobiles day and night for new placements. She's scarcely home at all, and when she does come through the front door, she's almost rigid with exhaustion.

During the day Alice goes to the Family Records Centre in Islington, and searches through their huge volumes, trying to winkle out some evidence of her grandparents' existences. This might have been achieved pretty quickly – three of them yield up their registrations in the first few hours. Only her mother's mother remains elusive. Neither Macintosh nor Mactavish proves a fruitful line of enquiry; nor does her supposed date of birth.

But persistence pays off, that and the absurd grandeur of her Christian names, for how many Jenista Alexandra

Ariadnes born on 8 June can there be? The initials JAAM must have been a trial, mustn't they? For she does turn out to be a Mac, but it's Macintyre – oh, and she was also a liar. After two days of hunting, and nearing despair, Alice finds the entry – born in Redruth but ten years earlier than she had always claimed. A sudden memory from earliest childhood returns – of Granny's bedroom, and Granny stuffing her paper-white body into one of those ghastly all-in-one corsets like medieval armour and turning to Alice with a 'Shh, darling, lady's secrets.' Had she ever told Grandad she was eight years older than him? And, if not, did this particular 'lady's secret' haunt her?

Alice would love to share some of this speculation with Lally but there doesn't seem to be any time. She feels hungry for a good old gossip, like they used to have in the Bristol days, before Lally went off to university. Alice had prided herself that Lally always told her everything – no 'ladies' secrets' for their generation. Only of course she hadn't – Alice realizes that now. It was just the nineties' version of 'everything' in which Alice made sure Lally booked her appointments with the family-planning clinic, but actually knew nothing of the substance of her life. All the emotional truths were kept cleverly hidden, as ever maintaining the time-honoured parent/child divide.

The problem is that Alice now finds herself longing to reveal her own emotional truths, to a real person, face to face, rather than down the disembodied emptiness of telephone lines from Vieilleville. She hasn't even felt able to write to Lally about what's been happening – far too dangerous to commit to paper and leave a permanent record of what might just be passing moods and fears. Since the divorce, she can see that what she most misses is the ordinary daily rhythm of living with somebody, the sort of communication that doesn't need permission or preamble. But by the time Lally arrives home she's already yawning. She kisses Alice on the head – as if it were Alice who now counted as the child – and crawls away to bed.

It's not just Lally who works these shattering hours, the other girls here do too, and work seems mostly to extend into late meetings and/or business dinners, which probably sound a lot more fun than they are. They all stagger in blitzed with exhaustion, change into tracksuit bottoms and sit around the television eating Pringles and American ice-cream out of tubs, like glazed zombies.

Alice feels sorry for them, really, despite their glow of youth. She herself had scarcely been touched by the birth of feminism. She'd already been too immersed in that other birth – of the twins – to take much notice. But, seeing its inheritors at such close quarters, she can see how very hard it is to 'have it all'. It even looks hard now, when none of them has started down the road towards permanent commitment and children. There just doesn't seem to be room for everything any more. How on earth are they going to be able to fit it all in? Alice finds them extraordinary – sweet, touching and generous – still searching and seeking out their loves and life choices, biological clocks ticking but presumably alarms not yet set.

Their dreams of a future seem all tied into structures she didn't begin to imagine at their age – maternity leave, child-minders, hoping they'll earn enough for nannies instead.

But following this route they'll never turn into an Alice, will they? If their versions of the Self-Proclaimed Finest Gynae in the West dumps them for a Hillary Aldyce, they'll just be able to give the two-fingers, and have another spin of the wheel. Alice admires them intensely – but doesn't envy them at all. Maybe there are no 'answers' – it's all too complex. Meanwhile she's aware of feeling useless to requirements as well as ancient, backed into the corner of the sitting room, trying to keep her eyes open, until the last of them decides to go to bed and leaves her to flip open the futon and curl up – alone and spare.

*

'Of course we all knew you'd only gone there to find a man,' says Deirdre, and her tone heaves with satisfied relief.

'I beg your pardon?' says Alice, hoping she's misheard.

'It was perfectly obvious – this Riviera business. I talked to Jilly and Jilly talked to Kate – and we all knew, it was *obvious*. Such a pity,' and she sighs.

'Excuse *me*,' is what Alice wants to rasp, 'excuse me, but you're telling me I wanted *what*? A man? Go stuff yourselves' – no, that's not strong enough, 'Go boil yourselves in acid and feed yourselves to Satan.' Yes, that's more like it – very much the sort of thing she wants to rasp. Instead of which she just shakes her head and tries to retrieve her hand from Deirdre's soggy sympathetic grasp. God almighty but this was a bad idea.

Alice is back at Deirdre's house again, in the familiar spare bedroom, only this time as a non-paying guest. This wasn't part of her original plan. She'd intended to stay at an hotel whatever the cost, but Deirdre's assumption of her visitor-status has been hard to shake off, and despite misgivings, the financial saving seemed just too tempting to turn down – particularly considering that the entire purpose of this trip back to Bristol is to see if she can rejig her finances. A meeting with the manager at the building society is planned; an independent financial adviser may be called.

Still, Deirdre's evident glee at Alice's less than glowing account of life in Vieilleville, is hard to take. It's beginning to feel as if the additional hole in her bank account by way of a thumping hotel bill would have been a small price to bear. Harder by far is Deirdre's sorrowful crowing. Alice already regrets her innate tendency for honesty – why hadn't she just said everything was marvellous? Why go and give Deirdre the opening?

'You poor thing,' says Deirdre now, sitting on the end of Alice's bed, 'it has been hard on you. When I think of all you've done for that man – and that woman hasn't had to lift a finger, not a finger.'

'Well, she's had the babies – and twins aren't exactly a picnic. I speak from experience, remember,' says Alice, wishing she wasn't having to expend energy defending Hillary Aldyce of all people, and wanting to let the subject drop. But then she can't resist a sneaky question because, after all, she's bursting with curiosity. 'In what way "hasn't had to lift a finger"?'

'Whole house Colefax and Fowlerized – top to bottom. Didn't have to choose a tassel let alone stencil a wall.'

'No?' says Alice, now really feeling sick. 'What about

my hall ceiling?' Thinking of the gilding and all that careful effort.

'Entirely painted over – designer thought the whole gold concept terribly eighties. Gone for something pale and simple, lemon yellow, I think. Better for the patients' calm – or was it karma?'

'Really,' says Alice, sicker and sicker.

'Are you finding it all *very* difficult?' Deirdre leans closer across the candlewick, looking increasingly sorrowful.

'Yes – well – obviously it's all very new but it's marvellous in so many ways – the weather of course . . .' Possibly too late by now, Alice plumps for the positive.

'Oh, yes, the weather – mind you we've kept an eye out when John Ketley does his European round-up on BBC2 and it often seems to us it's not quite so pink as it's painted.'

'No, it's marvellous,' says Alice firmly, retrieving her hand. 'And the life – the French – '

'I expect that has its trials.' Deirdre's ever more soulful.

'No, it's *marvellous*,' says Alice again. What a useful all-embracing word. '*Marvellous*' – why hadn't she just stuck with it from the start?

'You've been very brave.'

'Not at all.'

'It must be so lonely.'

'Not so very lonely.'

'And then on top of everything else, the money.'

'Well . . .' tricky – hard to deny the money problem when Deirdre was being so free with her hospitality ' . . . obviously it would be easier if things weren't quite so tight.'

'That bastard! When I think of what Hillary's been able to spend on curtains alone – you wouldn't believe – '

'Really?'

'But then I suppose you *were* a bit rash.'

'What?'

'Well, don't get me wrong but this French business – well, it was a bit sudden, wasn't it? Surely it would have been better to rent, wouldn't it? If you were hell bent on doing it.'

'Well, not hell bent exactly – '

'But could we dissuade you – did we try?'

'Well, obviously I'd made some plans – had to stick with them.'

'You always were headstrong, Alice, in your funny little way. Hidden depths – Bill's always said so.'

'Really? Me – hidden depths?'

'But there you are – '

'Yes – there I am.'

'Gone and burnt your boats, haven't you?'

'Well, in a manner of speaking.' Too right. Burnt boats. Crossed bridges. No bridges more like.

'Well, there you are, then,' sighs Deirdre, though on her face rests the ghost of a smirk.

12

Interlude of Hope

Initially Verona can't believe her eyes and leans further out of her window to have another look. Extraordinary.

A huge pantechnicon has been parked across the bottom of the rue d'Espoir, blocking its flow, but instead of the usual hiss of fury from the constipated traffic, a gendarme is in charge, laying out a stream of cones to create a diversion. *Cones* in Vieilleville? *Planned* diversions in Vieilleville? *Impossible.*

The locals think so too. Several come out to examine the novelty. There's that funny Madame who looks like a man, always leaning out of her ground-floor window to chat to passers-by, wearing a shirt and bow-tie – only ever displaying her top half, so that Verona's often wondered if she's permanently naked from the waist down. But here she is, fully revealed as fully clothed – the bottom half being a very tight stripy skirt and white stilettos, which don't go at all with the rest of the garb – and now she's being joined by Monsieur-the-rather-effete-wine-merchant from the other side of the square, and here comes the woman from the launderette and they're all having a lively debate.

From this upstairs vantage-point, Verona can't hear much, just gets a general view of arm gestures and lots of shoulder-shrugging. She decides to risk discovery and leans right out, pushing the shutter flat back against the wall to get a better look. And sees the mighty word PICKFORD'S written down the length of the huge lorry. And now its back doors are being opened, its ramp lowered, and there below are dear darling Pickford's men in green baize aprons, heaving great pieces of furniture up the rue d'Espoir towards . . . towards the Maison Puce. Well, no, actually past the door . . . along the road . . . to the other door, the one to the top flat – the penthouse or *appartement de grand standing*, as Monsieur Gerontin has always proudly labelled it. Someone is moving into the penthouse and using dear old Pickford's to do it. British, reliable and pukka as they come, which instantaneously leads Verona to draw similar conclusions about the new owner/owners. How intriguing. She rushes to get out as quickly as possible, only turning the key in one of her locks (unheard-of carelessness) in her urgent need to have a glimpse of the newcomers as soon as possible.

She starts off up the road swinging her basket, as if on her way to the market, even though this is the wrong direction. All she sees is the open front door in the other tower, and a glimpse of a hallway and identical spiral staircase, both every bit as shabby as their own, plus the back view of a Pickford's bottom, braced against a chest of drawers at the turn of the steps. She continues to the top of the road, through the archway under the clocktower of the rue de l'Ange, and doubles back down the other way. This time all she gets is the radiator front of the lorry, blocking the entrance to the square. She squeezes through between lorry and wall, and wiggles down to the end where she gives a sideways swipe at its contents as currently on display. Gratifying. Good furniture, looks mostly modern and pale but obviously high quality – very Sunday supplement. Very satisfactory. Then as a couple of the Pickford's men are coming back down the ramp with a rather splendid limed oak bookcase she has, regretfully, to move aside. She thinks of questioning them, but the streams of perspiration on their straining faces indicate that this is not perhaps the best moment for an inquisition. There's nothing for it but to have another little nonchalant troll back up the road, past the other door. Just as she reaches it, one of the Pickford's men comes out, accompanied by a slender woman in black trousers and a white shirt, immaculate – imagine being thus dressed on moving day, thinks Verona, in a flash of envy, for her own moving days have always been agonies of tea-chest-heaving and floor-scrubbing, in which Edmund never deigned to join. This woman has a shiny asymmetrical bob of dark hair, which has fallen forward, masking one side of her head, and Verona can hear her saying, 'Well, in that case you'll simply have to take it apart – it can't be *that* difficult,' in an authoritative tone – and, here's a surprise, an *American* accent. And the woman raises her head quite sharply, so that the hair swings back to reveal a familiar face. Verona is caught in a moment of hesitancy. It's *such* a familiar face that the first briefest instinct is to step straight forward and greet it like an old friend. But then not a friend, not at all, though familiar enough, goodness just *how* familiar, so that Verona knows the exact way one of the incisors is chipped, and that cheeky ironic lift to the right eyebrow, used with such devastating effect on screen. Verona stands watching them walk back down to the lorry, as the limed bookcase is being heaved steadily towards her. She only hesitates for a second, then leaps forward, intent on an introduction.

*

Alice is still away. Such bad luck. Only leaves Imo to share the news – and she might not relish it as much as she should. Still, Verona is bursting – *can't* keep it to herself much longer, simply *can't*. 'She's *Hope Boscombe*!'

'What?'

'Oh, Imo, you must know who I mean – on the box, that American woman, does that consumer programme, scares the wits out of drug companies and travel firms, something to do with cameras – God, my memory. Wednesday nights – I used to be *glued*.'

'Not *Sharp Focus*?'

'That's the one.'

'Oh. Her? Hope Boscombe?'

'That's what I said – that's who's moved in.'

'Are you sure?'

'Seen her – talked to her face to face. She was down there with Pickford's men – frightfully nice stuff, masses of it, the flat must be huge. Introduced myself, just quickly.'

'What's she like?'

'Well, shorter than she looks on the screen and her manner was actually a little on the brusque side – but then it was hardly the best time for a chat, what with the gendarme out there, and the traffic all held up, with *cones* – can you *believe?* – but you know, when things have calmed down a bit . . . Well, isn't it a *coup*? I couldn't believe it when I saw her – thought I must be imagining things – thought I'd give her a few days to settle in and then I'd go and ring her buzzer, say hello properly, and suggest a *leetle peek-neek* to break the ice – that would be nice, wouldn't it?'

*

Inside her head Imo's groaning. God almighty, what that woman doesn't understand about cool. What a bit of bad luck she got to Hope Boscombe first. I mean, for Chrissake, breaking into a celeb's private space like that. I mean, this could be really useful, right? It might be a real opportunity – not quite sure for what, not yet, but there might be something in it for me. But you've got to stay *cool* – why can't these women get it? They don't want Hope Boscombe thinking they're in any kind of awe, that she's in any way special – even though she is.

*

Word's got round the town pretty quickly and Josette is curious. She'd scanned this morning's *Nice-Matin* and there hadn't been a word on the new arrival so she can't be all *that* famous – not to the French anyway. Her recent favoured informant on life at the Maison Puce has been Alice Barnes, but as she still seems to be away, she'll have to opt for one of the others. But that Imogen always leaves her feeling uncomfortable, *mal à l'aise*, with her cockiness and slangy fluent French. Better to go for Verona – far more predictable and easy to pump.

Easy to find too: just make sure you get to the cheese stall in the market by 9 a.m. and join the queue.

'So zees 'Ope Boscombe, tell me,' says Josette.

'*H*ope,' says Verona, 'you really have to say your aitches to get it right.' She turns to Monsieur Paquier, who is holding his knife aloft over a hunk of Parmesan – '*Non*, Monsieur, *beaucoup plus petit* – like *that*.' Josette feels entitled to an internal snigger – talk about the pot calling the kettle black.

'She is famous, zees *H*ope,' says Josette, aspirating hard to sound the aitch (would that the *Eeenglish* ever made such an effort).

'She's got her own television show – on consumer affairs, you know, sort of like *Which?* magazine?'

'Which magazine?'

'No, *Which?*. That's its name. I'm sure you've got something similar here – to do with fair trading, shopping, that sort of thing.'

'*Shopping* – you mean like ze *Minitel*?' Josette's excitement is abating.

'No, on television.'

'But this is like satellite shopping?' Not in the least exciting – on their screens, dime-a-dozen, two-a-*centime*, trying to make you buy complicated egg whisks and useless things for chopping nuts.

'No,' says Verona, wanting the quality of their new neighbour made absolutely clear, and thus falling slap-bang into Josette's trap. 'Not at all like that. This is a big national television programme, on every week, and she does all sorts of other things – writes for the Sunday papers and she's always being quoted in magazines.

There was even a big feature on her in *Vogue* last year.'

'*Vogue*?' At last a name Josette can recognize with approval.

'Oh, yes, and all sorts of other things. She's *terribly* well known – quite a "somebody".'

'She will 'ave nice 'ouse in England . . .' Josette, never one to let an opportunity lie around going to waste, speculates out loud.

'I've no idea.'

'And she *will* play bridge,' says Josette, in a glow of certainty.

*

Hope Boscombe has really thrown herself into the unpacking. Of course, the movers have cracked the back of it but it's down to her to arrange things now – get the details right.

So far it's been kind of fun, doing things for herself, having time to breathe – with no secretaries and assistants breathing down her neck. And it's not as if it's heavy work. The apartment is all newly renovated and someone's obviously been in to clean – although not quite to her high standards. Still that's okay: she doesn't mind donning a pair of rubber gloves – quite amusing really, like playing house, quite soothing. And being soothed is part of what this French exercise is all about. Get herself some space, ease back, let it all calm down. Kick the Valium and avoid the Prozac – and, God only knows, she *needs* some space after all the recent pressure.

Not that this morning wasn't a little pressured too, with that big fat Englishwoman jumping out at her like that –

just terrible, trying to take her hand and telling her what a fan she was and what a thrill it was to have her as a neighbour. I mean, can you beat it? I've come all these hundreds of miles for some peace and privacy and find the goddam public right here on my doorstep?

In the middle of her beautiful new slate floor, her beautiful new silver telephone starts ringing. It's Jerry Slater, her agent. 'How's my baby?'

'Well – okay, I guess.'

'You only "guess"?'

'No, it's terrific. It's just – I don't know, I hope I haven't made a mistake.'

'How could you, darling? I looked at the satellite reports this morning – it looks heaven over there and it's pissing down here. I could *kill* you with envy.'

'Yes – but you haven't met the natives.'

'Oh, the *French*. I know, darling, but just give them time. You know what they're like – I think they just do it to annoy, love to put the wind up us with all that fucking *sangfroid* business.'

'It's not the French I'm thinking of. If only – '

'Tell me.'

'I don't think I dare.'

'God. You bitch. Now I'm gasping.'

'No, it's probably nothing. You'll have to wait and see – that's what I'm about to do. I'll report. Meanwhile, anything cooking?'

'Nothing that needs you back in the kitchen, darling – remember what you promised. Just you sit back now, relax and enjoy.'

Relax and enjoy. Okay, yes, and this should be perfect. Hope looks around her new space, still holding the telephone, then puts it back on the floor, uncertain yet exactly where it should go. Yes, the apartment's really very pleasing now it's finished – so she's made the right choice after all. When she'd first been shown it last September by that Monsieur Whatchamacallit she hadn't been that impressed – she'd had her doubts. It was a mess then, of course, no doors, dust everywhere, and small. Never one to dawdle through her life, she must have done her preliminary exploration in two minutes flat. Of course, the fittings weren't all in then so she'd had to use a lot of imagination – just this open-plan area down here with the kitchen and guest bathroom off, and then up the steel spiral a couple of bedrooms and another bathroom, pretty compact considering the price. And then while she was just standing there, considering, Monsieur had pulled back the shutters at the far end and flung back the tall windows on to what she would have called a balcony but which he proudly labelled a *terrasse* – and of course she'd gone straight out.

'But I thought there was a view,' she'd accused. 'I'd understood from Mr Allenby in London that this would be an apartment with a view.'

'Of ze mountains. *Vue des montagnes.*'

'Where?' She'd scanned the layers of roofs in front, starting with curvy old terracotta but rapidly climbing to modern blocks in shades of apricot and pink that crawled up the hill behind.

'Now is too much *nuages* – too . . . *cloudy*, yes? And too dark. But on a good day you can see right across to ze

Alpes-Maritimes – you can see ze snow up there while you lie down 'ere making ze tan. It is most *agréable*.'

'But the sea? Where is it from here?' she'd asked.

'Over there perhaps?' Monsieur had pointed vaguely in the direction of the windowless galley kitchen.

'Through there? On the other side of that wall?' she'd asked. 'I guess I could knock a window through.'

'T'rough? What is t'rough?'

'*Through* – the wall. A HOLE through the wall?' Hope had made what she thought was an appropriate gesture.

'Madame, you do not understand, there is another *maison* on the other side. You cannot make ze window like that – *impossible*.'

'Oh. Well, that's very disappointing. When Mr Allenby told me about this place I understood there was a view of the sea.'

'Avec *vue de la mer* here in Vieilleville you would pay *ten* times as much,' he said, getting purple round the jowls. '*Dix fois*,' he added, and for extra emphasis held up both hands and shook all ten digits somewhere up near her nose.

'Well, I don't know,' she'd said, walking around, injecting as much disappointment and gloom as she could into the phrase (she's not known as a hot negotiator for nothing) because inwardly she was thinking otherwise . . . It's not bad . . . not bad at all . . . Well, frankly, it's really kind of *got* something . . . and already she was seeing herself here, out on that *terrasse* (yes, it didn't take long for it to lose its iddy-biddy status as a mere balcony) – it was a *terrasse* (!), her very own *terrasse* (!) on the Côte d'Azur – not bad, eh? No, indeedy, not bad at all. And the price seemed do-able, very much within her fairly extensive budget, and she could have it finished to her own spec . . . pick out everything to echo her own particular tastes . . .

'I'll have to think about it,' is what she said out loud, though, dismissively. 'I've got lots of others to see . . .' though she hadn't – and she hadn't any time for hunting either, had only squeezed this visit into an an early-evening gap in her schedule at the Cannes Video Trade Fair, really had to get back, vital meeting at seven thirty . . .

'This will go *verrry* quickly – *très vite*, *comme ça*,' said Monsieur, with a snap of impatient fingers. 'Already I 'ave been saving thees for you because Meester Allenby in Londres says you are *verrry* special lady – *célèbre* – that you need somewhere discreet.'

'Well, I do,' she'd said. 'Of course I do.'

'And this place is, you know – *mignon* – cute.'

Which is, of course, what she was beginning to think too – because she'd gone ahead and bought it.

Now she looks around her, and even in the newly moved-in chaos feels a glow of achievement. So maybe she hasn't made it big back home in the good old US of A – but look what she *has* done. Struck out for Europe, all on her own – with no contacts, no family backing – and made a real impact in Britain. So okay, maybe she's not Oprah – not yet anyway – but she *figures* all right, oh, yes, she's right up there with the best of them. And now this . . .

Oh, Daddy, Daddy – just look at your little girl now. It's a long, long way from Lavaho, Texas to the South of France – didn't she do well?

13

Burnt Boats

For supposed economy, Alice takes the train back to Vieilleville. Not, of course, 'Le Tunnel' and the Eurostar, far too expensive, but a special low-season offer, involving the Dover ferry and a change at Paris – struggling across with her luggage by Métro from the Gare du Nord to the Gare St-Lazare. When she'd made the booking it sounded fun, as well as cheap. Verona's talked about how romantic this journey used to be – of how you took the Blue Train from Victoria, got into your *wagon-lit* at Calais or Boulogne, tucked yourself between crisp white linen sheets, and found by morning that you'd left the cool green plains of the north, and had awoken to the rocks, red-earth bluffs and olive groves of the south. Magic – *then*.

However, this version of the journey is a little different. Her special concessionary ticket threw in a couchette for free – which turns out to be something of a mistake. As the beds have already been lowered for the night, Alice and her travelling companions have either to stand up or lie flat from the very start of the journey. Lying down makes Alice feel like a naughty child who's been sent to bed early, but standing up is too knackering after all the travel so far. Her companions are a cheerful group of Italian plumbers' mates bound for Genoa. They're standing up all right – in boisterous mood – making lots of mini-baguettes out of *saucisson* and bottled antipasti, which drips oil everywhere. She retreats up to one of the top bunks to leave them to it. Gradually, as the train rattles through the French interior, they subside into sleep while she lies awake in boiling heat, surrounded by a chorus of snores and smells. Morning seems a long way off – and there's a lot to think about.

So she's going back to Vieilleville – but then what? The awful thing about the Deirdre/Bill wafts of 'I told you so' is that they're right. What lunacy could have made her believe that the mere physical act of moving to a different place and climate was going to conjure up a whole new life? Basic common sense should have told her that anything she wasn't able to rustle up at home, in her own language and culture, was hardly likely to materialize in Vieilleville by the wave of a wand – except . . . except that it *was* a sort of magic that got to her last year. It was wonderful to leap over all the dullness of 'being sensible' into the great void of the unknown possible. And these sort of things seem to work for other people – so why *not* her?

Of course, the tightness of money is definitely a major issue – perhaps it's the *only* issue. If it wasn't for that, she could just ride out the other problems of Vieilleville life and see if things improve naturally. As it is, with money problems looming so large, she doesn't feel she has any leeway. Having slogged through all those meetings at the bank and the building society, and paid for the services of the blasted independent financial adviser (what a farce), it's perfectly clear that she's not going to be able to increase her current income. In fact, as interest rates are now falling, she may have even less. The IFA man was full of schemes, which all had acronyms for titles. Her head was reeling by the end with all the ISAs and CATs and MINIs and MAXIs or whatever they're all called. *He* didn't even seem to understand them particularly well, so why should she? The only consistency she noticed was that every single leaflet he dropped on her lap had somewhere, in tiny print, 'The value of your investment may go down as well as up.' The prospect of having even *less* money is *truly* dire – so nothing's been sorted out in that direction.

Of *course* she shouldn't have committed herself irrevocably, of *course* she should have rented – given herself a taster of the new world and seen how it went and whether she could make a go of it. This visit back to England has brought her down with a real bump. Until now it hadn't quite sunk in how definitively she's cut her ties. There simply isn't any cosy refuge for her back there, representing safety and certainty. On the surface she'd known this before – but underneath, she now realizes, she'd always had this feeling that the children were there for her. But she'd been wrong – they can neither be expected to save her nor to provide her with a safe harbour. She's on her own.

If she wants to backtrack now, the only way will be to try to sell up. She's no idea what that would cost. Now that she knows Vieilleville better, it seems that the Maison Puce wasn't the bargain she'd been led to believe, so she doesn't even know if she could get her money back on it – and then she'd clock up a whole new stack of bills. Meanwhile property prices seem to be shooting up in Bristol, even though she wouldn't want to live there any more – too full of memories. And if not there, where? London is obviously out of the question financially. Whatever she does, she'll end up broker than ever.

But then last summer *was* a sort of madness – in the sunlight, under the influence of that soft red wine . . . was that it? Had she simply been pissed? 'With beaded bubbles winking at the rim' – Keats, wasn't it?, Ode to something or other, yes, Keats has a lot to answer for. And now, for her, nothing so romantic – just that clumsy refrain 'Burnt boats, burnt boats', keeping time with the rhythm of the train, a staccato rap of loneliness till dawn.

*

Hope jumps when the doorphone buzzer goes. Who the hell could that be? Too late for the post and she isn't expecting any deliveries. The last few days she's settled to a quiet rhythm of unpacking and arranging – so far it's all working as it should, calming her right down. And then the buzzer goes.

She picks up the receiver warily, automatically answering in English.

'Yes?'

'Miss Boscombe?'

Something in Hope instantly freezes. How? Who? Who knows she's here?

'It's Verona Grange, Miss Boscombe, your neighbour – one floor down, and up the other staircase?'

Oh. That's who. The fat English woman who'd pounced on her the other day.

'So sorry to bother you only I wanted to make contact, welcome you to our little clan, and of course I don't have your telephone number.'

Or ever will, thinks Hope grimly.

'I'm *so* glad your doorphone works . . . Ours don't, you know . . . I only gave yours a little push . . . just to test it . . . only now I've actually got you . . . well, I wonder if I might tempt you to come and join us for a *leetle peek-neek*?'

'A what?'

'On the beach – say, Saturday lunchtime?'

'No, I'm sorry, no – it's very kind of you, but I've got a lot of work to do.'

'Oh, I'm *sure* – poor you – up to your eyes. It wouldn't be for long.'

'No, I'm sorry but I can't possibly break into my daytime schedule at the moment.'

'Well, how about a drink, then? Very briefly, just to meet up – with some local French friends too?'

'Well . . .' My God but this woman is persistent, the sort who won't take no for an answer. Maybe it's best to give in – just this once – meet the neighbours . . . could be useful? 'All right, just briefly as you say. It's very kind of you.'

'Oh, *super* – six p.m. Saturday, then? Dress code comfortable but clean – that's what we always used to say up at the *bastide*. I'm flat three but don't bother to ring my bell – doesn't work. Just shout – I'll be all ears. Toodle-pip.'

Hope's regretting it before she's even replaced the receiver.

*

In Alice's absence, an early summer has happened. Even though it's still only the middle of April, she senses it the moment she gets off the train at Bonneville, and feels a great wave of honeyed sunlight hitting her back.

Because of her baggage, she takes a taxi down to Vieilleville. She'd intended to go straight to the Maison Puce, but she catches a glimpse of the market, still very much in full flow, and asks to be dropped off at the rue des Fleurs. After the gloom of last night's thoughts on the train, and the lack of sleep, she's suddenly whirled into the essence of the town. Dragging her case with all its appendages of plastic bags – her luggage seemed to have doubled its volume since she left – she walks in under the covered area of the market and stands for a moment, just drinking it in. She thought that by now she'd have grown *blasé* about it, but being here, in the flesh again, she's completely overwhelmed by its sights and scents.

Here at the entrance is old Madame Lafranier's small stall – the stuff she raids from her own garden. In a long green line piled down the trestle table are all the salad leaves and herbs, each of them labelled: *blettes*, the local Swiss chard, in two heaps, one of leaves and a separate pile for stalks, *mesclun* including lots of dandelion and rocket, then the lettuces, batavia, rougette and *feuilles de chêne*. Then the herbs – too early for a lot of basil, all good things have their own time and season; instead, bundles of chives, rosemary, thyme, sorrel, chervil and mint. Bay leaves in sheaves. A huge pile of golden courgette flowers for making *beignets*. Then she's got wispy little asparagus like tiny birds' quills next to pink and white stalks as fat as a thumb.

And miniature purple artichokes tied up in bouquets of five. And gleaming *oignons blancs d'Antibes* like giant spring onions. And *haricots rouges* in a heap next to the *haricots verts*. And goose eggs/duck eggs/quail eggs plus four different sorts of free-range bantam and hen eggs and last of all *bouquets garnis* made up like bridesmaids' posies (as big and as pretty) for five francs a time.

Further along the lines, the fruit men have mounds of strawberries and cherries – *fraises du pays*, *fraises carros* – *fraises des bois*, special *garriguettes* from the Dordogne, then cherries from the Ardèche and others from the Var, everything marked up on their little blackboards as to variety and price.

Monsieur Raoul, the cheeky chappie of the market, has also raided his garden – big buckets full of bunches of *roses de Mai*, cerise pink and puffing out great invisible clouds of scent, priced from ten to twenty francs the bunch depending how open and far gone the blooms, and cornflowers, sweet peas, a vast pot of arum lilies, and another of syringa, with that luscious orange blossom perfume and already dropping its petals. He greets Alice warmly – he's noticed she hasn't been around these last weeks. Could it be that, after all, she has started to belong without even realizing it?

Further on the spice woman also says hello. She keeps all her wares in bags made of Provençal cotton – ochre/saxe blue/scarlet/emerald – opened up on platters so you can see (and, more important, *smell*) their contents. There's a huge range and mixture – *spécial salade*, *spécial pâtes* (red), *spécial poulet* (green), *préparation huile piquante*, *safran de Chine* in a great mound, mace, little dried chilli peppers called 'birds' tongues', and 'exotic pepper' mixed up with rosebuds and dried lemon grass and spiced tea, black tea, a huge basket of Sardinian sun-dried tomatoes and another of dried aubergine slices . . .

And then the cheeses, all in a state of taste perfection in the humid air (even if prey to the odd fly but who cares?) – all those *tommes*, big flat lumps like curling stones, '*chèvre pays*', 'savoie blanc', the cheeses of Ariège, Piémont and Sardaigne, and the charolais/pavé vache/St-Julien – and on and on and on.

Alice is reeling, instantly half drunk again, on the luscious beauty of it all. Of course, this mood is what it was all about, *this* is why she came.

She's scarcely started to unpack before there's a knocking at her door. Tired and grubbily travel-worn, she opens it resignedly to Verona, whose face is a glowing pink orb of excitement.

'Alice *dear*, you'll *never* guess who's moved into the top flat!'

*

Verona's pulled her entertaining stops out, even ordered hot savouries from the ritzy Boulangerie de L'Évêque – though usually she'd have baked her own – and tidied up the flat quite a bit. Even so, her drinks party is a crush, even with only the five of them – six, if you count Fred.

'And this is our next latest arrival – Alice Barnes.' Verona has a proprietorial grip on Hope Boscombe's arm and is manoeuvring her around the crammed room as if it was a formal salon. Already Josette has been abandoned on the maroon Dralon sofa, while Imo and Fred are next in line by the kitchen area. 'Alice arrived not that long ago, didn't you, dear? Only just settling in – early days.'

Alice examines the familiar face. The last time she'd seen it had been on television – a repeat of *Sharp Focus* only a week ago when she'd been staying with Deirdre. It was a programme on cellulite creams, and Hope Boscombe had had a whole band of women standing in their M & S undies by the Serpentine, on what looked like a freezing morning, judging by the puffs of breath – and all having to expose their jiggling thighs to her scrutiny. Very sharp focus indeed. Odd to have that same face here, now, in real life. It seems much larger in proportion to her really quite short body than it looks on the screen but otherwise it's exactly as expected – weirdly so, like a puppet come to life.

'Hi,' says the puppet, and holds out a limp hand in greeting. There's an awkward pause – how does one talk to celebrities? A dilemma. Alice, for example, knows quite a lot about Hope Boscombe already, from random newspaper gleanings, whilst clearly Ms B. knows nothing about the subtleties of Alice Barnes. Hope's trouser suit, for example, more than likely Joseph, though it may well be Armani or Donna Karan – Alice has read about this in *Hello!* magazine at the dentist's. Details of Hope Boscombe's wardrobe and house in London have eased many a queasy moment before root-canal work. But what to say to her now? All the usual conversational openers – 'What do you do?' for example – are total non-starters: everyone in the room knows what she does, and Verona's already used up 'What brought you to Vieilleville?' and only got a brittle laugh in reply. Nothing Alice can remember of Hope's public persona is specific enough to be of any real help. Wasn't she a vegetarian? Hadn't there been some article in praise of eggs? Or maybe it was that she specifically *wasn't* a vegetarian, in that article about Lent. Too late, she remembers the Burmese cats in that spread in *OK* – or was it the *News of the World*? She could have asked who was minding them but, then, wouldn't that have shown an unhealthy interest in low-level tabloid journalism? – and already Hope is being ushered towards Imo and her chance is gone. Blast.

The kitchen area is half masked by a free-standing screen – a bamboo affair ruched to match the rest of the room in maroon velvet, and strategically placed to hide the sink. Imo has stuck herself here to make sure she gets a really good quota of the *boulangerie*'s nibbles – they're yummy and if she can scrounge enough of them she'll do without supper and get straight out to the Bar du Quai to suss out the weekend talent; the pickings in that direction have been lousy recently. In between swallowing as surreptitiously as possible she's been eyeing up their celebrated guest. Hmmm – not so impressive really, pretty bog standard, if you take away the name and the fame. Not difficult then to hang back, stay cool – look cool. She's had Fred more or less clamped between her legs, from where he's been looking up at her, dribbling, driven mad by the luscious food aromas. As Verona propels Hope towards her, and Imo prepares to greet, she loosens her grip on the dog. Fred uncoils like a spring towards the platter sitting on the hotplate. As he does, the screen topples sideways, revealing the sink and its unwashed, greasy contents. Then, as Imo tries to make a grab, it catches the edge of a bucket of Verona's soaking smalls, which she'd tucked back here for the interim. Before anyone can stop it, the bucket is tipping – bras, knickers and thick grey water are flooding across the floor, and Verona is turning as green as her pesto tartlets.

14

Reveries

In going back to England, Alice has restarted the clock on her *carte de séjour* application so, if need be, she can leave it for another three months. In any case she's going to have to wait for the copies of her grandparents' birth and death certificates to arrive by registered post, plus the document from the commissioner for oaths in Bristol. This last was Bill's idea – his solution to the problem of proving to the Bonneville *mairie* that she'd never been in prison. So, all in all, it's a case of dawdling towards a resolution, which suits her mood of procrastination only too well.

The burst of hot weather has changed the mood of Vieilleville. It's an early burst, even by Côte d'Azur standards, and everyone's enjoying it. On the day after the disastrous drinks party, Alice slips down to the beach. As it's a Sunday quite a few of the locals are here too, though only the foreigners are crazy enough to swim – *far* too cold for sensible people.

Alice stretches out on her bamboo mat, a bit ashamed of the ghost-whiteness and overall hairiness of her legs. She'll have to do something about both. Never mind. At this moment, as far as she's concerned, who's to notice? She props herself up on one elbow and observes the scene. In the warmth this place is already becoming very sexy. There are couples everywhere – and not all of them young and glamorous: they come in all sorts of shapes and sizes. There's a middle-aged pair down at the water's edge, nutmeg brown (that *does* help) – she with cellulite saddlebags and he with vast *embonpoint* – embracing, absolutely enchanted with each other and completely oblivious to the rest of them. It's a touching sight – but also enviable, and Alice feels a cold, covetous shiver in the heat of the sun.

It's a bit sad to be in such a charged atmosphere and yet so totally alone that she can't even spread her sunscreen on to the middle of her back. She can't reach it herself and there's no one to do it for her. A bit symbolic, that. And yet what Deirdre said was outrageous and terribly patronizing – she didn't 'come here for a man', though if she's come for a life, then she might well hope that a man would eventually be part of it.

She sits up and, under cover of her sunspecs, starts to have a good look round. Is there anyone here she'd truly want if she had the chance? Well . . . ummm, actually so far . . . no. There are some beautiful young Apollos, of course, but even playing this game, she's not *that* unrealistic. There are one or two good-looking middle-aged men – but they all seem to have younger wives and children in tow. Very few lone men . . . one over there with sad, flaccid calves . . . and one dipping his toe in the water with back hair like a fur rug . . . Now here's one just spreading out his towel . . . All right, Alphonse, *impress* me . . . shirt coming off, stomach held in . . . Oh, no, huge volcanic moles erupting with grey hairs . . . but how dare she be so critical with her own lumpy arms and unruly pubes? With Philip none of this had seemed to matter . . . They'd grown older together and when she'd looked at him she'd always managed to see his younger beautiful self. She'd always assumed he was doing the same thing when he looked at her . . . but obviously in that she'd been mistaken.

'Coo-eee – oh, *there* you are!'

Alice is rudely awoken from her erotic beach reverie. It's Verona, looming over her, complete with mat / towel / parasol / windbreak / canvas-and-metal-sit-up-and-beg contraption plus the inevitable bloody *peek-neek* bursting out of a fluorescent orange 'cool' bag (*what* a misnomer). She kneels down and proceeds to unravel / unpack / erect the whole lot.

'This *is* fun, isn't it?' she says. 'After the disappointments of yesterday I wondered if I'd feel up to fun, but there you are – just one of those things, wasn't it? I did try so hard to give a good impression – for *all* of us.'

'It was lovely, Verona – it was a lovely party,' says Alice, stretching the truth – but impossible not to.

'Do you really think so?'

'Well, yes – I'm sure Hope Boscombe appreciated the gesture.'

'Well, I hope so. I tried to contact her this morning – asked her if she'd like to come to the beach – but she was really quite short with me. Still, she's probably busy – I expect she was pleased, really – whatever she looked like – and it's no good crying over spilt smalls, is it?' She removes her summery orange tent dress to reveal an odd latex two-piece, with horizontal stripes at bursting-point barely containing her breasts.

Verona's breasts turn out to have a life of their own: they can practically go out for walks unaccompanied, and throughout the afternoon they seem to escape from the rest of her body with regularity. No one is more taken by surprise at this than Verona herself, who squeaks a little 'Oh' every time one pendulous brown nipple works its way free. Everyone else on the beach suddenly looks like a paragon of sleek, bikini-bronzed beauty in comparison to them – even Alphonse of the moles. None of the others seem to have brought anything with them, apart from towels, mobile phones and Ambre Solaire. Alice and Verona are the lone over-equipped island of solid British suburbia. Alice feels increasingly humiliated and wonders how she can avoid repeating the experience. Is this what's going to happen all summer long? How on earth can she keep herself to herself, hidden from Verona's gaze? So far the wearing of a paper bag over her head is the only solution that occurs.

An hour later and the constant burble of Verona's conversation, drowning out the soothing happy seaside noise, has given Alice a headache. She lies there stretched out with her eyes closed behind her dark glasses, planning her escape, then suddenly sits up, claims she has to write an urgent letter and makes a quick get-away while Verona is still engaged in deconstructing her entire beach edifice.

Sunday, late afternoon, and the whole of Vieilleville is *en promenade*. Alice settles at an outside table at the Café des Fleurs, toying with a notepad and pen just in case Verona tracks her down – it wouldn't do to be trapped in a lie – then orders an Americano and sits back to absorb the scene. Everyone is parading, from ancient, miniature little ladies with equally miniature dogs, to great butch, bronzed fellas striding down the road with ribboned patisserie boxes dangling from one forefinger. Deliciously absurd vision – and just as delicious, the communicated sense of anticipation of the enjoyment of the boxes' contents, the mysteries of *le dessert*. There's a real sense of communal pleasure – of people emerging from wintry cocoons, and flapping their new fine-weather wings, particularly the women, so appreciated by the long, lingering stares from the men. They're like birds, these women, literally . . . she could classify them as to species:

(1) Âgée *Golden Wrens: miniature, frail, skinny and nut-brown. Plumage: embroidered silken suits with as much gold as the body can carry; always accompanied by matching miniature dog with rhinestone leash.*
(2) Âgée *Golden Egrets: taller but less robust version than (1), extremely elegant. Plumage: scallop-edged suits in sugar-almond colours; attenuation such that even small dog might pull them over – that, or merest puff of wind – hence no dogs, no appendages at all, though often followed by solemn thin old men carrying overcoat or cushion to place on park benches and relieve buttock bones of stress. Imminent death of either a distinct possibility.*
*(3) Middle-*âgée *Golden Pouter Pigeons: very well looked-after, svelte forms, narrow hips and waists, voluminous bosoms. Plumage: delicate linen suits with Bermuda shorts, little golden pumps, little golden handbags strapped diagonally across said*

voluminous bosoms; often carrying beribboned pastry boxes, though from narrowness of hips must assume they do not consume the contents. On the whole Josette and her troop of Augustines fall into this category, although possibly they are in fact stronger versions of âgée *Golden Egrets* masquerading *as Pouter Pigeons (Josette is very coy about her age).*
(3a) Lesser Stouter Golden Pouter Pigeons: sub-species of (3) above – numerous examples. Plumage as for (3) but, because of solidity through the beam, opting for skirts, which are always slightly too short. Very busy *– thus slightly puffed and laden with too much shopping.*
*(4) Middle-*âgée *Golden Hippie Dippers: primavera corkscrew curls in brass blond. Plumage: transparent white muslin or cheesecloth suits revealing nipples; huge dogs, preferably mastiffs or, failing that, bulldogs with fierce Disney faces.*
(5) Solid Local Sparrows: no daytime gold, but come the early evening (as now) emerge from nest-boxes in gold-net cardigans, sparkly specs and ormolu metallic hair.
(6) Les Oiseaux du Paradis*: these are the stunners, the partners of the beach Apollos. Presumably hibernating all winter, and now revealed in full glory. The men all* melt *as these creatures pass. All are impossibly thin except for their cantaloupe breasts, clingfilm wrapped in black elastic and Lycra; precipitous heels clicking on the pavement, mobile phones clamped to one ear. Plumage: involves much less* GOLD *than other categorics, restricted to any bit of anatomy which can be pierced, plus hair and skin, which glow so much they can probably see in the dark.*

Alice is sketching doodles of these creatures down the

margin of the pad. She would like to be one of these golden women – she has aspirations. Obviously she couldn't make it into Category (6) – but who knows, perhaps with a little effort she might make it as a Hippie Dipper? She already has the use of the dog, of course, and by helping Mother Nature along a bit with some hair bleach, even if hers is a bit short, plus some judicious shopping? Alice can feel a taste-transplant coming over her . . . bad monetary timing, for her existing summer wardrobe contains nothing in transparent linen or GOLD, only sensible things from Principles and Laura Ashley. Perhaps on Friday when the street market comes to town? She may just have to indulge in some retail therapy before total financial continence takes control . . .

*

Very rapidly, in a matter of mere days, Hope Boscombe has learned that the entire *point* of her flat is the terrace. She loves it up here. It's an eagle's nest, giving her a real sense of what this place is all about without sacrificing her privacy. She can hear the swish of the sea, just a little traffic noise, and can sense the movement of people, of what's going on out there beyond the winding alleyways. But she herself doesn't have to engage with any of it physically – essential.

She can't imagine how those other women in the building manage without one. She thought Verona Grange's so-called flat was a total nightmare – she's known location trailers with twice the space. And only one window, looking straight across the street into another flat. And the décor!

Are you kidding me or what? Who'd she get to do it – Morticia Addams?

Not that Hope's had much time yet to enjoy her own space. Too much to get on with – finds it impossible to chill out until she's got everything just *perfect*. She hasn't really had a chance to enjoy the weather yet, though it's kind of what she came here for. Warmth and light – that's what you crave when you spend your winters in the northern chiaroscuro. They'd given it a name now, hadn't they? She'd done a feature on it – that deep, dense depression born of sodden days and leaden skies – SAD, Seasonal Affective Disorder. Hope guesses maybe she's been suffering a touch of the SADs for she hasn't seemed in command as usual – lost her habitual buzz. Where is her get up and go? Got up and gone, she'd joked with Jerry, when he'd queried her lack of forward planning – so unlike her. But you didn't get SAD in Lavaho, Texas. Maybe you got MAD a little, specially in the heat of high summer, but that's not the same. Perhaps her genes have been rebelling at their enforced endurance of grey English Januarys. So she'd upped her Valium dose when no one was looking, hoped her GP wouldn't notice, and he hadn't – so accommodating these Harley Street guys, wrap them round your little finger. But of course she can't go on like this for ever – even in her worst moments she's clear-headed enough to see that. Which is what this French adventure is about – freshen her up in pastures new.

This morning she'd given herself some time off, wandered the town for a bit – even went to the market where she'd gotten a selection of olives, *basilic* and *à la façon de la maison*, black, oily and smothered in herbs and garlic. For the rest of the day she'd made herself get back down to it – mustn't shirk – arranging and rearranging her closets for maximum ergonomic efficiency. By early evening, though, she's got to admit she's pretty well set. That's it – she's done. What now?

She opens herself a bottle of chilled Bandol, puts the olives in absolutely authentic Provençal bowls and takes everything out on to the terrace, where she places them on the *japonaise* teak table with matching cream pagoda parasol. Then she stands back to take a look – the burnt-sienna tiles, the low encasing wall with its stone balustrade painted cobalt blue, the terracotta pots already planted up with spiky, hot-looking bushes. It's like a photo-opportunity – pretty damn delectable. And that Monsieur Gerontin guy had been right about the view. The distant Alpes-Maritimes did appear on clear days, and tonight there's a softening glow of sunset to her right and a puff of peachy cloud hanging between her and their snow-capped peaks. Spectacular.

She stretches out on the *chaise-longue*, sipping her wine, getting a mental picture of herself – hard to break this habit when you spent so much time looking at yourself in editing suites. Just suppose you're up there, up in those hills right now, training your binoculars down on the town, and you happen to chance upon this vision, what sort of conclusion would you be drawing about this woman, so sleek, so gathered together, long-legged, toenails painted *rouge noir* and sticking out of stiletto Jimmy Choos (whatever the weather)? Quite a cookie, you'd think – hardly a *babe*, not her thing at all, but a woman of consequence in her own right. She finds herself seeing this vision so strongly that she suddenly feels quite self-conscious, and looks up towards those very hills a bit anxiously to see if she can spot the spy of her imaginings, pick out the tell-tale glint of a lens. Then she realizes she can't reach the olives on the far side of the table so has to stand and rearrange the set-up before sitting to begin the whole process again. She starts on the olives appreciatively, trying to forget the imaginary observer in the hills.

Well, this is fabulous, isn't it – this is what she came for? The slowly darkening sky, streaks of apricot light merging into the velvet blue, the mountains already faded into abstract masses on the horizon. The combination of images and tastes is already bleaching out the irritation of those women – for, God almighty, who'd have believed that you could come all this way, create yourself a whole fresh existence, and land slap bang in the middle of a gaggle of fan-bait? Because that's what they are – that's how she's always secretly thought of those people, mostly women, who stand outside the studios, waggling their autograph books, always wanting a piece of you, cackling with laughter like bloody witches. Fan-bait – just imagine landing herself by accident in a nest of female fan-bait. Never mind, though, she need never see them – except perhaps that girl, Imogen, she'd had a certain something, quite attractive in a tough, gritty way. Quite stirring, actually – possible pussy-pulling? Not that she'd envisaged any of that for here – uh-uh: Vieilleville is supposed to be her retreat from *everything*.

It's about now that it first starts, from somewhere behind her – the sound of an accordion. Would you ever believe this? This is so cute – the unlikely delight of it. How French could you get? This made up for that gaggle of women – this is so Gallic, it's a goddam cliché. The musician, wherever he/she is, seems to hesitate at first, then gathers momentum. She can recognize the tune, 'Under the Bridges of Paris', and in her mind hears Eartha Kitt's oiled murmur of a voice joining in – '*Sous les ponts de Paris* . . .' Then how did it go? Da da di da di-di . . . Is this perfect or is this perfect? And she sinks back, purely to enjoy.

*

The next day is equally warm. Back in England you'd be kidding yourself it was spring, and then a blustery April gale would knock you right out of your hopeful complacency, whereas here she's had the doors open, and when she's been able to wean herself off the telephone to the London office, and stop her fingers and toes from restlessly tapping at the unaccustomed lack of activity, she's sat outside again relishing her *terrasse*.

At about the same time, during the sunset vigil, the accordion starts up again, 'Under the Bridges of Paris' – lovely. Hope hums along, sips, absorbs – just *lovely* . . . Then – well, there it is again . . . charming . . . And *again* . . . Maybe whoever it is will switch tunes in a minute . . . *And again*. The only variation is speed. Sometimes it's slow and lilting like last night – but then it gets faster and faster, whipping itself into an energetic kind of barn-dance.

Hope cranes over the wall of the terrace to see if she can work out where it's coming from. Nothing's happening down in the street . . . and then it starts up *again* – 'Under the Bridges of Paris' . . . *Paris* . . . *Paris* – but not a sign of an accordion player. A momentary silence and Hope relaxes for a second – but, oh, my *God*, no, there it is *again*, one of the quick versions this time . . . She stands very still and tries to work out where it's coming from . . . Somewhere across the roofs, perhaps? But where?

By the third night she can't even pretend she's enjoying it any more – it's definitely beginning to tug at her nerves. She stands listening, trying to get a fix on the source. As on the first night it seems to be coming from somewhere behind, but with this dense maze of tall old buildings, most of which seem to overlap each other in some way, it's very hard to see where one place ends and another begins. It's a will-o'-the-wisp sound, sometimes seeming to come from the left, sometimes the right.

On the fourth night she realizes she's going to need some information. Much as she loathes the idea, maybe she's going to have to make contact with those ghastly females after all.

She'll start with the young one – Imogen. Maybe she can find out everything she needs to know from her, which would save any further unnecessary contact with the other bags. Imogen may be something of a fellow spirit, actually. Hope had caught her eye when Verona's soaking scanties had crashed to the floor, and she was definitely working hard to stifle laughter, whilst ostensibly grabbing the dog and bawling him out as Verona scrabbled around on her knees, gathering up flowered knickers and sturdy flesh-coloured bras – 'scanties' being a bit of a misnomer in this instance, not a thong or G-string in the lot, of course. A woman's basic attitude to her underwear can tell you a lot – and whether she has any hopes or expectations. Verona's clearly given up on hers, thinks Hope – and then wonders if there's a programme idea lurking in there somewhere, on the lines of *Candid Camera* . . . *Visible Panty Lines*? Possibly for Channel 5 – but perhaps not. Anyway, as her first line of information, Imogen will do.

15

Sussing the Enemy

Imo's not admitting it, even to herself, but she's flattered to get Hope's phone call. A blessing for once to have her name listed in the France Telecom directory. Hope's asked her for a drink – alone. That's one up on the old biddies – a chance to wangle her way in. Perhaps Hope needs some kind of helper down here – they all have gofers don't they, these sort of people? Imo reckons she's perfect gofer material.

Having been buzzed up via the intercom, Imo climbs the stairs, quite curious to see what's been done by way of renovation to the *appartement de grand standing*. So far, so similar. The tower staircase is identical to their own, even down to its scabby condition: surprising – she'd have thought all this would have been done up by now. It's a different story upstairs, though. A bit of all right. All gleaming white and silver and steel and pale wood. Not that Imo's expression shifts a centimetre – she's not going to give away a hint of what she's thinking. Instead she has a bit of a laugh, talks about the state of the staircase, tells Hope the tale of the dubious sexual history of the Maison Puce, and observes this doesn't faze her new neighbour one little bit. What a contrast to those bloody women next door.

*

Hope is surprised to feel so welcoming – but it's actually kind of *nice* to have some youthful bloom around the place. Well, possibly 'bloom' is stretching it a bit, but dressed now in a crop-top, with bare brown legs in platform trainers, Imo looks quite pleasing. Hope leads her out, together with the dog, on to the *terrasse*. Imo doesn't seem the slightest bit impressed with the glories of the apartment, a welcome display of detachment that Hope heartily approves. Frédéric pads along behind and flops down as Imo props her legs on the balustrade to catch the rays. Hope has a good look at them – very slim, but not bony, surprisingly unfuzzy, lightly tanned – *quite* stirring, actually. Ummm. Now, now – get to the business in hand, don't complicate your issues.

'So, as you can imagine, it's been a nightmare,' says Imogen, swallowing the urge to say 'fucking nightmare', her usual description, in the interests of potential employment. Because despite her impassive face, she's rather loving the attention – and the unaccustomed space and air up here. The Moulin à Vent isn't bad either, after all those carafes of rough rosé *vin de table*. Yes, she could get used to this.

'Well, I can see,' says Hope, putting on her concerned and understanding interviewer voice with the matching corrugated brow, 'of course I can see. My God, it must have been just awful – and the Verona woman in particular.'

'Yeah, Verona is a fucking nightmare.' Oops, she went and let that one out, but Hope doesn't seem to flinch. Imo hurries on, 'But then on top of that we get *Alice* – I mean!'

'Yes, I really didn't know what to make of Alice. She didn't seem to have a lot to say.'

'I mean, did I come here for this or what? It's enough to do your head in – it does *my* head in. I mean – what's the point?'

'You're *so* right. As you can imagine *I*'m not exactly thrilled at the prospect either. I can't believe this Gerontin guy managed not to mention it. I'd almost think of suing, but on what grounds?' Hope is laughing at her own joke. 'I don't suppose there *are* any legal sanctions against landing up with your own compatriots by accident – I mean, of course, I'm American but I kind of feel I'm an *honorary* Brit . . . I'm getting vibes about our Monsieur Gerontin – I don't think he's exactly generous with the truth.'

'Why? What else didn't he tell you?'

'The musical accompaniment.'

'In what sense?'

'In the accordion sense. Nightly.' Hope can sniff stonewalling.

'Really?' says Imogen, bending down to help Fred scratch his backside.

'You don't seem surprised. You wouldn't know whose?'

'Whose what?'

'Musical accompaniment I'm getting.'

'What's it like?'

'Well, if you stick around for the next hour or so you'll probably hear it for yourself. Real corny accordion music – loud. Seems to come from over there somewhere.'

'Dunno. With these old houses, could be coming from anywhere,' but there's something a little forced in her artlessness.

'You've never heard anything – or *of* anything? You've

never heard any complaints?' Hope's internal aerial is all alert.

'Well, there may have been been a comment or two . . .'

'What sort of comment?'

'Nothing much – from the Algerians who lived here. Big family – old grandma and her sons, one daughter-in-law . . .'

'All *here*?' Hope looks back into the shining white space of her loft living room and tries to envisage it full of this invisible Algerian family.

'And children – they'd be amazed about what's been done to it. It was – you know – pretty primitive before.'

'What happened to them?'

'Dunno. Gerontin got them out. Probably back to Oran – the men were working on the building sites up round Sophia Antipolis. Maybe they'd saved enough to go home . . .'

'You reckon?'

'No.'

'And they said something about music on the roof?'

'Dunno. They might have mentioned – I can't really remember – some old guy living up here?'

'Where?' Hope snaps out the word so fast, her jaw makes a cracking noise. Fred looks quite startled.

'Well, here – somewhere up on these roofs.'

'Someone lives on this roof? *My* roof?'

'No – I mean along here somewhere – one of the flats up at roof level, that's what I mean. This one's *all* our roof, if you come to think of it. I mean, it's the roof for all of us – the whole building.'

'But *I* have the penthouse – up those stairs are my bedrooms, that's the top floor. I've seen the plans for the renovations in Gerontin's office. This *is* the top of the building – that's what I'd understood.'

'Yeah, but there must be lots of people with flats up here. It's like another world, isn't it, with all the terraces and chimneys?'

'But this music I'm talking about is very much *here*, very in-your-face – you can't avoid it. I *wish*! You wouldn't know anything about that – this Algerian family never said anything?'

'I think they were too bloody knackered to worry about things like music somehow.'

'But they were bothered by something up here? By some*one*?'

'I don't know anyone actually *bothered* them, not as such. We always left each other *alone*. You see, that's what I mean, that's what it was like – but now, well, as I said, it's a bit of a nightmare – and you coming here, well, you're maybe like the saving grace.'

'I hope so,' says Hope, staring at her view of the mountains and absent-mindedly patting Imogen Prosper's calf – *en passant*, as it were.

*

That evening finds Hope alert and lurking, waiting for the music to begin. Right on cue, as the by-now familiar peachy skies begin to streak behind the mountains, it starts up – 'Under the Bridges of Paris' – tonight with an extra-cheeky syncopated rhythm. She shoots out on to the terrace and realigns her ears to the notion that the sound could be coming from above rather than the side. The house to the left is the same height as the Maison Puce, but the house to the right is taller, as is the one directly behind. From this angle there's no way she can see what's going on up there. The view of what she definitely thinks of as *her* roof – whatever Imogen says – is similarly limited. She drags the table over to the balustrade and climbs on to it – precarious and a tad wobbly, stuck up here, and in danger of toppling down into the street if she takes a step back too far, but the intrigue is getting to her. From this height she can see that the slope of roof above her bedrooms ends in a vertical plane of cement-coloured stucco, maybe six or seven feet high.

She gets down from the table and tries to match up what she's just seen above with the layout of the rooms below. Does that vertical wall line up with her back bedroom wall or not? So far she can't tell.

The next day she walks up to Bonneville and finds a large store, which seems to be some kind of French version of a five-and-ten – full of all those odds and ends that don't seem to have their own little shops any more. Just as well, for she doesn't know the French for 'step-ladder', and here she can just take one to the check-out and pay without any more ado. Supermarkets are a godsend for the linguistically challenged.

*

Given that Alice has been enjoying the process of procrastination, she's quite disappointed when the copies of her grandparents' birth certificates turn up so quickly from London. Annoying of the Family Record Centre to be so efficient. It's the first registered post she's received in Vieilleville and, unlike the system back home, requires her to collect the envelope in person from the main post office.

On the way up to Bonneville, she sees a very odd sight: Hope Boscombe struggling down the rue Nationale with a whacking great step-ladder, which she's trying very unsuccessfully to tuck under her arm. Alice almost stops to offer help, but as she's going in the wrong direction, and Hope Boscombe has her head well down, looking furiously touch-me-not, she decides against it. Odd, though. Wouldn't you expect someone as grand as *la* Boscombe to have minions available for such lowly tasks?

The certificates, when she opens them, are strangely touching – seeing her grandparents' lives laid out so formally like this, with the unknown great-grandparents' names at last exposed. She squeezes them into her cardboard file labelled 'Carte de Séj'. It's now full to bursting – only the certified translation of the affidavit confirming her lack of a criminal record still to come. Then she'll have to steel herself to face the men from the *mairie* again. She's dreading it, certain that whatever she produces by way of documents in triplicate, there'll be demands for yet another. Better by far to forget it for a while, let it all fade away.

*

Hope has one heck of a job getting the ladder up the twisting stairs. Maybe it wasn't such a good idea to have turned her back on all those super-streamlined modern blocks up the hill where she could have had some elements of civilization like elevators and air-conditioning. Sometimes she could curse her own need for style and individuality – and what, after all, *is* so bloody stylish about living in a place where the hall plaster is crumbling off the walls – wasn't that supposed to have been fixed by now? Time to come to some sort of reckoning with our Monsieur Gerontin – he won't know what's hit him.

She sets up the ladder on her terrace. The sun is fully out and beating down – the heat is soaking into the tiled floor and radiating back at her. She clambers up, then tries to scramble over to the roof. No good – impossible to bridge the gap, and it'll be even worse when she tries to get down again. She refolds the steps, and leans them against the lip of the roof, using them like a conventional ladder. This way, having deposited her Jimmy Choos on the floor and attacked the job barefoot, she's able to heave herself over the edge on to the tiles. These aren't like English roof tiles or even American shingles. These are more like terracotta drainage pipes split in half lengthwise – very curved – and, as it turns out, not attached to anything at all, just arranged in ridges, each one held down only by the weight of the one above it and so on.

As she tries to crawl up the slope she realizes she's dislodging this careful arrangement. Even as she thinks this, there's a crash as one of the tiles on the eaves tips off the edge and lands on the terrace floor. Dammit – where the hell will she find a replacement? It's hot out here – the tiles are baking. Still, having got this far . . . She crawls a bit further up the slope. Maybe by now, if she stands up, she'll be able to get a better view? She jams her poor bare feet into the valleys between the tiles to get a little purchase. She edges very gingerly up the slope sideways. God, is it ever hot up here? The sun's really hammering down now. She should have waited till later maybe . . . Still, good light to see by . . . She edges a bit further. Now she's reached the vertical cement wall. She eases her metal measuring tape out of her pocket, then pulls it out and back along the slope of the roof. Just as she'd suspected, her bedroom below is much bigger. So what's going on behind this wall? With arms stretched up she can just about reach its top with the tips of her fingers. She starts pushing against the tiles to give her some purchase – maybe she can pull herself up. She pushes, a little further, but she must have dislodged the delicate arrangement even more, for below another tile hits the deck with a crash. Oh, *God*. Now she'll have to buy *two*. And she's feeling kind of funny out here – dizzy and peculiar: how long does it take to get sunstroke?

Carefully now, and half sliding on her butt, but trying not to move any more of the tiles, she gets herself back to the edge of the roof and the ladder. The terrace floor is now a mass of terracotta slivers. By the time she's relocated her sandals, her toes are sliced and blood is mingling streakily with the tones of burnt sienna. This is crazy, she thinks, as she hobbles up to her bathroom trying to stem the flow with bits of tissue. All this bodily damage but still no information. Whether she likes it or not, she's going to have to make contact with those other women – get them talking, oil their wheels, prime the pump.

16

Priming the Pump

Verona is hammering on Alice's door.

'You'll never guess – Hope's asked us to lunch.'

'Us?'

'Both of us – you and me. Not Imo.'

'Why not Imo?'

'I don't know, Alice – what does it matter? The point *is* she's asked *us* and you'll never guess, it's at the Colombe d'Or – she's booked a table – in St-Paul-de-Vence.'

'Oh, *that* Colombe d'Or,' as if there could be another. Even Alice knows about the Colombe d'Or – it features in all the guidebooks. The most famous eatery on the whole Côte – possibly in the whole of France – celebrated not just for the authenticity of its cuisine but for its glamorous clientele and collection of art. Decades ago, so the legend goes, the likes of Picasso and Matisse had paid their bills in kind rather than cash, leaving a staggering legacy on its walls. The initial burst of surprise and pleasure is immediately pricked by a stab of doubt. 'Is it her treat?'

'What?'

'Or are we going Dutch?'

'I don't know, Alice, I didn't ask. Hers, I *suppose* – she's invited *us*.'

'Doesn't always follow.' Too right it doesn't – recent painful experiences still hurt.

'Whatever does it matter? The point *is* it's *super*, don't you think? Theo was going to take me once but it all fell through. I couldn't *be* more pleased – and she's ordered a chauffeured car, not even a taxi. She asked if either of us have cars and I explained how hopeless parking is in the town and I told her that driving here is more of a contact sport than a means of getting around – my goodness, she laughed. Anyway, it's tomorrow – she asked if that was all right and I said of *course* – we're to meet her at noon.'

*

Ironically, considering that for once Alice and Verona are not having to take public transport, Hope's hired car gets stuck behind a leviathan of a bus. As there's no space for overtaking, they're forced to observe it from behind, barely scraping its way past overhangs and between narrow walls. Alice alone is enjoying this crawl, enthralled to have the chance to look around.

So far the land is still predominantly crammed with buildings. Any postage-stamp site capable of use seems to carry some burden of masonry, most of it modern concrete in the regulation tones of apricot, cream and pink. Here and there an elderly, elegant villa remains stranded – melancholy reminders of a more gracious age – amidst the ubiquitous garnishings of oleander, umbrella pine, the odd isolated olive tree, a sporadic prickly pear.

Hope is complaining about this desecration. 'I guess if

you'd known the Riviera pre-war, all this could just about break your heart.'

'In many ways, of course, *yes*,' says Verona, enjoying feeling smug (how marvellous for once to have a more informed vision of the world than Hope Boscombe). 'Speaking from my own direct memory – not *pre*-war, of course, not exactly, I wasn't around *then* – I used to come down and stay with my godmother in Nice *after* the war, as soon as one could, of course. What with rationing and currency restrictions it was all very difficult – but I do remember it then, in the late forties, early fifties. I was *very* tiny, of course,' she adds hastily. 'They'd hardly started building – just a little bit, I suppose, but of course nothing like today. On the other hand look what an economic success they've made of things – and you can't support a thriving population just on beautiful views, can you? Oh, look – there it is.'

Across the steeply terraced valley is the vision – St-Paul-de-Vence, straight off those racks of postcards which deck all the *tabacs* and gift shops. There's an interval to enjoy its intensity of picturesqueness – almost indecently pretty – for they weave along the opposite side of the valley, sometimes losing it, then finding it again, only this time nearer and larger. A wedding cake of a town, tier upon tier of grey stone, precipitously perched on its hilltop and backed by a glittering azure sky.

At the Colombe d'Or they are seated out on the terrace. It hangs above the valley, a green bower of fig trees and ivy, punctuated by the cream of parasols, crisp white linen, scarlet and pink geraniums. Hope doesn't even want a menu, seems to know the fare well, orders for them all an item simply called *hors-d'oeuvres*, which doesn't sound all that exciting. Alice, who'd been looking forward to the subtlety of choice, feels cheated. But she needn't, for when they arrive these *hors-d'oeuvres* defy any dull preconceptions conjured up by the catch-all label. These are a trencherman's miracle, a great tray of separate dishes – of things marinated, dressed, filleted and stuffed, with a huge basket of salad, another of breads, a panoply of garnet *saucisson*.

'Oh, yeah, that's how I remember it,' says Hope, casually in the face of such magnificence for of course she's been here before. In fact, it seems it's one of the few restaurants she does know in the area, her acquaintanceship with the Côte d'Azur having been limited until now to various media festivals and conferences usually based at Cannes or Monaco. So it turns out that when she was last here with a group of executives from Channel 4, Gregory Peck was seated at the next table, the time before it was Robert de Niro and Bill Wyman was in the corner, or was it Michael Caine? Verona could happily wear this borrowed mantle of celebrity for the rest of the afternoon, and Alice would be content to nod occasionally in conversational support, whilst letting her eyes stray, trying to seek out a few glories from the famous art collection. But it's Hope who is calling the shots here, and her target rapidly turns out to be the workings of the *syndic*. Disappointing – an indigestible subject with no potential for glamour – and one on which the women are, in any case, a little hazy.

'As I understand the system,' says Hope, 'the *syndic* is

hired by us to look after our interests, manage the building – that *is* right?'

'In theory,' says Verona warily.

'What way is it theoretical? We have a *syndic* right?'

'Sort of. Monsieur Gerontin is our *syndic*.'

'How did he come to be hired?'

'Hired? I don't know he was ever *hired* in that sense – he was just there.'

'Really.' Hope's already sensing chinks in the armour. 'And he collects the various fees from us – right? Alice, is that right?'

Alice, who has let her eyes stray down to the valley floor and is watching the cypress trees bend in the breeze, turns back abruptly to their table. 'Er – yes, as far as I know. I mean, I'm new here too.'

'And these expenses would be . . .?'

'Just the usual – water, sewerage, communal electricity, insurance, of course.'

'And the renovations?'

'Well . . .' – Verona is sucking gently on the Puy lentils, trying to guess what spice was used, hating to split her concentration like this. You'd really think that having brought them up here, Hope might relax and enjoy it all a little more. 'Not really – I think he just puts down a token figure because we're supposed to vote on renovations.'

'Vote? How?'

'At meetings. We're supposed to have annual meetings.'

'Supposed?'

'Well, we tried to have one the first year I was here but it's all so complicated. It's done on a percentage basis and the people in Alice's flat were only tenants and no one seemed to want to track down the owners, Imo's a bit of an unknown quantity and yours was already empty by then.' Verona's feeling increasingly defensive. 'I mean, we did *ask* – it's not as if we didn't try – but no one seemed to know anything.'

'This "no one" would be Monsieur Gerontin, I take it,' says Hope, her lips tightening into a sarcastic purse.

'And neighbours and what have you – one's asked around . . .'

'So what's happened about the renovations?'

'Nothing much. I mean, they're due to be done – some time – but I'm not here all the time – and the thought of all the mess and everything . . .'

'Why does that matter?'

'If it was happening when I wasn't here – or actually even if I *was* – worse, if anything, the dust. It's been bad enough living underneath your flat while the work was being done – it took over a year.'

'Did it now?' says Hope approvingly, liking the idea of such lengthy attention to detail.

'But by that time I had a notion Monsieur Gerontin had his finger in the pie – involved with speculators. I think he kept running out of money.'

'Did he now?' says Hope, less approvingly, not liking this scenario half so much – a sniff of jerry-building.

'So it all just seemed better to let sleeping dogs lie.'

'Apart from Fred, of course,' says Hope laughing, remembering the tumble of soaking scanties.

'*Apart* from Fred,' says Verona grimly.

*

Hope is beginning to feel that perhaps this lunch was an expensive mistake. The women are eating greedily and she's just had to order another bottle of Bellet. This, frankly, ought to be quite enough oiling and pump-priming for anyone. Yet still the information gleaned is fractured and incomplete. And now she's beginning to feel more than a little oiled herself . . .

'I do wonder about you English sometimes,' she says, as her irritation begins to surface.

'In what way?' asks Verona, still taste-testing with vigour.

'It's these hidden depths,' says Hope. 'Everything seems so neat and tidy on the surface, and you think you know where you are with all these little rules and conventions, and then, bam, you find there's this maelstrom of emotional chaos underneath. It's so sort of *sneaky* – the schools, I suppose, at least with the upper-middle classes, and *there*'s a definition I didn't expect to be making in the twenty-first century. But what can you expect if you transport all your little boys off to educational prisons at the age of seven? It's just asking for sexual disaster. I mean, you may think I'm not qualified to comment but in a way, coming from outside, I can see things more clearly. And nobody – I tell you, *nobody* – could have tried harder to assimilate and understand.'

What is the woman going on about? thinks Alice, squiffily. Out loud she says, 'I would have thought these days, with the meritocracy and all that, I mean *does* anybody still send their children to "educational prisons"? It all sounds a little dated to me.'

'You'd be surprised,' says Hope firmly.

'No, I wouldn't,' says Verona. 'We did – Edmund and I sent Theo to Immingham. He *loved* it.'

'And Theo is?' asks Hope.

'My son.'

'How old?'

'Thirty-five now – but honestly he loved school, he's always told me he wished it could go on for ever.'

'That figures,' says Hope drily. 'Where I come from you couldn't get out of school fast enough – unless you made it to cheerleader or, better still, Homecoming Queen. Then maybe you'd want to stick around.'

'Where do you come from, in fact?' asks Alice. 'I mean, apart from America, of course.'

'America's a big place to come from,' says Hope, sounding sour.

'Of course.'

'Lavaho, Texas – my daddy was in doughnuts.'

'*Really*,' says Verona.

'Yeah – he was kind of a disappointed man because he'd invented all these kooky varieties only Dunkin' kind of got there first – made him bitter. Finally he drowned himself in the Gulf of Mexico.'

'Oh, my dear, how *ghastly* for you.'

'Actually it may have been an accident, we never knew for sure. It was where the sewerage pipe came out at Galveston – he may have slipped. Anyway, I was working in radio – little station out of Austin – because I didn't have a television face then. That didn't start till later when I got to England.'

'So *we* Brits discovered you, did we? Clever old us.'

'Well, don't get me wrong, I would've made it big at home given time – but the thing is I was born with the Scharnhorst nose via my mother. It looked fabulous on my granddaddy but on women, forget it, so I had this cranky adolescence – I mean *all* adolescence is kind of cranky, but this was crankier than most – until I got it done by Dr Sertorius when I was nineteen. He was the best plastic surgeon in the whole Dallas Fort Worth area – the first to abandon the ski-jump in favour of the Venus de Milo aquiline – you know? See?' She turns herself in profile and runs a finger down her admittedly very tidy proboscis. 'And I'd only just got the cast off when I was sent over to England by the radio station – that was in 'eighty-one to cover the Royal Wedding, Charles and Diana, and I guess it hadn't sunk in yet.'

'What hadn't?' asks Alice, who's finally abandoned her perusal of the ravishing landscape, and is trying to refocus her eyes on Hope – with difficulty under the joint influence of the sun and wine.

'That I was a *beauty* because at that stage I was – you'd better believe it – only the concept hadn't had time to take hold yet and maybe I wasn't as confident as I should've been, because that sort of thing takes a while to establish, and then suddenly there I was with a screen career, because even if KTVO Houston didn't want me suddenly Wessex West did. And that's how I got started. I never went home – and now here I am.'

'Yes,' says Verona. 'Here you are.'

A shadow crosses Hope's face – a puzzled look – and she leans across the table to make a fresh start. 'Listen, you guys, I wanna ask you something. You wouldn't have heard any accordion music coming down from the roof, would you, "Under the Bridges of Paris", for example?' And, rather to their amazement, she starts gently to hum.

*

Everything would have been fine if only Verona hadn't stuck her oar in. Hope had called for the bill and was clearly intent on paying it herself – had her platinum card out and ready, when Verona started on the oh-no-dears, the we-couldn't-possiblies, let's-all-chip-ins – and before Alice quite realized what was up, they *were* all 'chipping in', the whole substantial bill divided into three substantial portions.

Bugger. No *more* than that – Bugger, Bugger, *Bugger*.

17

Further Enquiries

Back at the Maison Puce, head still swimmy from the excesses of lunch, Alice surveys her latest bank statement. Any of the day's leftover glow fades to grey. The brief respite is over – none of the realities has changed. She's still got to face the fact that it isn't working down here. And if it isn't working – if she's going to admit it – then what? Is there any 'going back'? Horrible thought – tail between legs, broker than ever and Deirdre crowing.

She has to keep re-asking herself – what in the end is so very different from her original vision of life here?

Things I love here (still):
(1) Light/sun/yellows/blues/clarity/light, light, light – like today, a golden day until the bill came.
(2) Thus a Different Me without obligatory layers of thick clothing as per Bristol – with matching obligatory thick thoughts (how could I ever have been that chilly shrunken self?).
(3) Food – as ongoing concentrated work of art and life (scents/aromas/sizzling/luscious bounty of same).
(4) The Café Life – essential: see above, Food, but much more than that – is essential alternative to confinement of life at home (on that level Maison Puce isn't really a home as such,

more of a shelter, human version of dog kennel). Thus if keep to this analogy, without Café Life I could easily succumb like Fred to la claustrophobie.

(5) The Culture – as represented by more or less everything except the screaming suburbs, buildings/towns/villages – mellow-faded-elegant-soft-secret-intriguing-beautiful-funny. Museums/galleries/cathedrals/theatre-even-if-I-don't-always-understand-it/concerts – everything easily available on modest sort of scale.

(6) Trees – sculpted planes lopped to within an inch of their lives, lemons in full fruit hanging over the bus stop, palms by the dustbins, today's cypress trees and orange groves, all the daily norm.

(7) Frenchness *– everything clichéd I can think of: Françoise Hardy, Gauloises, Johnny Halliday, Juliette Greco, Françoise Sagan,* pétanque, *Ricard, elegance (both public and private) – everyone in their own distinct way, the waiters today, even the guards on station platforms, for heaven's sake, just oozing style and authority, Piaf –* 'Je ne regrette *bloody* rien'!

Things I loathe here:

(1) Frenchness *– see (7) above: sometimes hard* not *to regret* rien *a bit, the coward in me does, the feeling that however attractive and inviting it all is* I*'ll never belong – and who the hell did I think I was kidding when I dreamed I would? The lack of any sort of concrete help: I seek information, receive nothing. Josette and the Augustines treat all questions as mannerless invasions of private space. Sole level of communication with any local French is still only with shopkeepers, etc. – on one level, enchanting, welcoming, chatty, but that level is purely professional, i.e., lasts only as long as the specific transaction,*

as long as I'm buying and not asking. *But seething fury if I catch them on a nerve, not difficult with my linguistic shortcomings – even* I *wince when I hear myself. My French has improved a lot but I'm still light years away from anything like fluency. Am still completely banjaxed by all the rage I seem to attract if I query a bill or question quality or suitability or, heaven help me, return something shoddy or broken – this last seems to bring down a storm of fury and shrugged shoulders of despair. Never have been made to feel so utterly* clueless. *Sub-heading of above,* French Officialdom*: literally want to throw up at thought of facing the men from the* mairie *again . . .*
(2) Englishness *– the whole messy muddle of the Maison Puce, none of which would really matter if I felt able to escape it whenever necessary instead of being so trapped here –*

Alice reads back over her list. It's blindingly obvious that the fundamental problem is still money. Is it in fact the *only* problem? All the loves on the list cost money – even the simple admiration of nature and/or architecture has a price if she dares to get out of Vieilleville itself for a few hours. Until now she's felt as if she's been on an extended holiday – all the things listed 1–7 are the *stuff* of holidays. But she's not on one – not any more. This is supposed to be real and for earnest – the sum total. Her Life.

Meanwhile, rereading this latest grim bank statement, she sees that in order to get by she'll have to draw yet again on her dwindling capital. The slippery slope gets slipperier . . .

*

'Could I ask you something, Imo?'

'Depends.'

'I'm trying to work things out – you know, quite practical things.'

'Oh, yes?' The tone is immediately wary.

'Money and so on.'

'What about it?' Imo snaps.

'I just wondered how you managed down here – whether you find it at all difficult.' Already Alice can see Imo's hackles rising, and hurries on, 'I mean, I don't want to be nosy, it's just that I'm really finding it quite hard to manage and I wondered if you could, you know, if you had any advice . . .'

'Try working for your fucking living – it usually helps,' says Imo.

And, of course, she's right.

*

It's not that getting some sort of job hasn't occurred, just that putting the idea into practice seems fraught with insurmountable obstacles. Where to begin? There's an agency in Nice that seems to specialize in employing foreigners – Alice has heard them advertise on Riviera Radio, all in English, for bilingual secretaries, chauffeurs, cooks. She telephones them, hoping for an English voice at the other end of the line – someone to cosy up to.

'Allô? Sud Emplois.' Nope. French as they come – instant heart-sinking. Her opening at least has to be in French too: '*Excusez-moi*, Madame, *de vous déranger*' (the essential sentence, followed by the inevitable), '*mais pourriez-vous me donner un renseignement . . .*'

'Hi – English or Swedish?' says the voice in English, with an Australian accent.

'English,' says Alice, depressed. So even in that one sentence she's a dead giveaway.

'Got your papers sorted out?'

'Papers?' says Alice, knowing perfectly well what she means.

'*Carte de séjour* – usual stuff.'

'Well . . .' says Alice.

'Can't help you without.'

'Right. No, of course. It's all in hand.'

'Phone us again once you're sorted out.'

'Do you have any other type of jobs?'

'Such as?'

'Jobs that don't need you to be sorted out?'

'Just phone us once you're set.'

*

'Imo, you'd count as self-employed?'

'Who's asking?'

'I just wondered. If maybe that was easier, with papers and things – *cartes de séjour*, actually. I mean, supposing you always make sure you don't stay longer than three months each time, if it's easier to get by, because then I suppose you wouldn't necessarily qualify for things like the dole and so on – it could make it all simpler . . .' Alice's voice withers away under the force of Imo's glare.

'I really don't know what's the matter with you. I've told you before, *leave* things alone – got that?'

'Sure. Right. Sure.'

But there's no doubt about it, she's going to have to beard that lion in his den again.

*

In her mind, Alice labels it 'D-Day – Stage 2' and, full of foreboding, slogs back to the Bonneville-sur-Mer *mairie* at 7 a.m. This time the waiting throng is much thinner. She gets a ticket straight away, and once she's allowed into the inner sanctum is called in front of the same dishy young *fonctionnaire* she'd seen that first time. Her pulse is so loud she can hear it thumping in her neck. She hands over her documents – including, with a flourish of additional pride, the grandparental birth certificates and the sworn affidavit as to her transparent honesty and upright citizenry. Monsieur barely looks at these, then hands them back – unexamined, uncopied. Alice manages to splutter out an explanation that she'd been ordered to obtain them by the previous Monsieur. Perhaps he is just amused at her mangled French but *this* Monsieur smiles, shrugs and tells her in English that it's all unnecessary, everything is in order and if Madame would care to take a seat?

Alice sits steaming in turmoil – a mixture of non-believing delight and livid frustration. The whole certificate/affidavit business has cost a bomb and taken weeks of her life, and years of her nerves. But when Monsieur returns, waving a flimsy sheet of paper, explaining that this is just a temporary *carte* and that the real one will be posted to her shortly, the agony melts clean away. Alice has to stop herself kissing both paper and dishy young man right there in full view of all available remaining *fonctionnaires* and their quailing victims.

She dances back down to the Maison Puce and meets Imo in the hall.

'I'm *legal*!' she calls, flapping the certificate.

'Well, get you,' says Imo. 'Some people have all the luck.' She's just about to go into her flat when a thought strikes. 'You didn't put "Maison Puce" on the forms, did you?'

But actually – this time – Alice is pretty sure she had.

*

'Allô – Sud Emplois?'

'Hello, it's Alice Barnes again. I rang you the other day.'

'We get an awful lot of calls.'

'Of course. I'm the one who didn't have her *carte de séjour*.'

'Yes?'

'But everything's fine now, and I wondered if I could make an appointment to come in and see you.'

'What sort of thing are you after?'

'Well, I'm a trained secretary – St Hilda's in London.' There was a time when St Hilda's could open a few doors, but not now.

'Windows or Lotus?'

'I beg your pardon?'

'Which system?'

'I'm sorry?'

'Your training – Windows 2000? Excel? Lotus?'

Pitmans Touch-type, as it happens, on a big black Remington, but who's counting? Alice tries to recall the system she'd used to do Philip's letters before the advent of Hillary Aldyce. 'Does MS Dos ring a bell?' she ventures. There's a pause down the line, then the voice changes tone.

'*When* did you say you had this training?'

'Nineteen sixty-eight – or maybe nine?' says Alice.

'Oh.' There's a very long pause – then, was that a sigh? 'Bi- or tri-?'

'What?'

'Lingual – we try to go for at least French and Italian, though German's getting pretty essential, these days.'

'Oh.' Alice pauses in the hopelessness of it all. 'Do you have any other sort of vacancies?'

'Do you drive?'

'Yes, though I haven't down here yet.'

'Oh. So you don't have your own transport?'

'No.'

'That does rather limit the domestic situations. Most of our expat clientele live out in the back country, you see – up in the hills, a lot in the Var, round there.'

'Oh. I'm in Vieilleville – right in the middle.'

'There's not a lot of call for towns, apart from secretarial, but then you'd need the languages. Most of our secretarial placements are fully bilingual written and spoken, in addition to mother tongue.'

'In *addition*. Gosh, that's three.' Even as Alice says it, she can hear how ludicrous she sounds.

'That's right,' says the voice, with a patient sigh. 'Three

– otherwise there's not a lot of work around, you know, and it's all tourist-related. Most of the French down here have to make do with catering or shops unless they've got really good IT skills – then it's all right, of course, that and the languages.'

'Oh. Well, shall I come in anyway – get you to size me up?'

'I don't think that'll be necessary. We'll call you if anything comes in.'

'I'd be good with children, I think.'

'Trained?'

'Well, only as a mother – I've had two of my own.'

'Our clients usually stipulate trained – if you were Norland, of course . . .'

'Well, yes, of course, but I'm not – only St Hilda's . . .'

'You didn't do hairdressing there, by any chance?'

'Hairdressing?' St *Hilda's* – the very idea.

''Cause we've got a couple of vacancies in Cannes for hairdressers – but they'd need to be very skilled, good cutters.'

'Right.'

'We'll call you.'

*

Later the telephone does ring and Alice jumps on it. Could Sud Emplois actually be calling her back?

'Alice, love, it's me – Philip.'

'Oh.' Alice's insides turn upside down, inside out, and whirl through the window to the place d'Espoir.

'You sound surprised – '

'Well, I – yes – well – ' Come on, woman, pull yourself together. 'I am – I was expecting somebody else.'

'Oh, right, *were* you?'

And why not, Philip Barnes? Why wouldn't I, Alice Barnes, be expecting someone to call?

'Yes, an employment agency.' *Why* did she go and say that? Why not lead him on – pretend it was a lover at the very *least*? Cover it up now, quickly, sound brisk. 'Where are you phoning from?'

'Home, of course.'

'Oh, right. The Villa Guardi?'

'Of course.'

'Coming along, is it?'

'Pretty well. You should have dropped in when you were here – I heard from Bill and Deirdre you were back in Bristol for a bit.'

'Yes.'

'I do wish you'd let me know, Alice.'

'Do you?'

'Oh, yes.'

Alice's insides return from their flight round the *place* and linger on the window-sill. 'Why?' she almost whispers.

'What? What did you say?'

'I said, "why?" Why would you have wanted to know that I was in Bristol?' A warmth settles back in the gaping hole her insides have left.

'You could have helped me with a little problem.'

'What sort of problem?' As quickly, the warmth turns to frost.

'It's the silver candelabra – the pair we always had in

the dining room. You wouldn't know which tea-chest they got packed in, would you?'

'Why do you think I would?'

'Only it was you who did all the packing, wasn't it? And Hillary's had a good hunt around – can't seem to find them. Getting rather crucial, actually – we're getting back to entertaining at last, after the twins and everything, first big beano next weekend. Visiting profs from Harvard Medical School – you know the sort of thing – wanted to really give them the works.'

Oh, yes, she knows the sort of thing. Hadn't she done it for years – and years? She remembers polishing those bloody candelabra, working away with a toothbrush soaked in Silvo, bloody little curlicues, trapping all the tarnish. And she can see them again – that last suppertime on the night he'd announced his perfidy. But she'd cooked the supper anyway, a pork casserole with separate onion gravy – shame to let it go to waste. Just for a moment as she was handing him his plate, she'd thought to tip it on to his crotch but then she couldn't – not out of care for his genitalia but in the certain knowledge that it would be she, Alice, who'd have to clear up the gravy-carpet mess.

'They were already unpacked by the time I left,' she says now.

'No, they weren't. We've looked everywhere.'

'I can assure you they were – I can see them right now, on the dining-table without any candles stuck in them,' and she remembers too how she'd had just the shivering of a thought of what effective murder weapons they would be.

'Well, they're not there now . . .'

'Perhaps – well, if you've had builders in?'

'You're not suggesting Ballard and Green would have *stolen* them?'

'Oh, you used Ballard and Green?' The smartest builders in town.

'You wouldn't have . . . I mean by accident, of course?'

'What, Philip?'

'No . . . no, I suppose not. I mean, they weren't part of the settlement – you did know that, didn't you, Alice?'

'Your candelabra – *our* candelabra – are not hidden in the Maison Puce, if that's what you're hinting.'

'Good God, no, I wasn't suggesting . . .' But, oh, yes, he was. 'Just have to keep looking then, won't we? All the best.'

*

Imo's feeling low. Nothing good ever happens. No surprises – except the nasty ones. Nice ones *do* happen, of course, but only to *other* people, she's noticed. She feels like an animal gone to ground – something small and furry like a dormouse – which wouldn't necessarily be that fucking awful if she was sure she was safe but now, with all this sniffing around, all these questions, puts her on edge. If it wasn't for that she could put up with the boredom of it all – until something comes along. And surely something will? Maybe with Hope it already has.

'Imo sweetie, hi – it's Hope.'

Well, there's a phone greeting and a half. Imo's spirits rise like mercury – still remember to keep it *cool*. 'Oh. Hi, Hope.'

'I was wondering if you could help me – I've got a

communication problem which needs your skills.'

'Want me to translate a letter?'

'Need you in person, really, sweetie – want to have a little chat with our Monsieur Gerontin and if I try on my own we'll only stumble along in Franglais. In this instance I'd like to make myself absolutely clear.'

'Oh.' The mercury changes back into lead. Meddling again. Even Hope. And Imo doesn't like having to confront Monsieur Gerontin too much – not face to face. She's got a nasty feeling he suspects something – otherwise why give her that funny searching look? He doesn't *fancy* her, that's for sure – though here's a funny thing: Hope probably does.

'A letter's usually much better with him,' says Imo, trying to put off the evil hour, 'makes him concentrate a bit harder.'

'No. In this case I need to see the whites of his eyes,' says Hope.

'I'd rather write,' says Imo, but she's weakening.

'Could you spare me some time today?'

That's the get-out. 'Not a chance. Got lessons – booked solid.'

'Tomorrow then – I'll pay you, of course.'

'Will you?' That changes things.

'Definitely. Double your hourly rate times the number of pupils you'd normally have?'

'Oh. Right, then.'

'Come and ring my buzzer at ten.'

*

It's unseasonably hot, and Monsieur Gerontin sits stickily with his belly jammed against his desk, mopping his forehead. The two English women have arrived without an appointment. Outrageous. Nevertheless, he rises to greet them with courtesy. He's never had a lot of time for Mademoiselle Prosper, but this other one, this famous woman, well, there's obviously money there, and Monsieur has always known which side of his baguette is buttered.

It seems Mademoiselle Prosper is to act as interpreter.

'Explain to him about the noise,' says Hope, 'the music.'

Imo explains. A torrent of French ensues.

'He says you've got to understand that in a place as old as Vieilleville with all the houses so close together you have to learn to live with the habits of your neighbours.'

'Tell him that I understand that perfectly in the normal way of things – but that *this* noise is coming from *my* roof.'

Another torrent.

'He says that the way the town is built there are very funny tricks of sound . . .' Imo turns back to Gerontin, dissatisfied with this translation, tries again. 'Acoustic abnormalities, that's what he means.'

'Tell him I've been on the lower part of my roof and measured. I know there's something up there.'

Imo translates. Hope intervenes loudly, '*Sur* ma *toit*,' and stabs at her own chest with a forefinger.

'He says you must be mistaken.'

'Tell him that I want him to bring a big ladder and take me up there.'

'He says he doesn't know what you mean.'

'Ask him to come down with us and I'll show him.'

Another voluble outpouring.

'He says it's too dangerous.'

'Tell him I'm prepared to take the risk – and tell him he spoke a lot more English last September.'

An immense shrug by way of reply.

'It's a matter of safety apart from anything else – tell him I have a right to know what's happening on my roof.'

The torrent expands into a raging tornado. Lucky that Hope is immune to this kind of thing – nothing compared to the vicious fury of the fraudulent tradesmen and shysters she's had to deal with for years on *Sharp Focus*.

'He says it's not your roof,' says Imo, glad to have her own opinion confirmed on this point.

'But he sold me the penthouse, he *told* me – '

'He agrees.'

'But that's what a penthouse is, by definition, it's the top of the building. There was never any mention of there being another floor.'

'He says there isn't another floor.'

'Tell him I shall have to go back to my lawyers – tell him I know all about the concept of flying freeholds.'

But Imo doesn't like this turn in the conversation, or that funny stare she's getting from Monsieur G. 'I think I've done enough telling now,' she mutters in an aside, 'and I don't know the French for "flying freehold".'

*

Considering how unsatisfactory this confrontation has been, Hope's feeling a touch resentful about paying Imo. What with the unproductive lunch at the Colombe d'Or, and renting the chauffeur-driven car and all, her attempts at reconnaissance are getting too pricey in ratio to the results achieved. Still, she's a little surprised when Imo herself demurs about accepting the proffered notes, standing in the street outside Hope's front door, looking really quite shy and sweet.

'I was wondering, Hope . . .'

'Yes?'

'I mean, it seems to me you could do with some help – like sort of a, well, a real full-time assistant.'

'I've already got scads of assistants back in London.'

'No, I mean someone here, on a more regular basis – do your translating, bit of a gofer, run round for you.'

'I don't really want the entanglement,' says Hope, who's possibly imagining a tangle with Imo in another sense, though nothing secretarial. 'You have no idea how boring it gets – you find yourself all bogged down with their pathetic little lives, however detached you always start out. It weighs you down – and I'm supposed to be travelling light, so to speak.'

'Oh – well – a *part-time* assistant, maybe?'

'Uh-uh – *no* time.'

Well, fuck me, thinks Imo, another nice little dream down the pan.

*

Today Hope doesn't bother to wait for the evening musical accompaniment. Instead she watches for the sun to move round so that at least a portion of the roof is shaded. Then she crawls out of her bedroom window, dragging the step-ladder behind her. This time she's wearing trainers, for her feet still haven't fully recovered from the night of the smashed roof tiles, and she slides herself and the ladder carefully up the slope till she reaches the cement wall. Then she eases herself gently upright and leans the ladder against the wall, trying to steady it into the valleys between the tiles. It's precarious, of course, but she wasn't joking when she told Gerontin that she was prepared for risk. She checks back down the roof: not a tile dislodged this time. Right. She balances herself, then turns back and starts to climb. It's hot as hell – and around her swifts are reeling and swooping with their early-summer screams. This is nothing if not a tricky little venture. But now she's made it – and with her feet on the top step she can see right over the wall.

Running from left to right and blocking her vision is a swathe of woven dark green material, kind of like plastic raffia, attached at intervals to wooden poles, to make a huge screen now flapping in the wind. She can't see over or through it, but there's a seam slightly to her left, offering the temptation of a sliver-narrow view. She leans precariously over to take a peek. At first it only reveals more green – but this time waving fronds, with an acrid smell – familiar? Beneath she can see some sort of asphalt flooring, and on the far side, the base of what might be a chimney stack. But beyond that is a streak of blue – *blue* – what? She starts picking at the cloth, trying to widen the gap and then catches her breath – oh, my, oh, my God, I don't believe it – for beyond the chimney lies the wide brilliant blue of Vieilleville bay in all its staggering beauty. So there *is* a *vue de la mer* – it's been sitting here all along, awaiting discovery.

18

On the Beach

May – and suddenly the whole coast is *en fête*. May the first is a public holiday, but then so is Victory in Europe Day a week later, with Ascension Day and Pentecost to follow. Vieilleville shrugs off any lingering doubts and embraces the festival season. Definitely time for a *leetle peek-neek*.

Verona assembles them on the beach for Victory in Europe. Even Imogen's agreed to join them with Fred. Hope Boscombe's been asked but declined – quite sharply – citing pressure of work. None of the Augustines accepted, but Josette seems happy to attend.

The tartan rug is here (of course), but mercifully the sit-up-and-beg contraption and the windbreak have been left at home. Verona's allowed the others to bring the booze, but she herself has insisted on doing all the catering. She's been slaving away for several days wangling culinary magic out of her tiny excuse for a kitchen – only two hotplates and a combined mini-grill for an oven. Despite these gross limitations she's produced a feast. Any thoughts of 'goodies from home' have been firmly shoved aside as she sets out her own *tarte au chèvre*, *tarte aux poireaux*, two sorts of *pissaladière* – with tomatoes and without – *sardines farcies*, *terrine aux fruits de mer* and *salade de mesclun*. For dessert she's produced, as the sole flavour of England, good old Summer Pudding. A triumph of a spread, and she glows with the satisfaction of achievement.

Publicly, Josette applauds Verona's creations along with the others, though secretly she thinks the entire effort mad. Why go through all these extraordinary stresses and strains when each and every item on the menu (apart from the Summer Pudding – a disgusting concoction she remembers with a shudder from the old British Embassy days) could be bought ready (and exquisitely) made by the various *boulangeries*, *charcuteries* and *traiteurs* of the town? No self-respecting French woman would think twice about serving to her guests a tart bought from the *pâtisserie* – on the contrary, she knows they might almost feel a little slighted by having to make do with home-made. Still, remembering those old embassy days – New Delhi was it? Bangkok? – Josette feels she knows enough to understand the thinking of this Anglo species. Would that they could return the compliment. *Why* do they come here, these *Eeenglish*? They don't seem to comprehend us at all, they don't even seem to like us so very much. It's a mystery.

This is the first day she's ventured on to the beach, though of course the *Eeenglish* have been coming down for weeks. She looks at them now – *oh, la la*, dear Verona in that terrible striped *maillot de bain*, flesh erupting all over the place as she leans across to dole out ample portions, her face increasingly flushed with delight and the effects of the sun.

'Not for me, *ma chère* Verona – oh, no, leetle, *leetle* for me. I 'ave such not very big stomach,' she protests, smiling and ingratiating. She herself is in an *écru* linen sundress, sleeveless because she's managed to keep her upper arms so well toned, with lots of nice gold bangles and her Moschino sunglasses. She wouldn't dream of exposing her thighs in public like the others – if she needs to swim when it gets really hot she'll slip down to the little side beach in the early mornings and have a dip in private. Alice, she notices with approval, is at least wearing a sarong over her swimsuit – good thing too, for she really seems to have piled on the pounds since she got down here. Should avoid the cakes, of course – perhaps Josette should suggest a treatment . . . thalassotherapy can do wonders. But Alice shouldn't keep tugging at the sarong like that – if you're going to do a thing, do it decisively and with *style*. Josette isn't yet sure she's forgiven Alice for letting her down over that May Day trip to Juan-les-Pins for cocktails. Alice claims she'd had a bilious headache – *says* she was fast asleep under the effects of a camomile *tisane* so hadn't heard Josette shouting up at her from the street. But Josette doesn't quite believe her. There was something in the vague hesitancy of the excuse, and she looked perfectly all right the next morning, not at all like someone recovering from *la grippe*, and she's certainly tucking into her food now – *mon Dieu*, but they can put it away.

Imo, the only one of them who could surely bare all with abandon, is in fact the most covered up – even more so than Josette: virtually clad from neck to ankle in skin-tight stretchy black, with just a sliver of bare brown skin showing suggestively around her slender midriff, and platform trainers stuck on to the ends of skinny legs. Although Josette knows, of course, that this look is very *à la mode*, with Imo's build it gives an unfortunate hint of Minnie Mouse – all she really needs to complete the picture is a pair of ears and a bow in her hair. Josette smiles at the thought, and catches Verona's eye as she's about to tackle her terrine, fish-slice aloft.

'May I offer you a *tranche*?'

*

Alice is observing too – from this isolated tartan travel rug in the midst of the holiday crowds. Around are lots of French families enjoying their *jour ferié*, but there's not another picnic in sight, for these families have all rather sensibly lunched at a restaurant to give *maman* a day off. Friends arrive – modestly the women wrap towels around their naked breasts to stand and greet each other with evident delight, kiss, kiss, kiss Parisian-style, then sit together, dropping the towels, still talking nineteen to the dozen, quite nonchalantly with bosoms re-exposed. Then, fresh out of the sea, they stand and sluice themselves with care at the shoreline showers – above and below, legs splayed, inner thighs drenched, a permanent floor-show. But the moment it's time to leave, modesty reasserts itself, and the most elaborate changing rituals go on beneath the towels again – exactly like the charade on icy beaches the length and breadth of Britain, with wild squirmings to get knicks and bras on/off as secretly as possible.

Alice is squirming too, trying to wiggle the sarong around so that it fully covers her cerise pubic triangle – still not recovered from her foolish mistake with the Immac on May

Day. Women have to try so hard, she thinks, whereas men, in general, don't seem to give a damn. Even those here with handsome middle-aged faces unashamedly reveal puny legs or rubbery belly overhangs. And whilst the young of both sexes are often quite simply ravishing in their perfection – *Les Oiseaux du Paradis* fully revealed – the sight of the girls is particularly poignant, for it's such a fleeting moment, childbirth being the great leveller. It leaves its imprint even on the most lovely, the slight sag of a buttock, the silvery ghost of a stretchmark – Mother Nature making certain she's left her calling card on all the other mothers, lest they imagine for an instant they've got off scot-free.

Across the beach, assorted songs trill from mobile phones – what an infectious disease, bad as chickenpox. London is corrupted enough, but France seems to have embraced the *portable* like a lover. On the train journey from Paris, Alice had noticed that almost every hill and bluff the length of the land was topped by an aerial, where once a crucifix would have reigned alone. People used to go for their guns in old Hollywood Westerns, but now they go for their mobiles – no one quite certain for whom the latest electronic serenade might be. The William Tell Overture sings out for at least the twentieth time this afternoon and Imo leaps immediately for her bag.

'*Allô?*' she queries, with perfect French guttural, phone to ear, immediately pulling herself up into a sitting position from her previous sprawl, and expecting whom? A boy-friend, a pupil – possibly a *customer*, in Josette's suspicious gaze? As they all watch, her expression dissolves, and ''Ello, Mum,' she says, reverting instantly to Dagenham East. Out of respect for a parental call, the others immediately fade to silence, concentrating on chewing, each trying to disguise their eavesdropping.

'No, no,' says Imo, 'that's all right . . . No, I thought you was somebody else . . . I'm out on the beach wiv some mates . . . No, I don't suppose you do . . . No . . . Well, if you could – I mean, it's not easy for me, Mum, either . . . Yes, I know, Mum, but it's not as if I don't *try* . . . Well, I'm sorry, OK? . . . *Are you*? . . . Oh, fancy that! That'll be nice . . . No, I wouldn't do that, Mum . . . No, *don't*, cos I won't be here, that's why . . . No, *work* . . . Um, Italy, Milan – I've got this contract . . . Well, you wouldn't want me to miss out . . . No, I can't cancel – means money, Mum, you wouldn't want me to be *unprofessional*, would you? . . . Yeah, I'm sorry too, but there you go . . . Yeah, 'bye, Mum –'bye.'

Imo turns her phone off, looks at it with hatred and tosses it into her bag, so fast that Fred tries to snap at it like a bone but misses. 'Fuck,' she says. 'That was my Mum,' but they've gathered that. Imo seems to have shrunk to half her size in that brief conversation. 'She's coming down to Monaco – she's won a magazine prize, here and back first class, staying at the Grand.'

'How marvellous! What a *coup*,' says Verona. 'Have *un peu de salade*, why don't you, dear?'

'No thanks, Verona,' says Imo, shock having improved her manners. 'I'm not hungry any more. She wants to come *here* – fuck.'

'She hasn't been down here before?' asks Alice.

'Never. She's threatened but I've always managed to put

her off. *Fuck.*' Imo spins on her buttocks so she's got her back to the rest of them and is staring out to sea. Fred whimpers, and turns round also, leaving his plumed tail to mingle with Verona's chutneys on the rug.

'But you, of course, won't be here – Italy?' says Alice, then stops herself as she realizes she's admitting the eavesdrop – but, oh, what the heck, of *course* they all heard. 'What was all that about Milan?'

'I had to say *something*, didn't I? First thing that came into my head. I'll have to be away somehow – or hide. She says she wants to *stay*.'

'Oh, surely not, dear – not when she's got the lovely Grand! Why on earth would she?' Verona is laughing as she leans over to extricate Fred's tail from the feast.

'Because she's a nosy old bat – fuck her.'

Alice leans forward and gets a side view of Imo's face. A tear is running down her cheek, her back is hunched in misery. The mood is contagious despite their curiosity. The pastry suddenly dry.

Verona rushes to the rescue. 'Who's for *le dessert*?' she coos, and starts ladling blood-red pools of Summer Pudding into paper cups.

'It's funny this business of people coming to stay, isn't it?' says Alice, also caught by Imo's obvious pain, and wanting to create a diversion. 'My son Gavin's coming down too – at least, he's threatening to – next week for the Cannes Film Festival, and I know this'll sound awful, but I don't really want him to. At least, it's not that I don't want him here at all, I just don't want him here with me –

in the Maison Puce. I'm not quite sure why – it's just going to feel like an invasion.'

'Maybe it is ze size,' says Josette. 'These *leetle* studio, you know, are not made for ze party like zat.'

'Yes – perhaps it's that. I'm already feeling quite defensive about it.'

'What does this mean, "*defensive*"? You are not talking about war 'ere, Aleese, you are talking about your son!'

'I suppose I meant "apologetic" – I feel I'm going to have to apologize for the way I live.'

'Well, I think you and Imo are both very lucky,' says Verona. 'I'd be thrilled if Theo would come and stay with me – but there doesn't seem a chance. I'm always offering him the platform bed, but he never takes me up on it.'

'Yeah – but he came for the Grand Prix last year,' says Imo. She's suddenly perked up.

'But that's what I mean – *I* was back in Hove for the Grand Prix so it was a fat lot of use.'

'Yeah, it was,' says Imo, and now she's smiling.

'To tell you the truth I can't really fathom it – I mean, he loves it down here, has done from childhood, and he finds it very useful for entertaining clients, big investors, that sort of thing . . .'

'Surely he doesn't entertain his clients at the Maison Puce, does he?' asks Alice.

'Well, no, he generally takes them to an hotel – and Josette's right, really, the size of our flats is the fly in the ointment, isn't it? But still, you'd think he'd want to be with me – just occasionally. He was such a sweet little boy, very thoughtful, never forgot one's birthday, that sort of thing – but there you are, circumstances changed and so did he . . . I suppose he never really got over the Edmund business . . .' She's licking her spoon pensively, scarlet juice running down her chin.

'How old *was* Edmund when he died? Was it really so shattering for him?'

'What, dear?' Verona snaps out of her thoughts and turns her attention back to Alice.

'This change you're talking about – in Theo I mean. I've been thinking about my own children, what it's doing to them – the divorce I mean – but so far I can't see it's making much of a difference.'

'They may be keeping the hurt to themselves, of course.'

'Yes.'

'But on the other hand divorces are two-a-penny now, aren't they? They're not like a real *disgrace* – I suppose that's what got to Theo.'

'Disgrace – in Edmund dying?'

'Oh. Well, no – I meant the other thing . . . I shouldn't really . . .' Verona surveys her audience from sideways on. 'Oh, I don't know – it's ridiculous feeling I have to keep things secret any more, because I don't, really. It's not as if there's anyone left to hurt. It's only that I did keep it to myself for so long – it's become second nature . . .'

Her voice fades, and she seems to be concentrating on scraping her spoon round the bottom of the cup, whilst around her the atmosphere on the rug has sharpened. When she looks up again, she sees that the others have all turned towards her, their expressions identical, each brimming with curiosity. It's not the sort of interest she usually attracts . . . a shame to disappoint them. 'The thing is that Edmund had his little ways – I mean he'd always *cruised* and I never really minded as long as he didn't bring his assignations home – and, of course, as he was generally trawling round the Embankment, they never got as far as Haywards Heath . . . but then along came Burt and everything changed.'

'Burt?'

'Well, he was an Albert actually – chap from British Telecom who came to install their new modems or whatever they're called in the office. This is about ten years ago, I suppose, and Edmund had always had a thing about Burt Lancaster – so he changed his name and moved in with him to Tufnell Park.'

'What – full time? What about you and Haywards Heath?'

'Well, we kept it all on for appearance's sake – and Theo – and then they'd come back for high days and holidays, but it wasn't easy. There was the Christmas Burt revealed his pierced navel – Edmund's special little gift, a skull and crossbones from Brewer Street – and Great Aunt Tilly nearly collapsed into the brandy butter in shock. And then Theo didn't really take it at all well – it went *so* against the grain. Always seemed to blame me as much as his father.'

'So you never actually did that thing with the scarlet suspenders?' says Alice. 'All that stuff you told me – about when he was dead?'

'What about them, dear?'

'Well, did that happen?'

'Oh, yes, because then Burt dumped him, didn't he, poor

old Edmund with his dicky ticker – I suppose he wasn't up to much in the bedroom department – so he had to come home to me . . . But I never really gave up hope – I was always prepared to give it a go. You might say the scarlet suspenders were my secret weapon.'

'And he was bi-sexual all the time.'

'Gayer than bi I'd say.'

'But you still had a child.'

'Yes, though I'll never know *quite* how I managed the mechanics . . .' Verona's gaze falls on the ladle. 'Any more takers for Summer Pudding?'

'I remember Summer Pudding at ze embassy wiz my Billy-Boy,' says Josette. She hasn't actually eaten much of hers – all that cream and sugar, terrible for one's *ligne*. She stirs it reflectively.

'Which embassy was that, dear?'

''Ong Kong? My father was at ze consulate.'

'I thought it was Phnom Penh?'

'*Before* was Phnom Penh.'

'Your father was in the Diplomatic?'

'Ummm? What is this?'

'Your father?'

'At ze consulate – and my Billy-Boy was there, military attaché.'

'Wasn't that New Delhi?' asks Alice, a little tipsy now, stretching out on the rug, and looking up at the sky. This tale of Josette's has always seemed so hard to unravel.

'*After* was New Delhi.'

'My goodness, dear, but you did get around,' says Verona.

'Was this in the war?' For that would explain it . . . just about. Everyone on the rug is doing calculations.

'Ummm?'

'The WAR, dear,' shouts Verona, as if the volume will clarify her meaning.

'There were so many wars, *ma chère* Verona, it would depend on which one you mean . . .'

Verona's just about to stipulate when Imo pipes up. 'What was his name?'

'My Billy-Boy?'

'Yes, Josette, that's what we're talking about – what was his name?'

'Prescott-Smythe. *Capitaine* Prescott-Smythe.'

'I thought he was a lieutenant . . .' says Alice.

'Zat was *before*.'

'In Hong Kong?'

'New Delhi.'

'And what exactly happened, dear? What tore you apart?' asks Verona, her forehead wrinkled with concern.

'There was trouble wiz 'is family – I don't know. His *maman* was a witch,' and looking down at the blood-red mixture she's been stirring, she's suddenly wafted with nausea and feels again the shudder of cold metal on her most private skin.

'Men,' says Verona. 'In theory they always seem to be the answer but in practice they're often at the heart of the problem in the first place, don't you think?'

'What problem?' says Alice.

'Any problem. For us. Not that one wouldn't want another go. The trouble is, you seem to need the looks to be credited with the feelings – but looks aren't necessarily a very accurate guide. I've got *loads* of feelings but I'm not often given the benefit. I think I'd leap at it if I ever got the opportunity.'

'What opportunity?' says Alice. 'Look around you – look at this beach, at those bodies – none of us has a hope.'

'I should bloody well think not,' says Imo. 'God – it's disgusting. Women of your age – you've had your chance. You should move over and give the rest of us a go.'

'You might say that now, Imo,' says Verona, 'but once you get there you'll see it's not that easy. It's not a good feeling to have to step aside, find yourself becoming invisible, doors slamming in your face.'

'Tough fucking titty – about bloody time.'

'What makes you so angry, Imo?'

'I'm *not* bloody angry,' and she whips round again to stare out to sea.

*

They all help Verona to pack. By now Alice is too plastered to mind the curious stares of the French, who puzzle at these strange habits – foil packets and plastic pots piled into baskets, and crumbs scattered on the sand 'for the birds', according to Verona, though the Vieillois know for sure they'll be scavenged by the midnight rats.

They're a scratchy, untidy band as they weave up the beach towards the steep steps, dragging all the sandy detritus with them. Josette has been made to carry the bowl of Summer Pudding separately as Verona fears it may drip its staining juices over everything else. Josette holds it at arm's length distastefully – what with the sad sharp memories, and the prospect of its indelibility on the *écru* linen dress, she could have done without. Alice is also dragging behind, in charge of the empty bottles – rather a lot of them.

'You were *so* missed the ozzer night, *ma chère* Aleese, at Juan-les-Pins.' Josette is perfectly sincere about this – for she alone had been forced to pay all the cost of the taxi, never mind the hideous charges for cocktails at Boom-Boom.

'I know,' says Alice, 'it's sweet of you' (but it isn't, Josette's merely being practical and Alice is at last learning to read her signals), 'just one of those things . . . maybe something I ate – felt terribly sick.'

'And ze *migraine*?'

'Oh, yes, terrible – awful pain.'

'It is good to see you back so well.'

'One of these twenty-four-hour things, I suppose . . .'

'But of *course* . . . but you know you missed somezing – somezing wonderful. We 'ad *fun*.'

'Did Augustine go with you, then?' Alice never bothers now to stipulate which one of the Golden Egrets it might be – Marie-Auguste, Adrienne, one name seems to cover all.

'No, I met wiz zese two beeoootiful *men*, Alice – from Sweden. I sink zey are, you know,' Josette rubs her fingers together to indicate money, 'and I tell zem all about you because you know zey lurve ze *Eeenglish* too.'

'Swedish?'

'Or Danes . . . or maybe *Finns* – from up there

somewhere. One is very big wiz money in Cannes –'e is, you know, the *chef*.'

'A cook?'

'The *chief* of ze Bank, very big –'e does not know *zis* part of the coast so I invite him – and ze friend 'as good bizness in Nice, 'e is *antiquaire*, 'e sells all zese beeootiful chairs and tables and things.'

'An antiques dealer?'

'Yes – *antiquaire* – and he sell to all ze rich Scandinavians who 'ave their villa down here. 'E is lovely and you know 'e lurve ze Eeenglish – so I ask zem to come 'ere to Vieilleville, to come and meet my enchanting leetle Aleese, because I tell zem all about you and I say we will 'ave dinner *togezzer*. It will be *fun*. You know zis Imogen is not *sympathique* – I tell you zat, yes? She know nozzing if she think women like us cannot 'ave *fun – et voilà*, we show her, yes?'

Alice can sense another hefty restaurant bill poised to land on her dwindling bank account. 'Could we give them dinner ourselves?'

'You mean *cook* it ourselves?'

'Why not? It'd be much . . .' Alice stops herself saying the dreaded word 'cheaper' and comes out with 'nicer' instead.

'But you 'ave no space, *ma chère* Aleese. If you had like ze big apartment of zis *H*ope you could do it, but is much too small – we would 'ave to make like ze *peek-neek*.' Josette winks and Alice laughs, but sticks to her goal.

'What about your place, Josette?'

'My "place"?'

'Your place, Josette. Do you have a place now?' This is a bit wicked, for Alice knows perfectly well that Josette still only seems contactable via messages left at the Café Bleu.

'I am *encore* "flibbertigibbet" – that is good word, no? I tell you that before? My Billy-Boy teach it to me. I stay wiz Marie-Auguste.'

'Could we entertain them there?'

'Where? At ze 'ouse of Marie-Auguste? Oh, no, *impossible* – that 'usband is a pig, 'orrible man. 'E go to *Chine* with 'is secretary – she 'as *terrrible* time.'

'So no go there?'

'What is wiz zis "no go"?'

'We can't entertain these Swedes or Danes or whatever they are at Marie-Auguste's?'

'That would not be very *comme il faut* – she is sad, sad woman . . .'

The straggling band has arrived in the place d'Espoir, tired and disgruntled with too much consumption and heat, knowing that at least one of them is going to have to volunteer to help Verona with the washing-up. But there's a distraction. On the other side of the square, with her back towards them, Hope Boscombe is walking very slowly along the side wall of the Maison Puce, the one which extends into the dark recesses of the impasse d'Espoir. In high stiletto sandals she's carefully placing her feet heel to toe. They all stand watching her as she disappears round the bend into shadow. Then she reappears, still with her back towards them, bent low over a long metal tape measure. She pulls it out in six-foot lengths, the springy steel rattling against the cobbles, and scuttles backwards out into the street. At the corner, she stops and makes some notes on a pad.

'Hope *dear*,' calls Verona, as they approach. The others instantly seize up. No one else has dared call Hope their 'dear' yet – she's still far too much of an unknown quantity. Hope starts and spins round. Anybody less like Verona's 'dear' would be hard to envisage. She looks as if she might hiss or spit like a cat.

'So sorry to startle,' Verona continues, dropping the picnic stuff on the road and sponging off her face with a scrunched paper napkin. 'Can we help you – hold the end of the tape?' The others aren't so tight that they can't recognize Hope's wary look, and Imo in particular would like to make herself scarce before she's tainted with the Verona brush. Too late. 'Here, dear, do give me one end and then you can get a good clean sweep at it – such awkward things, aren't they?' The others all squirm, waiting for Hope to bite, but instead she hands the end of the tape to Verona and strides off back down the *impasse*, pausing to make notes as she goes. It's a very long tape measure, but even so from round the bend it tugs and Verona yells, 'Shall I follow through, dear?'

'Yes,' comes the answer, and Verona goes forward, disappearing round the bend too.

*

It's Alice who draws the short straw of the washing-up, but by this time curiosity makes it more worthwhile.

'What an odd thing for Hope to be doing,' says Alice. 'Did she say what it was for?'

'What, dear?'

'All that measuring?'

'Oh yes, dear,' and nothing more. God, Verona could drive you to distraction.

'What?' says Alice, throwing subtlety overboard. '*What* did she say she was doing?'

'Testing,' says Verona, and maddeningly leaves it at that.

19

Cannes Can

'What's with the sunflowers, Mum?' says Gavin, dropping his backpack on to the floor and striding into the studio as if it were just the entrance hall and there was somewhere else to go.

'They're very Provençal. The cloth is local. Traditional – well, the colours are. Thought I'd add a few of my own as well just to jolly it all up a bit,' says Alice – oh-oh, already the lady is protesting far too much.

'Yeah. Right,' says Gavin, and keeps looking about him. Within two steps he's yanking at the door to the shower room, 'And through here – oh . . .' as he catches sight of the porcelain. He closes it again with a slam, and looks back round the room. 'So . . . right . . . yeah . . . this is it . . . right . . . And you say Hope Boscombe's got a pad here – *really*?'

'Try not to sound too surprised, darling. Yes, she has, on the top floor, but hers is much bigger, of course.'

'It'd have to be – and you know her?'

'Well, I can't really say I *know* her – I've had lunch with her once. She's quite a private person, I think.'

'Well, yeah – she would be, someone like that.' Gav's

walked the other two steps now, down to the window, and is looking out. 'So this is it?'

'I did tell you it was small,' says Alice, but remembering the weeping flannels and pubic hairs of Fulham, she suddenly feels less apologetic. 'I've bought a Lilo.'

'What?' says Gav, looking startled.

'As you suggested – "I'll stump up for the Lilo", as I remember it . . . They're called *matelas* here – never to be mistaken for *matelot*, which means a sailor . . . could be tricky in certain circumstances,' Alice giggles, 'if you think about it.'

Gavin gives her a very penetrating look – as in 'This? My mum?'

'You seem a bit, umm . . .' He hesitates.

'Yes?' she says, fast.

'Different. That's what I was going to say . . . yeah – different.' Gavin surveys his very own mum – standing in the doorway in transparent white linen, with gold leather pumps . . . and are those her – God, no, not her *nipples* showing through the cloth? Gavin doesn't think he's seen those nipples since they represented six square meals a day.

Good, thinks Alice. So I have changed then. So I should hope. So I should damn well hope. 'Right,' she says, out loud. 'Dump your stuff, then, and we'll go off out.'

'Out?' says Gav, going all saggy at the knees, because he just happens to be knackered, right? Bloody awful journey on a charter flight – change at Brussels – garment bag lost, and God only knows how he'll manage without his DJ, sure to need it for the Cannes hot-spots. Had kind of hoped for soup and sympathy from Mum, and a blissful sinking into sleep. Not this ticking woman, talking dinner and bars and let's hurry up and split – get to where the action is, because tables get very booked these days, OK? Jeez.

And out they go. She insists. He can't believe it. Mum? His mum? Mum of the stew and baked potatoes? She of the 'Have you got your games kit?/You'll be late for Cubs'? She of the 'Don't worry, darling, it'll soon feel better,' is trit-trotting down the street, waving to barmen, blowing the odd kiss to strangers . . . *Mum*?

*

'But 'e iz *adorable*,' says the scrawny French one with the gold on her shades. 'You, *leetle* Gavin, Eeenglishman – 'Ow I adore ze Eeenglish – you remind me of someone *very* special – my Billy-Boy.'

'Super you could come down. Too sweet,' says the fat one with the grey wispy bun straggling into her soup. 'Such fun to have a chap down here – you'd never believe the dearth . . . Did anyone ever tell you you've got your mother's chin? Yes – just like that with the dimple off-centre, too sweet.'

'And you're in films?' says the slinky little one at the end. The one with the dog and the black stare.

'Oh, yeah, independent production.'

'Anything slated – I mean currently?' says the slinky one again. And Gav gives her a good second glance, because he wasn't expecting film speak here and now. Not yet.

'Oh, sure, full pre-production,' and he starts to give them the run-down (though really it's just for *her* benefit).

'My Billy-Boy was in films too,' says the French one, 'in 'Ollywood.'

'I thought he was in the army, dear,' says the fat one.

'*Before* was ze army,' says the French one, sounding exasperated.

'So you have accreditation, then, for Cannes?' says the little slinky one.

And he's thinking, Have I or have I bloody not? chest swelling with pride, as he brings out his business card 'GAVIN BARNES – Director – Roar-Roar Films' and an address in Wardour Street. What better fucking accreditation could she mean, not to mention letters written in advance, arrangements made?

'Can you get us tickets?' says the slinky one, flick quick, not meaning the others, of course, meaning 'us' as in Imogen Prosper – in the most single singular.

'Expect so,' says Gav, who's actually never been to Cannes before. Only heard the rumours.

'Cos you can't get anywhere in Cannes without tickets – *no*where.'

'*I*'ll be getting tickets,' says Gav firmly, with all the assurance of youth.

*

Alice has wanted to make Gavin's arrival a bit of an occasion – so despite the hole it was going to blow in this month's budget she'd arranged with the others to meet at the Taverne Vieilloise for dinner though this was firmly a Dutch treat. The women devoured him – like vultures picking at a corpse. Poor darling Gav – she'd had to sympathize – in his baggy shorts hanging at half-mast below his knees (was there *ever* such an unattractive fashion?), and the rest of his clothes *en route* for Tel Aviv or somewhere, he'd looked so exactly like himself aged seven it was hard to take him seriously.

By the end of the evening he was growing distinctly ragged, a bit drunk and sounding bombastic, boasting about this new project of his called *Deadeyes*. She's noticed his titles always seem to have 'death' in them – has asked him – but he just says, 'Death sells.'

When they get back to the flat she makes him blow up the Lilo, which, as she'd envisaged, only just squeezes into the space between the end of the open sofa-bed and the shower-room door. As the door opens outwards she has to ensure they've both fully abluted and (more crucially) peed before either can settle down. Gavin is instantly asleep, and already snoring as loudly as his father. It's quite comforting in a way – she hasn't slept in a room containing someone else (apart from the train couchette, which somehow doesn't count) since the day Philip first told her about Hillary Aldyce when she was up that scaffolding . . . not that there's anything of a reverse Oedipal complex here – she does *not* harbour unhealthy longings for her strapping son with spotty chin – but it does just feel warm and friendly to have someone near.

Hard to sleep, though, with all that steady snuffling rhythm going on. Aren't genes peculiar? Verona claiming Gavin's dimple is a dead-spit of Alice's own, and now Gav's snoring – is it his genes which mimic that double-held pause Philip always gives (gave?) in mid-gasp? And now Alice is really wide awake – a bit concerned about this project of Gav's, though it's been hard to pin him down and extract the full details. Something on the lines of Roar-Roar Films all lined up to do *Deadeyes* with what Gav called 'seed' money via the Lottery and the British Film Institute but only if they could raise huge X amounts from other sources – and he'd spent much of last year putting the whole deal together in his spare time from his day-job, and they've actually managed to film a trailer, which cost a fantastic sum like £50,000 for something lasting all of two and a half minutes, and everyone was very keen, even Viveca Jones who's prepared to star for peanuts and a share of the profits, when one of the biggest investors pulled out about three weeks ago, which is why Gav's come down. He has to rustle up some more money quickly or the whole deal's off – involving not just the collapse of the infant Roar-Roar Films, but imminent bankruptcy, unpaid overdrafts and howling guarantors in the shape of various parents inveigled into helping (though not Philip – characteristically. Gav had asked him evidently, but he'd refused to get involved citing the expenses of his new family and *Alice* – the cheek of it!). This, then, is what Gav had meant by the 'shit hitting the fan' – more of an entire sewage works, really.

*

Gavin's not having a terrific day so far. The train took far longer than he'd expected, wandering along the coast and stopping at all the little towns. Well, all right, so Mum had warned him but as she's always prone to fuss he'd assumed she was exaggerating potential problems the way she always used to. But it turns out she was right.

Then when at last he gets out at Cannes station he finds himself in swirling crowds of – like, well – *French* people, milling around, laden with shopping bags and pushchairs brimming with babies and non-stop conversation, bloody *French* conversation, not a movie mogul in sight. Don't these people realize there's a happening going on in their town? The whole centre of the fucking *universe* is what their town is and they're just moving around, blocking up all the spaces as if they haven't got a clue.

He follows his nose down towards the sea, fighting through dense and denser crowds. For the first time since he tumbled out of school he wishes he'd tried slightly harder at languages. GCSE grade C isn't getting him very far. He struggles along with '*Moi – anglais*,' all the way down until he finds himself below the bus station, looking at the Med. Not as glittery blue as it ought to be, clouds are looming, rain hangs in the sky, though the air is hot and humid. To the right are a whole load of old houses and fishing-boats, but towards the left looks more hopeful – banners are waving from the top of modern blocks. He walks along a promenade, past old men playing *boules* and old women knitting, and suddenly the atmosphere changes – this is more like it – flags, more banners and here come the first of the mega film posters, *Kong Kid* in giant letters hanging down the front of a modern glass-fronted block, *Scorched* interwoven through palm trees with huge polystyrene flames in three-dimensions licking up at the heavens. And here comes a pair of girls on rollerblades and very little else, blonde hair streaming, long legs rooted in minuscule stars and stripes shorts like Wonderwoman, heading straight for him, then splitting at the last second – yeah, this is more like it – the Croisette in all its mythical splendour. He can work out where to go now.

In the registration room at the Palais des Festivals, the queue stretches out on to the forecourt, stiff with twitchy people programmed for hurry and pace, already psyched for a fight. Gavin waits and waits, shuffling ever nearer, like the others, nervously consulting his watch and fingering his mobile as if there's a scud of ace appointments he's already in the process of missing. Maybe they're all like him, pretending to an importance and necessity they haven't yet earned. Who are all these people anyway? What do they think they're all doing here? Surely their needs aren't anything like as great as his? Journalists? Who needs yet another article on a feature not yet made, which won't get a look-see anyway – well, unless it's *Deadeyes*, of course, but that's different: *Deadeyes* can do with all the coverage it can get. He reassesses his fellow queuers with more interest and compassion. Maybe one or two of these guys could do with a good story, come to think of it . . .

The girl in front of him is being denied. 'You bitch – you goddam fucking bitch – who's your boss – I want your boss HERE, NOW. DO YOU HEAR ME, YOU BITCH?' she's shouting. The stunning girl on the other side of the counter has reverted to French in the face of this ugly barrage, though Gav was sure she'd been using English earlier to someone further along the line. But that's the way of it – no precious accreditation for the swearing yelling girl, not so much as a day-pass. The girl creeps away, labelled an outcast from the rest of them, the Golden Chosen Ones – for in a few moments that's how Gavin sees himself. The office in London had done its stuff: the right pieces of paper have arrived, the precious card mounted in a clear plastic holder strung on to yellow and black neck-tape is being handed over – and there he is, feeling a whole lot better, one of THOSE WHO COUNT after all.

When he gets back to the outer doors he sees it's raining now – tipping it down like a Satyajit Ray monsoon. People are scattering in all directions like snooker balls at the mercy of a cue. To one side is the fabled stairway – Les Marches de Cannes – climbing up to the main entrance of the *palais* in its gaudy dressing of scarlet carpet. Immediately in front across the concrete is just one of many metal hurdles, slotted together to make a huge barrier that snakes away down the Croisette. And down there amongst the beating rain and skedaddling people is a familiar face – the little angry slinky girl of last night, Imogen, standing smiling directly at him, umbrella in hand. He makes what he hopes is a laid-back kind of dash towards her, and ducks under the shelter of the brolly.

'Got it, then,' says Imogen. 'Get you,' and she gives a playful tug at the pass now safely strung around his neck.

'Yeah – like – piece of cake.' He grins down at her smugly. What a little thing she is – little, little thing – but kind of curvy in all the right places.

'You don't half look a prat in those shorts,' she says, without missing a beat, still smiling.

'Yeah, well, like it wasn't raining when I went in, was it?' says Gav, pride already melting away.

'Haven't you brought anything else?'

'In my luggage – lost, Tel Aviv they reckon. Maybe back tomorrow – if they trace it . . .'

'I shouldn't wait till tomorrow if I were you – those aren't going to open many doors . . .' They both look down at his bare shins – his socks sticking out of Nike Airs are already soaking. 'Why don't you get a pair of chinos just to see you through?'

'Well . . .' Doesn't particularly want to tell her money is an issue – not cool enough for a girl with insolent black eyes and curves in all the right places. 'Can't see the point, not with my luggage coming – '

'*If* it's coming – don't bloody bank on it. I can show you somewhere cheap, up the old town. Come on – get you sorted.'

They head back along the Croisette, Gav now holding the umbrella to keep the worst at bay, back past *Kong Kid* and *Scorched*, not looking so hot in the rain.

'Can you get tickets now you've got your pass?' asks Imogen. 'Tickets for screenings and things? Parties? There are some real mega parties.'

'Yeah, of course, no problem – I'm legit.'

'I think you need an assistant.'

'What?'

'Well, just look at you, wet through if it wasn't for me, going round in shorts when you haven't got the legs – or the language. Why don't you have me along – part-time, maybe full? I could be really useful . . .'

*

The squall has hit Vieilleville too and Josette is sheltering under the awning at the Café des Fleurs, sipping her morning *express* and opening up her copy of *Nice-Matin*. On the front page is a big colour photograph of a phalanx of stars climbing the red staircase at Cannes. Josette examines it carefully for a minute or two, critically checking out the evening dresses – the cut of a sleeve or the precise angle of a chiffon bias being of crucial fascination to her. *Quite* nice, she reckons, though if she had their kind of money what she couldn't do, what she wouldn't look like with her shape – just made for sequins and jet. Then she flips to the rest of the Cannes coverage inside the paper, eager for more stars to criticize and pull apart – the more youthful and Hollywood the better.

Ah, but there's the divine Deneuve, of course, always looks amazing – what a woman – could tell the world a thing or two about the art of ageing gracefully, not that Josette herself hasn't a useful tip or two in the same department. Now for the week's programme . . . She always looks for interest and amusement, though she rarely goes – as Imo said last night, without the right tickets and contacts it's a useless journey. Still, nice to know what's going on, have the right comments available should the topic arise socially – might be useful if she takes herself back to Juan-les-Pins, you never know . . . Here's the list – the Official Competition – then below *Un Certain Regard* (the Cannes version of 'Highly Commended But Not Quite There'), the Directors' Fortnight, the International Critics' Week, The Retrospective . . . and then she stops, hand at her throat – gasps aloud – 'The Retrospective' . . . but it *can-*

not be – and she reads it again. *Mon Dieu* – Billy-Boy is here.

Who to tell first? How to share this staggering event? Marie-Auguste is away – so is Adrienne. But then suddenly she sees that, in this instance, only Alice Barnes will do. *'Aleese!'* yelling up at that window again – come along, Alice, be *in* this time – *'Aleese!'* Josette is still shaking with the shock.

*

And what is Alice to make of the quivering woman and the crumpled copy of *Nice-Matin* shoved into her hands like this?

'Look – *look!*'

And 'What – *what?*' Alice is answering.

'Look *'ere*,' and at last the page is found, smoothed out and Alice is confronted by a photograph of a balding man with puggy face.

'It is 'im – Billy-Boy!'

And Alice gets her to sit down and runs her eyes over the article, capturing the gist without having recourse to her dictionary – 'In honour of his eightieth birthday, an *hommage* to the work of William Prescott, director of such Technicolor blockbusters as *Wide Awake*, *The Moll* and *Strawberry Fair*, to culminate with a presentation to the great man himself of a specially commissioned plaque made by the craftsmen of Vallauris.'

'You mean Billy-Boy is William Prescott?'

'But of course.'

'You never said.' But Josette immediately sends her that

look she's grown to know so well – that shaft of scorn, the one which keeps its own counsel as and when it pleases. But why, when this would have been so interesting? It's not that Alice is all that well up on film directors, of course, much to Gavin's on-going scorn, but names like Hitchcock, John Huston and William Prescott have managed to lodge themselves in her mind. Who could forget Hitchcock's *Birds*, Huston's *African Queen*, or the lovely joyous lilt and swing of William Prescott's fifties musicals – the sort that sent you out of the cinema on to dark, cold pavements still humming the tunes? Those were the days.

'So Lieutenant Billy Prescott-Smythe is William Prescott?' says Alice, just to make sure she's got this right.

'*Capitaine* Prescott-Smythe – yes. After that witch of a *maman* broke us apart, he went to 'Ollywood.'

'From New Delhi?'

'*Before* was New Delhi.'

'But he was in the army, wasn't he?'

'*After* he was in ze army.'

'From New Delhi?'

'Or Bangkok.' Josette heaves with irritation – *why* do these women have such an insatiable thirst for information? Don't they understand discretion? *So déclassé*. And why won't Alice let her get to the point? 'Your son, Aleese – your adorable leetle boy . . .'

So hard to think of lumpy Gavin as her little boy, but Alice tries. 'Yes – what about him?'

''E will 'ave ticket?'

'What sort of ticket?'

'For ze shows –'e can get ticket for us – for *me* – you zink so?'

'I've no idea. I should think he could try – we'll have to ask him.'

'Only you understand for me is *verrry* important – I 'ave not seen my Billy-Boy in over forty years.' Josette halts herself just for a second, but then, oh, what the hell – let them draw their ageist conclusions. 'Maybe more like forty-five. His *maman* keep us apart – was terrible, terrible thing. It broke my 'eart – I 'ave *neverr* been ze same . . . So you will 'elp me – because ozzerwise I don't know how I can reach him . . . You will ask your son when he come back to Vieilleville tonight?'

And of course Alice must agree.

*

Once Josette has gone, still babbling and clutching her mental straw of hope, it's Alice who's bursting to spread the word. But Imo's out and Alice hasn't seen Verona all morning. Typical. At last she's got some really juicy gossip she'd love to chew over, and Verona is nowhere to be found.

20

Pitching

Gav's beginning to reckon Imogen – resourceful or what? She's already thought of a plan of campaign – seems to know the ins and outs. And the way she speaks Froggy is a fucking miracle.

First she gets him sorted out with some black cotton trousers at a second-hand place round the back of the flower market – dirt cheap and pretty cool, might just count for Armani at a distance – plus, and this was her really great idea, a black jacket to match. Not equal to the missing DJ on its way to Tel Aviv but, as she points out, one black jacket (if sufficiently cool, right?) plus one bow-tie, is equal to most social situations at the Cannes Can. So he's already feeling much more up for it by the time she drags him into a stationer's on the rue d'Antibes and is photocopying his precious pass in the blinking of an eye. Before he's quite sussed her game, she's sticking her own photo carefully on to the copy and sliding the whole thing into a little clear plastic wallet.

Then she's eyeing up his official neckband – suggests if they cut it down it could double up for her as well. But he's not stupid – any self-respecting security guard would smell a rat, two people trying to get in wearing little necklaces like chokers instead of the long swinging real McCoys. But she doesn't give in easy, this one – goes for the next best thing: pins the pseudo-pass upside down on her breast, just below the left nipple which is jutting out so tastily into the stretchy black jersey, with a healthy eyeful of deep cleavage hanging an inch or two above it. And she's dead right – who's to check? Who's going to obstruct her passage, a fierce little thing, mobile clutched importantly in right hand just ready to take that vital call, clipboard wedged under armpit (board, notepad and clear plastic wallet specially purchased at stationer's there and then just to give the right image – oh, yes, she's got it all worked out)? Gav does wonder just for a moment if maybe he's putting his own precious professional status on the line here – but hey, what the fuck, it's only a little bit of fun. They're not out to hijack the joint – they only want Access.

Oh, but Access is like gold here – no, Access is like fucking platinum-plated plutonium: without it you're zilch. Nothing. *Nada*.

They start by tackling the main market down in the basement of the Palais des Festivals – but it's kind of depressing. A hundred thousand film dudes down there of both sexes, all desperate to sell their wares. More posters, pamphlets, stickers, trailers for more crap celluloid than the galaxy has a right to expect. Gav's got his own trailer, all precious two-and-a-half-minutes-fifty-thousand-pounds worth of it, on the laptop in his knapsack, just waiting for a chance to get a tasty prospect hooked and begging to invest. And they will be, once they've seen it, sussed the quality, seen the style and originality – not to mention its useful similarities to twenty-four-carat hits like *Trainspotting* and *The Full Monty*. This is, like, cutting-edge new True Brit film making for the New Millennium – like, get it or what? Like hell, yes. So when it comes to it, Gav can't get out of the official basement market fast enough. What he needs is hungry enlightened entrepreneurs – not starving overhung salesmen. Another tack is called for.

They head off down the Croisette, squeezing through the crowds. Plenty of pros – small stout middle-aged men with briefcases, talking non-stop into their mobiles, sweat staining the backs of their short-sleeved shirts, cheek to cheek with hard-assed women in tight little suits, pushing past luscious lovelies in flimsy nothings, and gaping, staring amateurs just here for the fun of the atmosphere, real nobodies without a jelly's chance in hell of getting into anything, anywhere, not a screening, not a meeting – and all complaining. Call this thing a 'festival', they all humph – what festival? Just a glorified trade fair, gilded by the Cannes sun.

Imo and Gav start darting into white-tented pavilions – here are the Algerians, there the Israelis, across the way the Danes – flashing their passes and slipping through barriers like a dream. In no time they're weighted with catalogues, brochures and cards – but no appointments. Then over there the British Pavilion where Imo's keen to linger for a while, not averse to a little spot of surreptitious star-gazing – not that she'd want to admit it. Gav, though, is suddenly self-conscious. Up until now it's all felt like a crazy game, played on foreign soil where he has no identity to squander. But now this feels more like dirtying your own patch, and for the first time he's nervous when Imo flashes her bogus pass at the very elegant, very *big* bouncer at the gate. Her cleavage does the trick, though – the guard doesn't seem to notice the deceit and ushers them through.

Imo's got flirtier and less spiky as the day's progressed. She's at it with a vengeance with the Brits, knocking back freebie lagers, and talking to everyone. But Gav sees only professional competition in every direction – lots of these guys already have their projects in the bag – and the last thing he needs is an eyeball confrontation with any of those generous bods from the BFI, asking awkward questions, when as yet he hasn't any answers. He catches Imo's eye, but she keeps turning away, ignoring him. In the end he has to slip his hand under her elbow and practically drag her out.

On the Croisette again where the rainclouds have rolled away leaving only hot thick sunlight, Imo is seething.

'Why'd you want to fucking do that? I was getting on really well . . .'

'But *I* wasn't,' says Gav, and explains about the men from the BFI, and his need for investment contacts rather than high-powered rivals.

'But that's what I was doing, you stupid arsehole,' spits Imo.

'What?' says Gav, like, doing what?

'Doing a recce? That's the word right? Doing your bloody recce – finding out who the good guys are, where they're staying. What did you think I was doing?'

'Flirting,' says Gav.

'Up yours,' says Imo. God, she's sexy when she's mad.

'Like what?' says Gav.

'Like now I don't even want to tell you.'

'Go on Imo, give us a break.'

'Like WarWorks are at the Majestic with a special brief to pick up new talent, first films a speciality – yours is a first?'

'In directorial terms,' says Gav, loving the word 'directorial' when linked to his very own self and nobody else.

'Well, that's one to go for if we can get an appointment.'

'We?'

'Can't do it alone, can you, Gav? Can't even buy your own sodding trousers. And there's another thing – a Pitch Fest at five o'clock up by the *palais*, open to all.' She thrusts a pink paper flyer in his face. 'There you are – everyone who's anyone'll be there. You get two minutes to pitch your film.'

'In public?'

'Well, sure in public.'

'Oh, no, Imo – sounds like Amateursville to me, kiss of death.'

'What's so Amateursville? Half of the big boys will be there, I told you. It's a market for ideas – can't do any harm. It might be *the* market for all you know.'

'Well . . .' Gav can feel his stomach shrinking.

'You have *got* a pitch, right?'

'Well . . .'

'How'd you get the money first time round?'

'Something called a treatment, Imo, something called a script, something with a bit of meat and substance – I don't want to fuck up my chances.'

'You're just a coward.'

'No, I'm not.'

'Do it, then. Pitch it – pitch it to me now.'

'No, I can't.'

'Yellow!'

'I'm not.'

'Prove it!'

So he pitches. Right there in the middle of the Croisette. Dumps all the catalogues and posters and brochures on the pavement, and does it there and then . . . 'There's these two geezers, right . . .?'

*

At roughly the same time, Hope Boscombe is also pitching – in a small boat, on a choppy sea in the middle of Vieilleville Bay. She's trying to focus her camera on the roof of the Maison Puce. After all her careful measuring and assessment of the building, she still needs some solid proof of her suspicions. She's already tried doing this from the hills above Bonneville, but without much success. She'd taken some photographs from up there, had them developed, then pored over them with a magnifying glass to see if she could pick out her own particular roof from the intricate maze of the town – but even though she's pretty sure that X marks the spot, from that angle there's still no view of the hidden garden behind the cement wall.

So now she's trying from the other side – hired a boat and headed out to sea. The skipper, a fisherman who does day-trips to expand his income, regards her very curiously as she makes him drop anchor directly in front of the beach.

This is as far as she wants to go, she says – '*Terminé, terminé, fini!*' is what she shouts, and though he might well puzzle as to where on earth she got *that* bit of lingo, he naturally understands the general idea. And as she's paying him exactly as if he was hauling her all the way to Monaco, why should he complain?

Amusing, though, to watch this woman with her binoculars and sketchpad and camera on a tripod, rocking with the waves and taking shot after shot of the town – as if you couldn't go and buy a perfectly good postcard for a couple of francs to save you the trouble.

*

At five o'clock, Imo and Gav get themselves admitted into the big white tent near the Palais des Festivals. It has a clear plastic front so that oh-fucking-hell the whole damn world can see – all the star-gazing gawpers have their noses pressed right up, staring in.

Gav's mouth feels like a dead plimsoll because Imo's right after all. This tent is *full* of people, all the right sort of people, out for a bit of early-evening amusement before they hit the big-time official screenings – and suddenly it's his turn – Gav – out there pitching *Deadeyes* to the world – two minutes to grab some motherfucker out there by the balls.

'There's these two geezers, right . . .?'

*

Afterwards he heads for the bar and the longest beer he can get his tongue round.

'Hi, there, liked your style – Bilt Claymore,' says a rich, round American voice, and a large hand is reaching out to grasp his.

Imo's mouth is half hanging open. 'Bilt Claymore – a name for real?' But Gav is already shaking the hand, grateful for any recognition, as the voice continues, 'From LA – Bad Boys Productions?' instantly changing mere gratitude into outright glee. Bad Boys? Weren't they the guys who did so brilliantly with *Haverstock* last year – American money allied to Brit Wit? My God, but maybe this is just the right sort of fish landing slap bang in the middle of the plate – already filleted and grilled.

'Hello?' says Gav, with a wide smile, accent instantly reverting to minor public school because Americans seem to like their English *English*. Imo's mouth hangs wider.

And before anyone knows quite where they are, Gav's got his laptop up and running on the table, and lager is changing into wine, and chummy-hummy happiness is breaking out all over.

'This is really terrific,' says Bilt – Dear Bilt, what a name, I *love* that name, thinks Gav. 'I mean I really like the whole kind of fundamental mood you guys have got going here,' and Imo thrills to be one of the guys after all – and they're talking meetings and dinner. Only Bilt says he's staying in Nice – a mess-up with his secretary, though really it's kind of nice to get out of Cannes sometimes because the non-stop craziness can just do your head in, do they know what he means? And Gav and Imo nod their agreement, and just happen to let on that they're in Vieilleville – 'I've got an apartment there, as it happens,' says Imo, whose voice has also changed, forsaken Dagenham for the shores of Malibu. And Bilt's saying, 'That's great, let's get the hell out of Cannes and really talk this thing through,' and Gav's saying, 'Great – at the Negresco?' assuming that nowhere less prestigious could house such a paragon, and Bilt's saying, 'Gee, no – let's meet at your place after dinner, ten p.m.' And that's it – they're stuck, superglued on to the rack of their own pretensions.

They sober up a bit on the hot rush-hour train clacking its way back to Vieilleville – quite a contrast to the dark-shaded stretch-limo world of the Croisette. For a brief while, Gav's still pissed and excited enough to do nothing but relive the triumph of his public pitch – did he do a great job or what? You bet your sweet arse he did – what a winner, what a guy – and some recess of his brain is already writing his Oscar acceptance speech. Would he thank Imo or not, after he'd run through the usual list of parents and God? Well, probably not because she's going all spiky again, forcing him back to chilly reality. Like what's he going to do with Bilt Claymore at 10 p.m.? Bilt who's expecting some cool luxurious Riviera pad, not a doggy hell-hole with the ceiling falling down in the Maison Puce. Because the first thing Gav's thought is could they use Imo's flat, of course, especially as she went and got them into this mess in the first place by going all West Coast and boasting? And Imo says, 'Like hell you won't,' thinking of aforesaid ceiling, plus the aroma of drains, which is just beginning to return for its summer sojourn. And Imo then says, 'Well, use your mum's, of course,' and Gav thinks of two major problems here. Number one being that his mum just happens to be there, in the all too solid flesh, right in the bloody way. And number two, though her ceiling may be currently *in situ*, so are all those sunflowers – chintzy winzty – smothering every surface. Not your actual film-maker's gaff: not the image for a cool, zappy, right-up-to-the-mark-and-minute-in-your-face Film Director of the Year, accepting his Oscar. No siree.

Still, in the circs – any port in a storm?

What they're not expecting, though, is what they get – a welcoming committee in the shape of Alice and a very jittery Josette, who leaps up as soon as Gav's staggered in, before he's even had time for a pee.

'Gaveen – darling boy – you can 'elp me? I need ticket for ze *hommage* to my Billy-Boy.'

And Imo's standing there in the doorway, because she's come upstairs too, and she's saying, 'Yeah – that should be all right, shouldn't it, Gav? You could do that for Josette, couldn't you?'

'I could do what?'

'Get her tickets for the Retrospective tomorrow – in the *palais*, is it? Yeah, no problem.' And she stands there looking all official, making notes on the clipboard – the crafty little bint. Except she's mad, you know, because he hasn't got the vaguest idea how he'd go about getting tickets – not a clue. Which is what he's about to start telling her, only she's interrupting, explaining to Alice how they've got this business meeting with the producer from Bad Boys, and what with one thing and another, she doesn't think her flat is quite up to the mark. And Josette is laughing at the very idea, and Alice is doing what Imo knew she would, especially with the kind offer of tickets just hanging in the air – bang on cue, without hesitation – offering to vacate her very own flat for their purposes. *Bingo.*

21

Night Moves

What Imo doesn't seem to realize, despite all her guile, is that Alice doesn't need buttering up with promises of non-existent tickets. That's simply not how motherhood works – on the whole. Where Gavin's best interests are concerned, she automatically wants to help. Despite any advance misgivings she'd felt about his visit, now he's here there's nothing she wouldn't do within her capabilities to ease his situation even when, as now, it's going to involve yet another evening of expense – because how else can she make herself scarce for the rest of the night, but in a restaurant or bar? Imo hasn't offered her own flat in exchange, and given that Alice knows only too well what a hell-hole it is, she doesn't ask. If Verona were at home, it would of course be all too simple to wangle an invitation, but there's still no sign of her. Odd this – for usually if Verona has been planning an entire day out, Alice has been regaled with every exhaustive detail. So it's off out with Josette yet again, trying to fill in time and leave the young 'uns to it.

*

Having got rid of the old biddies, Gav sends Imo out to buy some booze. Imo insists it's got to be champagne, nothing less will do, and nearly chokes when he suggests that sparkling Saumur might fill the bill as well. So off she goes – the elasticity of Côte d'Azur shopping hours being such a help in these situations – and comes back expensively laden with three whole bottles and a heap of nifty little nibbles in bags and boxes. They lay everything out, Gav puts his laptop on the table – and there they are, all set and ready to go.

They're expecting Bilt Claymore to arrive in one of those stretch limos – or at the very least a chauffeur-driven Merc. As it's Gav who's supposed to be the big-time player, Imo volunteers to go out into the square and keep a lookout; direct the driver if necessary to the nearest available parking and generally try to pre-empt the possibility of a noisy blockage in the rue d'Espoir. Don't want to send out the wrong vibes before they've even got started.

Gav meanwhile waits upstairs, nervously watching the screensaver on his laptop. Custom designed – but of course. DEADEYES, reads the caption, with winking blue eyes in each of the capital Ds – really wicked. Bilt'll love it, all over again – won't he?

*

He's late. Wouldn't you just bloody know it? Fucking typical. Imo strides round and round the place d'Espoir, already weary from checking whether she's missed this mythical car trying to nose its way into one of the other alleys, needing extra eyes round the back of her neck. By ten thirty he still hasn't arrived. Gav sticks his head out of the window and mimes a drinking gesture. Stupid little fucker.

'Wait!' she yells up.

Gav pulls the corners of his mouth down with his little fingers and has a go at miming clown sadness.

'Just bloody wait!' she yells again. At ten forty-five she's thinking of giving up, when Bilt Claymore rolls up the slope from the rue Maréchal Foch, very much on a wobbly shanks's pony – no vehicle in sight, and a distinctly drunken bend to the knees.

'Hi – ummm – beautiful . . .' He bends to give Imo a slippery, beery kiss.

'Hello, Bilt, glad you could make it,' says Imo, already full of doubt.

'My God, but this is one hell of a place to find – I asked some guys at the station but no one spoke English.'

Station? He came by train? Imo's doubts harden by the second, but how to get the message to Gav?

As she leads the way up the stairs, his hands keep straying up her skirt – pelmet-shallow, barely covering her bum in an effort to make the right impression. But now it turns out it's quite the wrong impression and what the fuck does the fucker think he's up to? Well, she knows damn well what he's up to . . . that's the problem. And now Gav has come out, hand advanced, shaking Bill's warmly, apologizing about the night, the light, the dark, the place, the space – shut up, Gav, and watch my lips, won't you? But no, Gav's already opening a bottle, splashing expensive champagne on to the floor, and Bilt's saying, 'Great, thanks, don't mind if I do,' looking admiringly round the flat, saying, 'This is really cute – you guys renting it for long?' And Gav – stupid fucking Gav – is practically on his knees with grovel,

grovel, offering nibbles and fags and sit here why don't you, it's the most comfortable, *are* you comfortable, and what I thought we'd do is take another look at the trailer – and then, like, well, we can talk about it? Right? And like I've got a copy of the script for you – take it back to your hotel – wonderful to have you on board – if you came on – percentages and gross – put in place – crew all lined up and ready to shoot – everyone so excited – what a project – what an opportunity – any questions?

And all the while Imo's trying to get behind Bilt and shake her head and scowl so that Gav'll get some sort of message, but he doesn't even notice because, of course, she always looks furious – that's just her norm – and, God, doesn't he fancy it? But some time into the second expensive bottle, Bilt's eyes have given up the effort to focus and, with lids dangling, he's talking rent – not film. Rent as in 'How much does it cost you guys for this place –'cause like I've tried crashing out on the beach at Cannes and the goddam police moved me on, which is why I'm trying Nice, because word's out on the grapevine that the Nice police – ' (but here he lisps and stumbles, the evening's booze having taken too strong a hold, stumbles and catches himself again) ' – the *Nice* police,' he re-emphasizes, 'well, they don't give a shit – they'll even let you light fires and stuff so you can cook, which saves you money, and like I've left my sleeping-bag there, just rolled up behind a rock, and do you guys think I could crash out here?' And finally the penny drops and Gav says, 'What about Bad Boys Productions?' and his mouth is going all twisted as if he's about to cry.

'What?' says Bilt Claymore, seeping innocence.

'Bad Boys Productions. I thought you were with Bad Boys – *Haverstock*?'

And Bilt laughs like a drain – except drains don't laugh, so why? – and says, 'Gee, don't get me like wrong, what I *said* was Badboyze – like all one word. You didn't pick up on that?' Knowing by now that of course Gav didn't pick up on that.

And Gav mumbles, 'No. So what kind of outfit are you?'

And Bilt says, 'Kind of a one-man band – I'm in soft-core just at the moment but I think big and hard's only just around the corner,' and he sort of leers at Imo and she socks him on the jaw. Just like that, no warning, and over he goes like a felled Christmas tree and just as awkward to get down the stairs, which they have to do, of course, otherwise how to explain his presence to Alice, who might very well resent the body of a fat, steaming, drunken pornographer taking up so much of her floor space.

But where the hell are they going to put him? By the time they reach the ground floor they're at least certain he's alive because of all the groans and spluttering as they bang him round the spirals. Gav's fertile imagination has already worked out a complicated scenario – might even make a film – involving a corpse, and the ugly necessity of contacting the Vieilleville *gendarmerie*, and the horror of trying to explain it all . . . and spending the next twenty years mouldering in some French jail, something like that place in *The Count of Monte Cristo* – oh, God, oh, God, why did I ever get myself into this in the first place? But Imo's perfectly practical. She knows the power of her punches – effective but not lethal.

She's all for sticking Bilt on a bench out in the place d'Espoir, where he can sleep it all off and be awoken by the street washers at 6 a.m. when he'll undoubtedly get his pants wet – dirty, rotten little bugger, wangling his way into their time and space, costing them well over three hundred francs in champagne. Bastard.

But Gav is nervous: supposing Bilt's concussed or something? 'So what are you expecting?' asks Imo, eyes already blazing. And Gav just kind of hints at *her* flat, for now they're right outside her door, and couldn't they just lay him out on her floor? And Imo says, 'Thanks a whole fucking lot – like what do you expect me to do?' And Gav says, 'Don't worry, I'll keep you company – just in case he wakes up,' and Imo says she's got the dog, and Gav says, 'Better to be safe than sorry,' and that's how it works out: Bilt slung across the floor with Fred growling at his feet, and Imo and Gav squashed up really close on the divan – which, what with the proximity, the effects of the champagne, and one thing and another, leads to what Gav reckons is a pretty satisfying consolation for the disappointments of the day.

*

For once Josette's been prepared to let her standards slip and she and Alice have the cheapest dinner possible in Vieilleville – pizza Napoletana at the bar on the quay. Even this she doesn't eat, just toying with the strings of mozzarella, round and round the plate. At this rate it's going to be a job to get through the rest of the evening.

'You're not hungry?' – hardly original, but Alice has to fill the time in somehow.

'*Trop d'angoisse – tu comprends*?'

'That bad?'

'Is bad – very bad. You really sink your leetle Gaveen will get ticket?'

'He seems to think so – at least Imo does.'

'What is *she* doing wiz 'im?'

'I haven't the foggiest.'

'You what?'

'I don't know, Josette – don't know what she's doing with him.'

'Because he does not need zat one, your leetle Gaveen, he is *adorable*.'

'Look, if I were you I'd try not to pin my hopes on Gavin.'

'"Pin" my 'opes?'

'We'll just have to wait and see – that's what I mean.'

'No, Alice, I cannot wait – I have been waiting already *so* long.'

'When did you last see him – Billy-Boy?'

'When . . . oh, Alice, I was just a girl, you know, and my father was ze chef at ze Embassy.'

And Alice, remembering her previous mistake, has to interrupt: 'You mean he was the *chief*?'

'No – he was ze *cook*.'

And now Alice swallows the question that's bursting to come out – Hong Kong? New Delhi? Phnom Penh? – because, after all, what does the detail matter? And maybe a lesson well learned, for suddenly it's pouring out – how Josette's father had to escape occupied Vichy France, wife dead, made a dash with his young daughter, got his employment where he could, British mad keen to have some *cuisine française* on board despite complications of nationality (but then de Gaulle was being such a good egg back in Blighty), and Billy-Boy's mother queening it over the entire legation as wife of the Biggest Bigwig. A total bitch/witch whose wrath was fearful to behold, and never more so than when her adored son Billy fell for the cook's daughter. And Alice can see the vision so clearly – the ravishing young Josette, smothered under the weight of all that Colonial British Snootiness and, on top of that, pregnant by the wretched louse, and carted off to the abortionist by the Mother Queen Bee. Josette's father was absolutely helpless and useless – needed his job, let the whole thing happen. But Josette was longing to have Billy's baby and live the full Prescott-Smythe Hampshire idyll as painted by Billy in happier days. Instead of which he'd been packed off to Hollywood to 'get himself a career'. She'd tried to keep in touch – not easy to track him via letters and Christmas cards – but he was soon married and their communication dwindled away. Josette had been left to rub along as best she could.

And it doesn't sound as if it's been all that easy. She's scraped a living for years as a sort of Riviera house-sitter, socially acceptable, thanks to all that close absorption of embassy etiquette – everything from an extra at bridge, to acting as companion to aged heiresses with grasping descendants to more or less anything. Current position involves house-sitting for Marie-Auguste, feeding her corgis and forwarding her mail, not exactly onerous – but no home of her own, scarcely any money, no security at all, as she looks old age squarely in the jaw.

This time Alice pays the bill without demur.

By now it's long past midnight. How long will this film meeting last? Alice should have arranged some sort of signal – a tea-towel stuck out of the window to indicate the all-clear? As it is, she feels that by marching into her own flat she may disrupt a delicate negotiation at the worst possible moment. Better go and assess the situation from outside.

Josette heads off towards Marie-Auguste's corgis, and Alice walks back to the place d'Espoir. There is a light shining out from her flat – but also, now, one from Imo's so perhaps she can risk it. She's just about to knock on Imo's door when she hears a noise – snoring . . . but with a familiar twist – that double-held gasp, the one inherited from Philip . . . Gavin? She hurries up to her own flat. The door is open, the remains of a party are all too evident, the laptop is still switched on with its horrible eyes winking and blinking. She knocks on the shower-room door – no answer. No Gav. She steps out into the hall again and listens – yes, there's that gasping snore again. So *that*'s the way of it – and she wishes the thought didn't make her even more uneasy than she already is.

The Maison Puce at 3 a.m.

On the ground floor, three sleeping humans and one twitchy dog.

On the first floor Alice half dozing, disturbed by the eerie light of the laptop which, for fear of wiping something, she doesn't dare switch off.

On the second floor, empty silence.

And up above, an anxious Hope is scanning today's photos with a magnifying-glass, reconfirming her suspicions for the umpteenth time. Tick, tick, tick – her nerves are prickling, her heart erratically thumping, her mind increasingly gripped by this new obsession. The View of the Sea is just sitting there behind her very own roof – the most perfect view in the world – with its great span of turquoise water, its fringe of palm trees, its rocky headland and lighthouse and boats, tantalizingly there, and yet not there. Not hers – but whose? It's outrageous. It's unsafe. It's unhygienic. It's . . .? What would she do back home? If this were a *Sharp Focus* issue she'd have sorted it out without a second glance. Why so different here?

She's called Jerry, of course – her first line of defence – but so hard to explain the situation. He suggests lawyers. And, well, yes, perhaps it will have to come to that. But the only lawyer currently on tap is the *notaire* who was in charge of the original transaction, and everything about that situation now fills her with doubt and dismay. There's the language, of course – so damn tricky when you're trying to express subtleties so she supposes an English-language lawyer will have to be found – and then somehow the papers extracted from the *notaire*'s grasp . . . for that's the other funny thing. Unlike any property transaction she's ever done, there's been so far no sign of any deeds or documents relating to the purchase of her flat.

Monsieur Gerontin is the clue here, really. If she could

only get through to him, he surely has the remedy at his fingertips. Whoever is playing that nerve-frazzling music is doing it from her roof. And once she's got it back, not only will she have secured herself essential peace but another *terrasse* as well – this time facing the other way round, leading off her bedroom and looking out to sea. *Vue de la mer* after all – just as it damn well should be.

22

Flying Flying High: Flying Low

The next morning, far too early, Imo takes a phone call – angrily because, bloody hell, it's only eight o'clock and, Christ, what a night, squeezed into the single bed with bloody Gavin, randy as all get-out (and, oops, she shouldn't have let *that* happen – bit of a slip-up there) and then turning out to be a mega fucking snorer, sending the whole room on to vibration alert. And then down on the floor Fred tense and unyielding, growling every single time that bloody fart Bilt burped or rolled over in the dark. Fuck the whole lot of them. Bastards. And 8 a.m., ring, ring, and Imo's fit to burst.

'Yes?' she spits.

'Imo – sweetie.' It's Hope Boscombe.

'Yes?' says Imo, made extra curt by double irritation, and enjoying the sense of not giving a bugger.

'It's *me*, darling heart, Hope,' because it's quite a good few years since anyone's answered the phone to the great Hope Boscombe like this and, well, it's really something – gives a woman a frisson in an area where she hadn't really expected to feel tickled again.

'Yes?' says Imo, for the third irascible time.

'Er . . . well . . .' (How unlike me, thinks Hope in a flash

– haven't started a sentence with a hesitant 'er' in years) '. . . well, I was wondering if you could spare me some time this morning. Something's come up – something pretty amazing, really, and I've got to gear myself up for another confrontation with Monsieur Gerontin.'

'Can't,' says Imo, 'busy.'

'Just for a couple of hours?' Hope puts on her *Sharp Focus* wheedling voice. 'Because you're such a *fantastic* linguist.'

'Up to my eyes all day,' says Imo, implacable. 'Working for Roar-Roar Films – PR liaison at Cannes.'

'You're involved with the Festival? But you never said . . .'

As if I'd have to, Hope, thinks Imo, and why shouldn't I have other irons in my fire? 'Non-stop,' she says, 'probably tonight too. I'm surprised you're not over there.'

'Well, this year I can give it a miss.' Too right – what was the point of coming down here for serious R and R, and then just throwing yourself back into the vortex? Best to explain, though – 'Frankly, it's kind of a relief to step aside for once – and in any case it's not that big a deal for me. Video's more my area than film. And the point is I've got *other* things on my mind this year – *real* important. Now listen, sweetie, listen good because I really want to persuade you. This could be real good for you too – and, of course, for me it would be so *wonderful* to have you on side.'

'Who do you think I am – fucking "Dial-a-Dyke"?' says Imo, and puts the phone down.

Up in the glory of her penthouse, Hope finds herself looking down into the mouth of the receiver as if it, personally, had snubbed her – something she'd always complained of actors doing in the sloppier soap operas. But now she can see they've had a point all along.

Gav has been half woken by the ringing of the phone. 'What was that?' he asks, as yet too sleepy to have put up his guard. 'Mind your own fucking business,' says Imo, bang on cue. Atta girl.

Slightly later, Gav watches Imo eject Bilt Claymore from her flat. Well, he'd help, of course, not as if he doesn't offer, but she just gives him one of her withering looks (and, phwoar, what that doesn't do to his love truncheon) and sets to like a tiny little whirling dervish. Bilt is rubbing his head, his stomach and his backside, glasses hanging lopsidedly off one ear, carrying his shoes, and limping in socked feet down to the place d'Espoir before Gav has even got himself out of the bed to think up an effective approach. No need, this time – amazing, this girl, in *all* departments.

But then, of course, she comes back and wants them to leave as early as possible for Cannes again, only he's gone and left both his laptop and the script – not to mention his toothbrush – up in his mum's flat last night, when he was still shit-scared they'd killed Bilt. So now he has to go upstairs and claim them back off her – which is awkward.

The laptop, which he'd plugged into the mains last night to preserve his battery, is still switched on. Mum says she was afraid of wiping something, so thought it best to leave well alone. The *Deadeyes* orbs are still at it – but now that things have got so difficult those bloody eyes are beginning to go sour on him. He's relieved to switch them off, gather the script, half apologize for the suddenness of their departure last night, 'Something urgent cropped up,' he mutters and, with head down, tries to slip away – but Mum's blocking the door.

'Excuse me,' he says.

'Tickets?' she says.

'Oh, right, yeah – tickets . . .'

'You promised, Gav, and Josette's desperate – you've no idea how important this is for her.'

'Yeah.'

'You *can* get some tickets, can you? Or at least one ticket?'

'Well . . .'

'Oh, Gav, you didn't make it up, did you?'

'Yeah – well, no, I'm sure it'll be okay. I'll go into the publicity office – can't be that difficult. It'll be fine – I've got full accreditation, you see, Mum,' and he waggles his Festival identity card in her face.

'I can't tell you how she's banking on this.'

'Yeah, all right,' because he wants to make the right noises – and how can he tell her that so far he hasn't had a sniff of a ticket for his own precious, privileged use, let alone been in a position to start handing them out like Smarties? Temporary inspiration strikes. 'Outside the *palais* – twelve thirty – meet us there,' he says, and that seems to satisfy her. Never mind that there are so many entrances to the *palais* and that he hasn't stipulated which.

It's with a sinking feeling that Alice dresses herself for the glories of Cannes. Gavin said all the right things – just about – but he had that same squirmy evasive look around the eyes he used to have as a child, when he didn't want to hand over his school report. She remembers it well. Still, as she doesn't have any other solution to Josette's problem, Gav will have to do.

What a lot of news to tell Verona – Alice wouldn't know where to begin. So ironic, all this Billy-Boy business and possible film deals and tickets for screenings – even one such titbit would have kept her going for days. Odd, though – hasn't been sight or sound of her. And then Alice feels a shiver of worry: supposing Verona's had a fall or a stroke or something?

By now she's already got herself into that transparent white linen suit again – the chicest gear she can muster – ready to meet Josette at the station. But she's worried, knows she'd better run upstairs and check. She knocks on Verona's door loudly, then shouts. No answer. Then she gets down on her precious clean white linen knees and squints through the keyhole. No key *in situ*, which means Verona must have locked it from outside, *ergo* she's not in. A relief . . . Odd, though.

*

In Cannes, Gav's depressed. It's all so unfair.

They get to the Palais des Festivals to find themselves embroiled in the same manic energy as yesterday. Everyone might as well be on E for this place is crazy, crazy, under the glare of the hot white sun. News cameramen and documentary-makers are filming anyone in sight who has the least smidgen of a chance of being *anybody* at all. On this basis alone, Imo will find herself on several cutting-room floors by tomorrow. Badged legitimate people in the biz are lined up waiting to be let into the different *palais* screens. Daily Festival agendas are readily available with the lists of showings and labellings, but with no hint whatsoever as to how the uninitiated might gain entrance. Vainly Gav wanders around flapping his pass, but on its own, without the magic tickets or invitations, it's not getting him very far.

In the British Pavilion, Imo gets at it again, yattering away over on the other side – bit of English here, touch of Venice Beach, California, over there, and a load of French in the middle, whenever she gets the chance to use it. She's scathing about his collapse into misery – 'Get your fucking finger out' is her chorus. But how – where?

Then there's the other detail, for inexorably the time is ticking towards twelve thirty when Mum and Josette will be turning up from Vieilleville all excited for the *entrée* he's promised them. He keeps looking over at Imo – his saviour – having unrealistic expectations of her powers, after the events of the last twenty-four hours. When she eventually comes back to him he can't believe she's empty-handed. He'd thought a couple of screenings and at least one of the good beach parties would be coming their way after all that chat – in the bag, surely? But no – she doesn't even stop, just whispers, 'Stick with me,' and hurries out on to the Croisette.

*

Imo thinks she may be on to a winner – it's up to Gav to catch her up and make the connections. The people standing right next to her were from British telly, she's not sure which company, but there's a cameraman with impressive apparatus locked on his shoulder, and a sound-girl with her equipment stashed into a trolley-bag, who'd been on her mobile for several minutes – 'All right, where are you?' she'd been saying. 'We're down with the Brits . . . Are you? . . . OK,' and then she'd turned to the cameraman, 'Dave's up at the Carlton Terrace – got the Bad Boys people all ready for their interview. We'd better split.'

Out on the Croisette, they haven't a notion they're being tailed.

'I've told him to wave,' says the girl. 'Keep waving!' she shouts into the phone, clamping her hand over her other ear so's she can concentrate on the answer. And she starts scooting along the pavement with the cameraman, plus Imo and Gav, in hot pursuit.

'If he's already on the terrace we won't see him from here,' says the cameraman, trying to zoom in on the Carlton as he goes.

'No, he's not, he's down in the street – he's going to get us in. WE'RE ON OUR WAY – KEEP WAVING!' she yells into the mobile, plunging through the crowd and using her trolley as a battering ram.

'Bad Boys' . . . 'Interview' . . . 'Get us in' are the three most pertinent gobbets of this eavesdropping, and Imo's intent on sticking like a leech.

By the time they've all four of them got to the main entrance of the Carlton, the girl is still bellowing, 'Keep waving!' into her phone, but Imo can already see the subject in question, a slightly familiar face – Dave Bruce from Youf TV or something? Not that she's exactly all that *au fait* with British media personalities, though when she has to go back home to the horrible house in Purley, the telly is her lone escape from the overall horror of it all, so she has been known to give it a go – especially in the long afternoons. And she's pretty sure this guy does some sort of jokey film and TV rundown aimed at the under-fifteens. Dave is waving frantically from the steps leading up to the terrace, but the girl isn't looking – she's got her head down and is still shouting, 'Keep waving,' and the guy's still swinging that bloody camera around like it would know something, and Imo just longs to grab both their stupid heads and crack them together, because why don't they stop panicking and just see what's staring them in the fucking face?

But in a way it's a blessing because Gav's now caught up with her, and as she hasn't time to explain, she just mutters out of the corner of her mouth, 'Whatever I do, stick with me,' and suddenly the other two have got the message and are heading towards the steps, where two big bouncers are very much on view in black sharp suits and even blacker, sharper shades wrapped around their heads so they look like bluebottles. And now Dave Bruce is leading the way, without even having to flash a pass, and Imo and Gav, being just a sliver behind the other two (so close, in fact, that Imo almost grazes the girl's sandalled heel), slip in behind them up the steps. So here they are, on the famed terrace of the Carlton and heading straight over to where the Bad Boys guys – the real ones this time – are seated in a corner, with loads of Perrier, just waiting to drop their pearls of wisdom to the Youth of Britain in the name of Blessed PR.

Phew.

*

In front of the Palais des Festivals, Alice and Josette are milling about. They've been waiting over an hour now, looking out for Gav and Imo, afraid they've missed them in all these crowds, milling about and getting nowhere. From the daily agenda, which Alice picked up at the Festival kiosk, they see that the *Hommage à William Prescott* is due to start at two thirty, and it's one thirty already. Alice leaves the quizzing to Josette and witnesses a deal of furious argument and shoulder-shrugging as the doormen turn her away and the women in the information office shrink behind the protection of their counters. It's just the way it is – without tickets you can't get in. Without passes you can't get in to see if you might get tickets. Impasse.

Gavin's reputation is already sinking fast. Alice is half livid, half resigned to the embarrassment of it all. But Josette is driven. Now she's asking passers-by if they might have a ticket going spare – particularly those beginning to line up for the event. Alice is even more embarrassed but for different reasons now: it's such a very un-Anglo-Saxon thing to do. The doormen don't like this pestering of their visitors either: another argument threatens to blow and Josette finds herself firmly led back down to the first level of barriers, frog-marched almost, leaching her elegant dignity by the second.

As two thirty approaches, she's almost hollow and bent with disappointment. It's the first time Alice has ever seen her anything but tall and confident – quite shocking in its way, her age suddenly revealed through anxiety and stress. In the road, the immaculate *gendarmerie* are already lining up in their braided *képis*, and the gathered crowd is surging forward – but only just so far as the barriers will allow. And here comes a big black limousine, and the door is opening, and several people from the *palais* have come down the steps, ready to greet, and Josette is straining to get a better view, using the base of the barrier as a step and leaning heavily on Alice's shoulder for support. And suddenly she's screaming out, 'Billy-Boy – Billy! It eez me! It eez *me*,' and Alice can't see a thing from down below, only a phalanx of minders guarding their precious hidden charge.

When they've gone, Josette lowers herself back to the ground and Alice reclaims her sore shoulder.

'Did you see 'im? My Billy-Boy – you see 'im?'

Alice decides to say she did – simpler.

''E is so – you know, I don't know 'ow to say this but you know 'e is somezing wonderful – what a man. You should 'ave known him at ze Embassy.'

Alice bites on the words 'In New Delhi?' for Josette looks stricken.

'I must get to 'im. 'Ow do you sink I can get to 'im?'

'It has to be possible to leave a message.'

''Ow? Where?'

'I'm not sure – at his hotel?'

'We don't know where 'e stay.'

'There must be some sort of contact office here at the *palais*?'

''Ow we get in?'

'That's something Gav *can* and damn well *will* do for us,' says Alice decisively, 'or he can find himself another freebie bed for the night,' but then, remembering that he already has, she clamps her mouth shut and wishes herself well rid of them all.

*

On the terrace of the Carlton Hotel, Youf TV as represented by Dave Bruce is well into its interview with the really rather charming producers from Bad Boys Productions. Imo and Gav sink down at a nearby table, and make themselves look busy and important. Imo does a lot of pretend-calling on her mobile, whilst Gav gets out the laptop and sets those orbs rolling again, whilst scribbling pretend notes on a pad. Neither talks to the other, as they strain to hear what's going on in the interview. All across the terrace, meetings are buzzing – American voices mingling with British and Australian. At the next table a woman with massive black hair is jabbering into her mobile in Italian, then impressively cross-translating the conversation for her German and Spanish companions, before delivering a complicated command to the waiter in French. Whatever she's asked for sounds expensive, and now the smiling uniformed waiter is heading towards them too. Gav groans and tries to think of something cheap to order. He goes for pastis – that's local and native – surely as inexpensive as anything? It arrives on a silver tray with its own little bowl of olives, a carafe of icy water, and a discreet bill for a hundred and ten francs.

Imo catches his look of pain. 'What you beefing about, chicken head?' she says. Chameleon-like she's latched on to the Youf TV lingo without even thinking. 'What else did you expect for the hottest seat in town? It's bloody good value for the company. Now, stop whingeing and *do* the biz.'

Easily said but yet again *how* to do the biz? Gav looks around hopelessly. How to break in? The Youf TV interview isn't the only one happening at this very moment. A woman's being quizzed to the right, tripod lights are being set up to the left, and immediately in front of them some deal must have come to a conclusion. There's a lot of noisy congratulation and hand-shaking going on, then one of the waiters arrives with tall fluted glasses like upturned trumpets and sets them out with elaborate care. A platter of strawberries is also laid with a silver sugar caster and a peppermill. There's a flourish of white damask napkin, a sense of ceremony and due deference, and Gav feels a stab of envy as the magnum of champagne arrives in its silver bucket on a stand. That's the way to do it. When you matter in this town that's what you get – deference and order and a platter of plump fresh strawberries to help the nectar down.

He gives up pretending to look important, and openly turns to stare as the ritual unfolds. The waiter is young, glamorous, pristine. He untwists the wire from the cork with professional precision, holding the bottle to one side – and that's when it happens. Without his exerting any additional pressure, the cork goes off with a tremendous crack and a fountain of champagne shoots up into the air, across their table and slap into Gav's lap and laptop. Everyone is instantly so aghast you'd have thought it was a bomb. The waiter is mortified – cringing with shame, now holding the still spewing bottle behind him, trying to explain he'd done nothing, nothing at all – and the men at the table are leaping to their feet, exclaiming over their wet trousers, though none is as soaked as Gav. Gav looks as if he's had a major urinary accident. Gav's crotch region is not a pretty sight, and Gav's laptop seems to have had a seizure, for the eyes have stopped turning.

Imo has escaped the worst of the flood, but for once she seems stuck for words, what with watching what's going on over there and wondering if anything can be done to help the situation here. For Gav is half rising from his seat to brush the liquid from his pants, then sinking down again in shame – no, oh, no – and he must be saying this out loud – 'Oh, *no*, oh, sodding, *no*' as he stares down at his wet-streaked crotch and then spies the paralysed laptop, and Imo, who's found her voice again, but is still stuck in Youf TV mode, says, 'Chill – just chill. Stop bugging out – it'll dry in a minute.' And Gav's pointing at the laptop and thinking, That won't and it cost me an arm and a leg and then some . . . and more waiters are gathering to apologize and mop up and down, and more champagne is heading this way in compensation, and altogether everyone's knickers are in the most terrible twist. But apart from Gav, they're all loving it, *really*, because when you spend all your days creating ersatz drama there's nothing like a bit of the real thing to add spice and anecdote to your life.

OK – being bombed in the Balkans it ain't, but this is a tale which'll go down a treat at Spago's or the Groucho, so everyone's already in the mood to forgive and forget, and the waiter's being comforted – not his fault, rogue bottle, just one of those things – and, yeah, we're all friends together and we'll look back on this one day and say, 'Remember when . . .?'

Then the guy at the other table, who'd had his back towards Imo and Gav but who'd also taken the brunt of the champagne attack, gets to his feet and turns around, also slightly self-consciously aware of the leaking-nappy look he's currently sporting, and starts to say something to Gav – and it's probably going to be of the 'Hope you're all right – anything we can do?' sort of order so that Gav can put in a plea for his laptop and consequential damage and start to mention tricky words like 'sue' and 'insurance' – when Imo says, 'Hi, Theo,' and the guy says, 'Hi, little Mouse! I don't *believe* it,' and bends down to do the double cheek-kissing business.

And would you, could you whack it? There's this big guy, big as in tall, and fleshy with it, thick thatch of auburn hair and an accent like victoria-plum jam with knobs on, and he turns out to be the son of Verona, that other old biddy at the Maison Puce. He's Theo Grange – her own very darling boy. And just at first, Gav thinks this is fan-fucking-tastic, because this is the kind of thing you read about, a touch of serendipity in your life or – what do they call it? that astrology malarkey – the magnetism of the stars, because Theo's actually staying here at the Carlton, and it's *his* client Aziz, who's just made the big film deal they were all about to celebrate. And Theo's here because he's in charge of this Aziz's investments and, would you believe it?, this Aziz likes to throw it about a bit – *mad* about film, I mean *mad* about it (wonderful or what? Gav's brain cells are *boiling*). And, hey, what's *that*? The question is directed to Gav's laptop, which has dried out in the blasting heat of the sun, so that the turning orbs have started winking again – which is, phew, kind of a relief, because it's all very well talking words like 'sue' and 'insurance' but bloody hard to make things stick when you get right down to it. But then Theo's calling over to Aziz and saying, 'Hey, come and get a look at this,' and suddenly here is Gav right in the middle of the Carlton Terrace with a full audience, because by now everyone's involved, from the Youf TV bods all the way to the waiters, and Gav is suddenly pitching *Deadeyes* for his life, flying high and thinking, Come on, I've cracked it this time, baby – I'm going to the stars,' only suddenly he's finished, and everybody's laughing and smiling, the champagne's being poured – but that's it.

Nobody says a thing. Suddenly they're talking about screenings and invites, and how's your trousers?, looking sympathetically at his crotch and Gav wants to scream, 'Sod the bloody trousers – what about my film?' and, worse than that, this Theo guy has slid his beefy arm round Imo's shoulders – keeps calling her 'Little Mouse,' the fart, the God-awful rugger-bugger – and Imo's smiling up, all soft and flirty, and letting her voice slip out of Youf TV and into Patsy Kensit, which is really rotten because she never did that for *him*, and as it happens he's been known to consider murder in the cause of Patsy Kensit. Justice or what?

*

Alice and Josette are having a hot, tetchy afternoon. Alice's feet are blistered fore and aft by the new gold pumps, and Josette's been hauling her to every stationer in town in search of the perfect writing-paper on which to express the delicate intensity of her sentiments for Billy-Boy. Her eventual choice – violet with an aubergine border – looks, to Alice, wildly unsuitable, a shady mix of Woolworth's and In Memoriam. Nevertheless they trail back down to the Croisette, where Josette settles on a bench in full view of the *palais* to settle to her task of composition.

She insists on Alice translating this into what she calls 'embassy *Eeenglish*', though as she sounds so utterly charming in the flesh, Alice feels it would be much better just to write the way she talks. It takes Josette nine goes to get it to her satisfaction and there are only ten sheets of paper in the packet. Alice doesn't relish having to limp back to the stationer's for additional supplies and heaves a relieved sigh once it's done, all the while scanning around for Gav.

By now Josette's opinion of her *adorable* leetle boy has sunk to *merde*, and Alice is weary of apologizing. However, as he remains their only means of Festival contact, he'll still just have to do. Naturally he could be anywhere in the town, but the *palais* is the hub of most events, and if he's going to be attending anything he'll surely have to come here at some time. She's been looking out for two people, of course, Gav *and* Imo as a pair, for that's how they'd left this morning. But it's a lone Gavin she now spies, climbing the steps towards the Festival office, looking depressed. She crams her swollen feet back in the pumps and, leaving Josette on the bench, totters up to catch him.

'Hi, Mum – you're still here.' At least he has the grace to look abashed.

'We've been here on and off since twelve thirty – as arranged,' says Alice sharply. 'How *could* you?'

'Look, I'm really sorry, Mum. I mean, it was hopeless – I did try, honestly, but it's all completely *hopeless*. I don't know why I came, Mum – I don't know where to start . . .'

'This isn't about the tickets for Josette at all, is it? This is about *you*.'

This time he has the grace to deepen his abashment to a full-blown blush. 'Yes – all right – I'm sorry – it's been such a pig of a day.'

'For all of us – just look at her.' Alice points out the slumped, defeated form of Josette.

'Yeah – you didn't get in, then?'

'Do we look as if we did?'

'Yeah – well, I'm really, really sorry – I just don't – I mean, I thought I knew how to work the system – for her as well. Okay, maybe not, maybe I didn't try that hard – but I couldn't even work it for me, right? I thought it was all a piece of cake and it wasn't . . .'

'Well, here's something you *can* do, Mr Piece of Cake, with your Full Accreditation.'

Alice tweaks the official pass still dangling round his neck. 'You can take this letter into the publicity office or wherever – whatever, *who*ever – you understand me, Gav?

You can take this and make certain it gets passed on to William Prescott's people. Got that?'

'All right, Mum, got that.'

The women sit and wait on their bench, It doesn't take him that long. Only about ten minutes later he's coming back down from the main *palais* entrance with a thumbs-up. Alice is immediately suspicious after today's experiences – could it have been that easy? – but Josette is so desperate she's prepared to believe anything. If Gav tells her, hand on heart, that the letter is to be passed on to William Prescott's office this very evening, well, she's going to believe every word. She may even reinstate him in her affections.

'Where's Imo?' Alice now has a chance to ask.

'Oh, gone off – met a friend.'

'Oh – girlfriend?'

'No.'

Alice waits for him to tell her more, but as nothing is volunteered she lets it drop, aware that she suddenly feels lighter – well, let's face it, Imo isn't the *ideal* prospect for a daughter-in-law.

'Well, we'll be heading back now,' she says. 'We've just about had it.'

'Yeah – me too,' says Gav and, to her amazement, joins them on their tired homeward trek.

Back in Vieilleville, they hobble down to the quay to get some air and supper, though as all three of them seem terminally broke, they limit this to bread and *tapenade* as a snack with their beers. It's just as they're leaving that Alice has her vision of Verona, walking in the deep shadow cast by the battlements. It's only a back view so maybe she's mistaken. She – if it *is* she – is with a man at least half a head shorter, with long pale hair, wearing the tiniest shorts ever sewn and very little else. He has his arm draped across her shoulders. By the time Alice has alerted the others, the vision has disappeared round the corner. A mirage?

*

Back at the flat, Alice and Gav go through the ludicrous palaver of blowing up the Lilo, and getting themselves showered and settled, exhausted and silent. In the dark, Alice stretches her aching limbs and thinks – about the day, about Josette, about Verona. It's peaceful and silent. Silent? Gav's not snoring . . .?

On the Lilo, Gav is wide awake, not thinking of the day – that's been too much of a let-down, put it away and look ahead . . . and that's what he's suddenly doing again because he might have had a brainwave. It came to him when they were walking back to Mum's. Coming up the rue d'Espoir, the whole building was in darkness – even Imo's flat, which made him cringe a bit, not wanting to think about her with that fat fart at the Carlton. All in darkness – except for a light gleaming right at the top. Not that you could see anything else from down here, just that light. Hope Boscombe's light. Hope Boscombe . . . and that's when it hits because maybe, after all, salvation's been here all along – right, so to speak, on his own doorstep.

23

Where Have You Been All the Day? (Billy-Boy – Billy-Boy?)

In the morning, Gav refuses to be roused. Alice tries to wake him and get him to co-operate, but all he does is groan and roll over. Goodness, but he *is* getting so like his father. She's forced to work round him, just about managing to fold up the sofa-bed and then sliding the Lilo plus its sleeping cargo a foot or so into the middle of the floor, so that she can get the shower-room door open a crack.

Once dressed, she goes up to knock on Verona's door – increasingly aware of the irony that it's now she who is coming after Verona and not the other way around. But there's still no answer and still no key in her lock. This is odder and odder. Then she goes down to the square to empty her rubbish into the municipal bin. It's now, as she's returning, that she bumps into her, coming out of the main front door, with an armful of post.

'Morning!' says Verona, flapping the envelopes as if all is normal.

'Hello! Gosh, I *am* glad to see you,' says Alice, surprised to realize she actually means it.

'And I'm glad to see you, Alice – all right, are you?'

'Yes – oh, yes, I'm fine – but how about *you*?'

'Oh, I'm fine too, never been finer,' and in fact she does look quite peachy, though maybe it's just that orange plaid tent dress which casts such a glow.

'I've got bags of news,' says Alice, expecting Verona's usual antennae to start quivering at such a prospect. But no.

'Me too,' is all Verona says, so that Alice is forced to turn inquisitor herself.

'Did I spot you last night on the quay?'

'You might have done.'

'With a man – would that be you?'

'Expect so . . .' and again that's all. Maddening.

'Well, go on, then, Verona, do tell,' says Alice.

Verona pinches her lips together tightly for one whole second, but then loses some internal battle. 'He's called Yogi,' she says.

'He *can't* be,' says Alice.

'Why not? I *knew* you'd laugh. Why shouldn't he be called Yogi? All sorts of people are called Yogi.'

'Like who?'

'Like that bear in the cartoon – *and* that American baseball player. I don't suppose people laughed at him.'

'No. All right. All *right* . . .'

'Yes. Well. So. Anyway, we met in the market – he was at the *saucisson* stall and I could tell he didn't realize he was buying that donkey stuff so I intervened.'

'What donkey stuff?'

'That Corsican one – made of old donkey, *de l'âne*.'

'I thought that was just a brand name.'

'Don't tell me you've tried it?'

'I rather think I might – quite, well, piquant.'

'Ugh – I don't know how you could.'

'I don't think I'd made the full donkey connection.'

'Well, there you are, that's what I mean – that's what I was rescuing Yogi from, because he was just about to buy seven hundred and fifty grams of the stuff, and that's an awful lot of sausage to chuck out once you've realized your mistake. Anyway, he was very grateful and absolutely *charming* – and later when I was passing Flipper's Bar, he popped out to say hello, and it just sort of took off from there.'

'What nationality?'

'English – from Leigh-on-Sea. And he's got a *boat*.'

'No. Not *here*?'

'Moored down at the quay. It's *bliss*. You've no idea of the fun – I can't tell you the difference it makes. It's a whole community – you get invited on to all the other boats. It really makes you feel part of it – gives you an entirely different perspective once you're *involved* and not just looking in. Well, you know how often one's just walked around staring at them, especially in the evenings, sort of imagining the goings-on – not any longer I can tell you. Now I *know*.'

'Gosh. Lucky you.'

'I *know*. I can't tell you how fortunate I feel – but lucky *you* too. I'm sure I can include you all when he's not so busy.'

'He works down here?'

'He's always terribly busy – bits of this and that – and now with the Film Festival he's off to Cannes today, he's taking all these people . . .'

'And you as well?'

Verona gives Alice rather an exasperated glare, 'Well, of *course*. He wouldn't be going without me – we're *inseparable*.'

'Gosh.'

'What do you mean "gosh"?'

'Just seems a bit quick that's all – sorry, that's all I meant – to be inseparable, I mean . . .'

'At our time of life I shouldn't have thought there's a moment to lose.'

'Perhaps not.'

'Anyway I must rush – we're embarking in an hour.'

'"Embarking" – gosh.'

'Alice, I do wish you'd stop saying "gosh" like that – whatever's got into you?'

'Sorry – no, I really am, no, that's great.'

'Now I must get a move on – got to put together a *leetle peek-neek*.'

'Oh.'

'For the voyage – nothing like the open sea to build up an appetite – a little treat for the crew.'

'The *crew* – ' but Alice manages to swallow the next gosh before it has a chance to slip out.

*

Alice has a sudden sense of what it must be like to be a Verona, because she can't wait to pass on the news to somebody – only to whom? Imo's not in and when she gets back upstairs, Gav is still deeply in the Land of Nod. She looks down at him now, quite fondly despite everything –

that topknot he always had as a toddler has reasserted itself, sticking up on the crown of his head. Even in mid-snore she can't help but love him. It's then that the telephone starts ringing and she has to clamber over his prone body to get to it.

'Aleeese!' Unmistakably Josette on the line.

'Hello.'

'Aleese, I 'ave 'eard from 'im – my Billy-Boy.'

'*No* – I don't *believe* it.'

'Why you no believe it?' says Josette. *'Why?'*

'Sorry – no nothing, just a manner of speaking – how amazing. Tell me all.'

'I went to the Café Bleu this morning and they 'ave message from his assistant zat I am to telephone – and so I do – and I speak to 'im.'

'You actually spoke to Billy-Boy himself – how *amazing*! What did he sound like?'

'No, Aleese, I speak to ze assistant but he tell me zat Billy-Boy want to make ze contact – and you will never guess where 'e is staying! On a yackt!'

'A "yackt"?'

'*Mais oui* – a yackt out in ze bay.'

'Oh, a *yacht*.'

'Yes, a YACKT – zat's what I tell you – so you see we would never 'ave found 'im no matter where we look yesterday so my message was good idea, yes?'

'Brilliant.'

'And ze assistant say zat Billy ask me to have lunch wiz 'im.'

'No?' This really *is* news. 'When?'

'Today – at Cannes – you will come?'

'*Me?* Gosh – why?'

'He ask me to bring a guest.'

'Surely he means a man in that case?'

'Why I bring a man? Aleese, zat wife of his is dead – I read in *Nice-Matin* zis morning in ze article about the *hommage*. She die last year, Aleese –'e is free man again, 'e is probably sad, sad man, I sink maybe he need me, no? And I need my *leetle Aleeese* because you are *Eeenglish* and my Billy-Boy is *Eeenglish* too – *eh, voilà*, you will come? Zis lunch is on ze yackt – you will be my leetle friend, Aleese, you will 'elp me through?'

*

There's no time to wash the transparent white linen, but it's still the only thing in her wardrobe that will do for a yacht at Cannes. She gives it a bit of a sponge down with a damp tea-towel, then irons it on a blanket on her table, still having to manoeuvre around the sleeping Gav.

She's about to write him a note when he comes to, heaving himself up on one elbow and yawning. 'Hello, Mum.'

'Hello, Gav – I'm just off to Cannes again.'

'Then you're a glutton for punishment.'

'Got an invitation this time – on to William Prescott's yacht.'

'No kidding.' Gav flops back on to the Lilo, shutting his eyes again.

'Don't you want to know how?'

'Letter did the trick?'

'Yes, it rather looks as if it did.'

'Well, I managed to get something right, then, didn't I?'

'Yes, darling, you did. Are you going back to Cannes too, later on?'

'No, Mum, I'm going to stay here – ' yawning ' – I need some time to think – get my head together, plan my strategy . . .'

'Right, Gavin,' says Alice, amazed that her only son has anything as directed as a 'strategy' up his sleeve, 'I'll leave you a set of keys.'

*

As soon as she's gone, Gav shakes himself awake and jumps into the shower, clicking with ideas. He's got a strategy all right – been plotting it half the night. Now it's a question of checking his facts, then sorting out a tactical advance.

As soon as he's dressed, he gets out all the bumph he'd picked up from the British Pavilion. In amongst the printed glossy flyers and brochures is exactly what he's looking for, a booklet, *The British Film Catalogue*, but for the previous year. He leafs through quickly – nothing under 'Features', but here at the back under 'Shorts & Documentaries' he finds what he's looking for. *Focal Point*, a TV documentary . . . fly-on-the-wall . . . consumer nightmares . . . produced by a company called 'Hope Springs Ltd' with an address in Chiswick. Producer Jan Tomelty, executive producer . . . Hope Boscombe. Yes–*Yes*–YES – Hope B. *is* a player.

*

Josette looks a picture on the train back to Cannes, stunningly dressed in something softly apricot and crêpey, with her blonde hair teased back into wispless perfection. She'd eyed the third consecutive appearance of Alice's white linen a bit balefully, particularly as Alice has been forced to swap the golden pumps for a quite sturdy pair of trainers in view of yesterday's crop of blisters. Still, Alice feels she's only coming along as a sort of token Ugly Sister, so it surely can't matter all that much.

Josette is, in reality, a seething bag of nerves. She'd rushed down to Chez Patrice for an emergency hair appointment, but after that has been forcing herself into a surface state of calm. The last thing she wants is to arrive breathless and perspiring on Billy-Boy's yacht. Cool elegance is what she wishes to project – that lightness of look and touch she's had to struggle so hard to maintain through all these long years, with minimal resources.

Sometimes she thinks she's truly a wonder. One can understand the *rich* being able to put on a good front – with sufficient funds, almost nothing is beyond the realms of possibility. But for her, without even a permanent home to call her own, well, at sixty-whatever-she-is (don't even *think* the precise number, let alone expose it for public scrutiny) she's a little miracle. And at long last the chance has come for her to offer up that miracle to its intended recipient. No wonder she's nervous.

*

Back in Vieilleville, Gav is searching through Alice's flat. Where's her address book? Where's the telephone directory? Where's Hope's number? After a fruitless search, he has to rethink. What would be the best way to make contact? Mum says she hardly knows the woman and, in any case, as a *bona-fide* professional in the tough world of media, you don't *want* your introductions set up by your mum, for fuck's sake, do you? You want to be up and out there on your own.

Write her a note? But then these crazy doors don't have proper letterboxes, so he couldn't do it right now-this-very-minute, he'd have to stick a stamp on and post it, wait until tomorrow for the mail to arrive. And he doesn't have the time for all that – he's up for it *now* and he's desperate. All those clichés come to mind – striking while the iron's hot. He sticks his head out of the window and looks along the road towards the other tower and Hope's front door. Ummm – perhaps he could just brazen it out and ring her bell? But Mum says she's quite private, she'd probably resent it, might even frighten her – don't want to put her back up before he's even got started. The best thing would be if she could just sort of come upon him by accident – yeah, he can see the whole set-up, could film it right now . . . There's this young guy – correction – *good-looking* young guy, sitting in the sun, picturesque setting – palm trees and cobblestones – but he's not lying back catching the rays, he's . . . well, what *is* he doing? Yeah, he's writing in a notebook, absorbed and centred, and by his side is his laptop, open and switched on, displaying this hypnotic vision – the turning, blinking orbs of *Deadeyes* – and the great Hope Boscombe comes out of her door, just strolling along and they exchange a casual glance – they smile (and he's got such a horny smile) and then she's captured by the eyes, mesmerized, asks the question, several questions . . . and before you know it half a million in the bag. Well . . . it's worth a try, isn't it?

*

In Cannes, Josette and Alice follow the instructions given by Billy-Boy's assistant and head down to the quay. Well away from the Film Festival razzmatazz, it juts out from the old town, a finger of concrete garnished with the usual ranks of pleasure- and fishing-craft. The tender to the *Golden Isle* is due to meet them at one thirty and Josette has got them there an hour early – 'just in case'. In case of what, though?

Alice props herself on a mooring bollard and watches the traffic of boats. There's no shade out here at the end of the quay and the sun is hammering down. Josette can feel her pulse beginning to quicken with nerves, the skin under her breasts dampening with sweat. Not what she's wanted at all – keep calm, keep very, very *calm*.

Then as Alice stands up, Josette catches sight of a great black oily smudge on her bottom. The calm snaps.

'*Aleese!*' The oily smudge is pointed out for all to observe. Several fishermen look up to see what the drama's about.

Josette is dabbing at the smudge with her hankie. Why go and wear something so *stupid* – white linen – on a day like today? *Why?* The smudge is getting worse under the ministrations of the hankie. Then a solution occurs. 'You must make like your Royal Family yes? Like your Prince *Philippe* – wiz 'ands behind ze back, so? Once we are sitting at ze table it won't show.'

'I don't think I can spend the entire afternoon with my hands behind my back, Josette.'

'But you *must*! Zat way you can cover ze dirt – we don't want Billy-Boy sinking you are not *chic*.'

'I couldn't care less what Billy-Boy thinks of me.'

'But *I* do.'

'Surely I can just explain. We can have a laugh about it – I'll make it into a funny story.'

'I don' want amusing *histoires*, Aleese, I want you wiz me, as my friend – at ze *back*, wiz 'ands at ze back too, you understand?'

*

Imo's had a lovely late breakfast in Theo's room at the Carlton, brought in on one of those trolleys swathed in white damask, which gets turned into a table by the waiter. Admittedly Theo did stick her under the covers while all this was going on – said he didn't want to 'rub their noses in it', the 'it' being that she's spent the night here as a not-necessarily-official guest. Still, once he'd allowed her to surface, she could wander round in his lovely thick towelling dressing-gown and sip freshly squeezed orange juice and nibble hot brioche while she spied on the Cannes craziness already whirling down below on the Croisette. That's definitely one of the perks of life with Theo Grange – you get all the trimmings.

She'd had the trimmings last night too – amazing party up at some villa in the hills, all done up like an ad for Fry's Turkish Delight. She'd even been provided with a *cosi* – shocking pink chiffon hareem trousers, a yashmak with sequins and a ruby in her belly-button. Bloody lovely. Champagne coming out of her earholes, dancing away with Theo, with his client Aziz and God alone knows who else – whole load of media bods.

And now she's squeezing back into her black clingy jersey crop-top with the new addition of her 'Screen International' baseball cap because they're just off out. Theo says he wants to 'troll around, Little Mouse' – yeah, he's quite a sweetheart in his way.

*

Ivy Prosper's having an exciting day so far.

That special plane trip for a start. First Class – smoked salmon and caviar – hot and cold running bubbly all the way – now there's an experience you wouldn't necessarily get in a month of Sundays. Mind you, it meant getting up in the middle of the night to get to Heathrow on time. Then meeting the people from *Woman's Way* in a VIP lounge – how's *that* for classy? Then flown with all the other prize-winners down to Nice airport, and then the helicopter ride directly into Monaco – and that was a first. Quite nice, really, as long as you didn't look. If you looked it made your tummy go all funny. She wasn't that struck on it, really, not to tell you the truth, though now at least she's done it, so if it ever crops up in conversation she'll be able to say, 'Yes – quite nice, really. When I go down to Monte I usually take the chopper,' which'll sound quite good at the Landlords' Convention in Bournemouth.

And they'd looked after her beautifully, the magazine

people from *Woman's Way*, you couldn't fault them. Quite exciting to meet them, really, almost the best bit of winning the competition. She's taken that book every single month since she was twenty – guided her through thick and thin, everything from men to the menopause, with wallpapering, recipes, childbirth and orgasm thrown in along the way. You'd have to admit that things have changed, though, wouldn't you? Whatever they said about the sixties and the Summer of Love, you didn't go on about your orgasms in 1967 – well, not in public down the Old Kent Road you didn't. So it was quite a thrill to meet them all, though they were a lot younger than she'd been expecting – girls, really. Probably in their early thirties like her Imogen, but then they all seem to hang on to their girlishness a lot longer these days. Look at her Imogen – thirty-three and still acting like she was seventeen. But, mind you, these magazine girls really had something about them – nice careers, going somewhere, not like Imogen.

You could begin to despair of Imogen. Never could seem to get herself together. Floating, always floating. Such a puzzle that girl. Always has been. A puzzle from the word go – a puzzle before conception, really. It would have been lovely if Imogen had turned out like one of these magazine girls – nicely dressed, beautifully spoken – and it's not as if she couldn't if she'd tried. She's certainly had the opportunities – she couldn't claim she hadn't. Ivy doesn't know where she went wrong with her. Can't see there's anything she'd actually have done different if she had her time over. It's not as if she hasn't bent over backwards to give her the opportunities, and you'd have thought that convent would've knocked some sense into her. But there you go.

And now she's in this taxi on her way to Vee-elle-ville – well, that's the way she said it to the driver, just the way it's spelt. Of course, Imo always says it different – something like 'Vee-ay-veel', which is what the taxi driver said too and he had a good old laugh – nice boy. And this road's amazing, really, high up in these cliffs looking over the sea – well, you couldn't really call them cliffs, could you? More like mountains – very steep anyway. Hadn't Princess Grace died driving off one of these things? Not surprising, now she's seeing them for real, not surprising at all. That was the subject of the competition, of course, the Monaco Royal Family, and she could have answered any question they'd thrown at her upside down and blindfold, because she'd always taken an interest since she'd seen Grace Kelly in *High Society* – lovely film, lovely woman. *There* was someone who'd got her act together – though of course *she*'d had difficulties with daughters too, hadn't she?

*

The tender to the *Golden Isle* is late – it's already one forty-five and Josette's wondering if she can hold this position much longer. On the basis that Billy-Boy himself may be coming to meet her, she's standing with practised precision, looking out to sea at a south-westerly angle, so that any approaching vessel will get the full effect of her magnificence . . . Only it's making her hip hurt and she's beginning to wish he'd hurry up.

Alice is wandering up and down the quay, not daring to repeat the convenience of sitting on a bollard in case she smudges oil on her other buttock. To pass the time she's having a really good look-out for Verona and her Yogi – but as she's no idea what sort of vessel theirs might be, nor its name, she doesn't have much hope . . . Now if amongst these scattered Red Ensigns there was an orange tartan tent dress flying at half-mast, that might give her a clue . . .

She wanders among the smaller yachts. How amazing that Verona's found herself part of this world. She knows from inspecting the window displays in various Vieilleville yacht brokerages that words like 'small' are pretty relative in this context. Even second-hand 'small' cruisers seem to cost something like a quarter of a million pounds sterling, and the medium-sized can easily creep up to the one or two million mark. Anything really big doesn't have a price tag at all, though she's heard sums like twenty and forty million mentioned. Silly, funny money with no relation to the texture of real life at all.

And now at last a long white speedboat is heading directly towards them with fat gold lettering along its bows – easy to spot – *Golden Isle*. Josette has a weird eerie grin stuck to her face, which she removes once she sees that there's no Billy-Boy on board, only a dashing young man in a white uniform with epaulettes on his shirt. Once she's had a good look at this paragon, however, she sticks the grin back on her face, takes his hand to step over the gunwale, and sort of floats aboard – rather like those women one used to see on *Come Dancing* doing the old-time section in tulle.

Alice is relieved to sit down and hide her oil-stained

bottom in the stern, while Josette settles herself in the cockpit. And then they're off, the boat turning slowly, then sweeping out of the harbour towards the open sea, with the engine gunning. Alice feels wonderfully lordly. Way out in the bay are several really big boats – which one is going to be Billy-Boy's?

Josette is animatedly gabbling in French to the lustrous young man, and Alice has been left to concentrate on the ride, and the glory of their destination. It looks as if they are heading towards a real whopper – more ship than mere yacht, spectacular, gleaming white and studded with gadgetry, radar domes and two helicopters parked on top. Gradually Josette has grown quieter, but Alice doesn't take much notice, because now they are coming to a sea-level landing-stage at the stern of the boat. A giant sign in three-dimensional letters smothered in gold leaf announces *Golden Isle*, just in case there's any remaining doubt.

Now Josette has turned and Alice sees that she's gone a peculiar colour – the shade of unripe greengages. Well, she supposes it was quite a rough trip once they got out of the harbour's protection, the speedboat bouncing from wave to wave, though Alice, not being prey to seasickness, has loved it.

They are helped out on to the landing-stage. Alice cranes her neck back to get a full view. Snaking above them is an extraordinary staircase like something out of a Busby Berkeley film, with swirly chrome railings and matching lollipop lamps instead of newel posts, layered right up to the top deck. And it's to the top deck that they are now bidden, by smiling uniformed flunkies.

Josette has lost her greengage hue, though she's looking very pale. The yacht is much steadier than the speedboat, though Alice can feel an underlying swell, and staggers slightly as she starts to follow Josette up the stairs, trying to keep one hand clamped to her buttock to disguise the offending oily mark. If it weren't for this encumbrance, she'd almost be tempted to try and tap-dance up – like that crazy routine in William Prescott's *Rhythm of Broadway.* But, as it is, decorum prevails.

On the top deck, a party is already under way. There are lots of Birds of Paradise plus a smattering of the sort of small, stocky men they saw all over Cannes yesterday with their briefcases and mobiles; also various Arab gentlemen in impressive robes and headdresses. Right in the middle is a round, bald fellow, a mixture of Buddha and Winston Churchill, in a white djellabah with gold frogging. Josette gasps and cries, '*Billy!*' and the Buddha turns round and says, 'My-oh-my, it's Toots! Hi there, Toots! Long time no see,' in a very American accent (so much for the glories of the *Eeenglish*) and suddenly he's slapping her on the back like some old veteran comrade-at-arms and telling everybody that he and Toots went back a long, long way. Then he's calling her 'Old Girl', and he's yelling for someone to come over – and someone does . . . A stunning creature who must be all of nineteen, with a yard of shiny black hair, about six feet tall in stockinged feet (only currently even higher on spindle heels). She comes tripping over, and starts rubbing Billy-Boy's pate with her thumbs.

'I'd like to introduce my fiancée. This is Marsha – is she a babe or is she a babe?' says Billy-Boy – and Josette, who'd been gripping his arm, suddenly lets go, as if she's about to shake the babe's hand, and promptly throws up all down the white djellabah.

The whole company erupts. Josette is apologizing and gasping, looking greener and greener. Billy-Boy is standing with his arms stuck out on either side yelling, 'Someone get this thing off me!' Flunkeys are rushing from all over the place – some to see to Josette, some to clear up the puke, someone running to get another djellabah. The babe Marsha is trying to get Josette to come and lie down, pulling her towards the staircase, and Josette starts slapping at her hand, shrieking, 'Let go, you bitch!' only being Josette it's coming out 'you *beeeetch*!' and by now she's looking really green, like boiled cabbage, as she totters down and away.

Meanwhile one of the flunkeys is offering Alice a tray of drinks, which turn out to be a choice of orange juice, Tizer or Vimto because the *Golden Isle* isn't owned by Billy-Boy at all, he's only a guest. The real owner is one of the elegant Arabs, and because of his strict adherence to Islam, no alcohol is allowed on board. But there's no Coca-Cola either because, as he told Alice most charmingly, he went to school in England and retains a nostalgia for the drinks of his childhood tuck-shop.

Despite everything, Alice is really rather enjoying herself, currently discussing the glories of Dartmoor with the Arab magnate, when Josette comes back with her hair all roughed up, most of her makeup washed off, and the skin beneath unhealthily waxen. She hisses at Alice that they must go. The babe Marsha suggests (very kindly in the circumstances, considering Josette had been so rude) that surely they should wait until she's feeling a little better. And then Billy-Boy returns in a different djellabah, and pats Josette on the back a bit cautiously as if he's afraid she's a bomb that might go off at any moment. And that seems to do it for Josette says, 'No, we must go at once,' and she and Alice hobble back down the staircase in full view of everyone leaning over the railings to get a look, with Alice hanging on to Josette, trying to keep her upright.

The trip back to the quay is ghastly. Josette hangs her head over the side, retching every minute or two and says she wishes she was dead – and that Billy-Boy was dead too. But that the bitch babe Marsha is *beyond* death. Purgatory being much too good for her.

*

Back in Vieilleville, Gav has positioned himself across the street from the Maison Puce, with what he hopes is a credible set-up. He's brought Mum's two small stools down, one for him and one for the laptop, and stuck them on the narrow pavement. He's also fished around in her cupboards and come up with a pad of cartridge paper so that he can look as though he's sketching – although why he'd be sketching with an open, switched-on laptop as his companion is something he can't quite resolve. He can't sit in the street pretending to write – the bench in the place d'Espoir is the only suitable possibility for a writer's location, but if and when Hope Boscombe emerges from her door, she might easily turn left instead of right, in which case she wouldn't come down as far as the square at all and would miss him entirely. In the street directly outside the house, though, he has a fighting chance of catching her eye whatever she does, even if he's in danger of getting his feet run over.

After two hours of this, with no sign of her, he's already growing weary. He can't draw for toffee, but he's got to have something on show to add to his credibility. He makes a miserable stab at the view towards the square. Every half-minute he looks up to see if anything's happening – after all this effort it would be maddening to miss her – but still the door remains implacably shut.

It's getting hotter too – the sun's moving round, catching the top of his head. What he wouldn't give for a beer – but if he goes back inside he'll have to take the whole boiling with him then start all over again – and in the interim she's bound to come out and he'll have missed her. Better stick it out, boy.

It's then that he sees a small, neat woman in a navy blue suit with gleaming white handbag and shoes come rather warily along the opposite pavement from the square. She's checking each of the doors as she goes, then looking at a piece of paper in her hand. She stops at the other door of the Maison Puce. She stands back and gives it a very obvious once-over, then steps up to the doorbells and pushes one of them. Could this be a friend of Mum's? He watches for a moment, loath to let his attention drift from Hope Boscombe's door, but also knowing that the bells don't work down there. She's giving them another go now – pushing . . . stepping back, looking. Perhaps he'd better say something. But how – in French? What's the French for 'not working'? He ought to remember that one . . . and doorbell?

No, but he can remember 'bell' and shouts out, '*Le cloche – non.*' The woman jumps – she obviously hadn't noticed him in the shadows. '*Le cloche* – not working,' shouts Gav now.

'Oh, you're English – what a relief.' She comes puffing over – not what he wants at all.

'Yeah,' he mumbles, trying not to look too welcoming.

'Do you know the people here – I mean in that building, number eight?'

'Yeah – well, some of them. My mum's got a flat there.'

'So's my daughter, Imogen.'

'You're Imo's mother?'

'Oh, you know her, then. Isn't that nice? Yes, Ivy Prosper, pleased to meet you. I can't tell you what a relief it is to hear an English voice. I've broken away from my group in Monaco and I may just have bitten off more than I can chew. I've had such a long day – do you mind if I sit down?' and before he can stop her, she's put his precious laptop on the pavement, and has flopped on to the other stool. Oh, *no* – this is *not* part of the master-plan.

Ivy Prosper ferrets around in her large white handbag and produces a small battery hand-fan, which she switches on and starts waving in front of her face. 'I mean, I had high hopes, really, when I started out this morning – well, really my morning started at Heathrow, only to tell you the truth it doesn't feel like it, it feels like the week before last but this place was further than I thought – and when we first come in at the top of the hill there I got all excited. That nice new bit's quite smart, I thought, nice blocks of flats, quite exclusive and classy, so I really got my hopes up, but then the taxi come further and further down here – I have to say it's fulfilling my worst nightmares and I've had a few where Imogen's concerned, I can tell you. Would you like a Polo mint?' She starts fishing around in the bag again.

Much as Gav would like to tell her to piss off, he'd almost kill for a Polo mint at this particular moment – well, no, he'd kill for a Kronenberg, but a Polo mint will have to do. He accepts one, still trying to keep his gaze fixed on Hope Boscombe's door, rather than Imo's mum's hot, damp face.

'Mind you, it give me a bit of a turn seeing our name up by the doorbell like that – "Prosper" – in a foreign land, so to speak. What my old dad would've thought, eh? Dear old Ivan Prosper – that was my dad – he was in fruit and veg, pioneered the slogan, stuck it up over all his shops – "I. Prosper" – always looked eye-catching and cheerful too, specially in the war with rationing – always raised a laugh. Of course, he'd have liked to turn it into "I. Prosper and Son" but there you are, had to make do with "and Daughter" instead. So you know my Imogen?' She's come to an abrupt halt, panting slightly, still waving the fan about.

'A bit, yeah.'

'You wouldn't know where she is, would you? Only I come over from Monaco on the off-chance . . .'

'No, I don't know. I saw her yesterday – in Cannes.'

'Oh? That's more hopeful – not Italy?'

'Italy?'

'Only when I rang to say I was coming she said she'd be in Italy . . .'

'Oh, well, I don't know anything about that – '

'But Cannes is only just down the road, really?'

'Not that close.'

'But in comparison to Italy . . .'

'Italy's not that far either – the other way – '

'Milan, I think she said.'

'Oh – well, much closer than that.'

'Only I get the feeling she doesn't really want to see me – well, it's more than a feeling, I *know* she doesn't want to see me – but she's artful, always has been, and now I get a look at where she's living I'm not surprised – I mean, look at the state of it!'

'The state of what?'

'The building. That plaster all needs hacking off for a start – God knows what's going on under there, it all needs doing with a good modern composite – I'm in property so I'd know. I mean it may look quaint – but as a place for living?'

Gav, who's now nursing his laptop and trying to maintain his vigil, feels a sudden defensive stab about the Maison Puce – after all, his mum lives there.

'It's not *that* bad,' he says.

Ivy Prosper lays a clammy hand on his. 'No, dear, of course it isn't. I'm ever so sorry, wasn't thinking. Your mum's got a place, you said.'

'And not just her – Hope Boscombe.'

'What?'

'Hope Boscombe.'

'*The* Hope Boscombe – from the telly?'

'That's the one.'

'Well I never did! That *Imogen* – you'd think she'd have

told me, wouldn't you? She knows I watch that programme – always got it in for landlords, hasn't she, that Hope? I've always meant to write in, have it out with her. You couldn't let me into the building, could you?'

'I don't have a key to Imo's.'

'No, of course not, dear – but I could take a look around while I'm waiting, get more of an idea, and, well, *really* to tell you the truth I'm bursting for the toilet. I couldn't use your mum's, could I, dear? I know it's a bit of a cheek asking but, then, being as you're English too we're all in it together . . .'

It's not for reasons of national solidarity that Gav agrees, more to (a) get her off his back and (b) get himself that lager, because by now though *she* may be bursting *he*'s gasping. He leads her upstairs, leaving stools, sketchbook and laptop down in the hall. While she's in the loo, he hangs his head out of the window to avoid the obvious tinkling noises, and swigs great gulps from the bottle. Below, a door slams and looking down he sees the crown of what must be Hope Boscombe's head passing directly beneath him and heading towards the square. Wouldn't he just bloody well know it?

*

On the Croisette, Imo and Theo are doing what he calls 'trolling about' – wandering, mingling with the crowds, absorbing the glitz and zing of the Cannes Can. Theo doesn't need *real* glamour as represented by the constant stream of Rollses and Ferraris disgorging their passengers at the Carlton. He's had a surfeit of all that. What he likes is mixing with what he calls 'the plebs'. Now if Theo weren't Theo, Imo might just sock him in the jaw for using that expression, but he is, so she keeps her punches to herself.

Ahead they can see a denser swelling of the crowd. It's gathering around a fenced-off stage, hung with lights and studded with cameras. Something must be cooking. It's like a giant electromagnetic field pulling in the crowd, which visibly grows as they walk towards it. There are shrieks from fans but no one back here can see anything – everyone's stretching to catch a glimpse of the real-life magic. Boys are shinning up trees. Girls in tiny tight mini-skirts are being pulled up on to the shoulders of black-vested dudes with bulging muscles, piggy-back, to get a better view. All Theo and Imo can see over the top of the packed heads, are banners being raised – 'Crazy Fred and the Fuckathon', they read. Imo squawks with laughter.

'Want to pop up, Mouse?' says Theo, holding out his hands, and she scrambles up on to his shoulders.

More shrieks and yells – something's happening at the front – cameras are rolling. Action! Where's Fred? Everybody's yelling now for the actor who plays Fred. Nobody's ever heard of him but it doesn't seem to matter. Everyone's straining at the leash. After hours of hanging around yearning for a real-life Celebrity, a newcomer will do just fine.

'Where's Fred?' the crowd chants.

'Fred's not here!' The crowd groans. 'But Fred's balls are!' The crowd shrieks. From the platform a hale of inflated beach balls showers on to the crowd. Screams of excitement – people are stretching and leaning, willing a ball their way.

Each is tattooed with the film's logo and *Fred's Balls* in orange lettering on a black base. They're hideous, yet everybody wants one. Imo wants one too. It's the Fred connection, of course. Imo suddenly wants one of those damn balls like nothing she's wanted in years. But they're not coming this way. 'Grab one, Theo,' she yells, bouncing around on his shoulders. But he can't grab one. They've gone off to the right and he can't get through the crowd.

The lucky ones clutch their balls to their chests, smirking at each other. Theo feels an urge to snatch one – it's like a medieval quest for his fair lady and he's failing her. Why should she have one – that fat old woman over there? What the hell's she going to do with a Fred and the Fuckathon Beach Ball – play croquet? And then the woman turns round and says, *'Theo!'*

'Mother?' says Theo.

'Verona?' says Imo, from over Theo's head, where she's still perched.

'Darling!' says Verona, and she lurches forward, beach ball still clasped to her breasts.

Theo instinctively jumps back. 'Eoww – watch it!' yells Imo, clutching at his hair, her knee slamming into the side of his face as she tries to save herself. He staggers, attempts to regain his balance, then topples forward, launching Imo horizontally into the crowd.

'Shiiiiiit!' shrieks Imo, a human projectile, flying through the air and bursting several of Fred's balls as she heads towards earth.

24

Queen of Sheba

After Ivy Prosper finishes using Alice's loo, she has a good old nose around the flat.

'You don't mind, do you?' she says, sniffing round the kitchen area. 'Only if Imogen doesn't come back tonight, this might be the nearest I get to seeing what hers is like. It's a bit on the small side, isn't it?, but I suppose for a holiday home it does the job – though you see in Imogen's case it's not a holiday, it's supposed to be permanent.'

'So's this for my mum.'

'Oh, sorry, dear – I mean, it's very nicely fitted and all that, what there is of it, I'm pleasantly surprised, really. Is Imogen's the same?'

'Not exactly.'

'Bigger?'

'Well, different . . .' Gav thinks of fighting through the piles of grot and dog to get to Imo's bed the other night '. . . yeah – a bit different.'

'I've always been curious – she's never even brought me a snap of the place and as I've got what you might call a financial interest . . . You see, it's not like me to get involved "sight unseen" but in this case I've just had to take it all on trust.'

'Whose?'

'Imogen's, of course. Well, sometimes you do with families, don't you? I mean, technically the mortgage is in her name – it was such a business, all in French, so I wasn't going to get myself directly involved – but I do make the payments, so where the nitty-gritty's concerned I'm in it up to my neck. Are these wardrobes fitted?' She's pulling at one of the sunflower cupboards.

'Look, Mrs Prosper, I've got to get back out now – I've got work to do.'

'Of course, dear – I interrupted your picture, didn't I? Professional artist, are you?'

'Well, sort of,' and Gav chivvies her out and down the stairs, while she keeps up a running surveyor's commentary on the state of the hall.

He reckons he can risk setting himself up on the bench in the square now. If Hope Boscombe went out this way, it's a fair bet she'll return the same way too, though with his luck, he'd better not bank on it.

He's left Ivy Prosper outside Imo's door, sniffing again. Thank God he and Imo left Fred round at Marie-Christine's bar before they'd gone back to Cannes yesterday otherwise she'd have something more substantial to sniff about. Although if Imo had had to come back to attend to Fred, maybe she wouldn't have dumped him at the Carlton and gone off with Theo Grange like that. Yeah, the way things have worked out so far, he'd really better *not* trust to his luck.

He switches on his laptop again and sets it next to him on the bench, turned at an angle so that Hope Boscombe won't be able to miss it if she comes back this way, then he starts fiddling around with the sketchbook to look busy again.

'Mind if I join you?' Ivy Prosper is standing over him. 'You wouldn't know if she's coming back tonight, would you – Imogen?'

'No, I don't know.'

'Only I might as well wait for a bit now I've come so far.'

'I can't help you – sorry – got to work,' mumbles Gav.

'Don't mind me, dear.' She sits down at the other end of the bench. 'I've left that door on the latch – is that all right?'

'What?' says Gav. She's like a particularly tenacious gob of chewing-gum that he can't scrape off his shoe.

'The front door, dear – it's safe, isn't it, to leave it open? I mean, we're keeping watch aren't we, so to speak? Only I didn't want to slam it and have you go off and then I couldn't get in again . . .'

'It's all right.' Gav tries to bury his head in the sketch-pad, but now she's leaning over to take a peek.

'Ummmm,' she appraises, 'professional, you said?'

'Abstract expressionist,' says Gav, wishing he could make her vaporize.

'You don't say,' says Ivy. 'Live and learn.'

*

Even after Alice and Josette reach dry land, the nightmare seems to go on. Having started being sick, Josette can't seem to stop, and in between the bouts of retching she's suffused with racking sobs. Stuck out on the quay in the hot late-afternoon sun, Alice doesn't know where to start. Josette clearly can't walk back as far as the station at the moment, even if she could travel in this state. Alice gets her to sit down on the concrete of the quay with her legs hanging over the edge – no worries now about oil-smudged buttocks. Then she settles beside her and waits. After a while, both retching and sobbing die down and just the occasional mammoth sniff heaves out, as Josette regains a modicum of control. Her damp, waxy hands lie limply in her lap. Tentatively, Alice takes hold of the nearest one and holds it lightly. Sometimes there's no substitute for the touch of another human being. They sit like this for a long while, as Josette gradually calms, and the sky begins to redden towards sunset.

'Is very sad, you know, Aleese, to lose a dream.'

'Yes.'

'And you – you lose a dream wiz your 'usband, your Philip.'

'You could say that, yes, though it didn't feel like a dream – it just felt like life, normal. It's only when you lose it that you think perhaps it *was* a dream – except, of course, it wasn't dream-*like* and it wasn't perfect.'

'Is terrible this thing he does.'

'Who – Philip? Well, it can't be as simple as that. He's not an evil man, only human – not very evolved maybe.'

'Evolved?'

'A bit insensitive – well, more than a bit – but there must have been something lacking in me too. Whatever I had or did, it obviously wasn't enough – he wanted more and he found it presumably. But it's never simple – I'd like him not to feel he's getting away with it, only then I realize *he* doesn't think he *is* getting away with it. He may even think *I*'m getting away with it on the back of his hard work – you see what I mean? It's not necessarily helpful to start chucking blame about too much – it usually cuts both ways, doesn't it?'

'I don't know these words – this "cuts both ways".'

'It doesn't matter. Do you feel well enough to walk? Because there's only one cure for you now, you do know that, don't you? A nice cup of tea.' Alice is smiling and from somewhere deep inside her, Josette manages to summon up a laugh.

*

Hope's not strolling this afternoon – her mind and pulse won't let her. This walk she's taking is more a form of prescribed medication than a relaxed amble. She had to get out of the flat because it's driving her crazy. She spent much of the day lying on her bed straining to catch noises from the roof – footsteps? Were those human footsteps? Then everything would go quiet for a bit – but her brain was already poised and alert to catch the next sound and the next, each one like a tiny hook picking at her nerves. So it's click, click, click on her high stilettos along the promenade, all the time craning her neck to see if she can spy anything incriminating from down here – and it's tick, tick, tick as a jumpy pulse jangles in her ears.

Coming into the place d'Espoir she automatically looks up at the Maison Puce, searching yet again for that elusive clue. But she can scarcely see her terrace balustrade from down here, let alone anything above.

'Hope! Hope Boscombe! I've got a bone to pick with you!'

Hope freezes, then returns her gaze to ground level. A solid, tidy little woman is getting up from the bench, extending her hand and laughing. Oh, my God, fan-bait – she's fallen into a trap. Fan-bait or a woman with a grudge – deadly possibility. Or a plot laid by paparazzi – is she being set up for tabloid humiliation? Has word got out she's turning recluse?

And then behind the woman, in a flash, Hope sees this young guy with a look of agony on his face – his jaw is hanging down, he seems to be trying to say something – and next to him is this weird thing, DEADEYES, flashing at her. Christ, it *is* a trap. Panic hits her – but the worst thing at such a moment is to make a run for it. Stay calm, avoid contact, move away . . . slowly away.

'Miss Boscombe,' says the man, getting up, 'look, I'm really sorry – it wasn't meant – '

But the woman's still walking towards her with hand held out, and Hope's instincts are to make a dash for it after all – only the woman's saying, 'Ivy Prosper. You might know my daughter Imogen. I'm ever so pleased to meet you' and the name 'Imogen' scythes through her panic and brings her to a halt.

'You're Imo's mother?' she asks, not going any nearer, but searching the podgy red face for any similarities – and yes, there is something in there, deep in the bones, behind the plump jowls, something which tweaks a familiar chord and brings Imo to mind, that and the cute button nose.

'Yes – Ivy Prosper. You know my Imogen, then? Isn't that typical? I'm always asking her what it's like down here and she's never let on – not a word.'

'About what?'

'About *you* – she makes damn sure I know about all the nasty things, anything that's going to cost me money, but something really nice and she doesn't say a thing. And she knows I watch your programme 'cos I'm always saying that you don't half have it in for landlords and we're not all Rachmans. I'm in students myself and I can tell you that's the mucky end of the market but it does a useful service. Fancy her not telling me. Can I ask if you've been here long?'

'Not long.'

'Well, that makes more sense, then. I don't mean about Imogen but the state of the place, because I've seen pictures of your house in London – Hammersmith, is it? Would it have been in *Hello!*? – and obviously you've got standards.'

'What do you mean by the state of the place?'

'The building. I was saying to this young man, that rendering needs hacking off for a start – look at that bulge – you'll never know what's going on behind if you don't. That's a scaffolding job if ever I saw one and it won't come cheap – another bill Imogen'll come crawling for me to pay on top of the mortgage. Sometimes I wonder will it ever end?'

'Are you a builder or something?'

'No. Like I said, I'm a landlord, but I know property and I wouldn't have touched this with a barge pole if I'd come and seen it with my own eyes – but there you are, I let myself be persuaded. It's not easy being a mother and I've always been on my own so Imogen can usually twist me round her little finger.'

'What was that you were saying about the rendering – you mean the plaster? It's due for painting, I know – '

'Needs more than that – I was telling this young man, wasn't I? That all needs coming off and replacing with a good modern composite. You can get them with the colour locked in now – saves you a fortune in the end. I never touch colour wash – you might as well stand on the street burning fifty-pound notes.'

All this time the young man in question has been bouncing around behind Ivy Prosper, putting his hand up, like a child in school. 'Miss Boscombe,' he says now, 'I was hoping to have a word with you.'

'What?' Hope snaps. Is he a journalist, the little creep?

'I'm Gavin Barnes – my mother lives in the Maison Puce too, first floor.'

'Who?'

'Alice Barnes's son.'

'The one who's in the City?'

'No, I'm in film production. I was hoping to discuss a project.'

'You what?'

'Only if it was convenient.'

'Well, it's *not*! Jeezus, how *dare* you? You've set me up to discuss a goddam film project?'

'It was just a thought.'

'Just a *thought* – trapping me in my own backyard? Are you crazy or something? Now, do you mind just butting out? This is a private conversation I am having here, OK?' and turning to Ivy Prosper, she continues, 'You wouldn't know anything about roofs, would you?'

It's then that a taxi turns into the bottom of the place d'Espoir and immediately begins to discharge a noisy cargo.

There's a loud female yell of 'Mind! Mind my leg!'

Hope, Ivy and Gavin turn to watch. Verona, carrying a pair of crutches, is getting out of the front passenger seat, and a big man in blazer and flannels is bending to help someone in the back with considerable difficulty. He gathers whomever it is, then slowly straightens up and turns round to reveal Imo, cradled in his arms. Wearing her customary skinny black jersey, but with white strapping now swaddling one leg from thigh to bare foot, and a baseball cap stuck jauntily on the top of her head, she rests triumphantly – it's the arrival of the Queen of Sheba with full retinue. The group turns towards the Maison Puce and heads a little unsteadily across the square.

'Girlie!' shrieks Ivy Prosper. 'It's my Girlie!'

Within two paces Imo seems to deflate like a balloon with a slow puncture. By the time Ivy has reached her, any sign of the Queen of Sheba has blown clean away.

*

In Cannes, Josette's still pretty wobbly, even after the enforced administration of two pots of Twinings in a tea-shop on the rue d'Antibes. On the packed train back to

Vieilleville, she looks more and more ill – hollow-cheeked and a nasty grey colour. When they pull into Bonneville station Alice suggests a taxi, but Josette says she needs the air, so they walk slowly back down to the old town.

Without demur, Josette allows Alice to accompany her 'home'. This current billet belongs to Marie-Auguste – the most glittering of the Augustines – and it turns out to be a very smart house indeed, right on the seafront at the western end of the promenade. It's totally shuttered when they arrive, looking severe and lonely in its empty magnificence. Josette is so trembly she can hardly get the key in the lock, and the glimpse Alice gets of the inside is dark and forbidding.

'Why don't I stay the night – just in case?' she suggests, not expecting for one moment to be taken up on the offer.

'Would you? Would you, Aleese? Is very kind.'

Josette's bedroom is a cubby-hole in the basement right next to the kitchen. It's full of expensive-looking luggage and a large wardrobe, but virtually nothing else by way of personal effects. Alice helps her to get settled, then creeps upstairs and does her best to flop in the rather grand salon. There must be at least four or five empty bedrooms, but as Josette hasn't offered, a kip on a rigid little Second Empire sofa will have to do.

*

While Verona, Theo, Imo, Ivy and the pair of crutches all try to squeeze into the Maison Puce at once, Gav watches in despair as Hope Boscombe retreats swiftly back to her own front door. What is it with him and luck? Is his ever going to change? Other people get breaks all the time, whereas he seems to be permanently cursed. Talk about bad timing. Those sodding eyes are still winking at him. He slams the laptop shut. For two pins he'd chuck it in the municipal bin. But he doesn't, just picks it up angrily and trails after the others.

There's a traffic jam in the hallway. Theo has tried to carry Imo over the threshold, but there isn't enough room, and in any case, the presence of her mother has immediately removed any desire Imo may have been harbouring to look helpless. She wriggles down and stands on one leg, searching through her pockets for the keys.

'Gimme those,' she says to Verona, who's still holding the crutches.

'*Ple-ase*,' says Ivy.

'Shut up, Mum,' says Imo, struggling with her lock.

Ivy's trilling laugh rings out. She turns to the others with a shrug: 'She doesn't half show me up.'

'Look who's talking,' mutters Imo, leaning heavily on the crutches and heaving herself into her flat.

'Mouse, you all right?' says Theo, and it's then that Gav sees he's got a huge red swelling around his right eye.

'Yeah – OK – see you later, maybe.' Ivy has already scuttled in behind her, and Imo kicks out with a crutch to slam the door conclusively behind her.

'Oh dear, what a business,' says Verona, from the bottom of the stairs. 'Are you coming up, Theo?'

'Well, of course I am, Mother.'

'There's no of course about it.' She turns her back and starts to climb.

No one seems to have noticed Gav at all. Isn't that absolutely typical?

*

'Someone's been in the wars,' says Ivy, watching for a moment as Imo fights through the general mess to get to her bed.

'Had a bit of an accident.'

'Nothing broken?'

'Ligaments torn and I've got a big cut – twenty-five stitches.'

'Nasty. What happened?'

'Someone dropped me. Look, why are you here? I told you not to come. I told you I wouldn't be here.'

'You've been telling a few porky-pies.'

'What?'

'Oh, Imogen, I don't know where to begin. This is a mucky little hole – whatever is that pong?'

'The drains, I expect – they always start playing up round about now.'

'You've got drains as well?'

'Of course I've got drains.'

'Dodgy drains, though?'

'Well . . . a bit dodgy.'

'It's *doggy* I can smell.'

'Yeah – well, I've got one of them too. I wish you hadn't come, Mum.'

'I bet you do.'

'I was all right – I was doing all right.'

'Yes, it looks like it,' says Ivy drily. She pulls open the

sliding plastic door leading into the bathroom. 'Oh, *Imogen*, however do you manage?' She regards the ancient pedestal *pissoir*. 'Call that a toilet?'

'No,' says Imo. 'I don't – I call it a *lavabo* or sometimes a "*vay-say*".'

'Now, don't get clever with me, Imogen – I can see right through you. I'll remind you, young lady, who's been paying for all this.'

'Oh, I knew it wouldn't be long before that came up – how long did it take you as a matter of fact?' Imo looks at her watch with an obvious flourish. 'Right, yes, as per usual – roughly four and a half minutes. Never miss a trick, Mum, do you? Can't wait to start turning the screw.'

'Now, don't take that tone with me, Girlie. We've had our little ups and downs, we've had our spats – '

'Not half.'

'Don't start giving me lip, Imogen.'

'Why not? This is my home. My space. Did I ask you here?'

'I've come a very long way – and I'm glad I did. I had no idea what I was paying for, and you made certain I didn't, but the game's up, Girlie, got to be. No more chequies without a bit of co-operation.'

'So what?'

'So you know what.'

'So maybe I don't need your chequies any more. So maybe I've got other fish to fry.'

'Out of the frying-pan more likely. Let's just call it quits, shall we, Imogen – I've had a long day and my feet are killing me.'

*

Up in Verona's flat, Theo pushes his way under the draped velvet of the pine platform bed and flops down on the sofa.

'How's your eye feeling?' asks Verona.

'Sore,' says Theo.

'It looks it. I'm afraid my fridge doesn't run to raw steak, only camembert and champagne.'

'Maybe champagne would help a bit, actually.'

'All right.' As Verona bends to the business of opening and pouring, Theo watches her. This is all very strange – this is Mummy, cosy, cuddly sticky Mummy, why doesn't she care more? Usually she'd be all over him – why this chilly proffering of a glass? Why no ministrations with damp towels and ice-packs? Why no fridge stuffed to the gills with tasty morsels? What's up?

*

In Alice's flat, Gav is all alone. He raids her fridge – picks at this and that, too weary to take himself out for supper – expecting her back any moment, not settling. By eleven, she's still not returned – bloody hell but that must be some lunch party on the William Prescott yacht. Mum? Who would have thought it of her? Off out in her flimsy white linen, hitting the high spots. Makes you think. Not that he grudges her a good time. She deserves it – no, really she does. What with what Dad did to her – did to all of them . . . never been a chance to think it through, talk to him, make any sense of it. We all sit in our little mental cubicles trying to work out our own scenarios. Now, if real life had the structure of a film, things would be a lot easier. He'd only just have got past the credits, wouldn't he, with a whole plot to follow.

*

On the very top floor of the Maison Puce, Hope Boscombe is lying in a hot, sweaty heap. Not the symptom of an early menopause, more in the nature of a tortured response. Every note must be seared into her cerebral cortex by now. How many renditions of 'Under the Bridges of Paris' can a body take?

25

Mornings after Nights before

For the second night running Gav doesn't get much by way of sleep. At first he was going to blow up the Lilo again, but as Mum still hasn't turned up from her Cannes jaunt, he decides not to waste his breath and kips on the sofa instead. But he can't drop off. The frustrations of the last days have got to him in a bad way now – missed opportunities, miserable luck, pathetic timing. And getting the timing right is crucial in this game – he's always known that, even if he hasn't sussed how to work the trick. He's been avoiding calling the guys back in the office, all anxiously awaiting news of his triumph: dreading having to admit to his total cock-up so far. And what now? Back to Cannes? Face it all again – alone – try to carve himself a path through the maze? Or admit defeat and go home?

By dawn he's decided. Haggard and stiff, he packs his backpack, writes Alice a note and heads off towards Nice airport in search of a stand-by flight.

*

Hope's had a poor night too, but by morning she's resolved to pull herself together and take some positive action. She starts by picking up the telephone, and putting her voice into its wheedling, persuasive mode.

*

Imogen and Ivy have had a terrible night. Ivy refused point blank to go back to Monaco – wouldn't hear of it, rang the hotel to explain to the *Woman's Way* people that something had cropped up and she'd make her own way home. In exchange for the luxury of a room ('with full *en-suite*') at the Grand, she has to squeeze in with Imogen on the divan – horrible. She'd insisted on making up the bed with clean sheets . . . well, clean*er*, because there was no way she was getting in those other things – what a way to live! – and Imogen with that great dressing on her leg. She'll get blood poisoning if she's not careful. As for that toilet . . . well, words fail her.

*

Imo is sore, angry and worried. There was a moment when, despite the pain, it had all seemed quite good fun. She'd been the centre of attention, everyone was making such a fuss of her – especially Theo, who'd felt directly responsible for the accident . . . For a brief spell she'd been a queen – but then when her mum turned up like that, it brought her back down to a thud of reality. Worse than her normal reality, in fact, for the hospital had asked a lot of awkward questions. Any one of her faltering answers may quickly reveal her dubious residential status – the absence of a *carte de séjour*, her failure to register with the *sécurité sociale*, which, if this weren't an emergency, would normally negate her right to treatment. Everything is coming back to haunt her. The painkillers are wearing off now and Imo's leg is seizing up. She can't roll over, has to lie rigid on her back staring up at the stripes of street-light cast through the shutters on to the ceiling. Ivy, also awake and brooding, makes do as best she can on the narrow slice of remaining bed. It's she who breaks the cramped silence.

'I've been wondering where I went wrong with you.'

'Don't, Mum, not now.'

'I did my best.'

'*Don't.*'

'And I was on my own. It's not my fault you never knew your dad – I couldn't have let on it was Pinker got me up the duff, it would've killed your grandfather. Pinker already had a wife and five kids and things were so different in those days – you wouldn't believe – the *disgrace* and with all his mates up Covent Garden too, and it was all an accident, my first time too – round the back of the exotic fruit. Not exactly what you'd call romantic, was it?'

'Thanks, Mum. Nothing like having it constantly shoved in your face that your entire existence on the planet is a total fucking accidental disaster.'

'Imogen, *language*.'

'Oh, shut up, Mum.'

'At least I kept you.'

'Yeah, thanks a whole lot.'

'If I'd put you up for adoption God only knows where you might be.'

'Probably somewhere lovely.'

'You never lacked for nothing, Imogen – you can't say you did. I wanted the best for you – I sent you to that nice convent, but what did you do? Threw it in my face – run off like that so I thought you were dead for all those months and months – got yourself in all that trouble with the law . . .'

'Might have been better off if I had been dead.'

'Don't say that, you silly girl. One day you'll be a mother and you'll see – we can only do our best . . .'

No, it's not a night of blissful slumbers for either of the I. Prospers, so the 7 a.m. ringing of the telephone is none too welcome. Ivy snatches at the receiver, 'Mrs Prosper? Hi, this is Hope Boscombe – sorry to call you this early but I wasn't sure if you'd stayed over and I thought if you did you'd maybe leave early for the airport or something. Look, I've been thinking – I wonder if you could come on up – I could really use a little advice – '

*

Theo's had a rotten night too.

He and Mother got thoroughly pie-eyed on the champagne, and what with his face blowing up and starting to turn a horrible yellowy purple, and the odd way Mother was behaving, he decided against going back to the hotel. She offered him the platform bed, which he'd had to share with piles of newspapers and stuffed carrier-bags. She hadn't seemed the slightest bit abashed by this situation – that was peculiar too – scarcely lifting a finger to help him clear a space.

And they'd stayed up talking very late anyway. Very late

indeed. There seemed to be a lot of emotional baggage to get out of the way, and in this the booze helped. Of course, it wasn't long before they got round to the subject of Father and all that funny business. So *un*funny in reality, though granted one might have had a good old laugh if it had been someone *else*'s dear papa who'd run off with the man from BT. But when you found yourself directly involved, it was pretty bloody lacerating – simply not the done thing, and impossible to shake off with any sort of aplomb. And with a man of Father's age and standing, there was something particularly obscene about it all – so shame-making. Could have wreaked havoc on his own career – very nearly did, when the Hemery-Blythes let the cat out of the bag. When all's said and done, a bit of good old rumpy-pumpy is one thing but full-blown in-your-face campery – not to mention *buggery* – involving your dear old dad is quite another. He's always felt a lot of it was Mother's fault, really. She should have put her foot down years ago – too bloody weak, too bloody forgiving. And now there's this new business – this bloke of hers – I mean, *honestly*, is his humiliation never to end?

*

Verona sleeps poorly too. She's missing Yogi. She'd had to leave him on the Croisette after it became clear that Imo and Theo needed hospital treatment. There'd been such a hullabaloo with the *sapeurs-pompiers* arriving to cut Imo free from where she'd got wedged into one of those metal barriers, and Theo complaining that the whole side of his face had gone numb – and those extraordinary people from the Fred and the Fuckathon film trying to clear everybody away – that she'd almost lost sight of Yogi in the crowd. Then she'd found him and managed to introduce him to Theo. They'd just got past the initial cagey greetings, when they'd had to split up again, he to gather up his clients and get back to the boat, and she to travel in the ambulance. She wonders if he's back yet. They'd had a lovely plan to go to St Tropez tomorrow – she can't wait. Wonder if they'll need a *leetle peek-neek*?

So odd to have Theo here. Utterly perverse. All this time she's been longing to have him come down, and now he's here, he's just a groaning, grumbling waste of space. Imagine his being at the Carlton all this time and not letting her know. *So* wounding – how could he? If it wasn't for Yogi she doesn't know how she could have coped. And to discover he's been there with *Imo* of all people too. She'd asked him if there was anything serious between them and he'd just laughed and said, 'Only the obvious,' and she'd said, 'Does Imo know that?' and he'd laughed again and said that of course she did, 'Got her feet on the ground, that one,' and she'd said, 'Though not when dropped from a great height it seems,' which had shut him up.

When morning comes she can't get him bundled into a taxi early enough.

*

Ivy's well impressed with Hope Boscombe's flat. She'd have to admit it – what a surprise. Hidden behind all this mucky old stuff, it's a real dream. A bit empty and short of ornaments for her own taste but that's what they seem to go for these days. This is all white and cool, beautiful fittings, lots of steel and marble – and *big*. It's huge next to the others.

'How come it's so big?' she asks, after she's had a good old nose. 'I mean, I know it's on two floors but even so . . .'

'Yes, I wondered exactly the same. Partly it's because I've got all the space from both of the towers, whereas for the others the tower is all taken up with their staircase – that's what gives me those nice curvy walls. But then also I go back quite a bit further than they do. I only know that because I've been doing a lot of measuring – and the way I figure it is that somehow this building interlocks up here with the house behind. I mean, these places are centuries old and I guess they put them up with no real planning. I can't really get to the bottom of it – that's one of the problems I've been having. Come take a look out here.'

Ivy trots out to the balcony, clocking a table of framed photographs on the way. Hope with Cilla. Hope with Sir Cliff. Hope with – *no* – Princess Diana. Ivy feels a little thrill run down her neck. 'Hope with Ivy Prosper' flashes into her mind. Oooh, this is *lovely*. Out on the terrace, she gives the roof an extra hard glare, clicking her tongue with what she reckons is a professional flourish.

'Definitely wants seeing to.'

'Do you understand how the co-proprietorship system works here? Imo's explained it to you?'

'Imogen doesn't tell me nothing.'

'But I thought you said you pay the mortgage.'

'I do – felt I had to help her out. The landlord here was getting stroppy, threatening eviction, and she seemed to like the town and – well, I can't tell you what it's always been like trying to get her settled – so I just went along with it. Mind you, I keep her on a tight string, give her the payments a few months at a time, otherwise I don't know what she might get up to – she's been a naughty girl, you know, hasn't half been a headache.'

'In what way?'

'Every way, really. She had the hump before she was born, that one. There was trouble with drugs at school – the police got involved – then she run off when she was sixteen, got mixed up with all sorts. Then she got herself a job on one of the boats at St Katherine's Dock, for some tycoon – just as a skivvy – but that's what got her started off down here, that's how she got the French, skivvied all round the world on loads of different boats for years – just sort of picked it up. That first job, though, when she started, she didn't get in touch for ten months. I thought she was dead.'

'Well, she's certainly mastered the language – you should hear her talking to Monsieur Gerontin – she's a natural.'

'Who?'

'He's the guy who runs our *syndic* – we're all freeholders, only it's not called that, it's called "co-proprietorship" and the idea is we hire this syndicate thing to run the building for us, only in our case the *syndic* is run by the same guy who sold us the flats in the first place and he's turning out to be almost impossible to pin down. Any repairs and renovations have to be voted on by all of us – only they never seem to have any meetings, and nobody but me seems to want one. It's done on a percentage basis – I've got forty-six per cent but even so I couldn't out-vote the others, always supposing I could actually get a meeting organized.'

'What percentage does Imogen have?'

'Ten, I think. It's on a sliding scale depending on square metres and Imo's is the smallest.'

'Ten plus forty-six equals a majority, according to my sums.'

'Always supposing I could get Imo on board.'

'Consider it done.'

*

Alice slept quite well, despite having to curl up on Marie-Auguste's hard little sofa, not an item made for lounging. However, it's surely been in a good cause. It wouldn't have seemed right to leave Josette on her own last night. She'd looked so ill and old, her skin still horribly waxy and pale after being so sick, her eyes shrunken in her skull. After all the shattered outpouring of grief, she'd even hugged Alice with limp appreciation.

Now, in the morning light, Alice is so stiff she can scarcely roll over, and she lies there on the slippery silk brocade, staring up at the refracted light patterns bouncing up from the sea on to Marie-Auguste's panelled walls, challenging herself to make a move and thinking about Josette. Poor woman – she's going to need careful handling. After such a depth of misery drawn from bitter disappointment, well, they'll all have to be very, very kind.

And she's thinking about this, and quite enjoying the moment of relaxation, when Josette bustles in. It's as if nothing whatever has happened. Josette's look of shrivelled defeat has completely disappeared overnight, and here she is back again to pristine Golden Egret form. She's washed and set her hair so that it's back to its metallic helmet look, and her face is perfectly made up with full precision warpaint. Her dress, in cool-looking aqua linen, is crisply ironed. Alice, who'd automatically composed her face to look concerned and helpful, immediately reverts back to her usual self-image as a tatty, crumpled creature who's still wearing yesterday's dirty white trouser suit, with teeth unbrushed and hair awry. Again.

'*Aleese*, my leetle Aleese, *bonjour*. It is a lovely morning. We go for *café* – we go down to ze *quai*, yes? We will 'ave *fun*.'

Needing a change of clothes plus the use of her own toothbrush, Alice says she'll go back to the Maison Puce. In fact she'd love to get away on her own now, for after all that outpouring of openness and honesty last night, it's hard to go back so instantly to the previous status quo. Perhaps if Josette doesn't need her help and sympathy any more she could get her own life back. But Josette insists on coming with her. They walk along the promenade towards the eastern end of the town. The sea is particularly glittery this morning, the atmosphere so clean that the view of the distant mountains is for once crisp and clear.

'Is *beeoootiful* morning, Aleese,' says Josette.

'It is. I'm so glad you feel you can appreciate it.'

'But of course.'

'I mean, after yesterday.'

'Well, life is life, you know, Aleese. We 'ave not so much time we can spoil it on a lost dream . . .'

'True. But I really am so sorry, Josette, that it all couldn't work out better for you,' and Alice reaches out to squeeze Josette's hand in sympathy. It feels as cold and rubbery as a dead squid and Josette seems to recoil at her touch.

'It is *nozzing*, you know, Aleese,' she says, rather grandly, looking past her, straight out to sea.

'Nothing?' says Alice, incredulous.

'Well, you know – as for my Billy-Boy, well . . .' Josette gives a hard little bark of a laugh.

'Yes?'

'Well, you saw 'im? He 'ave ze belly of a big pig – yes – and you know I have kept my *ligne*, you know? Why I waste my talent on such a man? I am better zan zat.'

'Of course you are.'

They're just turning into the place d'Espoir when they spot Verona coming out of the Maison Puce, doing her usual firm tugging at the door to make sure she's locked it properly. She's carrying the bulging orange cool-bag.

'Hello – if you'd come earlier you'd have met my son Theo,' she calls.

'You didn't say he was coming,' says Alice.

'I didn't know – it's a bit of a saga – '

'How was your trip to Cannes?'

'Well, fine, really, but that was part of the saga . . .'

'I looked out for your boat at Cannes but of course I didn't actually know what I was looking for – we were down at the quay for ages.'

'Really? Well, if I'd known I could have looked out for you too – which boat were you on?'

'The *Golden Isle* but it was moored right out at sea,' but

Josette is surely turning a shade paler again under all that foundation. 'Anyway,' says Alice hurriedly, trying to head off the subject, 'you're right about it being another world.'

'Isn't it just? I'm completely hooked – the *freedom*. Why don't you come down and see us, noonish, for drinkies – open house? Come down and I'll tell you all – '

'Not a *leetle peek-neek?*'

'Now don't tease, Alice, it's not very nice – third quay down on the right-hand side.'

'What's the name of the boat?'

'*Karma* – but we'll be ashore I expect, as usual. Once you're down there you won't be able to miss us.'

*

It's Ivy's idea to get a taxi to Monsieur Gerontin's office. Imogen can't possibly walk with her injured leg, even if it's quite near. As far as Imo's concerned she can't possibly go at all – the last thing she needs after the business at the hospital yesterday is to stir up her situation any further. But there doesn't seem any way out of it – Ivy's threatening to pull her financial plug, and Imo doesn't want to let on how deeply she's up shit creek, the proverbial paddle having been exchanged for a pair of crutches.

In search of rescue she'd tried to get hold of Theo while Ivy was up at Hope's flat. But when she rang the Carlton they told her that Monsieur had not returned last night. Could he have stayed with Verona then? Is he still in the building? Infuriatingly she doesn't have Verona's phone number and she can't find the directory amongst all this mess. She levered herself out into the hall on the crutches, but looked hopelessly up the stairs. Not a chance she could climb them. She tried shouting a few times, yelled Theo's name, but her voice echoed back down at her. The building seemed very empty.

When the taxi arrives, she kicks up a hell of a fuss – she's buggered if she's going quietly – but despite that, she finds herself bundled in the back, her leg propped up on her mother's lap, while Hope travels in front. Imo may be in a lather but, then, so too is Ivy. What did she always say about that girl – a puzzle? Always been a puzzle – and *why* would she set herself against challenging this Gerontin man about the state of the building? You'd think it would be in her own best interests.

They haven't made an appointment so Monsieur Gerontin might very easily not be there. That's what Imo's banking on, but today her gods of destiny must have gone walkabout, for here is Monsieur, taking his ease, squashed up to his desk eating a very large slice of creamy *tropézienne* for his breakfast. It's a lifetime's indulgence in this local delicacy that has mostly contributed so unctuously to his waistline. Delicious, but an inelegant substance to be caught with on the hop – custard cream bursting out from either side of the deep, sugary sponge, leaving a yellow moustache which creeps up the nostrils. Something normally best eaten alone – which at 9.30 a.m. with no scheduled appointments is specifically what Monsieur G. expects to be.

What a surprise, then, to have the door crash open and turn to see the little English girl come swinging in on crutches, yelling at the other woman in blue, with the rich famous American one bringing up the rear. The sight of them immediately starts the gnawing pain of indigestion in his gut – nothing to do with the cake, of course, just the certainty that this invasion can mean nothing but trouble.

They start in straight away, with the Prosper girl translating. What they want, what they don't want. What he must do, what he mustn't do. What *they* intend to do by way of lawyers and courts and bad publicity if the *syndic* doesn't get a move on straight away with the renovations. Terribly upsetting stuff. The pain in his gut sharpens. It's impossible, he explains, there will have to be a meeting of the co-proprietors. It'll have to be agreed. And there hasn't been such a meeting in years – and if there were no one, no consensus would be achieved. They should trust him, he *knows* these things.

But what about a majority decision? Well, yes, says Monsieur, possible in theory, but highly unsatisfactory in practice – terribly difficult to extract substantial sums of money from the other owners if they're not prepared to co-operate.

Consternation! What other money? How much? Weren't most of these renovations supposed to be in hand? That was the basis on which Madame Boscombe had bought her flat.

Ah, well, if Madame is simply referring to *those* renovations – the painting of the walls? – ah, yes, well, those are indeed in hand, sometime, sometime soon – or soonish. And here the older woman interrupts, 'Needs more than a lick of paint – you tell him, Imogen. That rendering needs hacking off for a start.' The girl translates and Monsieur digests briefly, then shrugs. Perhaps in a perfect world, ladies, but they don't live on such a planet and have they any idea of the possible expense and complication, what with the walls and the drains and the roof? If they were really to delve into such matters the costs could be enormous – and though he doesn't know much about the finances of Mesdames Barnes and Grange, he is certain that Monsieur Puce could never afford to contribute such sums.

Imo, who's been swinging her head from side to side between the parties, trying to keep up with the flow of increasingly heated debate, feels suddenly dizzy and sits down abruptly on the edge of Monsieur Gerontin's desk. 'Monsieur Puce?' she says again. There is a brief vacuum of silence – then:

'Monsieur *Who*?' says Hope.

'Puce,' mutters Imo.

'There's a Monsieur *Puce*? *Where?*'

'He's got the roof garden,' translates Imo.

'I *knew* it. Tell him I'm going to report this to the authorities,' says Hope.

'*Mais*, Madame,' says Monsieur Gerontin, despair breaking his determination to stick to his own language, 'you do not understand – Monsieur Puce is very, very old, he is ze last of ze *famille* Puce, you understand? One time they own all ze *maisons* there, many, many years . . .' He turns to Imo in French again.

'He says this Monsieur *Jean* Puce is the last direct descendant of the Puce family. They've sold off various buildings bit by bit over the years – he lives in the top-floor flat of the house immediately behind ours and he's always had a garden up on the roof.'

'I *know*,' crows Hope, triumphant. 'I've *seen* it. Tell him this is completely out of line.'

'The Puce family only sold their building in the first place on condition that Monsieur Jean could keep his garden,' Imo translates.

'I cannot have some goddam garden on *my* roof,' yells Hope.

'Madame,' says Monsieur Gerontin, without waiting for translation, 'you buy – *non*, you bought *un appartement de grand standing*. You did *not* buy a roof.'

'But it can't be safe – has it ever been tested? The weight must be humungous and I'm living right under it.'

'Please – what is "'umungous"?' begs Monsieur.

'I'm not standing for it – tell him that. Monsieur, you understand? And what's all this about a Puce family – what about all that stuff you told me, Imo, about the whorehouse and the fleas?'

'I must have got it wrong, that's all,' says Imo, and for once she's blushing crimson.

'Tell him I shall be contacting the *mairie* immediately about the safety of this so-called garden. Go on, tell him, Imo.'

But Imo doesn't have the chance, for Monsieur Gerontin has leaned towards her and whispered something very fiercely in her ear. She looks shaken and edges herself back off the desk.

'What did he say – I mean, really what did he say?'

'It doesn't matter – it wasn't about you.' Imo's teeth clamp into her bottom lip.

'What about her *drains*?' Ivy suddenly intervenes, and

then in case Monsieur hasn't quite caught her drift, adds extra loudly, though still in English, 'Drains!'

'Shut up, Mum – please,' Imo mutters.

'You ask him – go on.'

'It's no use, Mum. Believe me. Leave it.'

*

Verona's instructions turn out to be vague, and Alice and Josette have trouble locating the third quay on the right – on the right from where? They wander through a maze of bollards, parked cars and gangplanks. They've already passed the main part of the marina, and way down ahead is the finger of harbour that sticks out into deeper water, where some of the much larger boats are moored. They walk and walk, getting ever more hopeful. She couldn't have meant out here, could she?

They walk right out to the end of the longest, grandest quay and then head back again – past the chunky hunks of white cruisers and slender sailing yachts, reading the names off bow or stern. Here's the *Genevieve* from Hamilton, the *Dawn Chorus* from Georgetown, the *Swift* from Nassau, the *Joker's Trick* from London. Deck-hands scrape and sluice. There are very few owners on view, though virtually every cruiser displays a giant flower arrangement on its stern deck dining-table, in permanent readiness for a phantom feast. No *Karma* so far, flying either Red Ensign or orange plaid dress.

By now they're almost back at the port entrance. So where is it? They stop and scan right across the marina. Directly ahead is the area for fishing-boats and local-hire craft for diving or day trips. They'd walked straight past in their earlier search. Most of the fishermen are by now in the local bars, having a well-deserved rest from the midday sun with a pastis or two thrown in. A few are mending tackle. Ropes, nets, floats, jerry-cans, bikes, dogs, the odd deck-chair lie scattered. At the farthest end in the midst of this dense clutter, a group of people is gathered. Too distant for exact identification – just a bubble of laughter around a table. But there's something in the tone of that laughter which is Anglo rather than Gallic – a high-pitched cackle rather than a guttural gabble. And suddenly that familiar call, the very same one which has caused such heart-sinking over previous months, 'Coo-ee! I say! I say! Coo-ee – we're down here!'

And there is Verona, frantically waving.

Amongst the same scattered fishermen's debris, the group is gathered on white plastic chairs around a white plastic table laden with bottles and packets of crisps. There's an instantaneous impression of bare chunky legs coming out of very short shorts, plus multi-coloured Hawaiian shirts.

'Yogi, I'd like you to meet my friends, Alice, Josette – all of you – Yogi!'

'Pleased to meet you,' says he who must be Yogi, rising from a chair.

He's five foot four inches of tanned flesh stretched tightly over a small muscular frame and his age is completely indecipherable. In daylight his hair turns out not to be grey at all, but dazzling platinum blond, thinly shaggy on top, but hanging to a shoulder-length page-boy at the back. The skin around his eyes is deeply furrowed, his neck the texture of crêpe de Chine, but the rest of him is smooth and shiny as turned wood. From the ground up, he's wearing rubber flip-flops, a minute pair of bathing briefs in stretchy purple, a heavy gold necklace, a gold hoop earring – and that's it. The rest of him is entirely nut-brown naked, and leaves absolutely nothing to the imagination. It's a question of small but perfectly formed. Verona looms over him, at least half a head taller, squeezed into the striped two-piece, heaving with bosoms and happiness. She's pointing out the other occupants of the chairs.

'And here's Bruce and Mandy Allnut, Terry and Tanya Potterton, and Jake. Everyone's from Leigh-on-Sea except Jake. Jake's come from further afield, a real foreign interloper – Southend!' and Verona roars.

'Cheers!' says Jake, not getting up, but raising a very English-looking pint tankard of stout in greeting.

'Cheers!' say all the others.

'Now what can we get you?' says Verona, bustling about to seat and sort. 'We've got everything you can imagine, what with duty-free. Have a little vodka, why don't you, or how's about a Bloody Mary? We've got lots of ice on board.'

'On board' – the magic words. So far they haven't bothered to take on the significance of where 'on board' might be. So which is it, the good ship *Karma*? Well, here, right behind the gathering, is a vessel, a small, earnest little motor vessel – maybe ten, fifteen feet – painted sky-blue and currently spiked with rods and lines. A blackboard is propped up in what might be perhaps its fo'c'sle (though neither Alice nor Josette would actually recognize a fo'c'sle if it stood up and said good afternoon). '*À Louer*' is chalked up on the board and then underneath in English, 'To Rent – Day Trips – Fishing – Diving – Phone for Rates', the mystery of Yogi laid bare.

Verona has jumped aboard and is descending past the blackboard into what must be the cabin. It's clearly of miniature proportions, for her head is still fully visible as she fiddles with her hands down below. She emerges with a tray of ice. In the act of leaping back on to *terra firma*, one of her breasts has escaped, and she looks down at it with mild surprise. 'Oh,' she says, putting the ice down and pushing the offending mammary back where it belongs, adding, 'This *is* fun, isn't it?' as she starts passing round the Twiglets.

Somehow throughout the afternoon, Alice manages not to crack, though it's a close-run thing. Initially she tries to avoid Josette's eyes, lest any connection should release the pent-up force of giggles. But in fact Josette develops quite a concerned, puzzled expression and focuses on the group from Leigh-on-Sea, as if it's a recently discovered tribe and she an enraptured anthropologist.

As a whole group, though, they all laugh – laughter in this instance taking on a completely different significance from that of illicit giggling. *How* they laugh. Yogi is a generous host, keeps the booze flowing, and the cackles build. Laugh – you could've knocked me down with a feather. Laugh – I nearly *wet myself*. Lordy, lordy, the things that went on aboard the little *Karma* on the way to Cannes and back. Mandy sick as a dog – well, you were, weren't you, Mand? Bruce nearly lost his drawers. Tanya got burnt on her bum – serves you right, you rascal, sunbathing in the nud. Where's she think she is – back in Canvey Island? And throughout it all Verona's smiling and passing round the crisps.

'You're my little blossom,' says Yogi suddenly, as the party begins to break up, and he tweaks the stripy top so that it twangs against her breast, as Verona flushes a becoming rose.

'You know – ' says Josette, as they make their way a touch warily home, for the afternoon heat is high and Yogi's measures very generous, 'you know, I sink we can do better – yes?'

'What do you mean?'

'Wiz men. Better zan zis Yogi, you know?'

'We have a saying in English,' says Alice, 'goes, "the chance would be a fine thing" – do you have something similar?'

Josette winks. 'Trust me, Aleese, some zings I just *know*.'

*

Ivy is flabbergasted when Imogen agrees to go back to England with her. She'd been thinking up all these cast-iron reasons why Imogen couldn't possibly stay here on her own with her leg in its current condition – starting with that terrible toilet, but she could have gone on, the list is endless, and if necessary she could pull out the usual financial threats again to make her point. But she doesn't have to – Imogen caves in straight away, doesn't bother to put up any objection at all. She *is* a puzzle, that girl – Ivy'll never work her out – and now she's looking a bit peaky since that meeting with Monsieur Whatsisname, really pale and shaky.

The taxi to the airport is air-conditioned so the driver insists the windows are kept closed. Suits Ivy nicely – doesn't want to get her hair messed up. Doesn't suit Imo, though. Feeling caged already, the thick glass increases her sense of isolation from the sounds and smells of what she's come to consider home.

But paralysis has crept over Imo, and she can't seem to gather up the power to fight back. Misery. They've got her cornered, haven't they? It's what the bastards have always wanted and she's fought them like a wildcat – but they've got her all the same. Her 'freedom' was always a sham and in her heart she's always known it. If she'd wanted true freedom she'd have had to cut her family financial ties and she's never quite felt able to shape up to that challenge. It would've been different if she could ever have landed herself a really decent job – not as if she hasn't tried. Meanwhile, like a secret addiction, the conduit of money – but only ever just *enough* money – has always been there to cushion her through constant falls from grace. Not just rents and mortgages, but bail and fines as well, when she'd been busted for possession or petty theft. Not that she hadn't been clean for years now, mind – but probably not clean enough.

And Monsieur Gerontin knows. His icy little sentence in the midst of all that effusion of hot argument has sealed her fate. Somehow he knows that not only does she have no papers, but also that with her record she has very little chance of ever getting them. With a history of petty teenage crime, acceptance is almost out of the question. It's a serious offence, this illegal paperless state, and she's been living within it for years. He knows and she's always known. Time to call it a day.

It's all the fault of those bloody women. She'd always thought they were bad news. Simply couldn't leave well alone. Fixated on some deep need to get to the root of things, uncover and lay bare. Why? Things that were perfectly all right as they were – left alone. Like poor old Monsieur Puce on his roof. Left as they had been for contented years.

26

Le Marrakech Express

Alice had thought she was longing to get back to the peace of her own flat again, but now she's here it feels very strange. The frenetic activity of the past few days since Gavin arrived has caught her up in its whirl, filled her mind with other people's concerns, rescued her from the chilly dullness of her own. But now that everyone seems to have gone and the panic has died down, she feels flat and lonely again.

Gavin's note was brief. 'Heading off home – other leads to chase in London. Thanks a million for the Lilo – hope to use it again some time. That must have been some party you went to?!!! We'll catch up on the phone. LUV – Gav' and a series of XXXX along the bottom. Sweet, he'd even had the grace to deflate the Lilo and put it away in the *right* place – bless him. 'Other leads in London' . . . sounds promising. It's then that the telephone rings, a charming voice, someone called Dominic Flight from Bad Boys Productions wonders if she could put him in touch with Gavin Barnes as he's anxious to set up a meeting at Cannes later in the day. And she has to explain that Gav's gone back to London, and the man laughs and says, 'For a change of trousers?' and then starts to tell her some story about a champagne fountain on the Carlton Terrace, and Alice gives him Gav's London number and leaves it at that. But wasn't that American man who came the other night supposed to be from Bad Boys too? And that seemed to have been a disaster . . .

All that was yesterday, before she'd gone off with Josette to meet Verona and her Yogi. Today is altogether different, for the morning has brought a postbox stuffed with hideous communications – and all in one terrifying lump. There's a horrible credit-card bill, which doesn't even include the excesses of these last few days, plus her bank statement with OD printed down all the columns, plus an additional letter from the bank telling her that they are sure she would wish to be informed of this unauthorized overdrawn situation, plus a brown envelope from the UK Inland Revenue demanding to know what has happened to her self-assessment form, which should have been returned by 31 January – and threatening hanging, drawing and quartering plus a fine in consequence of its non-arrival. Well, all right, so she was exaggerating – but she immediately feels as if the world is tumbling in again all over her, drowning her more like . . . Oh, and there is also a note from Hope Boscombe – would she come round that very afternoon to discuss something to their mutual advantage? In old detective stories 'mutual advantage' usually meant unexpected legacies leading to murder most foul. Alice's mind boggles.

*

Verona received a note too – same invitation, same time. She and Alice decide to arrive together, interested to have their curiosity in this much-vaunted apartment satisfied at last. They're duly impressed by its expansive glamour as Hope leads them out on to her terrace and seats them round a big teak table. It's set up with notepads, pens and bottles of water as if they're in committee, very formal, so clearly not a social occasion, and in fact she launches into her subject with no preamble.

'I had a meeting with Monsieur Gerontin yesterday and I have to tell you that it was very far from satisfactory.'

'Yes, he always has been – what's the word? – *oblique*. Would that describe him?' says Verona.

'I'd call it crooked.'

'Oh, no, dear, not that – it's simply his *way*. I mean, we've always had to nag a bit – well, *quite* a bit – but there's a particular method of doing things here and on the whole it's usually best to let it all take its course.'

'What?'

'On the old basis that "if it ain't broke don't fix it"?'

'But it *is* broke. It's very, *very* broke.'

'Well, yes – but it's all cosmetic, he'll get round to it in the end – there's no point in putting his back up. Obviously it would be nice to have our doorbells working again . . .'

'I'm not talking doorbells here, I'm talking fundamentals – do you know for example that all the exterior plaster has to be removed and entirely renewed? I was tipped off by someone in the know and I called in a builder yesterday afternoon – from Nice, an English guy, lives down here and does a lot of work for expats. He's only made a quick inspection so far but even from that he confirmed the problem – and that's only the start. We've probably got major issues with the whole drainage system, the roof – God knows what. Here's his very rough estimate for just the stucco work.'

Hope passes round a piece of paper headed 'Côte Construction'. Alice regards the preposterously huge figure in front of her before passing it on to Verona. The numbers seem to swim along the paper's surface – even divided by ten to get an approximate amount in sterling, they still make her feel sick.

'Actually,' Hope continues, relentless, 'he suggests we bring in a structural engineer to assess the whole building – and I have to agree with him, because I've also just made another very disturbing discovery. We have an interloper using part of our building for his own purposes. There's a Monsieur Jean Puce living in the top-floor flat of the building immediately behind us – right through that wall there.' Hope stabs with her finger into mid-air towards the back of her sitting room. 'Living right *there*, and taking advantage of my – correction *our* – roof.'

'There's a Monsieur *Puce*?' chorus Alice and Verona together.

'Oh, yes. Evidently the family used to own the whole block – trying to keep his finger in the pie of this place too, got a whole damn garden on the roof.'

'Are you sure?' asks Alice.

'Oh, too right I'm sure – I'm sure as sure. Now I've got a proposal for you guys. I would be prepared to make a substantial contribution to the cost of the repairs we need – I mean in addition to my percentage payment as set out in the co-proprietorship – leaving you all with let's say ten to twelve per cent each to find, which I think you'll have to admit is pretty generous, and in exchange I'd like your full back-up in getting this man evicted from the roof. It may not involve lawyers – with the full support of the whole building I think we could get the *mairie* involved and those guys are pretty powerful, it has to be against some regulation or other. Then once we've got rid of this guy we can incorporate the roof back into our building – it's my theory that the weight of what's going on up there is putting the whole building out of whack. It may even be that which has affected the drains. I may tell you that I already have the full support of Imo and her mother.'

'What would happen to the garden?' asks Alice, trying to imagine it through Hope's wall. What a romantic notion.

'It would go – that's what I'd envisage – and the space eventually be reincorporated into my apartment.'

'Yours?'

'That's what I'd envisage, yes. Well, obviously it couldn't be part of anybody else's, could it? But you'd all have the peace of mind of knowing that the major problem was all taken care of . . . It's a very fair offer I'm making.'

Alice is working out what even 12 per cent of the proposed bill would be. It remains a horribly daunting figure – impossible for her to conjure up in fantasy or fact.

'Well?' says Hope.

'*Well* – ' says Verona, 'I don't know what Alice thinks but for my part – and I think I may have said this to you before . . .'

'Yes?' says Hope.

'Best to let sleeping dogs lie . . . don't you think?'

*

Josette has worked out a wonderful plan but Alice doesn't seem anything like pleased enough. It's a real 'date' with the Scandinavians – the ones she'd met at Juan-les-Pins. They won't even have to take a taxi. Jürgen has said he will pick them up – has an idea to drive them to the new Moroccan restaurant way out in the back country beyond Grasse. This is nothing short of a miracle, but Alice isn't showing anything like enough appreciation. It's doing wonders for Josette's battered ego, though. She'd only met the men that once at Boom-Boom – and the antiques dealer one had said this is *fun*, we should do it again, and had given her his card. The lighting in Boom-Boom is, of course, very forgiving with its thick red lamps, but it can't simply be that. She must have been *fun* too – just as she's always seen herself – exciting and *fun*. Eat your heart out, William Prescott-Smythe, you don't know what you're missing. The vintage wine is best.

But when she telephones Alice to tell her this good news, she gets quite the wrong response. Alice is gabbling, talking about the Boscombe woman, Hope (still so difficult to say), and huge expenses which none of them can afford. How the building may even be falling down. But that is surely nonsense. Vieilleville was first settled by the Greeks, the foundations of many of these buildings are *Roman*, so what is this foolishness? That this woman says the plaster needs replacing, that otherwise the damp will penetrate, the walls will crumble. But these are walls of rock – don't they realize that? And what is this damp? Can a little rain now and then crack the rocks and mortar of centuries? But Alice won't seem to allow herself to be consoled – refuses to discuss the arrangements for Saturday night (so crucial to getting the evening off on the right tack), says Josette hasn't grasped the seriousness of the situation, that Hope Boscombe seems determined to get things done, but in the most expensive way possible – talks of architects and engineers and lawyers. Even Verona's worried. And then there's this strange business about the man on the roof, and Josette says, 'Well, what about him?' and Alice says, 'You know who I mean?' and Josette says, 'You mean Monsieur Jean?' and Alice says, 'You've known all along?' and Josette says, 'But everybody knows that,' and Alice says, 'Why didn't you ever tell me?' and Josette says, 'You never asked.'

*

Hope's wondering if she's made herself clear enough. The women don't seem adequately worried about the situation. They'd hardly seemed to react when she'd explained it all to them, and no plans have been actioned. She's not used to this way of living. For years now people have jumped to it when she's made a suggestion. But from their dozy reaction she's wondering if the women even really *believe* her. They should come up in the evening – she should make them. They should sit out here and have to listen to the umpteenth rendition of 'Under the Bridges of Paris' then they'd know what she's up against. Ridiculous to be left almost high and dry with only one solid ally in the unlikely shape of Ivy Prosper.

Still, better one than none, she thinks, as she punches in the number.

'Hi, Ivy – just thought I'd keep you posted with what's

been happening down here . . .' and she tells Ivy about the man from Côte Construction and the meeting with Alice and Verona. Ivy lets her run right through to the end. Hope expects a smattering of 'fancy thats' or at the very least a few 'well I nevers' but Ivy says nothing.

'Ivy, are you still there?'

'Yes – oh, yes, Hope, I'm still here . . .' Through Ivy's brain is skittering that vision of a prospective framed photograph 'Hope with Ivy Prosper' – lovely thought. But then she's always been a practical woman, and this talk of structural engineers is starting to sound seriously expensive. And why should any of them make waves just to give Hope Boscombe a view of the sea? Because it's beginning to look as if that's what all this is about.

'I was thinking, Hope, that perhaps we should hold our horses.'

'You what?'

'Whoa there – you know what I mean? – because once you start using words like "eviction" things can get very complicated. Don't forget I'm a landlord, I know what I'm talking about. I mean, French law may be quite different and all that but, well, we could be getting ourselves involved in a very tricky can of worms.'

Horses? Worms? 'What are you actually telling me Ivy?'

'Better leave things be, eh, Hope?'

*

Josette already thinks of the Scandinavians fondly as 'boys'. They're boys quite as much as she's a girl – and, boy, oh, boy, she doesn't half intend to be a 'girl' this evening – she'll never have been girlier.

At first she thought the boys could pick them up from Marie-Auguste's house – a perfect, stylish kick-off for the evening. It would set quite the right tone, and place the two 'girls' in exactly the right context. She would arrange delicious little morsels and champagne, and Alice would reimburse her for the expenses. Maybe Josette herself would contribute a bit, though if she was providing the venue it was really up to Alice to shoulder the rest of the burden. After all, Josette's made all the running so far. Alice really ought to be grateful. And then, out of the blue, Marie-Auguste decided to arrive back from Zurich on Friday night with a crowd of friends, so that Josette was reconfined to the maid's room next to the kitchen, and the whole plan had to be cancelled.

Alice's flat will have to do after all. Oh dear. Not such a perfect spot. Sends out the wrong signals – but what's the alternative? A bar would look even worse, as if they're a pair of alleycats. No. Alice's must suffice.

Tactfully Josette suggests a few improvements. Alice never really seems to have come to grips with the realities of one-room living. Why, for example, is there no screen to hide the kitchen sink? A judicious tidying-up is called for, plus how's about killing some of those sunflowers? Sunflowers everywhere – makes the whole place look like some stall at the cheapo market in Nice. Let's at least put the artificial ones away in a cupboard – quite bad enough to have to cope with them printed all over the curtains and cushions, plus the painted ones she seems to have stuck on every available surface. *Mon Dieu*, but what can have possessed her?

*

With all the fuss Josette's making, Alice is beginning to feel nervous about this wretched date. And then being so sniffy about the flat – quite insulting. She almost caves in and goes off to buy a screen on Saturday morning, but the thought of clocking up yet another bill for something she'd never thought she needed is just too depressing. Bad enough that she's having to shell out for yet more booze and eats, when the original idea as described so enthusiastically by Josette was that the whole evening should be the 'boys'' treat. What she actually feels like doing at this very moment is rolling herself up into a ball like a hedgehog and staying there for the whole foreseeable future.

''Ow long is it, Aleese, since you 'ave a man?'

'Would that be "have" in the biblical sense?'

'What is zis "biblical"?'

'Never mind. A long time, Josette. It's been a long time.'

'Me too – I 'ave fun, you know, but it is always wiz women. Men don't want us – they see us as dried up and old. Men want ze women young and juicy.'

'Birds of Paradise.'

'What?'

'Nothing. You're right, of course – on the whole. It's all to do with natural selection, isn't it? Men can carry on planting their seed till their dotage, so in evolutionary terms they want it in fertile ground – like Hillary Aldyce.'

'What is "dotage"?'

'Old age. Doesn't matter.'

'So zis evening will be – you know, *fun*, is somezing special, and next to this Yogi man zese Scandinavians are very . . . well, you know . . . You say "a bit of all right", yes?'

*

It's back to the transparent white linen again, freshly washed and ironed, with some particularly sparkly gold earrings which show up really well, now Alice has stuck her hair up in a sort of joosh-thing on top of her head. Gives her quite a wild look of Primavera – watch out, Golden Hippie Dippers, here I come.

Once she's taken in the overall long-distance effect she goes in really tight to the mirror so as to see clearly enough to get her mascara on without smudging. Here she is, staring into each of her eyes in turn. Eyes – the windows of the soul, they say. Where's my soul? Where's 'me'? Am I just 'me' as in this outside shell done up like a party cracker, casing beginning to show signs of wear? Is this 'me'? I never used to ask myself questions like that. They never occurred. I always knew who I was. I was 'me' as Alice Barnes. I was Philip Barnes's wife. I was Gavin and Lally Barnes's mother. I woke up in the morning and knew exactly what the day promised. I went to bed at night certain of sleep and periodic sex. Nothing needed questioning. There was always pain – but it was out there. It was mostly someone else's. Hence periodic guilt – the charity work, raffles and dances and auctions and rattled tins.

She closes both eyes now, tightly, then opens them.

Winking, blinking like the eyes on Gav's laptop, which he'd shown her so proudly. Those Deadeyes. What am I doing this for, going on this date? What do I need with a date? No Scandinavian 'boy' is going to turn me back into me. Somewhere below, a great big pit has opened up, a muddle of fear and loneliness, and it's nothing Hope Boscombe can put to rights with architects or structural engineers.

*

They're called Jürgen and Hugo – and by the time Alice can hear them coming up the stairs she's caught a full case of Josette's jitters – feels really quite nervous. Josette came early and has been hanging her head out of the window to catch them, for the doorbells still don't work. Once she's spotted them she calls out in English, 'Good evening – you make good time!' and dashes down to let them in.

At first sight they're certainly better date material than Yogi, though calling them 'boys' is overstretching the point. They're probably both in their well-preserved late fifties to early sixties, with tanned elastic skin and washed-out blue eyes. There the similarity ends. Jürgen is tall and willowy, Hugo short and solid. In a rapid series of proprietorial gestures, Josette makes it clear that Jürgen is hers. She takes his elbow oh-so-lightly and steers him to the sofa – then perches herself on the arm with the smiling poise of an *ingénue*. Hugo is left standing, as Alice is busy with glasses and pouring.

'This is so nice,' he says. He has an American accent. 'So nice . . . This was a great idea of Josette's. You know we had this great evening with her – we were in Juan and we were, like, two guys out alone and far from home, and you know the French have this reputation, but we've found everybody *so* nice. Josette was very kind. She was translating the drinks for us – '

'Really. Translating the drinks?'

'You've been to Juan-les-Pins?' he asks.

'Actually, no. I was supposed to go that night but something cropped up.' But no – something had come *down*: the slide of Immac pulled by gravity. What a pointless thing to do. Who cares if she's got pubes like Brillo pads any more?

'Well, if you ever go you'll see. They have these huge cocktail menus – dozens of ingredients, oceans of potions!'

'And I 'elp because you wonder if a "Boom-Boom Special" is a bomb,' says Josette, 'and I tell you, no, it is tequila and Campari and Americano and Blue Curaçao all mixed up wiz egg-white and sugar on ze rim.'

'And we said, "Well, we're right, it is a bomb after all!"'

'Yes, you did – and 'ow we laugh.' Josette turns to Jürgen to laugh all over again, but suddenly realizes her neck is probably at the wrong level, for she's sitting slightly above him. *Disastre*. She gets up to fetch the platter of the Boulangerie de l'Évêque's delicious little *fours salés* in order to hand them around and reposition herself on the sofa at Jürgen's other side, where she can safely look upwards and let her eyelashes bat with impunity.

'Actually,' says Hugo, bending into Alice's ear, 'the menu was also in English – but we let her have her little game.'

'Oh – right.'

'Nice cupboards by the way – nicely distressed. Who did your sunflowers?'

*

The restaurant is called Le Marrakech Express and is surely a mistake. Whose choice could it have been? It's at least an hour's drive into the back country up bending, terrifying roads, which teeter over precipices. Alice bitterly regrets plying their chauffeur Hugo with that second glass of fizz, but it's too late now.

When they arrive, dizzied and disorientated, they are led down into a cellar hung with carpets and swags of embroidered mirrored cloth. There are no chairs, only squashy leather pouffes – how wonderfully authentic, they all cry. What fun. Oh, the fun. They each arrange themselves as carefully as twingey backs and trick knees will allow – this is wild, isn't it? This is life?

The menu features Hareera and Ulk'tban, Bastela and Frackh, L'Hootz F'Tadjeena and L'Hootz Bcharmeela Mneedan Ltaff, Sjdeda Bi Zatoon Bi Lima and Bibi M'Ahmarh – but who's counting? Who cares? Never mind no one knows what they're eating. It's warm and dark and the food arrives in giant bowls. Nameless to them, it takes on a uniform consistency, like spicy baby food – and the wine helps, of course. Doesn't take long for the mood to mellow – not so long at all. And the light is kind, and the music sinuous.

A long time later, after the sweetmeats (not puddings, not possibly, these are definitely 'sweetmeats') of fruits and aniseed and honey and nuts – well, a long time after, the live music starts. There's a pipe and a drum, a rhythm and a hum and a wiggle – and Josette's rising to her feet. Somehow, despite the lowness and the angle, which should have tweaked out a groan and gasp, she's got herself upright with lithe grace and is joining the dance. The tabor player in hooded robe has taken the centre of the room and Josette joins him. Beating out the rhythm, she bends herself backwards, so that her top rides up to reveal an inch of navelled belly and starts to undulate. Jürgen and Hugo lean forward to watch. The whole room leans forward to watch. The clapping starts, slowly at first, as Josette circles the drummer – perhaps it should be obscene, but it isn't. At sixty-plus, whatever she is, it should be embarrassing – Alice thinks for a moment that she's prepared to feel ashamed – but no, it isn't. If it were being done with more self-consciousness and less aplomb it might be comical, but as it is, it's perfect – an essence of female staking a claim.

The audience appreciates, erupts into applause, and Josette takes a slinky bow, loving her moment. Then, as the music continues, she shimmies towards their table and gestures in a come-hitherish way to Jürgen. Alice is holding her breath – this is when embarrassment will take hold? But no, for as she advances the whole room begins to spill on to the floor and Jürgen looks happy to join in. Everyone is dancing now – with nothing like Josette's mesmerizing skill but in a happy, sexy, rippling scrum. Apart from a few sticklers, of course, for there are always a few whose inhibitions rob their bodies of spontaneity – among them Alice and Hugo.

Possibly Alice would like to have been asked, though as she already knows how hopeless she'd be, it's almost a relief that he doesn't offer. Maybe it's the imbalance of their heights so that both instinctively know the vision they've just witnessed would in their case descend into farce. Or maybe it's simply that he doesn't fancy her. She's felt nothing coming from him all evening except polite objective interest, and now they're stuck with each other as the dancing builds its intensity around them. The music is too invasive to allow much in the way of conversation, so to fill in some of the gap she asks him for a cigarette.

She hasn't smoked since 1968, and she didn't like it all that much then. It was a thing you had to do in those days as part of the mating ritual, involving arcane and specialized equipment like Zippo lighters and silver cases, all in the hope that he, whoever the 'he' happened to be at the time, would light two cigarettes in his mouth at the same time, and hand one of them over to you, preferably post-coitally, so that you could glimpse each other through the faint glow of the burning tip.

Like riding a bike, the initial part of the ritual comes back to her with certain instinct. Hugo leans across the table with his lighter, and Alice accepts the flame, staring into his face for a moment. Is there anything there for her? The last man who could have done this for her would have been Philip – yes, before they were married, because they'd given up together, partly to help their tight finances and partly because as a habit it was already becoming unacceptable in medical circles. She sees a flash of Philip's young face through the smoke, overtaken by the fleshed reality of Hugo in this semi-light. It's not a pretty comparison.

Hugo has turned away from her and is watching the dancing. Josette and Jürgen are at the centre of the throng circling the drummer, heaving with the rhythm. He couldn't be making it more obvious that he has no interest in her at all. The cigarette tastes vile, but Alice puffs on it lightly, grateful to have something to do. Now just supposing that the signals were different and that this man was coming on to her – only thinking in the abstract, you understand – but, yes, well, making that sort of assumption, in such a scenario, could she be attracted to him? She observes him sideways – the wide thickish lips, supposed to be sensual, the folds of skin around his neck, the fluff of greying chest hair peeping over the top of his shirt – and feels only revulsion. What's got into her? How can she dare be so choosy? Is this what it will always be like, from now on, a life of lonely celibacy? 'The chance would be a fine thing?' they've all joked to each other, but here presumably is a chance, and neither in the least degree prepared to take it on.

And then he turns back to her, and leans in to shout, 'My business is kitchens – did you know that?' As a topic this puts the final lid on any lingering doubts she may have been harbouring, and it's a relief to admit romantic defeat and shout back at him.

'Josette said antiques – but she likes to embroider.'

'There's probably more money in kitchens.'

'Every home needs one.'

'Mine are specialist.'

'Yes?'

'Handmade, hand-painted – rich clientele, expects the best.'

'I see.'

'So tell me all about your sunflowers . . .'

*

Tick, tick, tick – for Hope the tensions haven't eased.

It's a beautiful mellow evening, but impossible to relax. Sitting out on the terrace her senses are all alert and waiting. Tick, tick, tick – her skin is scratchy, her heart is crashing around in her chest.

She'd called Jerry this afternoon to complain and demand. Get her an English-speaking lawyer fast. She's had it up to here with trying to unravel this situation for herself – it's like wrestling in molasses: the more she's tried to attack, the more stuck she's feeling. Jerry had irritated her too, using his soothing atta-girl-how's-my-baby voice – the one he always tries when he thinks she needs placating. Sod him. Cut the crap and just get that lawyer fast.

As on those earlier evenings, she's set herself a still-life of wine and olives, but the Bandol tastes bitter to her tongue, the olives rancid. She sits and stares back into her living room towards the solid wall on the far side. A mere nine inches or so of barrier – just through there lies the magnificent view. A totally tantalizing waste. And then it starts – just as she'd known it would – the accordion from up above. She tenses herself, ready for the familiar hated opening chords, only to realize that tonight the repertoire has changed. What is it this time? She allows herself to ease back just far enough to pick out the tune. '*La Mer*' – Charles Trenet in the original, wasn't it? But she's remembering Bobby Darrin's American version, 'Beyond the Sea' . . . beyond the sea . . . My God. He's *laughing* at her.

*

The dancing is still going on when Alice excuses herself and heads for the loo. Within the time it's taken for the rest of the company to work from belly-dance to conga via Moroccan variations on the hippie-hippie shake, Hugo as potential love interest has transmogrified into Hugo as potential employer. His company is based in Nice, builds high-specification fitted kitchens for rich expat Scandinavians who buy retirement villas in the hills. He's newly arrived from head office in Stockholm for it's reckoned to be an expanding market, they're getting into bedrooms soon – pauses for a laugh – fitted bedrooms would be lucrative too. But it's highly competitive out there, so he's always searching for that extra spark. Distressed paint finishes on his cupboard doors have been something of a speciality – a very Nordic look, of course – but he's been on the lookout for something extra. Likes the way she's done her sunflowers – the Danes would like sunflowers. Can she do other things too? An edelweiss kitchen might go down really well – but it could be anything. The rich like individuality above all else. And shouting over the din of tabor, pipe and shrieking laughter, Alice tells her Bristol tale of gesso and colour-washed walls and ceilings of gold leaf and size.

After she's peed and washed her hands, she stands, looking back at her face in the mirror. She's pretty drunk, of course – better do something about her makeup, cheeks too red, eyeliner smudged – but something's changed since she was doing this earlier, back at the Maison Puce. Possible salvation lurks around the corner – and even the prospect makes an involuntary smile of her lips.

She's just applying powder when the door opens and

Josette comes in. Alice sees her reflected in the mirror, and in her squiffy, happier haze she continues dabbing at her nose, whilst saying through the glass backwards, 'You were great – where did you learn to belly-dance like that?'

'Ummm?' Josette is leaning against the door now, panting slightly, the flat of her hands pressed in against her breasts.

'Are you all right?' Alice turns round now.

'Aleese, zey are *gay*.'

'What?'

'Hugo and Jürgen – zey are like zese.' Josette holds her crossed fingers up to indicate unbreakable intimacy.

'Oh. Right.' says Alice. 'Of *course*.'

'What you mean "of course" – you *knew*?'

'Not exactly,' but it's all making more sense.

'You should 'ave told me if you knew. I am so embarrassed – we are all dancing, and 'e can dance, that Jürgen, you see 'e can, and I am telling 'im we can take rooms 'ere because we cannot drive so drunk all ze way back to Vieilleville, and I give 'im a leetle wink, you know, and zen I give 'im a *leetle*, *leetle* kiss and *voilà*, you know what he call me?'

'Tell.'

''Is *leetle* Fag 'Ag – and he laugh. You know what is Fag 'Ag?'

'Fag *H*ag – you have to say the aitch like in *H*ope – and yes, I rather think I do . . .'

*

Tick, tick, tick – Hope is pacing. Tick, tick, tick – and, up above, '*La Mer*' is playing for at least the twentieth, thirtieth time, several different syncopations reverberating across the roof and settling right over her – a missile of sound aimed, she's sure of it, directly at her.

'Belt up!' she yells into the night sky. 'Cut it out, you little fucker!' There's a moment of silence, and then the opening chords of the thirty-first rendition. But she'll get him. Playing games, is he? She'll see about that. She drags the step-ladder up to her bedroom, kicks off her shoes and climbs out on to the roof. Then, as she had last time, she hauls the ladder through the window and crawls up the slope of the tiles pulling it with her as she goes. At the top she leans it against the cement parapet wall, with its legs resting in the valleys between the rows of tiles, and starts to climb.

The music, which had seemed louder, has suddenly stopped. She creeps now, and having reached the top she peers again through the slit in the green material. Then she takes a pair of scissors from her pocket and starts working at the seam as quietly as she can until she's made quite a sizeable hole. She pokes her head through. Clear ahead is the wonderful view – the sea and sky in matching inky midnight blue, just touched and sparkling with lights from the promenade and the distant beam of the lighthouse. It's so still she can hear the wash of the waves on the shore.

In front of her and on both sides is wooden staging, packed with terracotta pots. Green fronds are waving in the wind and wafting a familiar acrid scent in her direction. She sniffs and tries to recall – what is that? It's so familiar and yet – what *is* it? . . . sniffing again . . . could it be? . . . yes, of course . . . It's pot. She'd always had a sneaky feeling it must be something strange up here. Got Him. *Got him.*

And then it starts – *La Mer* – all over again from the far side of the plants and she's leaning over trying to hook one of them – further and further over – fingertips stretching, and now they've closed on a leaf, now a stem, just gently pulling, but too far, for the plant tips sideways off its shelf, its container crashing to the floor, though she's still clinging on to the stem, her vital proof. At the sound of the crash the music has stopped. There's a guttural sort of yell – and she's scrabbling with her feet to find the ladder, as she tries to hang on to the wall and the plant. And now she's found it – feet safely on the steps – and she's easing herself back down from the wall – when the plants in front of her are parted and a head is poked through, brown and wizened as a walnut, with eyes which look wide and fearful, and it's then she realizes that it's a tomato plant in her hand and just as she's about to dip down the legs of the ladder lose their grip on the tiles below. Suddenly she's slithering down the wall, and it's raining tomatoes all over, and the careful arrangement of tiles is slipping, sliding and crashing into the sky over the rue d'Espoir.

*

It's Verona who hears it first – that splintering smash. She and Yogi have slipped back to the flat for a shower and a late-night supper after their trip to St Tropez, and as she looks up from serving dear Yogi a slice of quiche, she sees tiles shooting past her window in a terracotta rain. She's in her dressing-gown, he in just a towel – and together they scoot for the stairs.

*

After all that, Alice and Josette have to take a taxi.

Jürgen and Hugo have decided to stay. Le Marrakech Express offers rooms at a very competitive rate with bathrooms *en suite*, but after her misapprehension, Josette feels it would be too embarrassing to stay. It's bad enough now, when drunk, but will feel truly terrible tomorrow morning when sober. Best not have to face them over croissants and coffee. Particularly humiliating to be seen to share a room with Alice Barnes, when she'd made it so clear to Jürgen that she'd expected the night to hold such promise. The shame is too much to bear.

So a taxi it is – at vast expense. For once Alice doesn't really care. It's partly the booze of course, but mostly this new hint of optimism born out of the offer of work – and at least she hadn't tried to seduce her new boss before she'd clocked his sexual preferences. Sometimes in life you can just feel grateful.

They doze on the journey back to Vieilleville, and when they reach the place d'Espoir, stay sitting for a moment while Alice pays with her credit card – double rate because the driver from Cannes will never get a return journey at this time of night. Josette mumbles about paying her back. Then they get out, the taxi draws away, and they stand, swaying slightly from wine and sleep, in the warm still air.

Until they hear the first crash – and the second – and

turning towards the Maison Puce see a hail of terracotta tiles tumbling from the sky and Verona and Yogi standing below, smudged and streaked with blood, as all around, the lights of the old town are switched on and shutters flung open to view.

27

Endgame

The For-sale sign goes up in August even though the front of the house is still masked by a jungle-gym of scaffolding.

À VENDRE
Agence Gerontin

Hope would have a fit if she knew Monsieur Gerontin was having anything whatever to do with her property, but as she's still buried in the seclusion of the Abbey Clinic in Wiltshire she doesn't know. Jerry's had quite enough to contend with in getting her out of the hands of the French police, without having to go to additional trouble finding another estate agent in Vieilleville. Gerontin knows the property – Gerontin will have to do.

There was also all the trouble with the press. The headlines weren't that original – 'HOPE'S HAIR-RAISER', 'BOSCOMBE BEDLAM' – usual run-of-the-mill stuff. One of the red-top tabloids went to town with its print-run, though, adding painted splashes of red to a photograph of the Maison Puce below a snatched shot of Hope at Nice airport, looking wild and woolly – 'HOPE ON THE (TOMATO) SAUCE!'. According to the *Sunday Scourge*, French locals were 'amazed to see the Famous Warrior for Consumer Rights Very Much the Worse For Wear – hurling half her roof plus a ton of tomatoes into the street on top of innocent bystanders'. One woman had been knocked unconscious, blood and tomato juice mingled in the dust. '*C'est* Froggy *formidable*!'

The *gendarmerie* in Vieilleville seems, on the whole, prepared to let it all drop. From an examination of the roof, it seems there had been some sort of collapse. The men from the *mairie* came to inspect, giving Monsieur Gerontin's stomach a nasty roller-coaster ride for a few days, but after initial mumblings about negligence, everyone seems to have come down on the side of an accident. If old Monsieur Jean hadn't died of his heart-attack he might perhaps have shed some light, but as it is, everyone's inclined to leave it be. The insurers are prepared to pay for a large proportion of the damage and Monsieur Gerontin has surprisingly agreed to cough up the rest. Thus the rapid erection of scaffolding and, after so many years of prevarication, the arrival of real *bona-fide* workmen.

Jerry's got this idea of sending Hope to Arizona as soon as she's fit enough to travel. There's a really remarkable funny farm out there in the desert where people learn to tap into their feelings – good idea to get the girl back to her American roots. Also Arizona sounds a nice long way from Telly Centre – the further the better for the foreseeable future, though if Hope comes out of this all right, maybe they could get a series out of her experiences? Waste not, want not.

*

A lot of it was exaggeration. No one was actually knocked out – not cold. It was Josette who caught the glancing blow and she needn't have staggered right into the line of fire like that. It was probably a bit to do with still being half asleep from the long drive down from Le Marrakech Express – that and the wine and the accumulation of disappointments over the previous weeks. And it did look for a moment like some vision of the Apocalypse – with Verona and Yogi standing like statues in the street, both swathed in white terry-towelling, looking upwards, all streaked with blood. No one was to know at that stage that it was mostly tomato juice, though Yogi had cut his big toe really badly trying to move some of the smashed tiles off the front doorstep, so there was a little genuine gore flowing around too. And then Josette had staggered forward, straining to look up, with her arms outstretched, in a gesture of supplication to the gods, and was felled by one of Monsieur Jean's flowerpots containing a handsome specimen of his own hybrid, the phenomenal early-fruiting *Gloire Rouge*, which he'd spent a lifetime perfecting up on the roof.

Josette's made a remarkable recovery, lapping up the attention and treating the few days she spent in hospital as a rest cure. *Nice-Matin* carried the story on its front page and printed a charming photograph of her from their files – that time she'd won the Vieilleville Ladies Bridge Invitational. So charming, in fact, that she's received several rather promising messages from gentlemen in the town, which she'll get round to checking out once she's on full form again. When she was allowed home, Marie-Auguste set her up in the second-best guest bedroom even though she still had her Zurich friends staying – and Josette's been enjoying every moment of it. The Swiss play a mean game of backgammon, but not so mean that Josette isn't stashing up a nice little pile of winnings, which is just as well for her wardrobe is pretty depleted and new clothes for autumn are a looming necessity. Of course, she still has nowhere she can truly call home, ever a cause for regret – but who knows what might come from these new contacts? If one doesn't let oneself go, keeps one's *ligne*, well, who knows what's just around the corner? One of Marie-Auguste's friends is a widower and Zurich can be wonderful in the spring . . .

*

In the Maison Puce, Verona is at last tackling all those piles of newspapers. Dear old *Torygraph* – time to go. Anyway Yogi prefers the *Sun*. Got to make some room in here somehow. She's only just got back from the UK, seeing to the Old Folk – still going strong, bless them. She hasn't told them about putting the Hove flat on the market – it would only disturb them. They hate the idea of change, and in this case it's surely a question of what the eye doesn't see, the heart doesn't grieve for? Isn't it? That's her perception anyway. They won't really notice the difference, will they? The fact that she'll be living on a boat in Brighton marina when she comes to visit them, rather than the flat, is quite beside the point. And she will visit – often. Well, apart from when she and Yogi are sailing round the world, but they can't even start to plan that until she's sold the flat and bought their big new boat with the proceeds. Terribly exciting. They've nosed around the yacht brokerages in

Antibes and Cannes but Yogi's really got his eye on the Boat Show in January so there's plenty of time to plan. Lovely. Often the best bit.

Meanwhile they've decided to share their living quarters for the winter – half on board the *Karma* and half in the Maison Puce – snug as bugs in rugs. Theo is still being very sniffy about this – as if it's any of his business. He'd been happy enough to leave her horribly alone when it suited him, but now he's always ringing up, asking questions about Yogi, making snide comments. Such a cheek. It's not as if she doesn't know Yogi's a bit of a rough diamond. She's not stupid, for heaven's sake. But he's very kind and very loving. More loving than anyone she's ever known. Mummy and Daddy were cold fish – and Edmund really rather hateful now she looks back. Always calling her Bully Beef in front of their friends, expecting her to skivvy for him non-stop – and then treating her like a leper in their bed. When she looks back she wonders how she put up with him all those years. Except even now it doesn't take much explanation. On the surface, at least, he made it seem as if he wanted her, and no one else had – not until then. She thought she had a place, that she knew where she was with him, but it was all a front. Now she's been with Yogi she can tell the difference. And how dare people hint that he's only interested in her money? How dare they? He's her Yogi and she's his Blossom – and she can feel her petals open just at the thought.

*

Imo's leg has mended well, but other things are happening to her body. It was the chucking up which alerted her – that and being late. She's never late and she never chucks up so it wasn't difficult to draw the inevitable conclusion. She'd loathed the enforced recuperation in Purley, but it hadn't been all that long before she'd been able to limp about on her own. Bought a testing kit in Boots, did it in the loos at McDonald's – positive, of course. Some little children were banging on the loo door while she was waiting, said they were going to pee in their pants if she didn't get a move on. She told them to fuck off and just went on sitting there with the lid down, waiting for the little line to turn blue. Knowing it would. And it did.

Went on sitting there a while longer – let the little darlings pee their pants. Just sitting there hugging herself – as in, all right, about time too. This is someone for me, little person whoever you are, and we'll be mates, you and I – I'll make it different. I won't land you in the shit, I'll just keep you safe and warm – and *free*.

It's a few days later that the practicalities begin to dawn. As a full-time home, Vieilleville's out of the question anyway now – at least until she can get her legal status sorted out. No access to maternity care and benefits without that sodding little *carte de séjour* – and only God and the Bonneville *mairie* can tell if she'll ever get one. Of course she can still visit – as often as she wants – and that'd be good. Assuming she could ever afford to be so indulgent to herself and Prosper junior.

She tries contacting Theo first but he's away in New York. Then she has a go at Gav – very much a second-rate solution. Gav sounds really pleased to hear her. Things are going great – well, great-ish. Got back to London to find that the real Bad Boys Production team are really quite interested in *Deadeyes* – well, interested enough to commission another draft of the script. This means that the Lottery money is sort of on hold – not confirmed, alas, but at least not yet down the drain altogether. And actually things are really looking pretty good – yeah? Bloody good, really, and yeah, he'd love to meet her for a drink.

Well, all right – but you should have seen his face when she told him in the pub. They met in the Chelsea Potter – music so loud she could feel it in her tum – had to shout to launch her little rocket. Poor old Gav – green? He went the colour of cheese mould before you could have said gorgonzola. And she was a bit rotten because she could have let him off the hook if she'd wanted, but thinking of little Prosper junior she reckoned she might as well keep all balls juggling – just for the moment.

The same with Theo – once she'd managed to track him down. He gave her dinner at Mezzo and she told her sorry tale. Poor little Mouse, he said, my little manky Mouse, we shall have to see what we can do, shan't we? And though she'd considered kicking him in the balls right there and then under the table for the 'manky', for the moment she smiled and simpered – looking grateful.

Of course she's pretty certain Prosper junior's going to arrive with almond eyes and a softly olive skin. She hopes so – Lin Ho was a beautiful man and a bloody good cook. Don't know quite where he is, though, that's the problem – somewhere in the Gulf aboard *Lady Karla* practising the use of his English adverbs? Well, who knows. Might be safest to run with Theo for the moment – with Gav as an understudy.

*

'Alice? It's me – Philip.'

'Oh.' (Good God.) 'Hello. Where are you phoning from?'

'What? Here, of course. Home.'

'Oh. I thought perhaps you were down here.'

'No. I'm at home.'

'So am I.'

'Oh. Yes, I suppose you are. All right, is it?'

'Oh, yes – quite all right.'

'Well, I'm glad.'

'Good. I'm glad you're glad.'

'Quite.'

'Can I do something for you?'

'What?'

'Did you phone for a reason – any more lost candelabra?'

'No, no. Well, in a way . . . yes . . .'

'Are you still there? Philip?'

'Oh, yes – just thinking. It's . . . well – '

'Yes?'

'It's Hillary.'

'What about her?'

'I don't know quite how to put it . . . She seems terribly low.'

'Does she?'

'Well, with the babies – it's such a strain, of course, twins – and what with everything else . . .'

'What "everything else"?'

'Well, you know – the house, my practice, entertaining – it's quite a lot to cope with I suppose.'

'Yes?'

'And she just can't seem to snap out of it. I've told her to pull herself together – '

'That must have helped.'

' – but she just doesn't seem to have any will or energy.'

'Post-natal depression?'

'Well, obviously that's one's first thought.'

'*Obviously.*'

'But I just wondered – I mean, *you* always managed and you've had the experience too – I mean, I just wondered if you might have a word with her, help her get things into proportion, get her to brace up a bit.'

'Brace up?'

'Yes – you know the sort of thing, I'm sure, word of advice from one who's been through it, that sort of thing.'

'You want *me* to advise your new wife on her post-natal depression?'

'I haven't phoned you for a *diagnosis*, Alice. Don't let's get medical – '

'Of course not. *You*'re the gynaecologist, Philip.'

'Only wanted to enlist your help – give her a sense of perspective.'

'No, Philip.'

'What?'

'No. I think that's something you'd better do yourself. *Va te faire voir chez les Grecs*!'

'What – what was that? Something about the Greeks?'

'It's a new expression I've just learned – I mean new to me. I think it may come in quite useful – means "go to hell" – *va te fairè voir chez les Grecs, mon cher* Philip, and *adieu*!'

*

It's been a boiling, blazing day.

After Philip's phone call, Alice doesn't feel like sleeping, so she gets up at dawn and takes Fred for a quick lone swim. The beach is deserted, and the water like soft, warm satin. She stops for coffee at the market *tabac*. The traders are still setting up their stalls. Just like last year, the aroma of basil and ripe melons is as heady as a drug. She doesn't think she'll ever tire of it. She buys a plump red mullet for her supper, plus some chanterelles, *mesclun* and a huge white peach for pud. She doesn't have to go in to work today, probably not all week as Hugo's got her painting roses on a stack of small cupboard doors for the Sorensens' bathroom, and he brought them over last night. They want each of them different, nothing matching at all, so she's using Redouté for inspiration – today 'Fantin-Latour' and 'Duchesse d'Orléans'. Through the blistering heat of the day, she paints in the vine-fringed cool of her flat, sometimes in silence, sometimes to Bach, sometimes to Riviera Radio, while Fred lies stretched out on the blissfully cold tiled floor, panting. Imo has rung from England and asked her to look after him, and she couldn't think of a single solid reason to refuse.

Josette turns up at six, shouting for Alice to come and join her for a night of jollification at Juan. As the doorphones now work there's no need for all this public messaging, but since she got into the newspapers she sees herself as something of a local celebrity, and sure enough, after the second yell of *'Aleese!'* there are heads poking out of every window in the street. Alice buzzes her up, though she can tell Josette is disappointed to have her performance cut short.

Josette takes one look at Alice's paint-spattered condition, and sees there's no chance of her making it to Juan tonight – not without a radical body overhaul – and the truth is that Alice doesn't want to go. What's the point of a night of Boom-Boom's cocktails for her? She can't afford them for a start. Hugo's piece-rate wages don't exactly add up to the riches of Croesus, though in another way they've changed things radically for her: it's now at least possible to stay here and give it a go, though not if she keeps blowing her money on Boom-Boom specials. In any case she's not short of busy evenings, so it's good to stay in for a change and continue to work. Hugo's taking her to Genoa at the weekend to visit a client who wants painted cupboards all over his new sea-front villa, and the week after they're off to Val d'Isère to work on some chalets – Fred can come too. There'll be dinners and laughter as well as work, and she may get asked to do that edelweiss kitchen yet.

So Josette is still standing in the doorway, probably not wanting to risk paint on her cream chiffon, for the flat looks like a tip, and she says, 'But, Aleese, it will be *fun*,' and Alice says that she doesn't need 'fun', not today, not at the moment, and Josette starts laughing and says, 'Aleese, you *Eeenglish*, what *do* you need? *Why* you come 'ere?'

Alice sits back from her easel. Josette has a point. It was a year ago last Sunday that she first discovered Vieilleville and fell for that whisper of an idea, her 'Dream of Glory'. So what has she found here? Certainly not glory – or not in any obvious sense. But she's definitely found *something* because the pit of loneliness and fear seems to have dried up, and the feeling she's got right this very moment is what she was after all along.

Josette is still waiting, tapping her foot, laughing. And Alice says, 'I came for a day like today – it's been a good day.'

Well, that's what she tells her and it'll do – to be going on with.

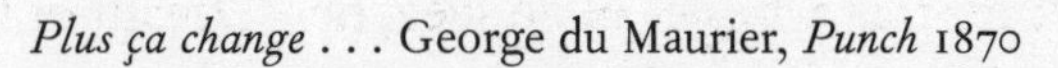
Plus ça change . . . George du Maurier, *Punch* 1870

OUR COUNTRYMEN ABROAD.

Sketch of a Bench on the Boulevards, occupied by Four English People who only Know each Other by Sight.